D1630489

OCCUPIED

Joss Sheldon

www.joss-sheldon.com

Copyright © Joss Sheldon 2015

ISBN-13: 978-1516821808
ISBN-10: 1516821807

EDITION 1.0

First published in the UK in 2015.

Cover design by Mareeniv.

FOR THE PALESTINANS,
KURDS & TIBETANS

"Every generation has to fight the same battles as their ancestors had to fight, again and again, for there is no final victory and no final defeat."

TONY BENN

CONTENTS

SECTION ONE: 'CHILDHOOD'

SECTION TWO: 'ADOLESCENCE'

SECTION THREE: 'ADULTHOOD'

SECTION ONE

CHILDHOOD

1. TAMSIN

"Do you know why our village is called *'Doomba'*?" Papa Tamsin asked his eldest daughter. He was lying on a rug, surrounded by piles of cushions, and an assortment of empty mugs.

"No papa," Tamsin replied. "I've always thought it was a bit of a silly name."

"Silly!"

"Yes papa. It's a silly word, *'Doomba'*."

Papa Tamsin smiled.

He exhaled some apple flavoured smoke, stroked his chin, and passed a rosary bead between his fingers.

A candle flickered and a lantern gleamed.

"Do you know what doombas are?" He asked.

"No papa."

"Well, that's why you think Doomba is a silly name then!

"You see doombas are animals. They look a bit like foxes, but they have bright red stripes and pointy grey goatees. They're ever so rare. But they're special; they protect everyone who is lucky enough to see them!"

Tamsin giggled.

"Have you ever seen one?" She asked.

"Oh yes! Just the once though, many years ago, when I was the same age as you are now."

"What was it like?"

"It was as wise as a monk, as wily as a raccoon, and as old as time itself. It looked me in the eye, winked, and then disappeared in a puff of smoke!

"I've never seen it since, but I've often felt its presence. Why, I do believe it's still living up there in the hills. Perhaps you'll see it one day, whilst you're playing hide and seek."

"Perhaps, papa. I'd like that. If a doomba is hiding in the hills, I'll definitely find it. I'm the best at hide and seek!"

Papa Tamsin chuckled, sucked on his water pipe, and looked at his daughter. He smiled. The lines on his face deepened, and his prominent teeth poked out through his leathery lips.

"Many years ago, our clan lived in a village to the south. The land was fertile there. It brought forth juicy fruits and plump vegetables every single year.

"But our clan was as small as a cat's forehead, and a bigger clan wanted our land. They howled like hyenas, charged at us with spears, and chased us all away. We had to flee to the hills, and hide in the long grass.

"It was there, after many hours had passed, that a little girl saw a doomba. That little girl had shiny black hair, chubby cheeks, and a tiny round nose. She looked just like you!

"Well, she looked at the doomba, and the doomba looked back at her. The doomba winked, and then it scuttled away.

"But the little girl didn't let the doomba out of her sight. She stayed awake for a whole week, and followed the doomba wherever it went. She climbed hills, traversed gorges, and scaled snowy mountains. Our clan followed her, because they knew that doombas brought good luck.

"Well, after several days had passed, the doomba went to sleep in a beautiful valley. Our ancestors were exhausted, so they fell asleep as well. All they had were some clothes, grapes and bread. But they were happy, because they had survived.

"And so they had happy dreams. They dreamt that the valley they discovered would become a prosperous village, filled with their descendants.

"They slept for forty years!

"When they awoke, their bread and grapes were still by their side. But the doomba had gone, and a village had grown up around them. They wiped the sleep from their eyes, and fell in love with that place, which stretched from the mountains in the east to the sea in the west.

"That village was named 'Doomba', after the animal which had led them there. And we've lived in this *Garden of Eden* ever since!"

Tamsin gazed up at her father in awe.

She loved spending time with him in that tent, which was affixed to the side of her family's home. And she loved attending to his guests; replenishing the coals in their water pipe, serving them homemade beer, and handing them quilted cushions.

Those men visited Papa Tamsin every evening. They played cards until their pockets were empty. They smoked until their eyes were red. And they talked until their throats were dry.

Tamsin enjoyed their conversations. There was no school in her village, so the stories she heard were her sole form of education. They were lessons in the sort of history which was only written down in the minds of old men.

"But our lands don't stretch to the sea, papa," she challenged.

"That's true," Papa Tamsin chuckled. "Not anymore."

Tamsin gazed up at her father, a wizened man who smelt of tea and tobacco. His body was shaped like a Coca Cola bottle, and his face was perfectly ageless. It was neither young nor old. Papa Tamsin could have been twenty, or fifty, or eighty. Tamsin could not be sure.

"What happened, papa?" She asked.

"Well, in the past, there weren't any policemen here. There weren't prisons, courts or judges. There wasn't a government. We didn't need it. We policed ourselves, without any outside interference.

"The only time that proved problematic, was when conflicts arose with neighbouring villages.

"Well, one day, many years ago, three thieves from a neighbouring village broke into a peasant's house. The peasant caught those thieves red-handed! He snuck up behind one of them, and slit his throat with a scythe. Blood squirted everywhere, and his voice box fell out of his neck!

"That murder put Doomba in a great deal of danger. The neighbouring villagers were planning to kill a member of our clan to avenge their loss. They were demanding '*A life for a life*', to settle that '*Blood Debt*'.

"So our elders arranged a peace meeting. And, after many days of heated negotiations, they agreed to pay a hundred gold pieces as compensation.

"Our clan didn't have that sort of money, but our elders were determined to pay. They didn't want any more blood to be spilt. So they sold the land nearest to the sea to some *Holies* for one hundred gold pieces, and gave that money to our neighbours.

"That is why our lands no longer reach the sea."

Papa Tamsin thought he had answered his daughter's question, and was about to retire to bed. But Tamsin had other ideas.

"Surely that land belonged to members of our clan," she challenged. "What right did the elders have to sell it?"

Tamsin stared at her father with eager eyes.

A lantern flickered and flashed.

Papa Tamsin ruffled his daughter's hair.

"You really are an inquisitive one, aren't you?" He said.

Tamsin did not respond.

"Well, back then no-one owned the land. The land belonged to everyone. Each man was free to farm whatever land he wanted, as long as no-one else was farming it already. So no-one became rich, but no-one became poor. God provided for all.

"Private ownership was only imposed on us when we were colonised. The Colonisers allocated parcels of land to each villager, so they could collect a land tax.

"We still pay that tax today, although our money is never invested here. The Colonisers keep it all to themselves. But that's another story for another time."

* * *

When she was not listening to her father's stories, Tamsin played games. And when she was not playing games, she worked. Everyone in Doomba worked, from the day they were born till the day they died.

In the summer, men cut the grain, women gathered it into bundles, elders threshed it, and children sifted out the chaff. The men harvested vegetables, and the women dried them in the sun. The children picked fruit, and the elders preserved it.

In the spring they planted crops. The men ploughed the land, the women uprooted the weeds, and the children sowed the seeds. In the winter the men helped to build each other's homes, and the elders made baskets out of dried reeds. The children collected firewood, whilst the women cooked traditional meals.

Even the animals had jobs. Horses pulled ploughs, chickens laid eggs, and dogs protected the village from wild animals. Only the cats lived a life of leisure.

Everyone had something to do, and no-one was ever idle. The work was hard, the adults often worked from sunrise to sunset, but people were happy. They were their own bosses, no-one ever told them what to do, and they produced almost everything they needed.

Most work was done collectively, but everyone had individual responsibilities too. There was the Midwife, who called her house '*The Department of Life*', on account of the copious amount of births which took place in Doomba each year. There was the Medicine Man who, with help from the voices inside his head, used a mixture of witchcraft and wizardry to chase evil spirits away. And there was the Humpbacked Priest, a member of the Godly religion, who evoked God's blessings on behalf of all the villagers.

It was Tamsin's job to get up early each morning, whilst the stars were still in the sky, and milk her family's yaks. When she finished, she slapped those animals' bottoms. They ran off into the woods, where they dined on a feast of weeds and wild flowers.

The yaks were well disciplined animals, who returned to Doomba at four o'clock each evening. They stood in an orderly line, and waited to be milked again. Then they made their way back into Tamsin's house, where they lived alongside Tamsin's family.

Tamsin never had any problems with those powerful beasts. She even gave them names. Her favourite was called 'Stripy', on account of the two stripes which ran around her belly. The others were called 'Tilly', 'Misty' and 'Tiger'.

Tamsin had one other job. She collected water from Doomba's spring several times each day. She put it in a terracotta pot, which she carried on her head.

Everyone said that Doomba's spring was magical, that its water could cure headaches, backaches and toothaches. Some people said it could cure any sort of ache. Papa Tamsin said it had a story of its own.

"When our clan first came to Doomba, there wasn't a single spring nearby," he told Tamsin one night. "Our forefathers had to walk several miles to get water.

"Well, at that time, two young men were competing to marry a beautiful maiden. One of them shot an arrow at his foe!

"But his arrow missed. It hit the leather water sack his foe was carrying. That sack split. Water gushed out, and poured over the rockface.

"The water continued to flow. It never stopped flowing! It formed the spring we use today.

"But as a result of that sorry affair, love marriages were banned in Doomba. These days, marriages have to be arranged."

Papa Tamsin seemed to have a story for everything in Doomba. For the peach trees, which flowered pinkish white, and the air which smelt of sweet tea. For the wild daisies, which sprouted in olive groves, and the views which looked like a painting. His ancestors had lived in Doomba for so long, his clan had become part of the scenery, and the villagers knew about every inch of the land.

Tamsin loved that land. She loved the shade cast by the village pomegranate tree, whose branches spread out like an umbrella. She loved the springtime sunsets, which brought clouds with mauve underbellies, and horizons which smelt of ginger. She loved the purple flowers which carpeted Doomba's orchards, the bees who searched for pollen, and the white butterflies who swarmed overhead.

But most of all, Tamsin loved to play games.

She dressed up in her mother's clothes, which were way too big for her. She put on her mother's dress back to front, and turned her cap the wrong way round. She invented tales, which she acted out to her younger siblings, using dolls made from twigs. She played tag with her friends. And she chased them with a rash-inducing sap, which she extracted from wild cacti.

The children were not the only people who played games in Doomba. Each week the adults had an afternoon off, when they joined in the fun. The girls took on the boys in choreographed bouts of tug of war, and won as often as they lost. Then the adults wrestled.

Tamsin always cheered for her mother, Mama Tamsin, who was one of the best wrestlers in the village. She was a stout woman, who had wide shoulders and cobalt eyes. Her movements were large and balanced, like those of a wild gazelle. And her skin was as craggy as a gorge.

The other villagers cheered as well. They had good reason to. Before the wrestling began, everyone put walnuts, apricots and apples, into a large wooden bowl. If the women won, they got to share those prizes. But if the men won, they took the spoils.

Yet of all the games Tamsin played, hide and seek was her favourite.

It allowed her to discover every inch of her village.

Tamsin hid in Doomba's fields, orchards and caves. She climbed trees, slinked between plants, and crouched behind rocks. She stood still and silent for minutes on end, whilst her friends struggled to find her. She anticipated their every move, and snuck away whenever she was about to be caught.

"Papa! Papa!" She yelled when she returned home. "I won again! No-one can catch me! Won't you come and play with us next time? If anyone can find me, it'll be you. I love you papa. You're the best!"

"Now come on," Mama Tamsin interrupted. "Your daddy is a busy man. He doesn't have time for children's games."

That rebuttal did not stop Tamsin from playing with her friends. Nor did it stop her from meeting other adults whilst she played. She met the locals, and she met people like the Bedouin; a man who had a flowing white beard, and a flowing white gown.

The Bedouin led a simple life. He meditated in his cave, brewed tea in a blackened pot, and played his oud whilst his goats wandered off on their own. Occasionally he visited Doomba, to exchange meat and wool for grain. But he spent most of his time in the hills, where he lived with his tribe, in a tent made from yaks' fur.

Tamsin could not understand how the Bedouin could be happy without a permanent home. It was not because her house was a palace. It wasn't. It consisted of one large room, with an annex for the animals. Wooden beams supported a thatched roof. The walls were made from stones, mud and leaves. But Tamsin's home offered her family a sense of security which the Bedouin, she reasoned, must have craved.

"Don't you want to live in a proper house?" She asked.

"No," he replied.

"Why not?"

"Because I like moving around. It makes me feel free.

"I live wherever I choose. The whole planet is my home! No government can rule me! No border can box me in!"

"Oh," Tamsin replied.

She fidgeted with a piece of grass, looked up at a soaring eagle, and changed the subject.

"My papa never plays hide and seek with me," she mused.

The Bedouin looked at Tamsin and smiled.

"Don't worry," he replied. "Be happy!"

"Don't worry, be happy?"

"Don't worry, be happy!"

The Bedouin sipped some tea, tilted his head, and closed his eyes.

* * *

Tamsin filled her father's water pipe with apple flavoured tobacco, and added some glowing embers from the fire. She passed the mouthpiece to the Medicine Man, who put it to his lips.

Those lips were stretched taut. The whole of the Medicine Man's face was stretched taut. His skin clung so tightly to his bones, he wore a permanent look of bewilderment. But Tamsin could still tell that he was in a crabby mood.

He had spent the whole day sucking the life out of a corpse.

That corpse had woken in the middle of the night. It had sat by the fire, and smoked a pipe. So his Widow had called the Medicine Man for assistance.

The Medicine Man had hit the corpse's torso with a yak's shinbone, clamped his lips onto the corpse's mouth, and sucked.

After many hours, the corpse's blood had shot out of its mouth. It looked like a devilish fountain.

The Medicine Man drew some spiritual motifs on a piece of parchment, dissolved it in vinegar, and gave it to the Widow to drink. He only left when the Widow was calm.

But, having made it to Papa Tamsin's tent, the Medicine Man was far from calm himself.

"The Humpbacked Priest was there as usual, muttering to himself and bickering," he complained. "He said the corpse should have been cut into little pieces and fed to the eagles.

"But what does he know? He thinks he can connect with the spirit world, just because he carries a Godly book. The man can't even read!

"If he'd gotten his way, he'd have created a ghoul which would have haunted our village forever. I tell you, there's no place for men like that in Doomba, with their Godly books and their temples and their prophets.

Pfft! Whatever next?"

Papa Tamsin comforted the Medicine Man. He shared his homemade beer. And he greeted each new guest who arrived.

A Frail Elder said, "May all auspicious signs come to this tent."

A Skinny Villager said, "I salute the God within you."

And a Stout Villager said, "Peace be upon you."

Everyone wore baggy trousers and tight-fitting plimsolls. Everyone lounged around a shimmering fire. And everyone shared the water pipe.

It did not take long for the Singer to break into a series of odes. Sweet notes filled the air, and melodies danced from wall to wall.

"*This is the cradle of civilisation,*" that small-headed man crooned. "*We've been here as long as the sun, and longer than the stars. Our clan is as old as time itself!*"

The evening continued on as normal, until the Midwife's Husband entered. His frazzled hands trembled as they scratched his mottled skin. His constricted eyes flickered beneath his sweaty brow. And his lips quivered as he opened his mouth to speak.

"The Colonisers have lost their war," he said in a whispered hush. "The Colonialists are splitting up their empire. They're going to give our land to the Holies!"

The Skinny Villager dropped the water pipe.

The Frail Elder spilled his beer.

The Singer stared at Papas Tamsin.

"They've wanted our land for years," he replied. "They want our oil, minerals and gold."

"They want our magnesium," the Medicine Man concurred. "Don't forget the magnesium. Our magnesium has magical powers!"

"I don't believe it," Papa Tamsin disputed. "The Holies by the sea have been our friends for eight generations. They eat our food, wear our clothes, and speak our language. They buy our fruit and sell us their fertilizer. Their fertilizer is the best! No, they wouldn't harm us."

Papa Tamsin's comments earned a murmur of approval.

The Skinny Villager picked up the water pipe and passed it along. The Midwife's Husband stoked the fire. And Tamsin grinned. Even the Singer nodded in agreement.

"I remember when one of their priests came from abroad to survey our valley," the Frail Elder concurred. "He said he'd tell his people, '*The bride is beautiful, but she is married to another man*'. He realised that this land belongs to us."

"Yes, that's true," the Midwife's Husband explained. "But the Colonialists have promised our land to the Holies. Their diplomats have signed a declaration. They're going to create a new country called '*Protokia*'."

"Protokia?" The Skinny Villager mocked. "Pfft! Don't be so silly. What sort of a name is that?

"What right does some foreign diplomat have to give our land away? The Holies only represent five percent of the population. They'll never be able to rule us. They don't have any right to our land. They've only been here for a couple of hundred years."

"They're claiming that their descendants lived here thousands of years ago," the Midwife's Husband explained.

"I heard we share the same ancestors," the Singer added. "We're all brothers, cut from the same cloth. We're distant cousins!"

"Piffle!" The Frail Elder retorted. "Most of them descend from converts.

"My grandfather remembered the day they first arrived. He said they were a right motley bunch. A real gang of strangers from a million different nations. They only settled here because we helped them."

The Frail Elder shook his head.

The Midwife's Husband tutted.

The Singer rolled his eyes.

The water pipe went out, the fire fizzled, and stray cats meowed.

The tent fell into a state of eerie silence.

Only the Medicine Man had the energy to speak.

"They want our magnesium," he repeated. "Our magnesium has magical powers!"

* * *

Tamsin did not say a single word that evening. She went to bed in a silent state of fear and confusion. She feared her clan might be driven out of Doomba, and she was confused because all the Holies she knew were nice.

She saw the Holies whenever she went fishing in the sea, and she knew the Rotund Holy who sold fertiliser to her father. He was a welcoming man, who looked a bit like Father Christmas.

"He's an orphan," Papa Tamsin had told her. "We found him wandering around the hills, when he was just four years old.

"Well, I was five at the time, so he was like a little brother to me. We treated him like a brother too. Everything we did, he did with us. He picked tomatoes, just like you do, and he played hide and seek as well.

"Our family fostered him for three years in all. Then, when he was seven, he was adopted by the Holies who live near the sea. Your Grandpa thought it would be good for him to live with his own people. But we've stayed friends ever since. He's a good man."

Tamsin called the Rotund Holy 'Uncle'. To her he *was* her uncle. He brought her sweets for her birthday, ruffled her hair, and amazed her with his magic tricks. It didn't matter that he was a Holy and she was a Godly, as far as she was concerned they were family.

So she could not understand why his clan would want to take her land. She was so confused, that she started to feel queasy.

She could barely sleep that night. When sleep did come, nightmares came with it. She saw a holy army of God's soldiers goose-stepping towards her, pounding holy books against their breasts, and firing bullets of fire from their eyes. She saw a cloud of bats descend from the skies, with blood dripping from their teeth, and acid spraying from their spiny wings. She saw squadrons of bears with claws like daggers, battalions of witches with long tangled nails, and legions of demented tigers with heads which spun right around.

She woke up in cold sweats, she shook, and she shivered.

She continued to shake whilst she milked the yaks the next morning. And she continued to shiver whilst she worked in the fields.

She remained silent too, until she finally got Papa Tamsin alone. They sat beneath an oak tree and ate a homemade lunch, whilst the other villagers harvested some carrots.

"Are the Holies going to take Doomba from us?" She asked.

It was the first thing she had said all day.

"What? Hahaha!!!" Papa Tamsin laughed. "The Holies take Doomba from us? Hahaha!!! That's hilarious. The Holies taking Doomba? Whatever next? You do make me laugh."

He pulled Tamsin to his breast.

"But your friends were talking about it last night, papa," Tamsin protested. "I heard everything they said."

"Oh Tamsin, you are silly! Did you really think they were being serious?"

Tamsin paused. She did not want to seem naive.

"No papa," she replied. "I'm not stupid. But I couldn't work out why they were saying all those things. It was awfully strange."

"They were starting the snake game," her father explained. "It's the game we play whenever the snake festival comes around."

"Oh," Tamsin replied. She looked embarrassed.

Papa Tamsin chuckled, stroked his daughter's hair, and sprinkled some walnuts over his grape molasses. He looked across the fields, down the valley, towards the sea. He could see the Holies' village in the distance. He could see their temples, tents and trees.

"Do you know the story behind the snake festival?" He asked.

Tamsin shook her head.

"Well, it happened a long time ago, back when Doomba was just an empty valley.

"Back then, a nasty king ruled the land. That king was barely human. He had claws instead of toes, scales instead of skin, and snakes instead of arms!

"The king's cook had to catch two children every day, chop off their heads, and feed their brains to those snakes. He served them in a soup made of blood, which was as red as pomegranate juice!

"But the cook was downhearted. He felt ever so guilty.

"Then an angel came to him in a dream. Her wings were made of candyfloss, and her halo was made of honeycomb! She told the cook to swap the children's brains for goat brains. She said she'd protect him.

"The cook still caught two children each day, to keep up appearances, but he always let them go.

"'Run to the hills,' he told them. 'You'll be safe up there'.

"So two children escaped every day. They formed a community in the hills. They hid in the caves during the day, and foraged for food at night.

"Their community grew. And as it grew, it became stronger. The children wrestled, boxed, and armed themselves with swords.

"Then, when there were a thousand children in those hills, they ran down to the city together, swinging their swords in the air. They stormed the palace and slaughtered the nasty king. They cut the snakes from his shoulders, and threw them onto a giant bonfire!

"No child was ever killed by that despot again!"

Some worms peeked out of the muddy earth.

Some villagers uprooted carrots.

Some birds tweeted.

"Well, to commemorate that great victory, we recreate our ancestors' story during the snake festival. The Holies play the part of the nasty king, and we play the part of the children. The Holies drive us up into the hills, and we hide in the caves. It's a bit like an adult version of hide and seek!

"Everyone carries a juicy pomegranate. If you're caught, you have to squash it with all your might, cover your brains with its juice, and fall to the ground in a heap. It's most important that you lie there as still as you can, hold your breath, and pretend to be dead.

"Then, when a thousand clan members have found each other, we run down the hill together. We shout, we scream, and we drive the Holies out of our villages. Then we celebrate! We throw snakes onto a fire, sing, and have a giant feast.

"It's great fun!"

Tamsin smirked. It all made sense to her. The previous day's conversation was just an elaborate piece of theatre, setting the scene for the game which was to follow.

And what a game it was! Tamsin could not wait for it to start. She loved the thought of finally playing hide and seek with her father. But she did have one more question.

"Did a corpse really come to life yesterday?" She asked. "Or was that part of the snake game too?"

"That wasn't part of the game," Papa Tamsin replied. "But I don't think it happened either. It did sound a little bit far-fetched!"

* * *

Tamsin felt an overwhelming sense of excitement as preparations for the snake game got underway. She was in awe of Doomba's adults, who brought palpable a sense of realism to proceedings. She had to remind herself that they were only acting.

Some villagers had grey sacks under their eyes. Others wore a look of hollow despair. A Young Mother ripped clumps of hair from her head.

The Humpbacked Priest spent hours praying. He turned the pages of his Godly bible, and pretended to read. The Medicine Man went from house to house. He sprinkled every wall with a mixture of ram's blood and vinegar. And the Midwife woke up screaming in the middle of the night.

"It's happening! It's happening!" She shrieked. "I can hear the buzz of their machines. They have horses and trumpets and guns! They're coming! They're coming! They're coming!"

But the buzzing she had heard did not come from horses, trumpets or guns. It did not come from the Holies at all. It came from the mosquitos who were out in force that night, sucking blood from people's veins.

Tamsin scratched the bites which covered her arms. It created a rash which was so pink, it made her look like a flamingo.

"Stop that," Papa Tamsin demanded. "You'll scratch all your skin off!"

He took a long drag on his water pipe, blew apple flavoured smoke towards the roof, and looked across at the Midwife's Husband.

"I think we should form a village guard," he said.

"We should defend our village," the Skinny Villager agreed. "But we shouldn't be the first to fire. We're not the ones who want a war."

Everyone nodded.

"All this talk of fighting is a little melodramatic," the Frail Elder retorted. "Our first priority should be to ensure we have enough food and supplies. We could be under siege for weeks. We don't want to starve."

Everyone nodded again.

"We harvested the carrots today," the Medicine Man replied. "We'll harvest the cabbages tomorrow. Our stores are already full of grain."

"We can use those sacks of grain to protect our windows," the Skinny Villager mused.

"For sure," the Stout Villager agreed. "And I sold a yak yesterday. I'll use the money I received to buy rice, sugar, juice, chocolates and candies. There'll be enough food to supply a feast."

Papa Tamsin looked at his daughter and smiled.

"I told you there'd be a feast," he whispered. "Just you wait and see!"

Tamsin gave her father a cheeky wink, buried her head in her hands and giggled.

* * *

The whole of Doomba was busy with preparations the next day. The women piled sacks of grain in front of every window, the men harvested every vegetable they could find, and the elders guarded every path in the village.

The Stout Villager went off to buy sweet treats. He returned with a rifle and eight bullets.

And Tamsin told the other children about the snake game. But an awkward boy called Jon, who had buckteeth and wonky eyes, stared back at her and scoffed.

"That's silly," he said. "Everyone knows the Holies are going to attack us. Adults don't play games."

"You're silly," Tamsin replied. "Everyone knows the Holies are our friends. They'd never attack us."

The other children looked at Tamsin. Then they looked at Jon. They scratched their heads, and shrugged their shoulders.

"You must know the story," Tamsin challenged. "You must know about the king who had snakes for arms, and the angel who had a halo made out of honeycomb."

Jon turned white.

"No?" Tamsin teased. "What, are you a bit stupid? Pfft! You're such an idiot, you give the word 'stupid' a whole new meaning!"

Tamsin smirked. She knew she had taken control.

She looked at her peers, took a bite from her apple, and then told her father's tale. By the time she had finished, Doomba's children were hanging on her every word.

A Spotty Boy trembled with excitement.

A Freckled Girl sucked her teeth.

Tamsin wagged her finger.

"But the adults have forgotten one thing," she concluded. "They've forgotten to collect their pomegranates."

So Tamsin led her friends to Doomba's pomegranate tree. They climbed onto each other's shoulders, and picked every piece of fruit. Then they split up into pairs, and handed that fruit to each adult they met.

Most villagers took a pomegranate, said '*Thank-you*', and continued on with their work. Others politely refused. Only the Humpbacked Priest kicked up a fuss.

"I don't want any of your fusty pomegranates," he wailed at Tamsin. "The Holies are coming! The Holies are coming! Oi vey! I don't have any time for rotting fruit."

The Humpbacked Priest was right. The Holies *were* coming. They were marching over the horizon.

There were hundreds of them. They all had guns, which the Occupiers had left behind. And they all had a supply of bullets.

They all marched, side by side, behind a solitary tank.

Tamsin was awestruck.

She knew the Holies had a car, a battered old *Fort Model Tea*, but she had never seen their tank. She did not even know what a tank was. It looked like a mythical beast to her. It had the arced shell of an armadillo, the long pointy snout of an anteater, and the clunky movement of a caterpillar.

Tamsin watched it with wonder. And she watched the Holies with a sense of awe. From her position, hundreds of metres away, it seemed that they had all dressed up like the nasty king. Their armour looked like scales, and their boots looked like claws. The rounds of ammunition, which hung from their shoulders, looked a little bit like snakes.

When the Holies fired bullets into the air, it gave Tamsin an enormous thrill. She thought they were setting off fireworks. And when they entered her village, she knew the game was on.

"Stop staring little girl," the Humpbacked Priest scolded. "We need to run to the hills. Come on babushka. Get moving! We'll be safe up there. It'll only be for a day."

"I know," Tamsin replied. "We won't be there for long. As soon as a thousand of us have gathered, we'll charge down the hill and chase the

Holies away!"

The Humpbacked Priest grabbed Tamsin's hand, and ran with a jerky sort of movement. His right leg took longer steps than his left leg, and his stoop made his torso bob. But he still managed to pick up some speed. Tamsin had to sprint, just to keep up.

She sprinted through Doombas fields, which looked like giant rainbows. A different crop was planted along each furrow. Red tomato plants sat next to orange wheat, yellow sunflowers, green corn, purple aubergines, and pink grapes.

She ran past the Midwife's house, where the sign which read 'Department of Life', was dangling from one corner. Past the pomegranate tree, which looked naked without its fruit. And past the Skinny Villager, who was standing firm.

"Come! Come with us!" Tamsin shouted. "The Holies will see you."

"I don't care if they see me," the Skinny Villager replied. "I'd rather die than leave Doomba. This is our home, and I'll protect it with my life!"

The Humpbacked Priest dragged Tamsin on before she could reply. He dragged her past a horse, who was eating tiny yellow flowers. Past large tracts of barley, which shimmered in the early afternoon sun. And past Doomba's spring, which had dried up for the first time in centuries.

They ran alongside villagers who bumped into each other, and tripped over their own feet. They ran along muddy paths, over thorny brambles, and around rocky boulders.

They came together at a point where many paths met.

"Tamsin!" Papa Tamsin called. "Tamsin! Over here!"

Tamsin pulled away from the Humpbacked Priest, and ran to her father, who was carrying two of his other children.

"Papa!" She cried. "This is so much fun! Let's go before we get caught. The Holies will be able to see us here, we need to run for cover."

Papa Tamsin smiled, ruffled his daughter's hair, and led his family on. They traipsed through sodden bogs. They trudged through marshy fields. And, after several muddy minutes, they finally reached the next valley.

They faced another line of hills, each of which was bigger than the last. And they faced a line of mountains, each of which looked like a crouching giant.

Heather fluttered in the breeze, which blew pollen in every direction.

Audacious plants clung to the sides of jagged cliffs. And tangled weeds battled with defiant boulders.

The escapees found refuge in an ancient cavern.

Tamsin counted them.

"One. Two. Three. Four…"

She counted every single person.

"Three hundred and sixty three. Three hundred and sixty four."

She looked around and waited, but no-one else arrived.

* * *

The children played cops and robbers that afternoon. They ran around the hillside, and had the time of their lives. When the sun began to set, they found shelter in a bears' den. They played draughts, using stones for pieces, and a board they drew in the dust. It was pitch black by the time their parents called them back into the main cavern.

The fires which were dotted around that cave created an eerie glow. People's faces flickered into sight, and then vanished back into the darkness. A drip supplied an irregular beat, which reverberated off the uneven walls. Insects scuttled between their unexpected visitors.

Tamsin counted the escapees once again.

"Three hundred and seventy three. Three hundred and seventy four."

Tamsin's belly rumbled.

"I'm starving, papa," she complained. "It's freezing up here. Don't we have any food or blankets? I didn't think the snake game would take this long."

"No-one thought it'd take this long," Papa Tamsin replied. "The Holies played us really well. They caught us completely off guard! No-one had the time to grab any food or blankets."

"But I'm hungry, papa. I'm really cold."

"We all are, but that's part of the challenge.

"Our ancestors got cold and hungry when they ran away from the nasty king. We have to suffer like they did, up here in the hills.

"But don't you worry, we always win in the end. It's written in the rules. We just need to gather a thousand villagers. Then we'll have a great feast, and warm up by a roaring fire. Just you wait and see!"

Tamsin nodded. She kissed her father, curled up into a ball, and fell asleep at his feet.

She was snoring like a wart hog when the Singer arrived, out of breath, and smelling of stale poo. His odour was so putrid, the other villagers had to cover their noses.

"I was in the village toilet when the Holies came," he explained. "The Holies stood outside, so I couldn't leave. But I could see them through the gaps in the wooden door. I could see a Holy walking towards me!"

The Singer shook his head. There was a look of shame on his face, and a look of horror in his eyes.

The rest of the escapees inched closer.

A beetle sat down by the Singer's foot.

"What could I do?" He begged. "What choice did I have?

"I unlatched the door and jumped into the cesspit. The sewage reached my waist. It came up my trouser legs and filled my pants.

"The Holy squatted down above me. His diarrhoea was like a shower. It washed right over my hair."

The escapees bowed their heads.

The Midwife tutted.

Mama Tamsin patted the Singer's back.

"That's terrible!" She said.

"That's nothing! Not compared to what they did to Doomba."

The sound of a howling wolf echoed across the valley.

The escapees all held their breath.

The Singer looked down at his groin.

When he lifted his head, he saw hundreds of eager eyes staring back at him. The cavern was silent. It was completely still. The fires no longer flickered, and the water no longer dripped.

The Singer shook his head.

"What happened?" His wife finally asked.

The Singer slouched.

"I don't know," he replied. "I heard the gunfire. It sounded like chickpeas popping in a pan; rapid and high pitched. I heard the screams. And then I heard the silence. It was deafening."

The Singer looked up at the villagers and down at the floor.

A bat flapped its leathery wings.

A star twinkled in the sky.

"I stayed in that cesspit for hours," the Singer continued. "I only left when I was sure the Holies had gone.

"The first thing that hit me was the smell. Ugh! It made the cesspit seem like a princess's boudoir.

"That smell was so strong, I could taste it. It was nauseating. It brought bile to my mouth and tears to my eyes. That smell of boiling human blood and scorched human flesh. That smell of fire and brimstone, which still lingers in my nostrils. That smell of kerosene, which made me vomit. Which made me choke up little pieces of my stomach, and fall to the ground in pain."

The Singer wiped a tear from his eye.

"I walked through Doomba's streets, between burning barns and burning homes, dead yaks and dead dogs.

"And then I saw it. That giant pyre. That glowing pyramid of human flesh and bones. With legs sticking out here, and arms sticking out there. With the dust of burnt human hair dancing on the flames. And with the Skinny Villager's head. With its hollow eyes and its twisted mouth."

The Singer stared at the opposite wall.

"Doomba is dead," he sighed. "Our houses have been ransacked, our supplies have been stolen, and our animals have all been killed. The embers of our dreams have been blown away by the wind."

A feather skipped across the floor.

A teardrop landed in the dust.

A spider buried its head.

The Singer looked at Papa Tamsin. Almost everyone looked at Papa Tamsin. But Papa Tamsin was lost for words.

"We need to get out of here," he finally whispered. "If we can make it beyond the mountains we'll be safe."

Everyone nodded.

Everyone shrugged.

Everyone went to sleep.

* * *

"I think we need to get out of here," Tamsin said the next morning.

Her comment took Papa Tamsin by surprise.

"Why is that?" He asked.

"The other villagers must have run to the opposite side of the valley," she explained. "We won't be able to reach them without getting caught. So we'd be better off heading towards the mountains. We'll be able to find some more Godlies over there."

Papa Tamsin chuckled.

"I think you're probably right," he said. "I think we should head in that direction too."

Papa Tamsin walked ahead and Tamsin followed. The other escapees walked behind. They traversed a narrow path which clung to the hillside.

When they looked up they saw mountains, and when they looked down they saw a craggy gorge. They passed rocks which were on the verge of rolling away, and trees which shot out towards the sky.

Tamsin took a berry from each bush they passed, and left the rest for the other escapees. Many of those villagers were struggling.

A Bony Villager dragged his twisted ankle along the ground. His shoe broke. He had to tie it together using long pieces of grass.

A Pink Baby was sick.

And a Blonde Girl was almost naked. Her shirt had been ripped from her torso as she ran from Doomba, and her feet were covered in blood. She had fled without getting the chance to put on her shoes.

After many hours had passed, they reached a mountain pool. A stream jumped off the cliff above it, and landed with a splash. A single water lily floated on its surface.

"I've been here before," Papa Tamsin told his daughter. "I know all about this pool.

"If you look at it hard enough, and pray to it long enough, you can see the future in its waters!"

Tamsin giggled.

She stared at the pool. She used all her energy to focus on its glossy surface. She moved her head from left to right. And then she jumped up into the air. She wore a ginormous smile.

"I've seen it, papa," she yelled. "I've seen the future!"

She had seen her father's reflection. Papa Tamsin was stood behind her, holding a curvy stick in the air.

"I saw you in the water," Tamsin shouted. "You were holding a curvy snake! I know what it means, papa. It means we're going to win the snake game! It means you're going to take a snake and throw it into a bonfire. We're going to win, papa! We're going to win!"

Tamsin was so confident, she skipped ahead without a care in the world. She did not feel hungry or cold that evening. And she was still smiling when she fell asleep that night.

* * *

The mood was mixed the following morning. Having put a day between themselves and Doomba, the villagers felt safer than before. No-one had seen a single Holy. But no-one had eaten a proper meal, and everyone was hungry.

Tamsin took the dock leaf she had just uprooted, put it in her mouth, and chewed. Its fuzzy surface tickled her tongue, and its bitter taste made her want to spit. She scrunched her lips together and winced.

Papa Tamsin slapped his own forehead.

"I think it's time to move on," he said.

"And where exactly would you have us schlep to?" The Humpbacked Priest challenged. He was sweating profusely. The Humpbacked Priest had a talent for sweating profusely. Beads of moisture covered his frog-like face. Sweat formed rivers between rolls of his neck-fat. And water dripped from his hairy nostrils.

Papa Tamsin looked around. He could see the path which led back to Doomba, but he could not see a path which would take them any further. They had reached a dead end.

Papa Tamsin looked around again. He saw a line of fir trees. He saw the mountains in the distance. And he saw the Spotty Boy, who was stroking a yak, which had a giant white dot on its nose.

"Where did that come from?" He asked.

"I don't know," the Spotty Boy replied. "She was here when I woke up this morning. Do you think we should eat her?"

"Let's eat her," the Midwife cried.

"It's a gift from God almighty, hallowed be his name," the

Humpbacked Priest cheered.

"Hunger be damned," the Singer chanted.

Papa Tamsin looked around again.

"Hold on one minute," he said.

He walked up to the yak, and slapped her bottom. The yak turned her head, grunted, and wandered off.

"This way," Papa Tamsin said.

"You're mad," the Humpbacked Priest chided. "You're a crazy yutz! A gonef! An amoretz!"

"Do you have any better ideas?" Papa Tamsin asked.

The Humpbacked Priest could not reply.

So the villagers got up, stretched their legs, and followed the yak.

The yak made her way around one hill and over another. By midday she had led the villagers above the tree line. And by sunset, she had led them over another three peaks.

Those hills were all covered in a rambling mesh of thorny bushes and prickly thickets. But the yak crushed those plants beneath her hooves, which created a path for Doomba's villagers.

The Blonde Girl had to be carried. Her bare feet had been cut to shreds by the thorns. The Bony Villager, who had a twisted ankle, stayed behind. And the other villagers plodded along at a snail's pace.

They did not see another soul until a Bearded Elder appeared on the hillside. That man had a hairy big toe, which stuck out of a hole in his shoe, and tousled hair which was caked with grey dust.

"There you are Dot!" He shouted. "Four o'clock! Just like normal! I thought we'd lost you when you didn't come home last night. I guess the Holies must have really shaken you up."

Tamsin had never seen that man before. She had never seen any of the people who came into view as she circled that hill. They were not from Doomba. But she was certainly glad to see them, even if they did all seem slightly strange.

An Elderly Spinster scooped up muddy water, and drank it down with real gusto. A Scabby Refugee shovelled bits of dirt into his mouth. And a Chubby Girl rocked back and forth.

"Five hundred and thirteen," Tamsin counted. "Five hundred and fourteen."

She ran off to find Papa Tamsin.

"Papa! Papa! Papa!" She shouted. "There are five hundred and fifteen of us now. We're more than halfway there!"

"That's nice," Papa Tamsin replied.

He ruffled his daughter's hair.

"I've just arranged our dinner."

Papa Tamsin had spent the previous half hour persuading the Bearded Elder to sacrifice Dot, his last remaining yak. The Bearded Elder had finally succumbed to Papa Tamsin's charms. And so they roasted Dot over a wood fire, and ate her flesh with some wild nettles.

That meal lifted the escapees' spirits for the first time in days. The Singer sung sweet odes, the Humpbacked Priest gave thanks to the Lord, and Uncle Tamsin decided to get married.

"My parents chose my bride months ago," he explained. "I was supposed to get married in Doomba today. Well I'm not going to let the Holies scupper my plans. Bugger that! Our lives must go on!"

"That's the spirit!" The Bearded Elder cheered.

"You tell 'em!" The Singer called.

"You go boy!" The Medicine Man chanted.

He walked away from the crowd, threw a rock in the air, and spat at the sky.

Everyone stared at him.

"Well someone had to scare off the ghosts and evil spirits," he said. "And it wasn't as if any of you were going to do it."

There was a brief moment of silence. Then the crowd replied with a mixture of nods, shrugs, and approving gestures.

The Humpbacked Priest shook his head.

"Bloody Medicine Man," he muttered. "What does that schmuck know?"

Uncle Tamsin and Auntie Tamsin exchanged glances.

Tamsin shed a tear. Mama Tamsin snivelled. And the Singer wept with joy.

The Humpbacked Priest hobbled to the front. He stopped to rub his bent back, picked some wild heather, and set it on fire.

"Let these scents release Auntie Tamsin from her protective deities," he said. "Bring her into the protection of her husband's angels."

The Bride's Father and the Groom's Father walked to the front.

They embraced.

"I am happy to give my daughter to your son," the Bride's Father said.

"I am happy to receive your daughter into my family," the Groom's Father replied.

The Humpbacked Priest smiled.

"I now pronounce you husband and wife," he said. "Mazel tov!"

Everyone cheered. Everyone clapped, chanted, and threw leaves into the air. The Singer sang. A group of women danced together in fits and starts. A Seductive Refugee shimmied with gyrating hips, wobbling breasts, and come-hither eyes. Little girls tried to copy her. And the men talked amongst themselves.

They continued to talk long after the children had fallen asleep.

"The Holies let us escape," the Bearded Elder said. "Dot was in the forest at the time, so we picked her up on the way. But we had to leave our other possessions behind. Oh, I do hope our village is okay."

"I wouldn't hold out too much hope," the Singer replied. "The Holies are burning every village they take. They're burning our homes, animals and tools. They want to make sure we never return."

"I heard they're lining villagers up, shooting them, and burying them in mass graves," a Curvaceous Refugee added.

"I heard they're stripping villagers naked, and hanging them from trees," a Petite Refugee concurred.

"I heard they're throwing villagers into acid wells," a Suntanned Refugee agreed.

They all tutted.

"But it'll all be okay in the end," Papa Tamsin consoled. "Twenty two neighbouring countries all follow the Godly religion. It won't be long before they declare war on the Holies. Our neighbours *will* save us! We *will* return home! This land is ours!"

* * *

The refugees set off early the next morning, and walked along a path which was older than time itself. The views were majestic.

Golden mists cuddled silver mountains. Candy floss shrubs grew from chocolate soil. Butterflies swam through the sky, and eagles surfed on the clouds.

Tamsin watched on in a state of wonderment, as Mother Nature revealed her naked body. As tiny yellow flowers turned to salute the sun. As gentle winds whistled ancient melodies. And as dandelion florets danced on the purple haze.

She found the tribal people they passed just as magical as the scenery. Stood there in the nude, or wearing animal skins, their faces seemed flat and their noses seemed thin. Their language sounded unsteady, and their movements seemed primeval.

Tamsin gave those people a wide birth, but she was not nearly so shy when she saw a grass snake. Her eyes lit up. Her pulse quickened. And she seized her opportunity.

She threw herself at that snake. She flew through the air, with her arms in front of her head.

But the snake was too quick for her. It slivered over a ridge, and slid down the other side the hill.

Tamsin ran after it.

She left the other refugees behind, and skidded down through an avalanche of scree. When the snake slinked between rocks, Tamsin skipped over them. When it slipped through a patch of shale, Tamsin gave chase. And when it turned into the next couloir, Tamsin swooped.

She dived through the air, and grabbed the snake with both hands. Her knee buckled as she landed. She stumbled and fell on her elbow. Blood streamed down her arm.

She grabbed a rock and smashed the snake's head.

"Ouch!" She shouted.

She had caught her finger. Blood streamed down her other arm. But she was happy nonetheless. Capturing that snake had made her day.

She grinned.

A *rat-a-tat-tat* sound, which reminded Tamsin of fireworks, rang out below. Tamsin looked down and saw three Holies.

To her, they all looked like the nasty king. Their ammunition looked like snakes, and their bulletproof vests looked like scales. They were standing over some Godlies, who were covered in a red liquid, which looked a bit like pomegranate juice.

Tamsin's pulse began to race. Her brow began to sweat, and her torso began to shake. Her heart beat so much, it felt like it was going to break through her ribcage.

Tamsin was Doomba's hide and seek champion. She had a reputation to protect. And she would have died of embarrassment if she was caught.

But there was nowhere for her to hide, and the Holies were heading in her direction. So she decided to play dead.

She took her pomegranate and tried to juice it. But her pomegranate refused to break. So Tamsin put it in her mouth and bit its waxy skin. She bit down so hard, she chipped her tooth. A river of blood poured over her chin, and dripped down onto her muddy chest.

Frustrated and in pain, she took the pomegranate and smashed it over a rock. An explosion of sticky red liquid sprayed in every direction. It covered her stomach, mixed in with her blood, and stained the ground behind her.

Tamsin fell to the ground. She was exhausted. Her leg was bent backwards, her hair was a tangled mess, and her body was covered in a sticky mixture of blood and juice.

When the Holies reached her, Tamsin stopped breathing. Her diaphragm did not contract, and her lungs did not inflate. Her nose tingled, and her stomach tensed. Her throat became dry. She almost choked.

Time stood still.

The Holies stood still.

The sun stood still in the sky.

A Sunburnt Holy, whose chest hair peaked out of his vest, kicked some gravel at Tamsin. It ricocheted off her shin.

He stared at Tamsin for what felt like an eternity.

Tamsin's head pulsated.

Then a Scabby Holy, who had a cut lip, trod down on Tamsin's belly.

Blood dribbled out of Tamsin's mouth, pomegranate juice trickled down her chest, and an ant climbed onto her wrist.

A Chunky Holy chewed a long piece of grass.

"Huh," he said. "Let's keep going."

And so the Holies left as quickly as they had arrived. They skirted around the hillside, away from the other escapees.

Tamsin took a deep breath, and beamed with pride. No-one could catch her!

She lay there, still and silent, until the Holies were out of sight. Then she returned to her clan. She ran past the back markers, jinked between some elders, and finally reached her parents.

"Oh my God!" Mama Tamsin screamed. "What on earth happened to you?"

"The Holies were about to catch me, so I covered myself in pomegranate juice," Tamsin panted. "I fooled those suckers! They thought I'd already been caught."

Tamsin paused. She pawed her foot and bowed her head.

"Papa," she asked. "Does that mean I lost the snake game?"

Mama Tamsin looked at her daughter with a look of ghostly horror.

Tamsin looked up at her father with puppy dog eyes.

Papa Tamsin chuckled.

"Did they capture you and take you back to their base?" He asked.

"No."

"Well then how could you have possibly lost? If the Holies didn't take you away, you're still in the game!"

"I thought so, papa," Tamsin cheered. "I knew I'd be okay. And look! I caught a snake for the fire!"

* * *

The long journey east started to take its toll, as days turned into nights, and nights turned into days.

The first person to perish was the Blonde Girl. Her father was so tired, he did not notice when she fell from his back. A search party spent hours looking for her, but she was nowhere to be seen.

The Singer's Wife died the very next day. She had a stroke, which was brought on by a mixture of exhaustion and sorrow. The thought of living anywhere other than Doomba was too much for her to bear.

The Singer carried his wife's body, because he wanted to bury her in Doomba. But he never sang again.

The other escapees continued on with heavy hearts and empty

bellies. They watched hills turn into mountains, whilst the air thinned and the temperature dropped. But their spirits warmed as freedom came into view. They had made it to the snowy ridge which marked Protokia's border.

Papa Tamsin led the way, but progress was slow. When he put one foot forward, his other foot sunk into the snow. Tamsin tried to walk in her father's footsteps, but she kept on sinking. The snow came up to her waist.

So Papa Tamsin put his daughter on his shoulders, and carried two of his other children under his arms. When his muscles ached, he jumped up and down. When his hands froze, he clenched his fists. And when he saw a dead body in the snow, he turned away, to protect his children from the gory truth.

That mountain was littered with frozen bodies. An arm stuck out here, and a leg stuck out there. Heads rested on the surface. Hands seemed to wave.

Any escapee who stopped walking, stopped living. Some escapees contracted snow blindness. Most of them contracted pneumonia.

Papa Tamsin protected his children from their suffering. And he protected his children from the Humpbacked Priest, when that man turned insane. The Humpbacked Priests' feet, which were only covered by a pair of sandals, had already turned black with frostbite. His lungs had already filled up with phlegmy liquid. And, as he climbed above the clouds, his eyes filled up with a kaleidoscope of colourful hallucinations.

"The snow is green," he wailed. "Oi yoy yoy! Where are the yaks? Why aren't they eating this green grass? Oi vey! God save us all!"

Papa Tamsin protected his children as they climbed that mountain. He cheered when they reached the top. And he was in a buoyant mood when they reached Collis, the neighbouring country.

He walked straight up to a Border Guard; a ragged man whose skin had been roughened by coarse soap and blunt razors.

"Papers," the Border Guard snapped.

"We're refugees," Papa Tamsin replied.

"Do you have papers to prove that?"

"Look at us."

"I'm looking. I don't see any papers."

Papa Tamsin held his palms up to the sky.

Little crumbs of snow tumbled down the mountainside.

Mama Tamsin removed her wedding ring, and gave it to the Border Guard

"Here are our papers," She said.

The Border Guard held the ring up to his eyes.

"Very good," he replied. "Everything is in order here. On you go."

Papa Tamsin gave his wife a sympathetic look, rubbed her back, and led his family down into Collis.

On their way they met another group of escapees, who were also fleeing from the Holies. To Tamsin they seemed both strange and familiar, the same but different. They spoke the same language, with different dialects. They wore the same clothes, with different motifs. Whereas her clan greeted each other by touching cheek against cheek, they touched forehead against forehead.

"Nine hundred and ninety nine," Tamsin counted. "One thousand!"

She tugged Papa Tamsin's trousers.

"Papa! Papa!" She cheered. "There's over a thousand of us. Let's go back to Doomba and kick the Holies out."

Papa Tamsin chuckled.

"All in good time," he replied. "But it'll take us days to get back to Doomba from here. Why don't we celebrate the snake festival down there?"

Tamsin looked up. In front of her was Natale; a town which covered a bulbous hill. At its top was a castle. And at its base was the biggest campsite Tamsin had ever seen. In its centre was a giant bonfire.

"Yes papa!" Tamsin cheered. "Let's throw my snake on that fire!"

* * *

With eyes which were full of tears, and a mind which was full of joy, Tamsin fell into a giddy daze. Her hands tingled and her veins throbbed. Goose-pimples covered her skin, and colour returned to her cheeks.

In that state of dizzy intoxication, she did not hear the Bald Local who was shouting at her family.

"Go back to your own country," he screamed. "You're not welcome here. Bloody foreigners!"

Nor did Tamsin pay any attention to the Mad Lady who scowled at her as she walked through Natale. The Mad Lady had an enormous nose, which dominated her face, and an enormous wart which covered her chin. She had raggedy grey hair, and eyes with tiny pupils. She wagged her bony finger as she spoke.

"You'll never return home," she wailed. "Never! You'll stay here forever. It's written in the stars!"

"Oh shut up," the Suntanned Refugee shouted back. "What do you know, you batty old witch?"

Everyone else remained silent. They were too tired to talk.

They continued through town until they reached the refugee camp. Then they waited there, next to a tall fence, looking like extras out of a science fiction movie; with alien faces and protruding bones.

When it was their turn, they walked through a turnstile. They were registered by a Female Guard, who had a moustache.

"Are we going camping?" Tamsin asked her father.

"Oh yes!" Papa Tamsin replied. "If we're lucky, we'll have a tent all to ourselves!"

Tamsin giggled.

Separated from the other refugees, her family walked down a boggy thoroughfare. A sea of white tents lined up on either side, reflecting the glimmering sun. Clean clothes hung from dirty trees. Soot rose from metal chimneys, and wafted over those clothes.

Tamsin followed her father towards the bonfire.

The closer they got, the more people surrounded them. It was claustrophobic. Refugees filled every road, path and alley. Their tents were overflowing, as were their loos.

The inhabitants of that camp came from forty eight villages, and they all looked slightly different. Some had bigger noses, whilst others had smaller ears. Some wore baggy trousers, whilst others wore patterned robes. They spoke the same language, but they used different phrases. They cooked the same dishes, but they used different herbs. They span the same wool, but they made different cloths.

Tamsin followed her father as he squeezed between those refugees. They were shoved one way, and shunted back the other. They were knocked in their sides, shoulders and hips.

After several uncomfortable minutes had passed, they finally broke through the crowd. A giant fire stood before them. Its flames seemed to stab the sky. They shimmied and they danced, in a majestic mixture of golds, yellows and reds. They radiated so much heat, Tamsin perspired.

"We've done it! We've done it!" She cheered. "We've won! We've won!"

Tamsin ran towards the fire, and threw her snake into its flames. Then she bounded back to her parents.

A local woman approached them there. She gave Mama Tamsin some lipstick, to make her feel human again. Then she squatted down in front of Tamsin.

"I think you're too young for lipstick," she said.

Tamsin shrugged.

"I'd like some," she replied. "I like presents!"

"I bet you'd prefer some lollipops."

"Oh yes, I'd love some lollipops!"

Tamsin took all the lollipops she was given, said '*Thank-you*', and handed one to Papa Tamsin.

"Papa! Papa!" She said. "They're handing out lollipops! The feast has begun! The party has started!"

The local woman laughed.

"The party has started," she replied. "Make yourself at home. You're welcome here. What's ours is yours!"

Tamsin held her head in her hands and cried tears of joy.

2. ELLIE

Ellie held her head in her hands and cried.

"Mummy! Mummy!" She whined. "Why can't I have any of those lollipops?"

"On the Godly bible!" Mama Ellie gasped. "How many times do I have to tell you? They're for the refugees!"

"But those country bumpkins can't even read or write. They're dirty and they smell. I'm your own daughter! It's just not fair."

Mama Ellie sighed.

A robin sang.

Ellie scowled.

She had never been close to her mother. Her Eldest Sister had taken care of her when she was young. She had put her to bed each night, read her a story, and slept next her on the floor. But her Eldest Sister had been married off to a foreigner. She had left Ellie behind, with her parents and three youngest siblings.

A glossy photograph was the only possession Ellie had to remind her of her Eldest Sister, and she carried it wherever she went. But it was starting to get tatty. Its corners were starting to fray, and the image was starting to fade. She had drawn a doodle on its back.

Ellie looked down at that picture, snarled through her nose, and then looked up at her mother.

"Those refugees have suffered tragedies we'll never be able to comprehend," Mama Ellie explained. "I swear on the grave of the prophet; they've got nothing! They've lost their land *and* their homes.

"But whilst they'll forget the people who harmed them, they'll never forget the people who helped them. Because the power of hatred is limited, but the power of love is boundless.

"It's important to have a white heart, Ellie. Don't you ever forget that!"

Ellie combed her shiny black hair, puffed her chubby cheeks, and tapped her tiny round nose. She stared into her mother's eyes.

Mama Ellie could tell that her daughter was not convinced.

"Why don't you come and see the refugee camp for yourself?" She asked.

"Can I have a lollipop if I go with you?" Ellie replied.

She pretended to apply some nail polish.

A chicken flapped its wings.

Mama Ellie sighed.

"Okay, okay," she said. "As long as you behave yourself."

And so they left their home and walked down the narrow paths which snaked through Natale. They passed thousands of tiny arches, which held up hundreds of stony buildings. They passed the djinns and fairies who lived beneath those arches. They dodged the donkeys who moved without instructions; serving as taxis, garbage collectors, water carriers and porters. They traversed the field at the bottom of town, where retired donkeys saw out their final days. And they arrived at the refugee camp's iron turnstile.

"Check." A Muscular Guard rattled. "Next. Check. Next. Check. Next."

The Muscular Soldier looked simply too big to be allowed. He looked wild. His head almost touched the ceiling, even though he was sitting down. He had mechanical movements and a robotic voice.

"Check. Next. Check. Next."

Mama Ellie stepped forward

"ID!" the Muscular Guard demanded.

"You know who I am," Mama Ellie spat.

"ID!"

"I swear on the evening prayers; you see me every day!"

"ID!"

"Really?"

"ID!"

"Huh," Mama Ellie shrugged. She removed a shabby piece of paper from her pocket, showed it to the Muscular Guard, and led Ellie into the camp.

The first tent Ellie saw was the Director's office. Its floor was covered in paving slabs, a sofa was placed at one end, and a television was placed on a portable table. It was powered by a generator.

Ellie had never seen a television before. But the only person watching it was a lonesome Tea Boy, who was dressed in a smart suit. The

Tea Boy had one responsibility; to occasionally make tea for the Director. He looked bored.

The other people Ellie saw also looked bored. But their tents were not nearly as nice as the Director's. They swayed in the breeze, and looked like they were about to fall over. Rainwater leaked through their roofs, and dripped onto the refugees who were crammed inside.

Outside, hundreds of other refugees were competing to get to the only water truck on site. They trod on rotting piles of rubbish, stumbled across the boggy floor, and slipped into the open sewers.

To Ellie, that place felt like an open air prison. She was shocked by the things she saw as she walked along its muddy streets. As she walked past an Orphan who was stroking a starving cat. Past a Moustached Refugee who was hugging two sheep; the only animals he had saved from his village. And past Tamsin, who was wearing a patched up dress, and holding out a bowl to beg for food. There was a defiant look in Tamsin's eyes, as if she had just waved goodbye to her childhood.

"That could have been you," Mama Ellie said. "I swear on my dead father's grave; we share the same land as these refugees, the same home. We have the same ancestors too. It's only by the grace of God that our town was not occupied as well."

Ellie shuddered.

An unattended Toddler picked up a handful of dirt.

Mama Ellie patted her daughter's back.

They continued on until they reached a billowy tree. A Pale Teacher was standing beneath its branches, and eighty small children were sitting in its shade. They had eager faces and mucky clothes.

"Who can read the alphabet?" The Pale Teacher asked. She pointed to a line of letters, which she had written on the blackboard: 'A, B, C, D....'

Her pupils stared back at her, with blank expressions and closed mouths.

"Can anyone read *any* of these letters?" She tried again.

At first there was silence. No-one moved. Then, in amongst the sea of tiny faces, a Cherubic Refugee tentatively raised her arm.

"Super!" The Pale Teacher cheered. "Please! Come to the front and read the letters you know. I think you're very brave!"

The Cherubic Refugee stood up. She wiped her runny nose, and tiptoed between the other children.

"C," she began. "H. N. R. U."

"Very good!" The Pale Teacher cheered. "Everyone give her a round of applause."

The children clapped, and the Cherubic Refugee blushed. Her embarrassment mixed in with her pride.

"Before you sit down," the Teacher continued. "Can you tell the class how you learnt those letters?"

The Pale Teacher was both confused and intrigued.

"They're all around the camp," the Cherubic Refugee explained. "They're written on the side of tents, on sacks of rice, and on the guards' jackets. My daddy told me they said '*UNHCR*'. It stands for '*United Nations High Commission for Refugees*'."

A little tear rolled down Ellie's cheek.

A little bird landed on a branch.

A little star appeared in the sky.

"Now do you understand why these people deserve our lollipops?" Mama Ellie asked.

"Yes mummy," Ellie replied.

She felt ashamed of herself for having questioned her mother. And so she walked on in silence, until they reached the camp's exit.

"Can we go home now please?" She asked. "My feet are really sore."

"Home?" Mama Ellie scolded. "Do you think we can survive just by walking around refugee camps? Pfft. On the three Godly months! Pull yourself together. We have chores to do!"

Mama Ellie led her daughter back through Natale. She went from market stall to market stall, haggled for food, and came out with bags dangling from both her arms.

She arrived home just as her other children returned from school. She fired up her wood-fuelled stove, boiled enough water to fill her bath, and bathed each of her children in turn. Then she washed some clothes by hand, cooked some dinner, and mopped her courtyard.

Mama Ellie's house consisted of five rooms, which surrounded that first floor courtyard. Below it was a front door, which was always left unlocked. And below that was a tiny basement.

Above it was a raised platform, where a shed housed the family's chickens. And above that was a flat roof where her children played games. They ran from roof to roof, whilst sparrows hid in the walls.

Each room in her house was built in the 'cross-wall' style; they were domed shaped and painted white. The lounge was the only room other than the kitchen that contained a wood burner, and so the children slept in there each winter. That room also contained an old radio, which had split along the middle, and was held together by tape. It was lit by a homemade lamp, which was made from a jar of oil and a fabric wick.

A rifle rested in one corner. Papa Ellie was a tailor, who spent most of his time at work in Collis's capital. He had insisted on leaving that gun behind, so his family could protect themselves.

The only other items in that room were five cushions. Ellie's family sat on those cushions to eat their evening meal, which was served on a large metal platter. Alternating sections of yoghurt and salad surrounded a mound of meat and rice, which collapsed as soon as they started to eat.

When they had finished, Mama Ellie turned towards her daughter.

"Would you like a lollipop?" She asked. "You've been a good girl today. I think you deserve one."

Ellie looked up at her mother, paused to think, and then shook her head.

"No thank-you," she replied. "The refugees need those lollipops more than I do."

* * *

Ellie and her mother grew closer over the months which followed. They shopped together, cooked together, and volunteered together.

Ellie helped her mother to set up an embroidery collective for female refugees. Mama Ellie sourced cloth and thread for those ladies, who made pencil cases which featured slogans like, '*Women can do everything – Men can do something*'. Then she sold their work to an exporter.

The women in that '*Women's Union*' laughed and joked whilst they sewed. They felt free. They felt human. They achieved a new sense of self-worth, learnt new skills, and earned money which their husbands never saw.

Their newfound confidence rubbed off onto Mama Ellie. She

welcomed new people into her home each day. They sat in a circle, drank an infinite amount of tea, put their arms around each other's shoulders, chatted and chortled.

Mama Ellie offered everyone the same warm welcome, whether she knew them or not. Whether they were good or bad, clean or dirty, local or foreign.

"Come in!" She would say. "You are welcome here. Have some tea. You poor things, you must be hungry. Eat something. Have some tea. Please! Share! What's mine is yours. Have some tea."

Mama Ellie's confidence rubbed off onto her daughter. And so when an international relief agency supplied two battered guitars, three broken drums and half a black recorder, Ellie volunteered. She helped them to form a music school for refugees.

'Natale Refugee All Stars' were born.

Ellie rounded up all the children she could find, and encouraged them to sing for their homeland. They whistled with their hearts and they hummed with their souls. They clicked with love and they clapped with joy. With smiles which were brighter than the sun, and eyes which shone like tiny white stars.

As their camp became cramped, those children grew closer.

As the days became colder, their hearts grew warm.

As their tents fell down, their spirits rose up.

Ellie's confidence rubbed off onto those children. She could see it in their postures; in the way they walked and danced. She could hear it in their voices; in the way they sang and spoke. And she could sense it in their auras; in the way they pranced and prattled.

She could sense it in a girl called Jen, who walked in fixed motions, like a chess-piece moving around a board. That little girl, who had tousled hair and ruffled clothes, played an instrument made out of metal scraps.

And she could feel it in a girl who taught herself to play the guitar. That little girl, who was a total wreck at first, became self-assured. Her health improved. She had chubbier cheeks and plumper arms.

"Hi," she said after band practice. "My name is Tamsin."

"Hi," Ellie replied. "I'm Ellie."

Ellie smiled.

Tamsin smiled back.

"Do you want to play hide and seek?" She asked.

"Okay," Ellie replied. "But let's get out of here and play in town."

Ellie led Tamsin past a Bread Boy, who was selling rolls out of a wooden cart. Past a Baker, who was scowling at that boy from inside his empty shop. Past a dusty café, where dusty men were smoking from dusty pipes. Past camels who proceeded at an inaudible pace, men who held hands, and fat cats who perched on the thin rims of rubbish bins.

"Okay, okay," Ellie panted. "Let's play here."

Tamsin closed her eyes and began to count.

"One. Two. Three. Four..."

Ellie ran away. She ran past a Mother, who was picking nits out of her Infant's hair. Past a Barber, who was cutting hair. And past the Bald Local, who did not have any hair at all.

She stopped, climbed a drainpipe, and hid on a rooftop bed. It was surrounded by a white sheet, which was supported by four black poles.

Beds like that one sat on every rooftop in Natale. People slept on them each summer. The sheets blocked out the sun, but they did not block out gravity. At least two people fell off their roofs each year.

"Got you!" Tamsin cheered. "Now it's my time to hide."

Ellie looked bewildered.

A white sheet rippled in the breeze.

Tamsin giggled, waved, and ran away.

Ellie looked for her everywhere. She climbed the stairs which ran from the valley below to the castle above. She trod on cracks and tripped on rubble. She slinked between homes with thick walls, and homes with small windows. She looked down their wells and up their wind towers. But she could not find Tamsin anywhere, and so Ellie became frustrated.

She wobbled her head, sighed, and stopped moving. She muttered to herself. And she jumped up into the air when someone tapped her shoulder.

"Got you again!" Tamsin cheered. "You're not very good at this, are you?"

"It's a silly game," Ellie whinged. "Hide and seek is for babies!"

* * *

Ellie and Tamsin never played hide and seek again. But they did play plenty of other games over the weeks and months which followed.

They fashioned kites out of sticks and scraps of cloth. Then they ran around Natale's castle, flying those kites, and shouting as loudly as they could.

They made toys out of any old rubbish they could scavenge. They hammered bits of wood into the floor, picked up pieces of metal using magnets, and made towers out of builders' bricks.

When it rained, they raced twigs on the water which gushed down the gutters, and bet on which stick would win. When it was sunny, they sat in the shade, playing noughts and crosses in the dust. And when the sun started to set, Ellie returned home to play-fight with her Middle Brother.

Ellie put her Middle Brother in headlocks, and her Middle Brother threw Ellie to the floor. They rolled on top of each other, and pulled each other's hair. Sometimes they got grazed. Occasionally they got cut.

"Mummy! Mummy!" Ellie whinged. "My brother cut me. Look!"

"Wash yourself up then," Mama Ellie replied.

"But mummy! He hurt me!"

"Well don't fight him then. I swear on the sacred bread; if you play like cats, you're bound to get scratched."

"But that's not fair! Why don't you ever punish *him*?"

Mama Ellie looked at her daughter with a look which seemed to say, *'Isn't it obvious?'*

"Really?" She replied. "Really Ellie? I swear on the twelve heavenly commandments; ever since you were able to crawl, you've been like a hyena with him. You used to come to my breast whilst he was suckling, push him away, and stick my tit in your mouth. You've got another thing coming if you think I'm going to stop him from protecting himself."

Ellie stomped away in a mood. She sat in an empty room, folded her arms, and grinded her teeth. She pretended to make herself look pretty. She put on imaginary make-up, and brushed her hair with a fork. She only left that room when Papa Ellie returned.

Everything about Papa Ellie was bent or off-centre. He had a cleft-palate, a hatchet-like nose, and a mouth which was shaped like Cupid's bow. If worn by another person, his body would have been described as 'unfortunate'. But Papa Ellie held himself well. He made his ugliness seem alluring, and imbued it with a certain sense of moreish-ness. Random strangers stopped to stare at him. Most of them liked what they saw.

Papa Ellie was bombarded by his children as soon as he entered. They hugged him and would not let him go. He had to walk up the stairs with four children attached to his legs. He made big, slow steps, like a tentative clown.

"Leave your papa alone," Mama Ellie scolded. "On my reincarnation in heaven! Give the man a break. He's only just come through the door!"

But despite her gentle scolding, Mama Ellie was just as happy to see her husband as everyone else. And her children's affection gave her a warm feeling inside. It made her smirk.

Papa Ellie sat down in the living room, emitted a big sigh of relief, and threw a handful of chestnuts onto the fire. He handed out some coconut pyramids. He looked at his children and smiled.

Ellie smiled as well. She was happy whenever her father returned home. She just wished they could spend more time together.

"I want to stay here with daddy," she said the next morning.

"I don't care what you want," Mama Ellie replied. "You need to go to school."

"But it's cold mummy. It's raining. I'll get wet on the way to school and spend the whole day shivering. They don't have a fire at school. I'll catch a cold. I won't be able to concentrate. I won't learn a thing."

Papa Ellie did not say a word. He was happy to let his wife do all the talking.

"On the Godly temple! I swear you've got an excuse for everything, young girl. Well it doesn't wash with me. You should count yourself lucky to be receiving an education.

"Do you know what happened when I asked my parents to go to school? My father said, 'No! You're not going. It'll only make you strong willed. You don't need an education to be a housewife'."

Mama Ellie scowled at her daughter.

"Would you rather I took that approach with you?" She asked. "Would you rather be an ignoramus like me?"

Ellie shook her head.

"Well get moving then!"

Ellie tutted, picked up her bag, and left for school. She had to wait another six days before she saw her father again.

But when Papa Ellie did return, he was not his normal self. His gentle persona had vanished. He seemed frustrated, agitated and tense.

"Listen up," he said once he had sat his family down. "I have some bad news."

Papa Ellie looked stressed.

His family looked worried.

Mama Ellie poured some tea.

"I've gone out of business," Papa Ellie continued. "I'm afraid we're going to have to make some cutbacks around here. We're going to have to stop all this hosting of guests. We're going to have to survive on a diet of rice and soup!"

His family stared at Papa Ellie. Their stomachs dropped. Their eyes looked hollow. Confusion covered their faces.

No-one said a word.

The silence lasted for minutes.

"It's those bloody foreigners!" Papa Ellie finally said. "It's those bloody refugees; coming here and taking our jobs. Pfft! We should have never let them stay, with their strange ways and peculiar habits. What have they ever done for us? Nothing! They're no bloody use to anyone. And now they're stealing our livelihoods. What chance do we have, when they're prepared to work for peanuts?

"We should expel those bloated leeches! Those circumcised ferrets! Those one-dollar whores!"

He glared at Ellie, slapped his thigh, and continued his rant.

"It was your friend, that Tamsin, who's to blame. It was her dad who's put me out of business; selling dodgy suits for half my prices. He can't even sew! He's got no bloody experience at all! Yet, because of him, we're going to have to live off rice.

"So I don't want you playing with that Tamsin, that dizzy-eyed midget, ever again. I don't want you going anywhere near that creepy elf!"

Ellie trembled.

She ate in silence that evening. She went to bed straight after dinner. And she went to school the next morning without making any complaints.

* * *

The weeks which followed were hard for Ellie's family. They spent their savings on rice, and their chickens supplied them with eggs. Some of her erstwhile guests brought Mama Ellie food, but others did not. Her family never had quite enough to satisfy their hunger.

Papa Ellie stopped being a passing stranger, a mythical creature whose absences added to his allure. He became an overwhelming presence, who seemed to appear at every turn. He brooded, he muttered, and he snapped at the slightest provocation.

"It's those bloody foreigners," he roared. "We need to kick those refugees out. We can't live with them; they're too needy. And we can't let this stalemate continue; it's killing us. They're playing for time, and we're playing into their hands. New refugees are arriving here every day! We need to fight them every day, or we'll never get our town back.

"They should bugger off back to their own country!"

"Oh give it a rest," Mama Ellie slammed. "Don't you think they've been trying? Protokian soldiers shoot them whenever they get close."

"Well they should go to another country then. Our town is bursting at the seams with those fish-lipped maggots. We don't have the resources to support them. They're stealing our jobs!"

"They're spending their money too," Mama Ellie argued. "I swear on my dead father's wounds! Our neighbours are doing a roaring trade with them. Some refugees are even employing locals!

"The opportunities are out there. If you'd only get up off your arse and look for them, we wouldn't be living off of rice."

"Poppycock! Refugees only do business with their own.

"Now listen here woman, I've had enough of your lip. I think you forget your place sometimes. I give you far too much freedom.

"Well I don't want you going near that camp again. You hear me? I don't want you mixing with those elfish aliens! Those hoary freeloaders! Those mad moustachioed malt-worms!!!"

Mama Ellie bit her tongue. She never questioned Papa Ellie once he had put his foot down. She never disobeyed her husband's rules.

But Ellie felt uncomfortable. She did not like it when her parents argued. So she left the room. She looked into a mirror, adjusted her hair, and went out to play with her friends.

They played *Seven Stones*; throwing a ball at a pile of pebbles. They played *Tag*; jumping from roof to roof. They played football. And they flew their homemade kites.

Those kites soared behind them as they ran down narrow alleys. As they ran between sloping graves. And as they ran through the field where retired donkeys saw out their final days.

Ellie's arm swung up into the air. Her kite's string had been caught in a tree. It pulled taught and yanked her back.

Ellie could only watch as her kite broke free, rose, and floated away. She paused to think.

And then she ran after her kite. She ran through the field, hurdled a stream, and sprinted down a stony lane. She reached the refugee camp.

She paused to think again.

She knew she was not allowed to enter that place. She knew she would get in trouble if she was caught. She knew there would be pain and sorrow.

She had never disobeyed her father before.

So she stood there and weighed up her options, whilst her kite floated above a sea of white tents.

Whilst refugees queued.

Whilst the Muscular Guard rattled on like a machine: '*Check. Next. Check. Next. Check...*'

The more she tried to hold herself back, the more she wanted to enter the camp. The more she resisted, the more she was tempted. She wanted to break her father's rule, simply for the sake of breaking it.

So Ellie simpered, puffed her chest, and walked through the turnstiles.

She felt an enormous thrill. Butterflies fluttered in her stomach, and her spine tingled. Her hands shook.

The first thing she saw was the Director's office. His tent had been replaced by a pink cottage; the only permanent building on site. Pretty flowers were planted by its door, next to three jeeps. Three drivers looked bored.

The second thing Ellie saw was the graffiti:

JOSS SHELDON | 55

'UNITED NATIONS RESOLUTION 194. *Refugees wishing to return to their homes, and live at peace with their neighbours, should be permitted to do so at the earliest practical date*'.

Beneath it Ellie scribbled, '*We are the 99%! The people of Natale support the refugees!*'

And beneath that, a peppermint plant fluttered in the breeze.

Ellie ran after her kite. But she ducked for cover as soon as she saw Tamsin. She felt guilty for abandoning her friend. She felt ashamed. And she filled with hatred for Tamsin, for triggering those negative emotions.

So she picked up a stone and threw it at Tamsin's foot. She regretted it straight away. She felt worse than she had done before.

But Tamsin did not notice the pebble which skimmed off the ground in front of her. She had other things on her mind.

"Why can't I see papa anymore?" She asked her mother.

"Your papa is working really hard," Mama Tamsin replied. "He's a real hero. He's working a hundred hours each week! But don't worry, hard work gets rewarded. His tailoring business is sure to take off. We're going to be rich!"

"I miss papa."

"I know, but he'll visit us in six months. You'll see him then."

Ellie's shoulders drooped, her torso slouched, and her kite drifted out of sight. She ambled back to the entrance.

A Brunette Refugee vomited in the middle of the street.

A Blonde Refugee sprinted through that vomit.

"Our neighbours are coming to save us!" She cheered. "They're going to drive the Holies into the sea! We're going to get our land back! Yippee!!!"

"We're going home!" A Noisy Refugee chanted. "Protokia has no right to exist!"

Hundreds of refugees turned to face each other.

"We're going home!" Half of them whispered.

"We're going home!" The other half cheered.

* * *

"They're finally going to bugger off home," Papa Ellie said. "Good riddance to bad rubbish, I say. Everything will go back to normal."

Ellie looked up at her father, and back down at his suit. She polished its brass buttons for the seventh time that evening. Then she ironed it with a box iron, until its corners were perfectly crisp, and its lapels were perfectly flat.

"My daughter, you've whitened my face," Papa Ellie said. "You really are worth ten sons!"

He did not realise that Ellie was only cleaning that suit to assuage her guilt. Ellie had gotten away with her visit to the refugee camp. So she exhaled. She clung to that small victory. And she felt triumphant.

She rolled over, brushed her father's suit, and grinned.

Papa Ellie also grinned. He assumed that his daughter was excited about his upcoming interview. He had spoken of little else for the previous three days.

"I'm going back to work!" He said. "Oh, I do hope I get that job. It pays almost as much as my last job! I'll get a day off every week! Every week!

"They're only interviewing three of us. Three locals! No refugees. I'm in with a chance, I tell you. Our days of rice and soup could be behind us!"

Mama Ellie passed her husband his seventeenth tea of the evening, sat down, and listened patiently without saying a word. She told her children to go to sleep, led Papa Ellie to bed, and made love to him for the first time in weeks.

But Papa Ellie never made it to his interview.

His whole family was woken up by the sound of gunfire and grenades. The walls shook and the floors quaked. The skies turned black with soot, and the sun hid behind the moon.

The Protokians had launched a counter-attack. They were grabbing as much land as they could.

Papa Ellie grabbed a sack of rice, and escorted his family into their basement. They huddled together, and waited for the bombardment to stop.

Ellie moved the charms on her necklace back and forth.

An ant ran away with a tea leaf.

A jar fell off its shelf.

But the bombardment did not stop.

They sat in that basement for what felt like an eternity. Their conversations ran dry. They played games until they were bored. Then they stared at each other's faces, without saying a single word.

Ellie had never paid so much attention to her mother's face. She noticed that it had three peculiar features. A round bone poked out of her nose, about half way down. It was not big enough to make her nose look bent, but it did skew her appearance. Her aural canals were asymmetrical. One was curved like a kidney bean, whilst the other was round like a chickpea. And her parting was slightly off-centre. It swerved to dodge a scar at the front of her scalp.

Ellie looked at everyone's face.

An ant ran away with a grain of rice.

The door rattled.

But the bombardment did not stop.

In the darkness of their basement, it was impossible to tell when one day ended and the next one began. Ellie's family slept to pass the time. Yet they were never fully asleep. They were in a permanent stupor. Their eyesight was blurry and their minds were numb.

Ellie looked at herself in a compact mirror.

An ant ran away with a splinter.

A chicken clucked.

But the bombardment did not stop.

"I'm scared," Ellie said.

"Our lives are in the hands of God," Mama Ellie replied. "Governments rule, but God is the only ruler. He'll protect us."

She gave Ellie her nail polish. Ellie spent hours applying it to her nails, slowly and methodically, with the utmost attention to detail.

An ant ran away with a grain of sugar.

A bottle of urine fell over.

A cat meowed.

And the bombardment finally stopped.

That war became known as the 'Seven Day War'. Some people said it had only lasted for six days, but no-one could be sure. Everyone in Natale had stayed inside on the seventh day, because they had been traumatised by the shelling. They only emerged when the Protokians announced their victory on loud hailers.

Ellie's family faced a scene of devastation.

Their stairs had been crushed. There was a hole in the roof, and a hole in the kitchen wall. Their courtyard had been turned upside down. Pieces of the ceiling were spread across the floor, and pieces of the floor were wedged into the ceiling.

It took Ellie hours to find the courage to leave her house.

When she did finally step outside, the first thing she saw was a dead donkey, whose corpse was attracting flies.

The second thing she saw was a group of Godlies, who were fleeing to a neighbouring country.

A Sinewy Local was wagging his fist at them.

"Cowards!" He shouted. "You should be standing firm! You should be fighting for our freedom! You poisonous toads! You good for nothing toe-rags! You clapper-clawed barnacles!"

And the third thing Ellie saw was a Hunky Soldier, who wore a smart uniform and a friendly smile.

That Protokian teenager squatted down, looked into Ellie's eyes, and offered her a sweet.

"I bet you'd like some lollipops," he said. "Help yourself. What's ours is yours!"

Ellie stared at the Hunky Soldier, cried, and ran back inside.

* * *

Everything changed slowly, but everything changed.

A barbed wire fence was erected around Natale's castle, which was turned into a military base. A Holy flag, which could be seen from anywhere in Natale, was raised in its centre.

A giant billboard, the first in town, was erected at the bottom of the hill. It featured a black and white poster, which said, 'Love the Protokians: They have liberated you'.

Ellie's school was renamed 'Atamow Elementary', after the Protokian prime minister; a man who was so cold, his facial features had frozen. His eyes had turned red, his lips had turned blue, and his hair had turned white. His skin was frosty and his voice was bitter. His blood was icy cold.

Hundreds of Protokian soldiers arrived in Natale each day, dressed in neatly pressed uniforms. And thousands of Protokian administrators followed them. What they gave with one hand, they took away with the other.

They assembled pylons which brought electricity to Natale for the first time, then closed every well in town. They repaired the houses which had been damaged during the war, then demolished those houses to build new roads. They tarmacked Natale's existing roads, then drove their vehicles into the walls which surrounded those narrow streets.

"They're here to stay," the Mad Lady told anyone who would listen. "They'll never leave. A magical toad told me so."

"Oh shut up," a Dairy Farmer shouted back. "What do you know, you batty old witch?"

The Mad Lady scowled at the Dairy Farmer; a man who smelled of stale manure. Her pupils became so small, they almost disappeared. Her wart seemed to wobble. She wagged her finger and walked away.

The Dairy Farmer walked towards his fields, which covered the hill adjacent to Natale. He waved at Ellie, who was playing catch with her friends. And he approached a group of soldiers, who had just fenced off his land. They stopped him from reaching his cows.

"This is my land!" The Dairy Farmer bellowed. "Bugger off and take your bleeding fence with you, or I'll call the police!"

"The police?" A Punky Soldier replied. He picked a piece of tobacco out of his teeth. "We are the police!"

"But this is my land!"

"Can you prove that?"

"I've been farming this land all my life, you can ask anyone in town. This hill has been in my family for generations."

"Have you registered it with the authorities?"

"The authorities? This land has been in my family since before there were any authorities!"

"Do you have any papers to prove that? Do you have any deeds?"

"Papers? Deeds? Why do I need deeds? I walk on this soil every day. Even the worms know that it's my land!"

"If you don't have any deeds, it's not your land, it's the government's land, and you're trespassing on it. So I suggest you move along, or I'll be forced to arrest you.

"The government has given this hill to a group of Holy immigrants, who plan to build a settlement here. It's Protokian land for Protokian people. It's not for troublemakers like you!"

The Dairy Farmer lifted his fist. But he stopped short of punching the Punky Soldier, because he felt an overwhelming presence behind him. He turned around and saw seven soldiers. Fourteen eyes glared in his direction. Seven fingers hovered above seven triggers.

So the Dairy Farmer made a quick retreat. He rushed past Ellie, spoke to his lawyer, and returned the following morning.

"You're in breach of the *Fourth Geneva Convention!*" He cheered triumphantly. "Article forty-nine point six states, '*The Occupying Power shall not transfer its own civilian population into the territory it occupies*'.

"You can't give my land to Protokians. It's against international law! You're in breach of the Fourth Geneva Convention!"

The Punky Soldier looked at the Dairy Farmer, furrowed his eyebrows and snickered.

"Does this look like Geneva to you?" He mocked. "Now I've warned you already. If you don't step away, I'll arrest you for trespassing. So bugger off. Get out of my sight!"

The Dairy Farmer shook his head, wagged his finger, and stormed off.

He stalked past the Muscular Guard. He stampeded past Mama Tamsin. And he cursed as he stomped past Ellie.

"Bloody Protokians! Bloody foreigners, coming here and taking our land! Bloody Holies, with their strange ways and peculiar habits. What have they ever done for us? Nothing! They're no bloody use to anyone."

Ellie shuddered. She was startled, shocked and stunned.

But she soon grew accustomed to that sort of behaviour. It became commonplace as the Holies moved in. As they built an aquifer, which sucked up water from beneath Natale. As they turned the green fields grey with concrete roads. And as they scattered their mobile homes across the hillside.

She finally understood Tamsin's ordeal.

She returned home, shook and shivered.

3. ARUN

Arun sat in his new mobile home, dressed in his new clothes, and began to perspire. A pearl of sweat rolled over his tiny round nose, and reached his chubby cheek. Arun flicked his shiny black hair behind his ears, and opened a window, whilst a wall-mounted heater rumbled away.

He turned around, sat down on a sofa, and beamed with pride.

It had taken his family years to get to Protokia. Years of hardship, years of sorrow, and years of pain. Years spent hiding in vast forests, cold and hungry, living with a strange mix of partisans and crooks. Years spent working on an assortment of different farms, never knowing when Papa Arun's crippled arm would fail. Years spent denying their names, their identities and their religion; not knowing who to trust, or who to avoid.

But all the dreams which sustained them during those years had finally come true. They had arrived in their homeland, and moved into their very own cabin.

Arun sat back and took it all in.

He took in a giant pouf, which sat on the linoleum floor, and a piano which ran alongside a plasterboard wall. Behind that wall was a shower room, which contained the first flushing toilet Arun had ever seen. To the side of that room, a tiny open-plan kitchen was flanked by three shelves, which supported jars of red paprika, orange cinnamon, and green herbs; rice, flour and lentils.

The kettle whistled.

Mama Arun, a stout woman who had wide shoulders and cobalt eyes, painted white flowers onto a turquoise light switch. A model giraffe, which was missing half a leg, watched her in silence.

Papa Arun scratched his bumpy nose, asymmetrical ears, and off-centre parting. He was sitting on the other side of a door which did not have a lock, in a marquee which was bigger than the cabin itself. Its walls were made from plastic sheets, and its roof was made from palm fronds. Two sofas and an armchair surrounded a table and a water pipe. A wood burning fireplace, which Papa Arun had made from an old oil barrel, rumbled away in the corner.

Papa Arun had spent every penny the Protokian government had given him. Every loan, tax break and grant. He had taken out a subsidised mortgage to furnish his subsidised home. And he felt satisfied. He was sure he would make a good impression on his guests.

The first person to appear was an Orthodox Settler, who wore lilac lipstick and pungent perfume. She introduced her husband, who had a bushy beard and straggly eyebrows. They were followed by a Militant Settler, who wore khaki trousers, and his wife, who wore a floral dress. They talked for an hour before an Economic Settler entered, ran his fingers through his curly hair, and glanced at his lover's plump derriere.

"It sure is good to be back in the land of the Holies," he said.

He talked about how cheap it was to live in a settlement, and how he had prospered there. The Militant Settler nodded along.

"God will provide," he said. "He gave us this land, and he will give us opportunities to thrive. We just need to ensure we protect his gift."

The Orthodox Settler scowled.

"We just need to obey God's rules, that's all," she said. "We don't need to do God's work for him."

She paused, glared at the Militant Settler, and then turned to Papa Arun.

"So what's your story?" She asked.

Papa Arun smiled.

A palm frond rustled in the breeze.

Arun, who had been listening from inside the cabin, ran into the marquee and sat down on the floor.

"Tell them your story, daddy," he pleaded. "Go on daddy! It's the best story in the world!"

Papa Arun ruffled his son's hair.

A cat wandered into the marquee.

Arun looked up at his father with eager eyes. He had heard his father's story hundreds of times before, but it still excited him. He loved it when his father spoke about his adventures. It gave him goose-pimples.

"Okay, okay," Papa Arun chuckled. "But first let me make some more chai."

Papa Arun went into the kitchen and returned with nine cups of tea. He fired up his water pipe, inhaled, and passed the mouthpiece along. He sank back into his armchair and began to speak:

"Well it all started on the *'Night of the Broken Glass'*. Of course the Holies had been persecuted before that. I was caned every day at school, my Sister was denied hospital care, and we all had to wear red suns. But things took a turn for the worse that night, when the Colonisers looted our shops and burnt our temples.

"*'The authorities will protect us'*, my father argued. *'I served in their army. Have some faith.'*

"But he was bundled into a car and taken away the very next day. That was when we went into hiding. People were saying the Colonisers were slaughtering Holies. They were calling it the *'Great Genocide'*!"

Papa Arun's guests nodded. There was an empathetic sort of sadness in their eyes, as if they had experienced similar tragedies themselves.

"I heard they lined Holies up, shot them, and buried them in mass graves," the Militant Settler said.

"I heard they stripped Holies naked and hung them from trees," the Orthodox Settler added.

"I heard they threw Holies into acid wells," the Economic Settler agreed. "I heard they dressed them up in striped pyjamas, locked them in cramped chambers, and poisoned them with Zyklon gas."

Papa Arun drank some tea.

"Well, I knew a Pharmacist who was kind enough to hide us in her attic."

"Tell them about the Pharmacist, daddy," Arun cheered. "Tell them about her nose."

"Oh, she had some nose on her, the Pharmacist. It was the biggest I've ever seen!"

"It was as big as a cavern!"

"It sure was. I swear there was a clan of goblins who lived in there, boiling up cauldrons of green snot. That snot used to fizz, bubble and pop. It sprayed out of the Pharmacist's nose and covered everything in her vicinity! If you weren't careful, you'd end up looking like a swamp monster after five minutes in her company!

"But she was a nice lady nonetheless. I wouldn't be alive if it wasn't for that Godly."

Everyone stared at Papa Arun.

"A Godly saved you?" The Militant Settler asked. He looked gobsmacked.

The Economic Settler looked astonished.

The Orthodox Settler looked amazed.

"Oh yeah," Papa Arun replied. "The Godlies have a saying in their bible; *'If you save another person's life, it is as if you have saved the whole of humankind'.*"

"We have the same saying in our bible," the Orthodox Settler said.

"For sure," Papa Arun continued. "Well, the Pharmacist took that saying very seriously. She saved our lives, but to her it was as if she was saving the whole of humankind. It didn't even bother her that she could have been killed. Her friend was executed for withholding information about some Holies, and the Pharmacist didn't even batter an eyelid.

"*'Besa, besa,'* she said. *'It's a matter of honour. I have made a promise to protect you. And anyway, you would do the same for me'.*

"So she hid us in the attic above her pharmacy, where we shared a single bed for over a year. It was dark and dingy in there. Only a thin sliver of light made it through a boarded up window, which rattled during the air raids. The rest of the time it was silent. We didn't speak, because we didn't want anyone to hear us."

Papa Arun drank some tea.

"You're going to tell them how I nearly got us caught, aren't you?" Arun asked.

"I sure am," his father replied.

Arun giggled.

His father gave him a mischievous look.

A spark flew off the fire.

"It was when the Colonisers came to search the pharmacy. Four of them rushed into the building. We could hear their heavy footsteps. We could hear their conversation.

"Arun cried. He was going to get us caught!

"So we crushed a sleeping pill, mixed it in with some milk, and made Arun drink that concoction.

"But that only made him more alert than before! We had to give him another pill before he passed out. I tell you, our hearts were beating like drums. We thought the game was up."

Mama Arun looked at her son, grimaced, and covered her mouth.

Papa Arun chuckled.

His guests shuffled towards the edge of their seats.

"Well the Colonisers left, and the Pharmacist came to check on us. Only Arun wasn't responding. He had overdosed on pills! We thought we had lost him.

"The Pharmacist tried to resuscitate Arun. She breathed into his mouth, and pumped his ribs.

"After several minutes had passed, Arun woke up. He vomited all over the Pharmacist, and kicked his legs in the air.

"We were ever so relieved, but we knew it was time to go. We knew it would not be long before the Colonisers returned. And we knew we'd be killed if we stayed.

"So the Pharmacist bought me an army uniform. She found us some fake papers. And she arranged for us to go to the port in the back of a lorry. We just had to meet that lorry on the edge of town.

"We made it to the meeting point without any troubles. But whilst we waited there, outside a bakery, I heard a sharp voice at my shoulder.

"'Well, well, well," it barked. 'What do have we here then? Why aren't you at the front?'

"I turned around and saw a Policeman.

"'I work in munitions', I replied. 'I'm on my way to check a shipment'.

"I was so nervous, I started to feel nauseous.

"The Policeman looked me up and down, read my papers, and whistled. I thought I'd gotten away with it.

"But the Policeman had received an anonymous tip off. He knew we were Holies. And so he arrested us, and took us back to the station.

"We thought we were done for."

The Orthodox Settler looked at her husband.

The Militant Settler looked at Papa Arun.

Papa Arun winked, sucked on his water pipe, and passed it along.

"We were put in a processing cell together. We hugged, we cried, and we attempted to save our lives.

"We swallowed some pills, and scratched ourselves all over. By the time the Policeman returned, we were covered in a horrific rash. It was pink, blotchy and raw.

"The Policeman took a step back and covered his mouth. He was aghast.

"We told him, '*We think we've got scarlet fever*'.

"Well, the Colonisers were really scared of infections like that. The Policeman didn't want anything to do with it. So he sent us to the hospital.

"The security was not nearly so tight in that place. There was just one guard on our ward. So we pretended to be asleep. And when the guard went to the toilet, we jumped out of bed and ran to the window.

"Our ward was on the second floor. But we didn't have the time to worry about that. I climbed onto the ledge, swung my feet outside, and jumped. I held Arun in my arms. But when I landed, my knee buckled, I stumbled, and I crashed down upon my side. My elbow shattered into a million little pieces. It's still crippled today."

The Militant Settler winced.

The Orthodox Settler grimaced.

Papa Arun rubbed his arm.

"I put Arun down, moved a pile of soft rubbish below the window, and watched my wife jump.

"Then we ran off into the forest. We hid there for two days.

"Eventually we saw a parked cart. We climbed into that waggon, which took us to the coast, without the driver ever knowing.

"We were almost free!"

The Economic Settler exhaled and sank back into the settee.

Mama Arun made some more tea.

Arun jiggled his legs.

"We had missed our boat, and so we asked around to find another one. It was a massive gamble. If we had spoken to an informant, we'd have been arrested within minutes.

"Fortunately for us, we found two fishermen who were happy to take us across the bay, to a vessel which was heading abroad. But those kind men were stopped at the opposite shore by a Customs Officer.

"We huddled together in the hold, shivered and prayed."

The Economic Settler looked up to the heavens.

Mama Arun poured some tea.

Arun cheered.

"Tell them what happened," he shouted. "Tell them what the

fishermen told the Customs Officer."

Papa Arun chuckled.

"Well, there were two empty bottles of rum up on deck. When the Customs Officer came aboard the fishermen grabbed those bottles, stumbled about, and slurred their words.

"'*Do you know that it's a criminal offence to be drunk at the controls of a boat?*' The Customs Officer asked.

"'*Go kiss a pig*', the Wide Fisherman slurred.

"'*It would be more enjoyable than kissing your wife,*' the Narrow Fisherman added. '*The pig would be more attractive!*'

"'*Right, that's it,*' the Customs Officer snapped. '*How dare you talk to an officer of the law like that? You're both coming to the station.*'

"So the Customs Officer arrested the fishermen instead of searching the boat. We were able to escape without getting caught!"

The Militant Settler shook his head.

"You're the luckiest person I've ever met," he said.

Papa Arun chuckled.

"Perhaps," he replied. "Most Holies didn't receive the assistance we did, that's for sure. We were the fortunate ones."

The guests bowed their heads, and shared a moment of silent contemplation.

Water dripped from a tap.

The fire rumbled.

A clock ticked.

"Well, we found the vessel and approached the Captain, but he wanted more money than we had to offer. We felt stumped. We felt that all our efforts had all been in vain.

"Then my wife spoke up.

"'*Take this*', she said. And she offered the Captain her wedding ring. '*It's worth more than you're asking for*'.

"The Captain paused to think. He took the ring, sold it in town, and then returned to the ship. He led us down into the hold, and locked us in a cage.

"We huddled together with a group of Holy escapees. There was a Doctor, a pair of beloved actors, an elderly couple who cherished life more than anyone else, a Young Mother and her three year old Child. That woman spent two sleepless nights teaching her Child to use an alias.

"Finally, we arrived on neutral land. We got off the boat and met a local lady, who gave some lipstick to my wife, and some lollipops to Arun."

The guests all exhaled.

A chicken clucked.

Mama Arun poured some tea.

"We stayed in that country until the end of the war, although it was a struggle at first. We had to go from farm to farm to find shelter. I worked to pay our way, but we had to move on whenever my arm packed in."

"Tell us the tales you told, daddy," Arun pleaded. "Please!"

"Okay, okay," Papa Arun chuckled. "Well, when people saw I had a gammy arm, they weren't prepared to employ me. I needed an ice-breaker to build rapport. So I told all sorts of tales to make them laugh.

"I told one person that my arm had been squashed by a rampaging tank. I told another that it had been mauled by a red-eyed tiger. And I even said it had been crushed by the Great Dictator himself!"

"Tell us about the owl man, daddy. Please!" Arun cheered. "Please! Please! Please!"

"Okay, okay," Papa Arun chuckled. "Well there was one Farmer, who looked like an owl. His eyes were bright green, and separated by a wide nose. He had a flat face and pointy ears.

"I told him that I had destroyed my arm during a fight with a naked sumo wrestler. That I had pushed that obese man out the ring, but he had stumbled over, and crushed my arm beneath his blubber.

"The Farmer didn't believe me, but he laughed, which was all I wanted. The Farmer warmed to me. And whilst he didn't have a spare room himself, he knew a Widow who did.

"We stayed with that Widow till the end of the war.

"She was warm-hearted and brave, but above all else she was practical. She dressed us like the natives, got us official documentation, and overwhelmed us with advice.

"'*Don't ever take your pants down or relieve yourself in front of a local*', she told us. '*Don't ever eat fish on a Sunday. And don't ever compliment a man on his looks*'.

"We still felt like refugees, but we felt protected too. So life was good, until the Colonisers occupied that country.

"But things never got as bad as they had been. The locals stood up for us. They protected us from the Great Genocide!

"When the Colonisers made us wear red suns, all the locals wore them too. Even the king wore one! When the Colonisers paraded through town with their arsenals of weaponry, the locals turned their backs and walked away. They left the Colonisers without an audience! And when the Colonisers asked for directions, the locals pointed them the wrong way.

"So we were able to keep our spirits high. And we had faith that the Colonialists would beat the Colonisers. That twenty two nations would come to our rescue.

"Of course, that's exactly what happened. The Colonisers were beaten, and we made our way to Protokia.

"I'll never forget that Widow though.

"'*Remember to be friendly to everyone you meet*', she told us before we left. '*Take care of persecuted people, like I have taken care of you*'."

* * *

Whilst Arun was comforted by the familiar story his father had told, he also longed for adventures of his own. And so the next day, when his mother sent him out to buy eggs, Arun snuck down into Natale.

He walked along a tarmac road, which was perfectly clean and totally empty. There were two lanes running in each direction, either side of a row of trees, but there weren't any other settlers in sight.

He walked past a rickety assortment of caravans, cabins and shacks, which had been scattered across the hillside in a hotchpotch manner.

And he walked through the established part of his settlement, where settlers had built identical homes. They were all big and bold, with front gardens and fat cats.

A bus passed by, carrying settlers to their jobs in Protokia. And then the silence resumed. The only thing that moved were the birds, who sang to their heart's content.

Waves of tiny flowers covered an ocean of empty hills. Yellow and blue petals fluttered in the breeze. And an eagle soared through the sky.

Arun walked around a concrete football pitch, an artificial pond, and a plastic playground. He approached the perimeter fence, which was three metres tall, and topped with curls of barbed wire.

He waved to the Muscular Guard, who was standing by the gate. The Bedouin, who was tending to his flock. And the Militant Settler, who was shouting at Papa Ellie.

He entered Natale for the first time in his life.

He felt claustrophobic as he walked down that town's narrow alleys, which were all surrounded by tall walls. Butterflies fluttered in his stomach, and his spine tingled. His hands shook.

He loved the thrill of the unknown.

He ran up stairs and skipped down lanes, before he turned a corner and saw some children who were playing football. Their pitch was marked by a low wall, a crumbling building, and some small stones. Bigger stones were used for goalposts. The playing surface was a mixture of dust, pebbles, sticks and wire.

A group of children, who were too young to play, watched on from the side. A Lanky Refugee, who was older than the other players, dominated the match. And the ball, which was made from scraps of old cloth, slowly fell apart.

"Hello," Arun said. "I salute the God within you."

Those were the only words of Godliness, the language of the Godlies, which Arun understood. He spoke Colonialist, and he was learning Protokian; the language the Holies had just invented.

He pointed to his chest, pointed at the ball, gave a thumbs up, and nodded his head.

The other children stared back at him.

Arun kicked his foot through the air.

"Hello," he said again.

He gave another thumbs up.

A Scruffy Refugee spat on the ground.

Tamsin sniggered.

"Let him play," she said. "Let's see what he's got."

Arun did not have a clue what Tamsin was saying. He just bounced on his toes and bobbed his head.

Tamsin waved him over and gave him the ball.

As soon as the game restarted, the Scruffy Refugee tackled Arun and passed the ball to Tamsin, who kicked the ball between Arun's legs. Arun fell to the floor. A puff of dust engulfed him.

The other children stood over Arun and laughed.

"Are you okay?" Tamsin asked.

She stretched out her hand, pulled Arun to his feet, and kicked the ball into the air.

Arun's team scored, then the opposition scored. They were losing by four goals to two when the Mad Lady hobbled past. Pus was dripping from her wart, and a beetle was crawling about in her hair.

"You play today, but you'll fight tomorrow," she wailed. "Oh yes! All the goblins are saying it!"

"Oh shut up," Tamsin shouted back. "What do you know, you batty old witch?"

They played football for another fifteen minutes. By the time they had finished, Tamsin was covered in sweat, and Arun was covered in dust. They both had stitches. Their ball had completely disintegrated.

They sat down on a low wall and tried to speak.

"Holy?" Tamsin asked. She pointed at Arun's chest.

Arun nodded.

"Godly?" Arun asked. He pointed back at Tamsin.

She nodded too.

They looked each other up and down.

They both squinted.

"You eat chickens, don't you?" Tamsin taunted.

Arun looked puzzled.

"Chickens," Tamsin repeated. "Chi–keh–nez!"

She flapped her arms to make them look like chicken wings. Then she moved her hand towards her mouth, as if she was eating.

"Ah," Arun replied with a smile. "Yes! Yes! But you eat cows!"

Arun moved his hand towards his mouth.

"Moo! Moo! Moo!" He said.

Tamsin giggled.

Arun giggled too. He pointed at Tamsin, opened his mouth, and pretended to be sick at the thought of eating beef.

Tamsin pointed at Arun, and waved her hand in front of her nose, to suggest that eating chicken made Arun smell.

They both guffawed.

They both slapped their thighs.

They both looked at a Geeky Refugee, who sat down beside them.

"I speak Protokian," she said. "I can translate if you like."

The Geeky Refugee began to translate.

"I heard you pray six times a day, facing north," Tamsin teased.

"Of course," Arun replied. "You know it makes sense. God won't hear you if you pray to the south. And only praying four times a day is just lazy."

"Lazy?" Tamsin spat back with fake disgust. "At least we pray properly. You don't even separate men from women!"

"You're not even baptised!"

"You're not even circumcised!"

"Your hymns are solemn!"

"Your hymns are brazen!"

"Your angel is a peacock!"

"Your angel is an elephant!"

"You write from left to right!"

"You write from right to left!"

"Your calendar is based on the moon!"

"Your calendar is based on the sun!"

"You worship fire!"

"You worship scrolls!"

Arun blew a raspberry.

Tamsin stuck her tongue out.

Arun scrunched his nose.

Tamsin blew a sarcastic kiss.

They both laughed in unison.

The Geeky Refugee rolled her eyes.

"Stop praying to a piece of wood," Tamsin continued. "Come with us and join the Godly religion. It's the one true faith."

"I'd rather not," Arun replied. "My dad would kill me."

Arun wanted to change the subject.

"What does your dad do?" He asked.

"He's a market trader," Tamsin answered. She was always happy to talk about her father. "He sells satsumas.

"He was a tailor, but a Protokian firm undercut his prices. They offered him a job in their factory, but he wanted to keep his independence. He didn't want to work for anyone else. He's an entrepreneur!"

"That's good," Arun replied. "His hard work will pay off in the end."

"Yes. We're going to be wealthy. Just you wait and see!"

Arun chortled, stood up, and left.

"That's right," Tamsin teased. "Off you go to your fake little village, with your plastic grass and your concrete cows."

Arun rolled his eyes.

Tamsin pulled a silly face.

They both went to their temples, said the same prayers, and glorified the same God.

* * *

Arun played with the Godlies several times over the months which followed. Papa Arun did not seem to mind. His son was being *'friendly to everyone he met'*.

After they played, Arun and Tamsin chatted, with help from the Geeky Refugee. And, as time passed, they learnt each other's language.

Sometimes they spoke about their long journeys to Natale, sometimes they spoke about their homes. They spoke about their favourite meals and their least favourite classes at school. Tamsin said her uncle was a Holy, and Arun said a Godly had saved his life.

They played in the field where retired donkeys saw out their final days, in the refugee camp, and near the Protokian prison.

"I heard it's full of Godlies who don't want the Holies to be here," Tamsin said one day.

"Don't be silly," Arun replied. "You only get put in prison if you're naughty. That place is full of two-headed madmen, rabid zombies, and walking skeletons! They've been locked away so they can't hurt us."

"I heard they dunk the inmates into tubs which are full of snakes!"

"I heard they rip off men's testicles with pliers!"

"I heard they chop off women's breasts!"

"I heard they tie inmates to the back of their jeeps, and drive around until their bodies completely disintegrate!"

Arun and Tamsin looked at each other with wide-eyed amazement.

"Let's explore!" They cheered in unison.

They giggled.

They bounced on their toes.

A leaf fell off a tree.

Arun and his friends snuck towards the prison, with trembling hands and sweaty brows. They tiptoed around the prison's perimeter, and looked up at the top of its wall. Tall concrete slabs stood side by side, decorated by a mixture of spikes and barbed wire. But the only things they were able to see, were three watchtowers; gangly contraptions which looked like garden sheds on stilts.

"It's impossible," the Geeky Refugee said. "There's no way in."

She shrugged her shoulders.

Arun tensed his cheeks.

Tamsin had an idea.

"Let's go to the stadium," she said. "There's a game on today!"

Arun's eyes lit up.

"But we can't afford the tickets," the Geeky Refugee replied. "We don't have any money."

Tamsin raised her eyebrows.

"Don't worry about that," she said. "The stadium's wall is nowhere near as daunting as this one."

Her friends looked at each other, grinned, and then followed Tamsin through town.

The game had already kicked off by the time they arrived. The only supporters who were still outside, crowded around two ticket office windows. Those at the back pushed those at the front, whilst the nimble tried to jink through, and the long-limbed passed money over their heads.

The Geeky Refugee, Tamsin and Arun, walked past them. They made their way to the opposite end of the ground.

Arun looked around. He put his foot on a padlocked gate and scrambled up. The gate wobbled. Arun heaved himself over, and jumped down on the other side.

"Come on," he called back. "There's no-one here. Hurry up!"

Tamsin and the Geeky Refugee followed. They sneaked towards the main stand, climbed the stairs, and traversed the terrace. No-one seemed to care. Everyone's eyes were firmly fixed on the match.

Elderly men worked their way through bags of sunflower seeds. They bit the husks apart, spat them onto the floor, and chewed the tiny kernels which were hidden inside. Middle aged men drank silty cups of coffee, which were as thick as cement. And boys ate boiled sweetcorn, which was covered in salt and spices.

At the front, some teenagers faced the crowd, and led their chants. When they saw someone who was not joining in, they wagged their fists, and gave that person a dirty look. Another teenager produced an uneven beat on a battered drum.

To the side was a concrete building. Armed police, and a small selection of fans, stood on its roof. They watched on as Natale scored.

The crowd went wild.

"Wahoo!!!!" Arun screamed.

"One nil to Natale!" Tamsin cheered.

"Natale! Natale! Natale!" The Geeky Refugee chanted.

Then she fell silent. A hand had clasped her shoulder.

"Well, well, well," a gruff voice rung out. "What do have we here then?"

The Geeky Girl, Arun and Tamsin, all turned around. Their hearts all sank. They all thought they had been caught.

"We're just watching the game," Tamsin said.

"I can see that," the Tall Policeman replied. He had a warm face, with round cheeks and soft eyes, but it was clear that he was flustered. "Tut, tut, tut! Do you think it's acceptable for little girls like you to be here?"

Tamsin shrugged.

"Look around," the Tall Policeman continued.

Tamsin looked around.

"What do you see?"

"Football fans"

"What sort of football fans?"

"All sorts. Young and old. Rich and poor. Fat and thin."

"Male and female?"

Tamsin paused, looked around, and shrugged again.

"Football matches aren't for girls," the Tall Policeman continued. "I'm going to have to ask you ladies to leave."

Tamsin and the Geeky Girl did not know whether to feel angry or sad.

They just froze and looked down at the ground.

The Tall Policeman looked down at Arun.

"Did you think it was okay to bring girls to a football match?" He asked.

Arun remained silent. He slid his thumb up and down his finger.

Tamsin clasped her hands together.

The Tall Policeman cleared his throat. He squatted, looked into Arun's eyes, and put his hand on Arun's shoulder.

"Where do you live?" He asked.

Arun translated the question.

"Liberation Village," he finally replied.

The Tall Policeman turned pale.

"Liberation Village?" He repeated. "You're a Holy? You're a Protokian? The horror! Protokians aren't welcome here. I'm going to have to take you back to your parents!"

He patted Arun on his back and led him away.

"A Holy?" He muttered to himself. "Here? The horror! Whatever next?"

* * *

Papa Arun welcomed the Militant Settler into his marquee, sat him down, and gave him a cup of tea.

Papa Arun sat down himself. He sank back into his armchair and took a swig of water.

The two men talked.

"It really is amazing to see how Liberation has grown," the Militant Settler mentioned.

"Oh yes," Papa Arun agreed. "I see new immigrants arriving here every day. Settlers are building homes everywhere I look."

"They're bringing the same prosperity to Collis that the first wave of immigrants brought to the rest of Protokia. This place was a dusty outpost, inhabited by a small handful of peasant farmers, before we returned. And now look at it! We've turned Protokia into a prosperous country, fit for the modern world!"

Papa Arun shifted in his seat.

"I'm just happy to have a home," he replied.

"You lack ambition," the Militant Settler continued. "I'm telling you, one day we'll be as rich as the Colonisers *and* the Colonialists! At the rate we're going, we'll be a superpower! It takes big balls to do what we've been doing; creating a Holy nation, here amongst the Godlies. Don't you ever forget it!

"We've come of age. We're not the weaklings of the world anymore. We're men, we're strong, and we're going places!"

Papa Arun wore an awkward smile.

Mama Arun made some tea.

The Militant Settler rubbed his hands along his thighs. It was clear he was about to broach a delicate matter.

"Your son," he said. "What's his name? It's Arun, right?"

"That's right," Papa Arun replied.

"I thought so. Well, it's come to my attention that he's been spending time down in Natale, mixing with the natives."

Papa Arun nodded.

"You knew?"

Papa Arun nodded.

"And you haven't stopped him?"

Papa Arun clicked his knuckles.

"I want my son to be friends with everyone," he replied.

The Militant Settler paused, tapped his knee, and shook his finger.

"People have been talking," he continued. "And the things they've been saying have been far from complimentary.

"You see, relations with the natives are, how do I put this? '*Delicate*'. We need to watch where we tread. We can't afford to kick the hornets' nest, so to speak. We need to keep our relationships professional."

Papa Arun tilted his head, as if to say, '*Go on.*'

"Look, it's okay to be seen with a Godly if he's working for you. If he's repairing your car or cleaning your home. But you shouldn't get too close. Too *personal*.

"The Godlies have been living rent free in our country for centuries. We can't allow those bloated leeches to think they can get away with such liberties. Protokia is the cradle of Holy civilisation. It's the land of the Holy people. Our people! Those Godlies, those circumcised ferrets, are our guests, nothing else. They're not our equals."

The Militant Settler gave Papa Arun a stern look.

"It's up to you how you choose to live your life. It's a free country after all. But if your family continues to pally up to the Godlies, I think you'll find opportunities hard to come by. I think you'll struggle to fit in with the other settlers."

The Militant Settler tapped his chin.

"You're new here, you need time to learn our ways. It's fine, I understand. But if you want to be part of this community, you need to act like a settler. You're a Holy, not a Godly, after all."

The Militant Settler smiled at Papa Arun.

Papa Arun smiled back.

The Militant Settler stood up.

"Thank-you for the tea," he said.

"Any time," Papa Arun replied. "What's mine is yours. You're always welcome here."

They embraced, the Militant Settler left, and Papa Arun sank back into his chair. He took a deep breath. And then he heard a knock at the door.

The Tall Policeman entered with Arun by his side.

"Good day sir," the Tall Policeman said in Godliness.

"Hello, come in," Papa Arun replied in Protokian. "Would you like some tea?"

"No. No thank-you. I can't stay for long. Things to do! People to see!"

Papa Arun wore a blank expression.

"He says he can't stay," Arun translated.

"Oh," Papa Arun replied.

"Your son was at a football match." The Tall Policeman explained.

"He said I was at a football match."

"Oh."

"Apparently that's not allowed."

"Oh. I see."

Papa Arun shook the Tall Policeman's hand, showed him out, and walked back into his marquee.

"Sit down," he told Arun.

Arun sat down.

"Do you understand how important it is that we settle here?" Papa Arun asked. "This is our home now. It's not just another random town we're passing through. We're here for good."

Arun rubbed his eyes.

"Well, that means we need to behave like the other settlers. We can't afford to be different."

Papa Arun paused.

The fire flickered.

Arun waited for his father to continue.

"You see, the other children in Liberation don't play with the kids in Natale. So I think it'd be for the best if you didn't either. It'll help us to fit in. It'll help us to become upstanding members of the community."

Arun turned pale. He was aghast. He felt betrayed, abandoned and cheated.

"But daddy!" He protested. "The Widow who saved us told us *'to be friendly with everyone we meet'*. I just want to honour her."

Papa Arun blushed.

"You make me proud," he said. "It's very important to be friendly with everyone you meet. Very important.

"But that doesn't mean that you need to meet everyone on the planet. You can pick and choose the people you meet.

"I'm just asking you to spend your time in Liberation. Be friendly with the children here. Forget about the children in Natale. That's all."

Arun's face turned red.

Tears dripped from his eyes. Snot dripped from his nose. And saliva dripped from his lips.

"But daddy!" He cried. "That doesn't make any sense. That's cowardly. Who cares what the settlers think? I only care about what the Widow would think."

Papa Arun looked at his son. He felt sympathy with Arun's point of view, and he respected his son for speaking up.

But Papa Arun was determined to settle in Liberation. He was determined to lead a trouble free life, after all the hardships he had faced. So he decided to put his foot down.

"I don't want you playing with that Tamsin, that dizzy-eyed midget, ever again!" He shouted. His face turned purple and his eyes turned red.

"I don't want you going anywhere near that creepy elf! I don't want you going into Natale again. Understand?"

Papa Arun had never shouted at his son before, and so his tone shocked Arun, who trembled in fear.

He put his head in his hands and hid from the world.

He never played with Tamsin again.

* * *

Over the months which followed, Papa Arun did everything he could to fit in, and establish himself as a pillar of the community.

He welcomed new people into his cabin each day. They sat in a circle, drank an infinite amount of tea, patted each other's backs, chatted and chortled.

Papa Arun offered everyone the same warm welcome, whether he knew them or not. Whether they were good or bad, clean or dirty, new immigrants or established settlers.

"Come in!" He always said. "You are welcome here. Have some tea. You poor things, you must be hungry. Eat something. Have some tea. Please! Share! What's mine is yours. Have some tea."

When he was not hosting guests, Papa Arun worked in Protokia, in a factory which produced cheap suits.

He spent his wages on an infinite array of bits and bobs; on cushions, cupboards and curtains. He bought a brand new bed and a second-hand desk. He even bought a television.

"Daddy! Daddy!" Arun cheered as his father entered. He grabbed his father's leg and hugged it as tightly as he could.

"Hey there," Papa Arun replied. "Look what I've got."

Arun gazed at that television as if it was a spaceship from another galaxy. It looked so alien to him; so modern, futuristic and strange. He stared at its screen without even turning it on.

No-one else in Liberation had a TV, so owning it made Arun feel special. Although the '*big magic box*', as he called it, did scare him a little at first. He was dazed by the rapid movements of the black and white figures who danced across its screen. His ears vibrated whenever they spoke.

That television was big news in Liberation. Everyone talked about it. And everyone watched it too.

Papa Arun hosted more people than ever before. Adults squeezed onto his sofas, and children sat on his floor. Their eyes were glued to the screen. Their conversations stopped. They were shushed whenever they spoke.

They watched the news. They watched nature documentaries. And they watched the prime minister address his nation.

"Holies should live in and around every Godly town in the land," Atamow said, whilst staring into the camera.

Everyone in Arun's cabin stared back at him.

"We must expel the Godlies and take their places. Because there is no Protokian colonisation, or Holy state, without the eviction of Godlies and the expropriation of their land.

"So everyone should take action, should run, should grab more hilltops and enlarge the settlements. Because everything we take now will stay ours. But everything we don't grab will go to them.

"If we can guarantee our right to settle peacefully, then we must do so. But if we have to use force, then we have force at our disposal!"

There was a brief moment of silence.

A cat rubbed up against a settler's leg.

And then everyone applauded. They gave the prime minister a standing ovation, hugged each other, and shouted:

'Whoop! Whoop! Whoop! Hip hip hooray! Long live Atamow!'

"That's our boy!" The Militant Settler cheered.

"He's got our back!" An Elderly Settler roared.

"We're in this together!" A Housewife cried.

The Militant Settler's son, Jim, looked at Arun. He gave Arun a sinister smile, and an ominous wink. He emitted a devilish snigger.

* * *

Arun went to school in a row of cabins which had been welded together and painted pink. It stood in the centre of Liberation, surrounded by a small playground, and a large line of flower pots.

Arun tried to befriend every other pupil. He tried to be friends with the Pale Settler who looked like a ghost, the Owlish Settler who had a hairy ear, and the Cherubic Settler who had a runny nose. He tried to be friends with Jim. It took them a while to accept Arun, but they grew closer as time went by.

They played games after school each day.

When it rained, they raced twigs on the water which gushed down the hill, and bet on which stick would win. When it was sunny, they sat in the shade, and played noughts and crosses in the dust. And when the sun began to set, the girls took on the boys in choreographed bouts of tug of war.

By the time they had finished, they were covered in a thick layer of sweat and dust. They breathed heavily. They sat down on a low wall and began to speak.

"Brother," Jim told Arun. "You're a nice guy. You want to be friends with everyone. I like that. But you're naïve. You need to understand that those Godlies aren't what they seem to be. They're fine on the outside, but you can't trust them. They're dangerous. You should treat them with caution."

Jim looked into Arun's eyes. He smiled. It was an unnervingly large smile, which made Jim look like he was about to go for Arun's neck. His cheeks were slightly too wide, and his eyes were slightly too narrow. They juxtaposed with Jim's broad shoulders, and his beautiful buttocks, which looked like a pair of flattened mangos.

"Protokia is our home," Jim continued. "Don't ever forget that. We had to wait two thousand years for the peaceful liberation of this land. And we have a duty to ensure those Godlies don't take it from us again."

Arun looked back at Jim.

"It's their land too," he said. "They've been here for hundreds of years."

Jim shook his head.

"No," he replied. "Look, if I went to live in a random country for ten years, I couldn't claim that country was mine. It would still belong to the people who lived there before me.

"Protokia is the land of our ancestors. We lived here first. The Godlies' can't say it's theirs, just because they've been here for a few hundred years. Their claims have no legitimacy."

Jim spat on the floor. His saliva sprayed in every direction. It glistened in the sunlight.

"Haven't you heard my father talk? Didn't you pay any attention to Atamow's speech? Haven't you realised that the supremacy of the Holies is absolute?

"I tell you, we should put the Godlies on a bus and drive them into the sea. Their nation has no right to exist!"

Arun was confused.

"Why can't we live together?" He asked. "I'm tired of all this hatred. I just want to live in peace."

Jim looked at Arun and laughed.

"You see!" He told the other children. "This is exactly what I was talking about."

He put his arm around Arun's shoulders.

"I like you Arun. You're a good guy. A genuine chum. A brother from another mother. But my word, you're naïve.

"My friend, we live in a dog eat dog world. There are only two types of people out there; the hunters and the hunted, the persecutors and the persecuted, the lion and the sheep.

"My brother, we've been the sheep for far too long. The Colonisers slaughtered millions of us. The Godlies took our land. We've been banished, chased and enslaved.

"But no more! It's time for us to take control. It's time for us to be the lions!"

The Cherubic Settler stamped his foot.

The Pale Settler saluted Jim.

The Owlish Settler cheered:

"The Godlies are a bunch of godless atheists!"

"I'll give you three out of ten for that insult," Jim laughed.

"They're rat-faced, fat-raced infidels who suck their own father's dicks!" The Pale Settler said.

"That's more like it! Eight out of ten."

"They're uncivilised mountain men who don't have any culture!" The Cherubic Settler added.

"Meh. Four out of ten."

There was a moment of silence.

Everyone turned to face Arun. He felt their steamy breath on his cheek. He felt their glaring eyes. But he did not say a word.

"Come on little brother," Jim cajoled. "It's fun. Insult the Godlies."

Arun bowed his head.

The Owlish Settler tapped his head.

Jim shook his head. He gestured for the Pale Settler to continue.

"They're the offspring of whores and rapists!"

"Six."

"They're red-headed devil worshippers!"

"Five."

"They're maggot-infested scrotes, who bathe in cow's semen!"

"Nine!"

Everyone turned to face Arun.

"Don't you want to give it a go?" Jim asked. "Don't you want to be one of the gang?"

Arun paused to think. He took a deep breath. And then he looked Jim in the eye.

"They're a bunch of sissies," he said.

Everyone cheered.

The Pale Settler howled like a hyena, the Owlish Settler punched the air, and Jim high-fived the Cherubic Settler.

"That's only two out of ten," he cheered. "But it was good for a first try. You're one of us now."

Jim made an approving gesture.

Everyone else sat back down.

Arun puffed his chest.

"They're animals," he said. "Animals! Like on the nature documentaries. All of Natale is a jungle. There are monkeys, dogs, gorillas and pigs down there. They drink their own urine. They throw their shit at each other. They're uncivilised. They're uneducated. They're not human like us. They're animals. Dirty filthy animals!"

There was a brief moment of silence. No-one could believe what they had heard.

And then everyone cheered. They jumped up and down, shimmied and danced.

"Ten out of ten!" Jim shouted.

He picked Arun up, put him on his shoulders, and strutted down the street. The other children skipped around him in a circle.

"He's one of our own," they sang. "He's one of our own. This boy called '*Arun*', he's one of our own."

* * *

Back at home, things followed a sure and steady routine. Papa Arun would not have it any other way.

As if by clockwork, Arun's family woke up and went to sleep at the same time each day. They ate the same food each week. They went to school, and they went to work.

Their lives had a calming rhythm, which only hit the buffers when the school holidays came around. Arun was left with time on his hands, which he filled by playing with his friends.

But they soon got bored of Liberation. It was a pleasant place, but it was sleepy and small. Every building looked the same. The birds made more noise than the people. There were only so many times they could go on a seesaw, chase a skittish cat, or tie each other's laces together.

So Arun and his gang explored the surrounding hills. They scrambled up rivers and bathed in pools. They hid in caves. They had picnics on hilltops, and they ate wild berries.

They were always on the lookout for new places to visit, and it was usually Jim who led them on. He led them over hills and he led them into valleys. He led them through woods, forests and thickets.

He faced his friends each morning, with his hands on his hips, and announced his plan for the day:

"Today, my friends, we're going to town!"

Everyone nodded.

Everyone walked out of Liberation.

Everyone walked into Natale.

Their senses were dazzled by the hubbub of constant motion. By the traders who moved supplies, the shoppers who carried bags, and the wild dogs who sniffed for food. By the call to prayer, which rang out from the Godly temples. And by the soldiers, who stood on every corner, chatting to their comrades and caressing their pitch-black guns.

Jim squatted down into a sniper position, and motioned for his friends to do the same. They were at the end of a shady alley. Ahead of them was a corner, beneath which was a set of stairs.

Jim put his finger to his lips. He picked up some pieces of rubble, and gestured for his friends to pick up some stones.

They waited there in silence.

A piece of paper danced on the breeze.

A cockroach scuttled into a crack.

A butterfly flew overhead.

Jim heard a group of children climb the stairs. Their footsteps created a chattering sound, which echoed down the passage.

Jim stood up, walked to the top of the stairs, puffed his chest and stood proud. He lifted a rock above his head and swung his arm with all his might. His rock flew through the air, and hit a Freckled Local on her chin.

"Aaaah!" She screamed. Blood poured out of her skull. She pivoted, pushed past her companions, and ran away.

Her friends ran after her.

Arun's friends lifted their arms and threw their stones. A storm of rubble and rock filled the air. Pebbles pounded the walls, and smashed into bodies. High pitch screams reverberated off of every surface.

Arun watched on until his vision was blurred by a cloud of dust, when an eerie sense of horror descended upon him. His whole body froze.

His friends emerged from the dusty haze, brushed themselves down, and high-fived each other.

"That felt amazing!" Jim cheered.

"I feel like a God!" The Cherubic Settler replied.

"I feel alive!" The Pale Settler chanted. "I'm on top of the world!"

He hugged the Owlish Settler.

Jim sniggered.

Everyone turned to face Arun.

"Why didn't you join in?" Jim asked.

Arun shrugged his shoulders and dropped his stone.

Jim grinned, winked at Arun, and patted his back.

"Don't worry, my brother. You'll get another chance. Just you wait and see!"

Arun nodded.

Jim nodded.

Everyone nodded.

Everyone followed Jim down alleys which twisted and turned, through passageways which clung to the hillside, and along lanes which squeezed in between wonky buildings.

"In here," he said.

He gestured for his friends to enter an empty house.

Arun explored that place with his eyes. He looked up at the shiny beams, which were a pale shade of gold. He looked across at some cushions, which surrounded a low table. And he looked out at a pretty mosaic, which decorated a shaded courtyard.

Jim went outside, and collected some stones.

"Take these," he said.

He took a stone himself, and chucked it through an open window. It hit a Disabled Local, who was sitting in a wheelchair.

Arun's friends all followed suit. The Pale Settler hit the knee of a Pretty Local, who was holding a baby. The Owlish Settler hit an Elderly Refugee's walking stick. And the Cherubic Settler hit Mama Ellie's belly.

Ellie gripped her mother's leg.

"Don't just stand there!" Mama Ellie screamed at a Greasy Soldier. "I swear on every verse in the Godly bible; do something, or the gods will!"

The Greasy Soldier leaned against a wall, ogled a Pretty Refugee, and touched his crotch.

"Settlers are throwing stones at us!"

The Greasy Soldier made a duck face.

"You're lying," he quacked.

Ellie clenched her fist.

"What's your name?" The Greasy Soldier snapped.

"Ellie."

"What are you doing here?"

"Shopping."

"Why aren't you at school?"

"It's the holiday."

"Where are you from?"

"Natale"

"Why don't you go and live somewhere else?"

"I was born here."

"Why is your mummy making unfounded allegations?"

"She's not!"

"You're a disgrace," Mama Ellie growled. "I swear on my sexual honour and betrothal! How dare you interrogate an innocent little girl like that? You're a disgrace! A disgrace!"

She grabbed Ellie's hand and stormed away.

The Greasy Soldier guffawed.

Jim sniggered.

"A Holy doesn't arrest a Holy," he said.

Everyone nodded.

Everyone waived at the Greasy Soldier.

Everyone watched as the Greasy Soldier waved back.

Jim gave Arun a vicious glare. He looked like a caged animal, locked inside an enclosure which was too small for him. He seemed to fill the whole room. He seemed to tower over Arun.

"My friend," he said. "You're up!"

Arun's emotions mixed within him, like liquor in a cocktail shaker. Guilt, despair and terror, merged to form one transcendent sensation. Shame and horror sploshed around his belly. Fear and fury made his saliva froth. Vulnerability made his knees knock together.

He hated his society. He hated himself. And he hated Jim for putting him in that situation. He wanted to beat Jim. He wanted to destroy Jim. He wanted to kill Jim. He wanted to see Jim's corpse, broken and twisted, in a bloody heap at his feet.

But he did not have the courage to dissent.

So he took a deep breath and looked out the window. He saw some locals, who all had bad hairdos. He saw some mice, who all had big teeth. And he saw Tamsin, who was hawking satsumas to everyone who passed.

Arun felt guilty for abandoning his friend. He felt ashamed. And he filled with hatred for Tamsin, for triggering those negative emotions.

So he took his stone and threw it at Tamsin's foot. He regretted it straight away. He felt worse than he had done before.

"That's my boy!" Jim cheered. "Doesn't that feel amazing?"

Arun winced.

"Come, come," Jim continued. He put his arm round Arun's shoulder. "You became a man just now. I'm proud of you. King Arun of Natale! King Arun the Conqueror!"

The Cherubic Settler patted Arun's shoulder.

The Pale Settler gave Arun a thumbs up.

The Owlish Settler winked.

Jim threw another stone. It hit a Bespectacled Refugee, who threw it straight back at Jim. The Greasy Soldier spat on the ground, arrested the Bespectacled Refugee, and dragged him away.

Arun dragged himself towards Liberation, with his head hung in shame, and a tear in his eye. He walked through Natale, across some fields, and along a stony lane. He approached his settlement's gate.

Jim approached the Militant Settler.

"Hi daddy!" He cheered.

"Hi son," the Militant Settler replied. "What have you boys been up to?"

"We've been throwing stones at the infidels! It was great fun, daddy. Really nasty!"

The Militant Settler took a step back, paused, and then smiled. His cheeks bulged so much, his skin became taut. His eyes, which were full of joy and wonder, almost popped out of their sockets. His lips parted.

"That's my boy!" He said. "You've done the Holies proud! If every boy in Protokia behaves like you have today, we'll have a bright future ahead of us. We'll drive all the Godlies away!"

The Militant Settler looked at Jim's friends. They all grinned. They all flushed with boyish pride.

"Come with me," he said.

He took them to an ice-cream parlour.

"Order anything you want. Anything at all. You boys deserve it!"

Jim devoured a chocolate-fudge sundae. The Pale Refugee devoured a bowl of cherry sorbet. And Arun devoured a banana split.

"Are you still hungry?" The Militant Settler asked him.

Arun tilted his head towards his shoulder.

"How would you like a milkshake?"

Arun's eyes lit up.

He drank his milkshake so quickly, his teeth became numb, and his head spun. He felt ill. He returned home, sat in a corner, and gripped hold of his aching stomach.

* * *

"Come and eat your dinner," Papa Arun told his son.

"No-thank-you," Arun replied. "I'm not hungry."

Papa Arun looked puzzled.

"You're always hungry at dinner time," he said. "It's part of our daily routine. Are you sure you're feeling okay?"

Arun nodded.

"Yes daddy," he replied. "But I ate quite a lot of ice-cream today. I don't have any space in my tummy."

Papa Arun tapped his lip.

"Where did you get ice-cream from?" He asked.

"Jim's dad bought it for us," Arun replied. "We threw stones at some Godlies, to drive them away, and Jim's dad rewarded us with ice-creams. He said we were '*patriots*'. He said we should be proud of ourselves."

Papa Arun's face turned red. It was a blood-curdling shade of red. A shade of red which was so dark it was almost purple, so bold it made his face pulsate, and so loud it seemed to scream.

In the blink of an eye, he had puffed his chest, lifted his hand above his head, and swung his arm with all his might. His knuckles crashed into Arun's cheek with so much power that Arun fell to the floor. His legs were tangled. There was a bruise on his cheek and a tear in his eye.

"What was the one thing the Widow asked us to do?" He bellowed.

Arun trembled.

"Ru-ru-ru-remember to be fu-fu-fu-friendly to everyone you mu-mu-mu-meet," he stuttered.

"And?"

"Tu-tu-tu-take care of persecuted people."

"And is throwing stones at people the same as taking care of them?"

Arun shook his head.

"So why on earth did you do it? Really! After everything we've been through. You should've known better."

Arun wiped his eyes, whimpered, and looked up at his father.

"Bu-bu-bu-because you told me *to 'behave like the other settlers'*," he replied. "And the other settlers were all throwing stones.

"Yu-yu-yu-you told me that *'we can't afford to be different'*. If I had refused to join in, it would have made me different."

Arun looked into his father's eyes.

"I did it for you," he said.

Papa Arun shivered. His heart sank and his face froze. He was completely lost for words.

* * *

Arun ate in silence the following morning. His cheek was still sore, and his confidence was still shaken. His trust in his father was shattered.

Papa Arun felt guilty.

"Son," he said. "This may cheer you up."

He went into his bedroom and returned with a long brown tube. He removed its cap and unrolled a large piece of paper.

"What is it?" Arun asked.

"These are the blueprints for our new home."

Arun's jaw dropped.

Mama Arun made some tea.

The Bedouin arrived outside. He unloaded his yaks, and left a pile of bricks on the ground. He waved at Papa Arun, turned around, and disappeared.

Arun watched as the Bedouin was replaced by a group of day labourers. They were a ragamuffin crew, with floppy sandals and unkempt hair. Their shirts were covered in a haphazard selection of holes, and their trousers were grey with dust.

"It's cheaper to employ Godlies," Papa Arun explained. "They'll turn up for an egg and an apple, and do double the work in half the time. They don't ask for holidays, their breaks are unpaid, and they don't mind risky jobs. They don't have any legal rights!"

Arun twiddled his thumbs. He ate a mouthful of toast, and looked outside. He saw an incredibly hairy man, who had a look of childish innocence. His clothes were still clean, as if he had not worked in them before. And he stood on his own, away from the other labourers.

That man looked back at Arun, and gave him a mischievous wink.

4. CHARLIE

"How could you?" Mama Charlie screamed.

She threw a mug at Papa Charlie, who ducked to avoid it. The mug smashed into the wall behind him, and broke into several little pieces. Its handle flew towards Charlie's Brother, and its base rebounded into Papa Charlie's nape.

"How could you? How could you? How could you?"

Papa Charlie rubbed the back of his neck; the only part of his head which was not covered in hair. His forehead was dominated by a pair of bushy eyebrows, which almost reached his scalp. His double chin was concealed by a beard, which was as coarse as wire. And his eyes were shaded by a set of pointy lashes.

"Those bastards have stolen our land, penned us in between their settlements, and installed aquifers which are sucking up our water.

"And what do you do to stop those mangy rats? Nothing! You go and build homes for them!

"Are you mad? Do you want us to suffer? Really! How could you?"

Mama Charlie, a stout woman who had wide shoulders and cobalt eyes, threw another mug at her husband's feet.

Charlie pressed his teddy bear against his chubby cheek.

Papa Charlie held up a small sack of rice.

"We can eat tonight," he said. "For the first time in four days! You want to know how I could do it? Well here's your answer. If it saves us from starvation, I'll do anything. Anything!!!"

A tear formed in the corner of Charlie's Brother's aquamarine eye. It rolled over his prominent cheekbone, and dropped onto his burgundy lip.

A piece of mug span around on the floor.

Mama Charlie panted like a dog.

"I don't want you going back there tomorrow," she whispered. "You're selling us out for an onion peel!"

"I don't have a choice," Papa Charlie replied. "I feel like a slave, but I have to put food on our table. If I could work anywhere else, even for a quarter of the money, I would. But there aren't any jobs. Half the village is unemployed."

He shrugged.

Gunfire rang out in the distance.

Mama Charlie wagged her finger.

"What sort of future are you building for our children?" She wailed. "A future penned in by occupiers, without access to our fields? Without food, water or work? Is that what you want?

"Our own people will hate us. No-one likes a turncoat. We'll be ostracised. We'll be social outcasts. Pariahs! Just like the other mercenaries here. The natives will dump their garbage in front of our house, throw rotten fruit at us, and piss in our well!"

Papa Charlie winced.

Charlie's Brother wailed.

Charlie patted his shiny black hair, and pinched his tiny round nose.

"What sort of future are you building for our children?"

Papa Charlie repositioned some items on the table.

"You're right," he mumbled. "We need to make plans for our children. They shouldn't have to live like this.

"I'll arrange for Charlie to go to Natale. He'll be able to go to school there."

Papa Charlie bit his lip.

"Education!" He concluded. "Education will save him from this mess."

Mama Charlie bounded towards her husband and hugged him. She gripped him so tightly, it affected his circulation. His hands turned white and his eyes turned red.

Charlie rocked back and forth. His nervous twitch made his cheek pulsate and his eye blink. But he did not say a word.

* * *

Liberation was not the only settlement to overlook Valley Village. Four other settlements dominated the surrounding hills. New mobile homes appeared there almost every day.

Without access to their pastures, the villagers watched on as their animals all perished. They were not allowed to reach their farmland, which lay beyond the settlements. And they were not allowed to cross a road, which surrounded their valley.

A crew of locals were building that road.

Those villagers used dynamite to blast the hillside flat. The men drilled the rock, whilst the women cleared the dust. Then they spread sticky tar across the flattened space.

At the end of every day, the Protokians always lectured them.

"There is a house in the capital," they said. "On the second floor is a long corridor. At the end of that corridor is a door. And behind that door is a wise man who makes decisions.

"His name is Atamow, and he wants you to be happy.

"He will bring about development. He will set up industries and bring progress. He will ensure that your hard work is rewarded.

"Just remember this: The supremacy of the Holies is absolute! All hail the Holy God! He'll make you rich. He'll make you happy. He'll make you whole."

The workers were never fully convinced. Some of them suffered from bad backs, whilst others got dust in their lungs. People died. Their fellow villagers called them '*skivvies*', '*sluts*' and '*skanks*'. But their jobs helped them to survive. Their work saved them from starvation.

That road was guarded by a Night Watchman, who was friends with Papa Charlie. He had found Papa Charlie his job. And so he was happy to turn a blind eye, when Charlie walked past with a bag of clothes on his back, a map in his trouser pocket, and a look of trepidation on his boyish face.

It was the midnight hour, and the moon was nowhere to be seen. Charlie wore a cloak of darkness as he descended down the other side of the hill.

Grass rustled in the breeze.

An owl hooted.

A wolf howled.

Rat-a-tat-tat. Rat-a-tat-tat. Rat-a-tat-tat.

The sound of Protokian machinegun fire burst in Charlie's ears. He heard a bullet bounce off a rock to his right. He felt a bullet whizz above his head. And he saw a puff of dust in front of him.

He dived behind a boulder.

His heart pounded. Butterflies fluttered in his stomach, and his spine tingled. His hands shook.

He looked down and saw that he had wet his pants. His genitals felt warm, sticky and moist.

His nervous twitch went into overdrive. His left cheek pulsated as quickly as the machinegun fire. In and out. In and out. In and out.

His left eye opened and closed at a manic rate. His eyebrow vibrated.

He concentrated on his breathing.

He waited there for hours. He looked up at the stars, and down at the earth. He looked down towards Natale.

When his pulse had settled, he continued. He crawled on his belly to avoid detection. Soil stained his hands, stones tore his clothes, and thistles pricked his skin.

He slithered like a snake.

Rat-a-tat-tat. Rat-a-tat-tat. Rat-a-tat-tat.

Charlie paused. He pressed his body into the earth and closed his eyes.

A rabbit ran into its burrow.

A squirrel ran up a tree.

Charlie caught his breath, paused, and continued.

By the time he reached Natale, his shirt had disintegrated and his chest was covered in bruises. He was exhausted. So he rested his head on a donkey's stomach, and fell asleep in a grassy field.

The stars faded and the sun rose.

A cockerel crowed.

A mouse squeaked.

A girlish voice rang out:

"What are you doing, silly?"

Ellie poked Charlie with a stick.

"Do you think you're a donkey?" She asked. "Donkey boy! *Eee-Or. Eee-or. Eee-or.*"

Charlie rubbed his eyes.

"Are you a tree?" He replied. "Who pokes people with sticks?"

Ellie laughed.

"Why are you sleeping here?" She asked.

"I just arrived. I was so tired, I passed out."

"You're a refugee, aren't you? I can take you to the refugee camp if you like. It's not far from here."

"Oh no, I'm not going there. I'm staying with my uncle. I just need to find his home."

Charlie passed Ellie his map.

"I know where that is," she said. "Follow me."

* * *

"Sit down," Uncle Charlie said.

Charlie sat down and looked at his uncle. He was a plump man, who had far too much hair. His mullet was greasy, yet also dull, whilst his chest hair was lustrous and dark. His facial hair was both black and grey. His back hair was as bushy as wool, and his toe hair was as thorny as wire.

"Now listen here," he continued. "I've heard good things about you, so I'm prepared to give this a go. Yes. Yes. But make no mistake, I'm not your pa. You're not my son. I'm a businessman, and if you're going to survive you need to buy into that. I'm not going to coddle you. Understand?"

Charlie nodded.

"Yes sir," he said.

Uncle Charlie beamed.

"'*Sir*,'" he repeated. "I like that. You've got manners. Good. Good. Keep on calling me '*sir*'."

Charlie straightened his back and looked into his uncle's eyes.

"Yes sir, uncle sir, Uncle Charlie sir!"

Uncle Charlie scratched his head. He could not tell if his nephew was being polite or sarcastic.

"Good. Good," he continued. "Very good.

"You know, I was about your age when I came over the hills? There wasn't a single hair on my chin back then. My balls were still stuck in my crotch! Yes. Yes.

"Like you, I didn't have a single penny to my name.

"And now look at me. I'm one of the most respected traders on the market! True. True.

"Outside my stall, I have open-topped tins full of pickles. I have white and yellow cauliflower, green leaves, gherkins, jalapenos, radishes, blood-red beetroot, and five different sorts of olives. Five different sorts! It's a sight to behold. A real smorgasbord of colour! Good. Good.

"I have big sacks displaying every grain imaginable. Yes. Yes. I have wheat, popcorn, barley, quinoa, couscous, rye, millet, brown rice, white rice, wild rice, every sort of rice!

"Inside I have nuts. All the nuts! Peanuts, walnuts, chestnuts, hazelnuts, almonds, cashews, pecans and pistachios. The lot! I have snack mix, Bombay mix, crisps, dried chillies, dried apricots, dried prunes, raisins, sunflower seeds, chickpeas and olive oil. Yes. Yes. Olive oil!!!"

Uncle Charlie grinned.

"Do you know that some traders only sell one product? Apples or satsumas or grapes. Just the one product, piled up on moveable wooden tables. Yes. Yes. But not me. Oh no. I sell hundreds. Hundreds!

"I'm one of the most respected traders on the market.

"I eat meat every day!"

Charlie looked up at his uncle in awe. He did not believe that anyone could afford to eat meat *every* day. Not even kings. The very thought of it made Charlie blush.

"Am I going to work with you on your stall, Uncle Charlie sir?" He asked.

Uncle Charlie paused.

"Ha! Ha! Ha!" He laughed. "Dear child, why would I need a boy like you on my stall? Ha! Ha! Ha!

"No. No. A market stall is no place for a child. Why you need to work your way up if you want to work on a market stall. You need to start at the bottom, as a trolley boy, just like I did. Yes. Yes. That's a tip top plan. Good. Good. Very good."

* * *

Charlie followed his uncle through the market. He had never been anywhere like it.

A labyrinth of narrow alleys with stone floors shot off in every direction. Slices of orange light peaked between buildings. Shoppers pushed between traders. Mice scurried between feet.

Charlie looked around. He saw two mothers and two sons, who were carrying two bags of shopping each. An Ugly Man, who was selling beautiful flowers. A Cobbler, who was fixing a broken shoe. And a Chandler, who was grinding coffee beans. The aroma made Charlie salivate.

A Toddler grabbed a strawberry from a table and put it in her mouth. The Toddler's Mother was about to apologize, but she saw that the strawberry was a product of Protokia. So she gave the Strawberry Seller a condescending look, ruffled the Toddler's hair, and walked away without paying.

Uncle Charlie led his nephew past a row of bird shops. Wire cages were stacked on top of each other. Pigeons, parrots, turkeys and budgies created a cacophony of chirps and tweets. A rooster sat above a cage full of hens, who declined the opportunity to escape through an open door. Two cats gazed up at them, purred, and waited patiently.

Old ladies sat cross-legged on the floor, behind piles of leafy greens. Like the other traders, they were all self-employed, although they had not produced their wares. Charlie glanced at them. Then he followed his uncle around a corner, into a hidden square.

He came face-to-face with a group of young boys, who stood next to a group of wooden trolleys.

One of those trollies was full of bananas. A Sooty Local pushed it away. The other trollies were much smaller. One had a wonky wheel, and another had a twisted handle. They all had wooden tops and metal bases. They all had seen better days.

"Here's your new trolley," Uncle Charlie said. He pointed at an oversized wheelbarrow. "And here is your new gang. Yes. Yes."

Uncle Charlie turned to face the other boys.

"I want you to take care of this young whippersnapper, and show him the ropes. If you give him any problems, I'll make sure the other traders never do business with you again. Yes. Yes. I have influence. I'm one of the most respected traders here!"

Uncle Charlie waved goodbye.

Charlie froze. Only his face moved. His cheek twitched and his eye vibrated.

He faced the other boys, who stood shoulder to shoulder, and stared straight back at him. A Shabby Local folded his arms. A Vain Local fingered his hair. And a Grubby Refugee looked Charlie up and down.

"Come with me," Oliver said. "Let's see if we can get us some work."

Charlie looked back at that boy, who had wispy blonde hair and chubby cheeks. He glanced at the other boys, grabbed his rickety trolley, and followed Oliver out of the square.

They approached a Butcher's stall.

A cow's head hung from a hook. Its tongue hung out of its mouth. And some herbs hung from pieces of its carcass, near buckets which were full of hearts, stomachs and spleens. Near piles of chopped onion and chopped parsley. And near the Butcher himself.

The Butcher was a potty-mouthed, gun-toting, whiskey-swilling, card-playing, kangaroo-shaped oaf. He blew cigarette smoke over his meat, sliced off a sliver of beef, and put it into a mincer.

"Do you have anything you need to be delivered or collected?" Oliver asked. "We'll do you a good deal."

The Butcher sniggered.

"Does it look like I can afford to hire lackeys?" He replied.

He turned his mincer's handle.

"I have to work as a history teacher because business is so slow here. Do you really think I'm going to waste my money on market rats like you?"

Oliver gave the Butcher an angry look, scrunched up his nose, and pushed his trolley away.

Charlie glared at the Butcher, turned, and followed his accomplice.

"Don't worry about the knock-backs," Oliver said. "You get used to it. We do enough business to survive."

Charlie nodded. He followed Oliver down the path. But he lost sight of his new friend when a Junior Priest jumped out of nowhere.

"Donation! Donation!" He demanded. "Give me a donation! I'll give you a blessing. The more you donate, the more blessed you'll be. God is watching. Don't invoke his wrath!"

The Junior Priest, who had long fingernails and short hair, rattled his money box in front of Charlie's face.

"Donation! Donation!" He wailed.

Charlie froze. The world passed him by. People crowded him. Light blinded him. Noise deafened him.

Chickens clucked.

Oliver disappeared into the distance.

"Donation! Donation!"

The Junior Priest rattled his money box again.

"I, I, I," Charlie stuttered. "I don't have any money, sir. I'm new here. Please don't hurt me."

The Junior Priest gave Charlie an angry look, and then disappeared.

Charlie pushed his trolley past a woman who was selling multi-coloured cake. Past a child who was selling fruit salad. And past a man who was sitting by his stall, asleep, with his head drooped over his chest.

He pushed his trolley past Papa Tamsin, who was selling mouldy satsumas.

"This is my last day on the market," he told an Apple Seller. "I can earn more by building roads. I'm going to be a contractor, so I'll still be my own boss. I'll be able to come and go as I please!"

Charlie kept walking. He looked in every direction, but he did not see Oliver anywhere.

A brave rooster jumped out of its cage and made a dash for freedom.

An eager Tea Boy rushed past, carrying a tray full of hot drinks.

The Medicine Man squatted down in front of Charlie.

"You look lost," he said.

Charlie looked back at the Medicine Man. He felt a little scared.

"I felt lost when I first arrived here too," the Medicine Man continued. "Don't worry. It gets easier."

The Medicine Man removed a set of cards from his pocket, split the pack, and showed Charlie the bottom card.

"Remember that card, but don't tell me what it is. Okay?"

Charlie nodded.

The Medicine Man caught a glimpse of the card as he put the pack back together.

"Now shuffle the cards really well."

Charlie shuffled the pack. He dropped the nine of hearts, picked it up, and continued shuffling.

"Now turn the cards over one at a time, and put them face-up on your trolley."

Charlie did as he was told.

The Medicine Man shook his head each time a new card was revealed.

"Ah!" He finally proclaimed. "That's the one! That's your card!"

Charlie looked back at the Medicine Man with wonder in his eyes.

"That's amazing, sir," he said. "How did you do that?"

The Medicine Man chuckled.

"A magician never reveals his secrets," he said.

"Oh."

"But I can tell you something a little birdy told me."

The Medicine Man paused for effect.

Charlie waited for him to continue.

A cockroach crawled into a sack of rice.

"There's a Confectioner down that alley, who has a bushy grey beard and a scar above one eye. I think he might need a trolley boy to help him."

Charlie grinned.

"Thank-you sir," he said.

He went to find the Confectioner. He pushed past dawdling shoppers and dithering old ladies. He weaved between traders and stalls.

Those stalls seemed to repeat themselves every twenty metres. Charlie passed fifteen perfume stalls, sixteen fruit stalls, and seventeen clothing stalls. The presence of so many similar kiosks meant shoppers could always find what they wanted. And the intense competition kept things affordable. All the traders sold enough to survive, but the low prices meant that no-one thrived. No-one was rich, but no-one was poor.

Charlie pushed past another five jewellery stalls, and another six crockery stalls, before he finally reached his destination. It was an Aladdin's cave full of chocolate and candy.

The sweet and sickly smell of sugar hit Charlie's nose straight away. A wall of colour bombarded his eyes. He could almost taste the sweets; the cola bottles, sour cherries and marshmallows; gummy bears, lollipops and jawbreakers.

A drop of saliva fell from his mouth. His eyes jumped out of his head. And his stomach rumbled.

"Do you need anything delivered or collected, sir?" He asked. "I'll give you a good deal."

The Confectioner looked Charlie up and down.

"You'll give me whatever deal I like," he said.

Charlie nodded. He did not say a word. He just gazed up at the Confectioner, who was missing all his teeth. He had wrinkled lips, which puckered into his mouth, and tiny eyes which stared at Arun.

"I have a delivery waiting for me at the bottom of the hill. Go down that alley there, turn right when you see a row of mannequins, and turn left when you see some Holy graffiti.

"When you get to the bottom of the market, you'll see a man with a lazy eye and an over-active hand. Show him this receipt. Make sure to take at least seventeen boxes of sweets, then come straight back.

"I'll be timing you."

Charlie sprinted away. He swerved around corners, jinked between shoppers, and skidded to a stop at the bottom of the hill. He loaded his trolley as quickly as he could, and pushed it straight back up to the Confectioner's store.

"Six minutes, twenty three seconds," the Confectioner said.

Charlie bent over, put his hands on his knees, and panted.

"Pretty good!" The Confectioner continued. "Pretty good indeed!"

He checked the seams of every box Charlie had delivered.

"You haven't taken a single sweet, have you?"

Charlie shook his head. The thought had never even crossed his mind.

A chicken crossed the road, to get to the other side.

The Confectioner chewed some tobacco.

"The other trolley boys always fill their boots, but you're different," he said. "What's your name?"

"Charlie, sir."

"Well, 'Charlie Sir', make sure to come back here at the same time next week. I could do with a trolley boy like you."

He stuffed a coin and a cola cube into Charlie's palm.

Charlie grinned.

He strolled along the alley, crammed with confidence, and touted for business at every stall he passed.

* * *

Charlie had been a trolley boy for over a month. He had earned himself a reputation, and built up a regular clientele.

Charlie helped traders to move stock. He helped bin men to move rubbish. And he was a firm favourite amongst Natale's housewives. He took their orders every morning, and delivered their shopping each afternoon.

He brimmed with boyish pride.

"My cart is a *Fastari*!" He boasted to Oliver.

"That piece of old junk ain't no Fastari," Oliver replied. "Pfft! You're blowing ducks! I've never heard so much nonsense in my life."

Charlie tapped his nose.

"When I grow up I'm going to be rich like my uncle," he said. "I'm going to earn so much money, I'll be able to buy a real Fastari. But until then, this'll have to do."

"Well if that old rust bucket is a Fastari, then my cart is a *Sheeporghini*," Oliver replied. "And everyone knows that Sheeporghinis are better than Fastaris."

"What?" Charlie shouted back with fake horror. "That's slander! Poppycock! Bunkum!"

"My Fastari would beat you Sheeporghini over any distance, on any race track, on any day of the week."

"Yeah?" Oliver replied. "Really? Okay, prove it then."

"Alright, I will.

"The Poultry Man, the one who's missing half an eyebrow, wants me to take his rubbish away. If you can make it to his stall before me, you can have the job."

"You're on," Oliver replied.

He spat on his palm and stretched it out to shake hands with Charlie.

Charlie cringed. He slowly lifted his hand towards his mouth.

Oliver swung around and pushed his trolley away.

"Oi!" Charlie shouted. "Come back here, you cheeky rascal!"

He pushed his trolley ahead, and chased after Oliver.

They ran down alleys which were made of cracked concrete, passages which smelled of rotting fish, and paths which swerved one way and then the other. They skidded around corners, scaled steep inclines, and slid down rutted stairs. They whizzed past stalls which sold spices, stalls which sold clothes, and stalls which sold fabric by the metre.

They ran past a Tape Seller who sold traditional music, in an attempt to keep his people's culture alive. His daughter, Jen, put a tape in a ghetto blaster. The sound of a folk song filled the air.

They ran past a poster which the *Holy Defence League* had glued to a wall. It said, '*Gas the Godlies*'.

And they ran past the Mad Lady, who was wagging her bony finger back and forth.

"You can run as fast as you like, but you can't change your life's direction," she shouted. "You're all owned by the bank. The seeds have already been sown!"

"Oh shut up," Mama Ellie shouted back. "What do you know, you batty old witch?"

Charlie sprinted ahead. But no matter how fast he ran, he could not overtake Oliver. The paths were always too narrow.

So Oliver reached the Poultry Man's stall before Charlie. He panted, turned around, and stuck out his chalky tongue.

Charlie shrugged.

"I'm here to take out your rubbish," Oliver said.

"Good," the Poultry Man replied. "Clean out the droppings from every cage, load them onto your cart, and take them all away. Don't get any filth on my floor. And don't complain about the smell. Shit stinks. Get over it."

Oliver grimaced.

He turned and wagged his fist at Charlie.

Charlie covered his mouth and giggled.

* * *

Charlie and Oliver raced through Natale every day. Sometimes Charlie's Fastari won their races, and sometimes Oliver's Sheeporghini came out on top. But those boys always shook hands once they had passed the chequered flag. They never bore a grudge.

When they were not racing, they ogled the knickknacks on display in Natale's market. The mandolins, skipping ropes, and blonde dolls. The toy guns, toy daggers, and toy soldiers.

They made their own toys by hand. They shaved stones in pencil sharpeners to make arrowheads. They made swords from sticks, and shields from pieces of wood. They used over-ripe fruit as grenades.

Then they ran around Natale and played their favourite game, 'Occupiers and Natives'.

"I want to be the Protokians," Oliver said. "The Protokians are strong. They have soldiers and tanks. They take anything they like."

"That's not fair," Charlie replied. "You were the Protokians last time. I don't want to be the Collisians again. They're as weak as a broken vase. They bow down at the feet of the Protokians."

They argued every time they played.

They also attended football matches, where they chanted as loudly as they could. They sneaked past the lingerie stall, where they gawked at ladies underwear. And they watched the weekly cock fights, where birds danced the tango; circling their opponents, and flapping their wings high above their heads.

But most of the time they spent at work. And when they worked, they raced.

One day, in the middle of spring, they raced towards the Water Pipe Seller. They sped down cobbled aisles, and sprinted up concrete tracks.

Oliver led the way, but Charlie was hot on his heels. They shot past a row of shoe stalls, turned into an alley full of hats, and snaked between a gaggle of fruit sellers.

The passageway widened. Charlie saw an opportunity to overtake. So he swung his cart out to the right and made his move.

He glanced at Oliver and ran past him. But, in doing so, he took his eye off the path. So he did not see an Old Lady, who was stepping out of a wool stall. He did not see the front corner of his cart crash into her hip.

Charlie turned his head when he felt the impact. He watched on in slow motion as his cart pushed through the Old Lady. As she flew back through the air and landed on one leg. As her knee buckled, her leg stumbled, and her elbow crashed onto the ground.

She lay on the floor, holding her crippled arm.

Charlie stopped, turned around, and looked on in pale-faced horror.

A Wool Seller, who had jug-like ears and orb-like eyes, ran out of his cluttered shop.

"Oi!" He yelled. "You little rascal. What on earth do you think you're doing?"

Charlie froze.

The Old Lady groaned.

The Wool Seller grabbed Charlie's ear.

"You're coming with me," he growled. "We'll see what your uncle has to say about this!"

The Wool Seller stormed off, with Charlie's ear between his fingers. Charlie scuttled along, bent over, facing the mucky ground.

They stepped over a row of turkeys, who lay on the floor, with their ankles tied together. They bumped into a man who was holding a pigeon by its feet. And they shoved past a woman who was carrying live chickens in a hessian sack.

They reached Uncle Charlie's stall.

"What's all this?" Uncle Charlie asked.

The Wool Seller gave Charlie a menacing look.

"This boy of yours has been assaulting old ladies," he said.

Uncle Charlie took a step back. He looked horrified.

"Is that true?" He asked.

Charlie looked down at his feet.

"It was an accident, sir," he replied.

"He wasn't looking where he was going," the Wool Trader interjected. "Accident or not, it could have been avoided."

Uncle Charlie shook his head.

"Is that true?" He asked again.

Charlie squinted.

"Yes sir," he replied. "Sorry sir. I was racing my friend, sir. His cart is a Sheeporghini. My cart is a Fastari. We were trying to win the Natale grand prix, and get to the Water Pipe seller first."

Uncle Charlie turned red.

"Fastari?" He screamed. "Sheeporghini? You're throwing cream into my eyes. Cream! Don't you go spouting foreign words near me.

"This is an honourable community. Yes. Yes. People work hard here. They work honestly. They produce everything we need, and trade their produce on this market. We don't need any imported muck in Collis.

"If God wanted us to have cars, they'd grow on trees. Yes. Yes.

"No sports car ever made anyone happy. No fancy gizmo ever brought people together. No gas chugging metal box ever helped people to find God. No. No.

"We don't need any of that filth here. It's just not respectable!"

Uncle Charlie turned to face the Wool Seller.

"Thank-you for bringing him to me," he said. "I'll make sure he learns his lesson. Yes. Yes."

The Wool Seller embraced Uncle Charlie, turned around, and left.

Uncle Charlie slapped his nephew's ear.

Charlie winced.

"What am I going to do with you?" Uncle Charlie asked himself. "You've done well as a trolley boy, I'll give you that. You've earned some respect.

"But you're just so ungodly. It's bad. Bad. Very bad."

Uncle Charlie tutted.

"Look, there are two types of people in Natale; the religious and the secular, the virtuous and the base, the godly and the ungodly.

"No-one likes a secularist. They're just not respectable. No. No. Do you really want to be like those one-dollar whores? Do you really want to sell your soul to the devil for a few shiny trinkets?"

Uncle Charlie put his finger on his lip, looked up to the heavens, and tapped his foot.

"I think it's time for you to start your education," he said. "It's time for you to go to school. Yes. Yes. School will save you. It'll make you rich! It'll be good. Good. Very good."

Uncle Charlie rubbed his hands together.

Charlie pinched his chin.

A cat chased after a chicken.

* * *

Charlie followed his uncle into the temple. He had never been anywhere like it.

Its dome shaped roof was covered in gold, its marble steps were pearly white, and its turrets were as tall as the clouds. Every wall featured paintings of religious scenes, icons hid in every hollow, and patterned carpets covered every inch of the floor.

The gaudy mix of colours made Charlie feel dizzy.

"Come, come," Uncle Charlie said. "And remember to honour the priest. He's a learned man. A spiritual man. A man of god! Yes. Yes. A man of God! *He's* respectable. Respectable!"

Charlie followed his uncle into a side room and sat down on the floor.

His uncle left.

Charlie looked at the other children. They were tidier than the trolley boys. Their clothes were new, their hair was tangle-free, and their fingernails were clean.

They waited in silence for several minutes.

Light spilled through a stained glass window.

A motorbike pulled up outside.

The other students shuffled their bottoms, pulled their shoulders back, and straightened their spines. Charlie copied them.

The Humpbacked Priest entered. He hobbled over to the donations box, emptied its contents into a brown leather bag, and put that bag in his pocket.

"Turn to page seventy six of the Godly bible," he said. "Let's read."

The sound of page turning filled the room.

"*Blah, blah, blah,*" the children read. "*Blah. Blah, blah. Blah, blah, blah, blah.*"

Charlie did not understand a word they were saying. He just sat there and pretended to read.

The Humpbacked Priest scowled at him.

Charlie twitched. His cheek vibrated and his eye blinked.

"Good," the Humpbacked Priest concluded.

He sprinkled some petals into a font.

A Chubby Local lit some incense.

A Haunted Refugee said a prayer.

"Good," the Humpbacked Priest repeated. "Let's begin our lesson."

He mopped his sweaty brow and stroked his crooked back.

"There once was a man who was generous and kind. As he was leaving for work, a monk came by and asked him for food.

"'*Give this monk something to eat,*' the kind man told his wife. '*It'll be a mitzvah. A good deed! Make sure his belly is full by the time he leaves'.*

"But his wife was greedy. Oi vey! She wanted to hoard her food. That shiksa wanted to discourage the monk from returning.

"So she locked the monk in her basement, and kept him there whilst she ate all the food in her house. She only released the monk after many hours had passed.

"She thought she had gotten away with her sin. But she died that week, and came back as a ghost. She didn't have any teeth, and her neck was too narrow to swallow food. That goy couldn't eat! She was made to exist in a state of eternal hunger!"

The Humpbacked Priest stared at his pupils.

His pupils stared back at their teacher.

A moth flew into a window.

"What does this story mean?"

At first there was silence. No-one moved. Then, in amongst the sea of tiny faces, a Cherubic Boy tentatively raised his arm.

"Super!" The Humpbacked Priest said. "Go ahead."

"It means we must be generous," the Cherubic Boy replied.

"Yes. But who should we be generous to?"

The Cherubic Boy paused to think.

"Monks?" He asked.

"Yes. And?"

The Cherubic Boy shrugged.

Ash dropped from a joss stick.

Sweat dropped from the Humpbacked Priest's face.

"Priests!" He continued. "If you give your money to priests, you'll have a great afterlife. But if you don't make regular donations, you'll become a hungry ghost, and starve for all eternity.

"My pupils, you must commit yourself to the lord! You must circumcise your hearts!"

The boys all looked aghast.

Charlie took a coin, and put it in the donations box.

A Shaggy Local and a Shaven Refugee copied him.

"Good," the Humpbacked Priest said. "Let's move on.

"Who knows a folk song?"

Charlie's hand shot up into the air. His eyes bulged and his head bobbed.

The Humpbacked Priest gestured for Charlie to start.

"Go on babushka," he said.

Charlie stood up, took a deep breath, and began to sing.

"Oh enemy, the Collisians live on,

"They have not been crushed by the weapons of any era,

"Let no one say Collisians are dead,

"They live on, and will never lower their flag."

The Humpbacked Priest's face turned red. It was a blood-curdling shade of red. A shade of red which was so dark it was almost purple, so bold it made his face pulsate, and so loud it seemed to scream.

"What do you think you're doing?" He bellowed. "What chutzpah! Oi vey! Do you want to get me fired? Do you want to get me arrested?"

Charlie shivered in fear. His twitch went into overdrive. And his cheek vibrated so much, he had to hold his head steady.

"You can't sing that in here. You're here to study the Godly bible, and learn the Protokian language. That's all. Oi va voi! Show some respect!"

The Humpbacked Priest hobbled towards Charlie.

"I don't want to hear another word from you today," he said. "You treasonous toad! You putz! You schmoe! You shagetz! I'll report you to the Protokian authorities."

A tear rolled down Charlie's cheek. It landed on a piece of dust, and rolled into a crack.

The Humpbacked Priest hobbled across the room.

The class sang the Protokian national anthem.

* * *

Charlie went to school every morning and worked on the market every afternoon. He always had something to do, and he was never idle. His life was hard, he often worked from sunrise to sunset, but he was happy. He had coins in his pocket, and faith that his education would make him rich.

His schooling followed a fairly regular routine. It always started with prayers, and a lesson from the Godly bible. It always finished with a literacy exercise, and a lesson on the Protokian language.

The only exception came on Protokia Independence Day.

Charlie walked through the temple, which was decked out in the Protokian colours. Every icon had been dressed in the Protokian style. Protokian flags hung from every wall.

He heard a motorbike pull up outside. He shuffled on his bottom, pulled his shoulders back, and straightened his spine.

"Stand up and face the Protokian flag," the Humpbacked Priest demanded.

The class stood up. They held their hearts. And they recited the Protokian pledge:

"I pledge allegiance to the flag of Protokia, and to the Holy republic for which it stands. One nation under the Holy God, and the home of all Holies, indivisible, with liberty and justice for all."

The pupils walked to the front, one at a time, and kissed the Protokian flag.

"Good," the Humpbacked Priest said, whilst mopping his sweaty brow. "We have a very special guest today. Please say 'hello' to Sergeant Officer."

"Hello Sergeant Officer," the class cheered in unison.

"Hello," Sergeant Officer replied.

Sergeant Officer stood tall in his pristine uniform. There were pips on his shoulders and medals on his chest. His hair glimmered with gel, and his moustache shimmered in the sun.

"Today is a very important day in Protokian history," he lectured. "It marks the anniversary of this nation's liberation from the heathen hordes who had occupied it.

"Great men risked their lives to drive those infidels away. But, thanks to their sacrifices, we're all able to live in this prosperous land together. We're all able to live in peace, in this nation where the supremacy of the Holies is absolute.

"All hail the Holy God!"

Sergeant Officer smirked.

The Humpbacked Priest swayed.

Charlie furrowed his brow.

"The Protokians brought freedom to this land," Sergeant Officer concluded. "And they brought wealth which is trickling down to us all."

Sergeant Officer removed a bag of silver coins from his pocket, and gave one to every child. He embraced the Humpbacked Priest, turned around, and left.

Charlie stroked his silver coin. He flipped it over, and rolled it back and forth. He had not seen such a valuable coin before.

The Humpbacked Priest raised his eyebrows.

The class looked back at him in silence.

The Humpbacked Priest glared.

"What are you going to do with your coins?" He asked.

No-one said a word.

The Humpbacked Priest gestured towards the donations box.

Charlie took a cheap bronze coin from his pocket, and swapped it with his silver coin. He stood up, walked across the room, and donated the bronze coin. He sat back down on the floor.

Slowly but surely, the other pupils all followed. They all donated their silver coins.

The Humpbacked Priest glowed.

Charlie giggled.

A chicken ran into the temple.

* * *

Charlie made his last delivery of the day, and then met Oliver at the Tape Seller's stall. That man, who had a hairless head and a hairy chin, fancied himself as a bit of a teacher.

"Music is the voice of the soul!" He lectured. "Each note echoes throughout the centuries. Each of our songs has touched the ears of our fathers, their fathers, and their father's fathers."

He pressed the play button on his ghetto blaster.

Charlie tapped his foot.

Oliver stood up and danced.

"So long as we have our music," the Tape Seller concluded. "We'll remember who we are. Our Collisian identity will live on."

Charlie and Oliver listened to three more songs. They danced three more dances. And they nodded three more times.

Then they walked through the market, and emerged onto a lane which ran through Natale. But they were unable to continue, because a large crowd was blocking the street.

People of every shape and size stood before Charlie and Oliver. There were refugees and locals, villagers and townsfolk, monks and lay people, youngsters and pensioners, students and workers. Some of them wore colourful gowns and patterned robes, baggy trousers and wide belts. But at least a quarter of the crowd, and at least half of the youngsters, wore denim jeans. They looked like a casual army; rebellious on the outside, but self-conscious underneath.

"What's going on?" Oliver asked the Midwife.

The Midwife pointed at a building. Its front had been replaced with glass. Its door was translucent. And its sign was illuminated by a halogen bulb, which spewed neon light into the sepia sky.

Charlie tried to read that sign. He tried to read Protokian whenever he could.

"Pa, piz, pizza," he read. "Ha, how, house. Pizza House!"

The Mad Lady ran into Charlie. She clutched her hair and shook her head. She tripped over her feet and landed in a puff of dust.

"The shareholders are coming!" She screamed. "They'll drive us out of town. They'll put a Pizza House on every corner!"

"Oh shut up," the Midwife shouted back. "What do you know, you batty old witch?"

Charlie and Oliver snickered.

They slithered through a mass of people. They weaved to the left of old men, and slinked to the right of young girls. They crawled between legs and ducked beneath elbows.

They reached the front of the crowd, and peered through the glass. They saw red tables, which were bolted to the chequered floor. They saw stools, which lined up along a tiled wall. And they saw a white counter. It hid a jungle of silver machines, silver utensils, and silver sinks.

To Charlie, it looked ridiculous.

To Oliver, it looked fantastic.

To the rest of the crowd, it caused confusion.

People scratched their heads. Old women ground their teeth, and old men muttered. Young women fidgeted, and young men frowned.

Oliver and Charlie listened to their conversations.

"What is it?" A Curvaceous Refugee asked.

"They sell pizza," a Petite Local replied.

"Pizza?"

"Foreign food."

"What's wrong with Collisian food? What's wrong with cooking at home?"

The Petite Local shrugged.

A spark flew off a Welder's soldering iron.

Oliver and Charlie listened to another conversation.

"I heard it's owned by foreigners," a Suited Local said.

"That's madness," his Brother replied.

"It's true."

"How will they get to know their customers, if they live abroad?"

The Suited Local shrugged.

A sparrow flew by.

Oliver and Charlie listened to a third conversation.

"I heard it's owned by Colonisers," a Tall Refugee said. "Or perhaps by Colonialists. It's definitely owned by one of the two."

A Short Local looked shocked.

"I thought we'd gotten rid of those fist-dragging bullies," she replied.

"So had I," the Tall Refugee sighed. "So had I."

SECTION TWO

ADOLESCENCE

5. TAMSIN

Tamsin, her parents and nine siblings, huddled together in their one room home.

That shack had felt like a palace when they first moved in, after two years spent living in a tent. Even though it was too hot in the summer, and too cold in the winter, it did not leak, and it did not fall over in the wind. It was a welcome upgrade.

Their home consisted of four asbestos walls and one zinc roof. It was four metres long and three metres wide. The floor was made of uncovered concrete.

Tamsin's family ate, slept and socialised, in that tiny space. They went to the toilet outside.

Papa Tamsin had wanted to build an inside toilet and two additional floors. He had applied for a building permit. But over three years had passed, and he was still waiting for a response. His neighbours had expanded their home without a permit, and some settlers had torn it down. So Papa Tamsin felt that he had no choice but to wait.

Instead of spending his money on his home, he spent it on thingamajigs and furnishings. His family was one of the first in the camp to own a television. They owned a pile of thin mattresses, a halogen stove, and a cabinet full of pots and pans. Their shelves displayed jars full of red paprika, orange cinnamon, and green herbs; rice, flour and lentils. A model giraffe, which was missing half a leg, stood in the corner, next to Tamsin's guitar.

Papa Tamsin bought his children new toys almost every month. His home was full of *Garbie Dolls*, *E. I. Joe* action figures, and plastic toy soldiers. Miniature model cars, *Lejo* building bricks, and juggling balls. Board games like *Risky*, *Battle Boats* and *Oligopoly*.

Their windows were adorned with black bars, and their windowsills were adorned with flower pots, which added colour to a white wall. A wire ran through that wall. It brought electricity when it was dry, but not when it rained. A large barrel of water sat by their door. The settlers controlled the water supply, so the natives had to hoard whatever water they could gather.

Two babies slept in a corner. The rest of the family sat around a blackened can, which contained a small fire.

That fire fizzled and popped.

An owl hooted.

Two soldiers walked by, and shone their searchlights through a window.

"What's that, papa?" Toddler Tamsin asked.

"That's the moon!" Papa Tamsin replied. "Isn't it amazing?"

A soldier moved her searchlight. It created a round circle on the wall, which moved from one side of the room to the other.

Toddler Tamsin, who had the most unfortunate set of ears Tamsin had ever seen, looked at that light with wide-eyed amazement.

Tamsin's Brother slapped his forehead.

"Don't be silly," he said. "The moon doesn't move about like that."

Papa Tamsin chuckled.

"Well, not normally," he replied. "It's the first time I've seen it move like that in Collis. But it used to move about when we lived in Doomba. It used to dance through the sky, as if it was happy to see us!"

Papa Tamsin winked at his eldest daughter.

"Oh yes," Tamsin added. "The moon always danced when it saw Doomba. It shimmied and it swayed! It did the foxtrot *and* the tango! It glowed in the brightest shade of orange you've ever seen."

Tamsin's Brother, a bony child who was five years younger than Tamsin, looked impressed.

"Tell us about Doomba, daddy," he pleaded. He was too young to remember it himself. "Go on daddy. It's the best village in the world!"

Papa Tamsin beamed with pride.

Tamsin's Brother looked at him with eager eyes. He had heard about Doomba hundreds of times before, but it still intrigued him. He loved it when his father spoke about their village. It gave him goose-pimples.

"Well, it was the most beautiful place in the world," Papa Tamsin said. "People called it '*Rainbow Village*', because of the wide furrows which spread out across the valley floor. A different crop was planted along each furrow, which made the valley look like a giant rainbow.

"The tomatoes were redder than any tomatoes you have ever seen.

We grew the most orange wheat in the world. The sunflowers were as yellow as the sun. The green sweetcorn stalks were taller than houses. The purple aubergines were so plump, it took two people to carry them. And the pink grapes were so sweet, they gave you enough energy to run around for a whole day!"

Tamsin filled the water pipe with apple flavoured tobacco, and added some glowing embers from the fire. She passed its mouthpiece to Papa Tamsin, who put it to his lips and inhaled.

Mama Tamsin drank some sugary tea.

Tamsin's Brother gazed at his father.

"You're going to tell us about the wild animals, aren't you?" He asked.

"I sure am," his father replied.

Tamsin's Brother giggled.

The wind whistled.

Papa Tamsin gave his son a mischievous look.

"Well, there was one wild animal which was called a '*wolf*'. Wolves had pointy ears. They looked a bit like dogs, but they had bigger, sharper, deadlier teeth.

"When I was young, I didn't know what a wolf was. So I didn't do anything when one entered Doomba. That wolf grabbed a chicken, and tore it to shreds! I got spanked, because I didn't do anything to stop it.

"I learnt my lesson though. The next time a wolf entered Doomba, I picked up my slingshot and chased it away. I ran and ran until that wolf was out of sight.

"I was a bit of a hero after that."

Papa Tamsin chuckled.

Mama Tamsin made some more tea.

Tamsin's Brother called for more.

"Tell us about the tiger, daddy. Please!" He cheered. "Please! Please! Please!"

"Okay, okay," Papa Tamsin replied. "Well there weren't many tigers near Doomba. It was a safe place on the whole. Our dogs scared off most of the foxes, bobcats and jackals.

"But a tiger did approach our village one spring. She had bright yellow eyes, a snotty nose, and two clumps of grey whiskers. I think she must have been elderly. She just lay down near a cave which overlooked Doomba, and went to sleep.

"Well, a group of us were sent to chase that tiger away. We had stones and rocks and knives. But the tiger didn't move. So we crept up on her from behind, and slit her throat.

"The Medicine Man sacrificed her to the gods. He ground her bones into a powder, which he turned into a special potion.

"That elixir kept the villagers healthy for years!"

Tamsin's Brother was open-mouthed with amazement.

Mama Tamsin rolled her eyes.

Papa Tamsin fell silent. He loved Doomba so much, the thought of it struck him dumb. He stood up and kissed the key to his village home, which hung on the wall. He polished that key every morning, and prayed to it every night. It was his most cherished possession.

"One day we'll go home," he concluded. "This place is just a bus stop for us. We'll wait here as long as we have to, but we're not here to stay. A giant bus is going to take us back to Doomba. Just you wait and see!"

Everyone bowed their heads.

Everyone sighed.

Everyone unrolled their mattresses and went to sleep, apart from Tamsin, who was too tense to drift off.

She had stomach cramps. They were not painful, but they were uncomfortable. They tapped her abdomen, and made her feel sick. They made her feel constipated. Her vagina felt sore.

So she cupped her belly, stroked her stomach, and put her hand inside her pants.

Her fingers felt moist.

Her palm shook.

She lifted her hand to her face, and investigated the gooey liquid which covered her nails. It smelt like the sea, and it felt like pus. Tamsin thought she was bleeding, but she was confused, because the liquid in her pants did not look like normal blood.

She tried to work out why her body was acting so strangely.

Perhaps it was because she had eaten too many jelly babies for lunch, she thought. Or because she had caught herself when she climbed over a wire fence. Or because she had spent too long in the same position, sat cross legged on the floor.

She thought about going to the toilet. But it was cold and rainy outside. She did not want to wake her family. And she did not want to encounter any Protokian soldiers.

So she picked up a cotton handkerchief, folded it into quarters, and pressed it between her legs. She rolled into a foetal position. And she stayed there all night, with her hand on her handkerchief, and her handkerchief on her genitals.

By the time the morning came, her handkerchief was completely brown. Tamsin went to the toilet and threw it away. Then she vomited.

* * *

"Come on," Mama Tamsin said. "Let's go."

"What?" Tamsin replied. "Where? Why?"

"You're dirty."

"No I'm not. I showered this morning."

"No, you're *dirty*. I've seen what you've been doing these last few days; holding pads against your bits."

Mama Tamsin raised her eyebrows.

"Look, it's fine if you don't want to talk about it. That's up to you. But you do need to be cleansed. There are rituals which need to be performed."

Tamsin scowled at her mother. She could have died of embarrassment.

"Haha!" Toddler Tamsin mocked. "You're dirty. You're a dirty girl. Oooh! Unclean! Unclean!"

"Unclean! Unclean!" Tamsin's other siblings chanted.

"Urgh!" Tamsin screamed. "Let's go."

She took Mama Tamsin's hand, and dragged her through the camp.

They walked past houses which were packed in so tightly, it was impossible to smell the wind or see the sun. Past pylons which sent a tangled mass of electricity cables in every direction. And past the items which hung from those cables; the old plastic bags, broken kites and broken wheels.

They walked down narrow roads, which turned into narrow alleys, as narrow houses crept forward on either side. The pastel coloured paint which adorned those buildings could not disguise their shabby state, although Protokian propaganda did hide patches of crumbling bricks. There were posters of Holy priests, etchings of Atamow, and spray-painted red suns.

Those symbols competed with propaganda from the Collisian rebels, the KPP, who hung flags from every pylon, and painted giant murals to honour their fallen rebels.

Signs marked 'UNHCR' seemed to look down on both sets of images.

Tamsin and her mother walked past a Butcher, who slaughtered a cow, who writhed on its back, with its legs held up in the air. Past the Moustached Refugee, who tended to the offspring of the sheep he had rescued from his village. And past a house which was full of flapping chickens and jumping goats. It was the only building in their camp which did not appear to have a television.

They walked past a Slick Refugee, who was eight years old. He was smoking a cigarette, and drinking a strong cup of coffee. They passed some teenage refugees, who were sitting in an internet café, playing the latest football game. And they passed a Gloomy Refugee, who was wearing a fake *Barcanal* shirt. He was holding a football, but he did not have anyone to play with.

Those children all looked different. Some had bigger noses, and some had smaller ears. But they all spoke the same dialect. They all used the same phrases. They all ate the same food and wore the same clothes. It was impossible to tell which village a refugee came from, just by looking at them. Forty-eight cultures had merged into one.

A stray cat leapt between bins. It licked the remains of a broken egg off the street, and then scuttled under a car.

That car waited to turn into Natale. But three blue barrels had been spread across the road, and a gaggle of Protokian soldiers were stopping citizens from passing.

A Frustrated Soldier wore a permanent frown. An Impatient Soldier wore skin which seemed to have been pulled back from his nose. An Officious Soldier had a hooked nose. And a Bored Soldier had a satiric smile.

A gaggle of protestors held up placards. They shouted, '*From the mountains to the sea, this land of ours will be free'*. And they ignored the gunfire which rang out in the hills.

The soldiers checked permits.

"This is a copy," the Bored Soldier told a Frail Refugee. "We only accept originals here. I can't let you pass."

"You're forty two," the Frustrated Soldier told a Tidy Refugee. "Only citizens aged under forty or over sixty are allowed into Natale today. You'll have to come back tomorrow."

"This permit is expired," the Impatient Soldier told a Red Refugee.

He tore it up and threw it away.

"It was expired when it was issued," the Red Refugee protested. "You can't get valid permits. It's impossible!"

The Impatient Soldier glanced at his watch.

A donkey swished its tail.

A pick-up truck loaded with bricks crawled towards the checkpoint.

"Bricks aren't allowed into Natale today," the Officious Soldier told the Driver.

"I came yesterday with cement, and you said it wasn't allowed into Natale. You specifically said that I could bring bricks!"

"That was yesterday. Yesterday you could bricks, but not cement. Today you can bring cement, but not bricks. Pfft! If you keep coming here with forbidden items, I'll have no choice but to arrest you."

The Officious Soldier clutched his gun. The Driver did a three point turn. And a Stumpy Refugee stepped forwards.

He approached a Ruddy Soldier; a man who seemed incomplete, as if Mother Nature had got distracted whilst designing his body. His cheeks were a little too boisterous, as if they had not been sanded down. And his eyes were a little too intense, as if they were made of solid rock.

"Are you a Holy or a Godly?" He asked.

"I'm not religious," the Stumpy Refugee replied.

"How old are you?"

"Thirty seven."

"Why do you want to enter?"

"To see my family."

"Show me your permit."

The Stumpy Refugee handed over his permit.

A sparrow landed on a donkey's back.

The Ruddy Soldier shook his head.

"You can't enter," he said.

"Why not?"

"Men aren't allowed to enter on their own today. You need to be accompanied by a woman or a child."

The Stumpy Refugee filled with rage. He looked like a bull who was about to attack its tormentor. His eyes bulged, he blew hot air out of his nostrils, and he dragged his foot back through the dirt.

"Put yourself in my shoes," he pleaded. "I just want to see my family. Tell me, what should I do?"

The Ruddy Soldier shrugged.

"Not my circus, not my monkeys," he said. "Do I look like your problem solver?"

"Are you my God?" The Stumpy Refugee shouted back. Spit sprayed out of his mouth, his knees buckled, and his legs trembled. "Am I your slave? Do I work for you?

"Where are my human rights? Show me! Show me where my human rights are, so I can go and look for them."

"Shut up!" The Ruddy Soldier snapped. "What can I do? What do you expect me to do? My hands are tied by the law. And the supremacy of law is absolute!"

"But I always pass through here."

"Well you're not passing through here today. Period. If you have a problem, go and speak to the Collisian police. They're the ones in charge of you."

The Ruddy Soldier picked up his gun and pointed it at the Stumpy Refugee.

"Go to hell you animal," the Stumpy Refugee barked. "I'll break your bones! Why are you doing this to me? Shoot me, I don't care."

He stormed off towards a portable table, which had hinged legs and a splintered top. For every Protokian soldier at the blockade, there was a Collisian policeman behind that table. A Bored Policeman and a Frustrated Policeman pushed some paper back and forth. And an Impatient Policeman argued with some citizens.

The sun emerged from behind a lonely grey cloud.

Tamsin and her mother stepped forward.

The Junior Priest undressed them with his eyes.

"Papers?" He asked.

A dog ran through the blockade.

Mama Tamsin handed over her papers.

The Junior Priest ogled her breasts.

"I'm going to have to pat you down," he said.

He ran his hands along the inside of Mama Tamsin's arms, under her armpits, and across her ribs. He cupped Mama Tamsin's breasts. He pressed them together, looked into Mama Tamsin's eyes and sneered.

"Open your bag," he said.

Mama Tamsin opened her handbag.

The Junior Priest held it upside down, and emptied its contents onto the top of a barrel. He rifled through Mama Tamsin's possessions.

"Batteries," he said. "I could really do with some batteries."

"Take them," Mama Tamsin replied. "Consider it a gift."

The Junior Priest smirked.

"Thank-you," he said. "You've got brains as well as beauty. On you go."

The Junior Priest winked at Mama Tamsin and licked his lips.

Tamsin and her mother walked into Natale.

The Stumpy Refugee ran after them.

"They're with me," he said. "They're accompanying me. I'm not on my own. See! I'm with a woman and child. You have to let me through."

Mama Tamsin turned around, and gave the soldiers a thumbs up.

The soldiers allowed the Stumpy Refugee to pass through.

Tamsin looked up at some shops, which all had neon signs.

On one street there was a *'Burger Queen'*, a *'McRonalds'*, and a *'Pizza House'*. On another street there was a *'Sandwich Way'*, a *'Greasy Fried Chicken'*, and a *'Pizza Home'*. On a third street there was a *'Star & Bucks'*, a *'Wompy Burger'*, and another *'Pizza House'*.

Amidst those foreign owned outlets, a few plucky locals had set up their own fast-food joints. There was a *'Collis Burger'*, a *'Godly Kebab'*, and a *'Natale Chippy'*. Tamsin was familiar with restaurants like those, because her father worked for *'Freedom Pizza'*; a pizzeria who gave him regular work, for a low but regular wage.

She followed her mother into Natale's market. Half of its stalls were boarded up. Whole alleys were empty. Uncle Charlie was sitting in his emporium, twiddling his thumbs, and staring at his unsold produce.

"Bad. Bad," he muttered. "Very bad."

There wasn't a single trolley boy in sight.

Tamsin turned onto a lane which was full of smog-emitting lorries. Shops with glass facades lined up on either side. There was a 'Toot's Pharmacy', a 'Superb Drugs', and an 'Accessories'. A 'Sparks and Fencers', a 'Tip Top Shop', and a 'High Mark'. A 'PC Universe', a 'Computer World', and a 'Dick's Sons'.

Tamsin turned another corner, and saw a building site. Big posters said; 'Window Mart is coming! Get ready for the cheapest food in town', 'Get all your groceries in one place', and 'You'll never shop anywhere else again'.

A Greengrocer, Baker and Butcher, all shook their heads. But no-one else seemed to care. Shoppers filled their bags with consumer goods. Small children stuffed chips into their mouths. And Tamsin followed her mother into the hamam.

They walked through the foyer, which was covered in blue and white tiles. They undressed in a small wooden cubicle. And they stepped into a pool of icy water. They were both completely naked.

Mama Tamsin dunked her daughter's head beneath the surface.

"There," she said. "You're cleansed! Your soul is clean. I'm proud of you. You've become a woman!"

Tamsin shook the water from her eyes, hugged herself and shivered.

"Come," Mama Tamsin said. "It's cold for me to see you like this. Let's warm up in the hot pool."

Tamsin followed her mother into the next room. She sunk into a pool which was so hot, it covered her skin in wrinkles. It made her look like a stewed prune. And it made her feel like a piece of chicken, in a steamy bowl of broth.

Mama Tamsin nattered to a Pink Local, but Tamsin did not say a word. She felt self-conscious, awkward and ill-at-ease, because Mama Jon was staring at her naked body.

That saggy lady, who had droopy breasts and floppy wrists, was exploring every inch of Tamsin's skin. Her eyes were skipping from

Tamsin's breasts to her inner-thighs, and from her stomach to her pelvis.

Tamsin shuffled along, but Mama Jon turned her head. Tamsin covered her breasts with one arm, and crossed her legs, but Mama Jon did not avert her gaze.

"I want to go home," Tamsin said.

She got up, got dressed, and left.

* * *

"I've lost my job," Papa Tamsin told his family. "I'm afraid we're going to have to make some cutbacks around here. We're going to have to stop buying all these bits and bobs. We're going to have to survive on a diet of rice and soup."

His family stared at Papa Tamsin. Their stomachs dropped. Their eyes looked hollow. Confusion covered their faces.

No-one said a word.

The silence lasted for minutes.

"It's those bloody foreigners!" Papa Tamsin finally said. "It's those bloody Protokians; coming here and closing our businesses. Pfft! We should have never let them stay, with their strange goods and peculiar services. What have they ever done for us? Nothing! They're no bloody use to anyone."

Mama Tamsin looked fraught.

Toddler Tamsin sucked her thumb.

Papa Tamsin shook his head.

"The Protokian soldiers built checkpoints on both sides of Freedom Pizza," he explained. "Our customers couldn't reach us, so the Boss had to close his store."

Papa Tamsin sighed.

"We're going to have to make some changes," he concluded. "We can't afford this lifestyle anymore."

Papa Tamsin clicked his knuckles.

Mama Tamsin made some tea.

Tamsin shook her head.

But hardly anything changed. Tamsin went to school, just as she had done before. She hawked fruit every afternoon, and she met her friends every evening. She had to live off a diet of rice and soup, but the rest of her life continued on as normal.

It continued on as normal for over two months.

Then, one day at the end of spring, she returned to a house full of guests. Mama Jon was sitting between Papa Tamsin and Papa Jon; a meagre man whose skin was covered in liver-spots. And Jon was sitting with his First Wife; a woman who seemed oddly complete, like a set of drawers which had been chiselled out of a single hunk of wood.

Mama Tamsin made some tea.

Tamsin looked at everyone in the room.

Mama Jon looked back at Tamsin.

"The meat is hung out for display," she announced.

Tamsin swung her head to the side, glared at the Mama Jon for the briefest of moments, and then turned back to face her father.

"Err, yes," Papa Tamsin stammered. "I'd like you to meet your fiancée. This is Jon."

Tamsin took a step back, looked Jon up and down, and then shook her head.

"I'm not marrying that lump of foul deformity," she said. "You've got to be kidding me!"

Papa Tamsin gave his daughter a stern look. He had been in the same position twice before, and he had learnt his lesson well.

When Tamsin was twelve years old, Papa Tamsin had tried to marry her to the Spotty Boy. But Tamsin had said, '*I'm not marrying him. Dad, he smells. Everyone calls him 'smelly smelly poo pants'.*'

Papa Tamsin had chortled, hugged his daughter, and relented. The Spotty Boy had run outside to cry.

Papa Tamsin had also tried to marry his daughter to Oliver. But Tamsin had objected again. '*I'm not marrying him*', she had said. '*He's not from Doomba*'.

Papa Tamsin had filled with pride, pulled Tamsin to his breast, and sent Oliver packing.

So it was easy to understand why Tamsin protested. She thought she could change her father's mind.

"I'm only fourteen," she said. "I'm far too young to get married."

But Papa Tamsin was determined not to be manipulated again.

"What's all this '*I'm only fourteen*' nonsense?" He snapped. "Last year you were '*only thirteen*', and the year before that you were '*only twelve*'. You'll be '*only seventy*-six', and you'll still be unmarried if you keep this up.

"Do you want to be some sort of old spinster? Do you want to be some sort of old witch, left on the shelf, passed over by every man in town?"

Tamsin put her hands on her hips.

"I don't want to be an old spinster," she snarled. "But I don't want to get married either. I want to wait until I fall in love."

"Enough!" Papa Tamsin snapped. "I didn't fall in love. My parents arranged my marriage, and that worked out just fine. Stop whinging!"

Tamsin turned red.

"Really, papa!" She screamed. "I feel like I'm being enslaved by two occupiers; the Protokians and you!"

"Well," Papa Tamsin barked. "You'll be better off out of my house then. It's settled!"

Mama Tamsin put down her tea and gave Tamsin a big hug. She held Tamsin away, with one hand on either shoulder, and looked into her eyes.

"This will be a good marriage," she said. "The Medicine Man has already drawn up your chart. You're a perfect match! Jon is a pig and you're a tiger. Pigs and tigers are ever so compatible. You'll be happy. You'll have lots of children. And you'll be rich!"

Tamsin wagged her finger. A tear rolled down her nose, and a bubble formed in the corner of her mouth. She looked at her father with puppy dog eyes.

"Enough!" Papa Tamsin growled. "You're marrying this man, and that's that.

"The dowry has been set at five camels. Five whole camels!!! That will pay for your wedding, and give our family enough money to survive for months. Months!!! Do you really want us to starve? Really, Tamsin? Think of us for once. I think you forget that I'm unemployed."

Tamsin shook her head.

"I want to get married in Doomba," she muttered.

"Well you can get married on the other side of Natale. There's a temple there which faces towards Doomba. We'll get the Humpbacked

Priest to perform a Doomba style ceremony. We'll invite the whole of bloody Doomba to come and watch!"

Tamsin looked at her father. There was a moment of silence. And then Jon spoke:

"I've been back to Doomba."

Tamsin's jaw dropped.

"How?" She asked.

"I have a blue permit. I'm allowed into Protokia to work."

Jon gave Tamsin a cheeky wink.

The fire fizzled and popped.

Tamsin stared at her fiancé.

"What's it like?" She asked.

Jon smiled. He paused. And then he spoke:

"The first time I returned to Doomba, I just stood there in silence. I was overwhelmed with emotion. I asked myself, '*Why? Why was this place taken from us? Why?*'"

"I felt our village greet me, with a face which was both smiling and weeping. The stones were so full of tears, I'm sure they'll cry for us when we return. I looked at the earth and whispered, '*This land is ours*'."

Papa Tamsin closed his eyes. An image of Doomba came to him.

Mama Tamsin clutched her husband's thigh.

Tamsin gestured for Jon to continue.

"The second time I visited Doomba, I went with the Stout Villager. That man wanted to steal his own fruit.

"We walked between the houses, which were riddled with bullets, and crumbling at their seams. Then we visited the land where our fields once stood. The Protokians had planted trees there. They had erected a picnic area where we used to plant carrots. A big sign said, '*Built by the Holy National Fund, with donations from abroad*'.

"Everything had changed. But as I walked around, I could still see where everything once stood. I could still see our peach trees, flowering pinkish white, as if they were really there. I could still see the wild daisies which sprouted in our olive groves, the yaks who gave us their milk, and the pomegranate tree whose branches spread out like an umbrella. I pointed to where one furrow began and another one ended. I smelt the fragrance of sweet tea on the air.

"The spring had dried up, but our fig trees had all survived. So the Stout Villager harvested what fruit he could.

"He felt humiliated.

"'*End this torture,*' he prayed. '*Dear God, please put me out of my misery*'.

"I tried to talk him around. I explained that UN Resolution 194 says we have a right to return. But he didn't listen to me, and God did listen to him.

"The Stout Villager went to repair the village toilet during a thunder storm. Lightening shot down from the heavens, and struck his hammer. It burnt him like a stick.

"God had answered his call."

Jon took a deep breath.

"I don't think he was the only person to perish when he returned. Other villagers died of broken hearts as soon as they stepped back into Doomba. It's a sad situation. It makes me cry."

Everyone bowed their heads.

Everyone shed a tear.

Jon tried to lift the mood.

"The third time I returned," he said. "I decided to act.

"The Protokians had put a sign in the village square, above a mass grave. It said, '*Godlies and the Godly state were buried here*'. I destroyed that sign! I replaced it with a sign which said, '*The Godly revolution, and the KPP, were born here*'."

Toddler Tamsin giggled.

"On my fourth visit to Doomba I took a cutting from a fig tree. I brought it home and planted it in our garden. It produced fruit for the first time last year.

"Now, each time I visit our village, I try to bring something back."

Jon passed Tamsin a small stone.

"This is for you," he said. "I found it outside your home in Doomba."

A tear of joy dropped onto Tamsin's lap.

"I'd like to visit," she said.

Jon smiled.

"Ok," he replied. "I'll take you. But let's get married first."

Tamsin nodded.

Papa Tamsin grinned.

Mama Tamsin made some more tea.

* * *

Tamsin's engagement do took place the next week. They held a street party, and barbequed a goat on a spit. Rings were exchanged, a wedding contract was signed, and citizens shoved envelopes full of cash into Jon's hand. Then their families prepared for the wedding.

Tamsin and her mother went to the temple on the other side of Natale. They were held up at the first checkpoint, which had been replaced by a permanent structure. Mama Tamsin gave some sweets to a Tattooed Soldier, who allowed her to pass. But they did not have any problems at the second checkpoint. An Athletic Soldier, who wore a look of complete disinterest, ignored them as they walked through.

The Humpbacked Priest was deep in prayer when they arrived at the temple. So Tamsin and her mother bowed down and prayed at his feet. Tamsin did not understand what the Humpbacked Priest was saying. She just closed her eyes, daydreamed, and cried a little.

The Humpbacked Priest swayed from side to side.

"Peace be upon you," he said.

"I salute the God within you," Mama Tamsin replied.

They both smiled.

"What can I do for you?"

"My daughter would like to get married here."

The Humpbacked Priest stroked his crooked spine.

"I remember when I had to drag this one out of Doomba," he said. "It seems like it was only yesterday. Oh vey! This babushka was so young back then! And now she's getting married. Oi va voi!

"How old is she?"

"Fourteen," Mama Tamsin replied.

The Humpbacked Priest rubbed his hands together.

"I can't wed anyone aged under eighteen," he said. "The Protokians insist on it. They're a funny bunch, those shmendriks. I really don't understand their support for gay rights, their policy of 'education for all', or their opposition to incest. It's a load of cockamamie, if you ask me. Oi gavelt! It's depraved. But what can I do?"

Mama Tamsin tugged her hair. She looked anguished and fraught.

"We need this," she said. "We really, really need this. Surely you can do something?"

The Humpbacked Priest wiped his sweaty brow.

"I can't wed anyone aged under eighteen," he repeated. "But I suppose we could make your babushka a little older. I mean, she doesn't have a birth certificate, does she?"

Mama Tamsin shook her head.

"That's good," the Humpbacked Priest said. "I'm sure I could make her eighteen in return for a couple of hundred dollars. Yes, that sort of mitzvah should definitely do the trick."

Mama Tamsin gave the Humpbacked Priest a dirty look, tutted, and then handed him some crumpled notes.

"Ah yes," the priest concluded. "I think you made a mistake when you said this babushka was only fourteen. I remember when she was born quite clearly. It was definitely eighteen years ago. I'm sure of it!"

Mama Tamsin laughed as she led her daughter away. They walked past hundreds of shops, which all had glass facades and neon sides. They walked through two checkpoints. And then they arrived at their home.

* * *

During the weeks which followed, Tamsin's family spent hour after hour preparing for the wedding. They bought vegetables, animals and ribbons. They made salads, butchered meat, and decorated their street. The only time Tamsin got to herself was late at night, when she went to visit Jen.

"I'm giddy with anticipation," she confessed. "I love being at the centre of attention, but I am a little nervous.

"You know what it's like. I've got a lot on my mind."

Jen fiddled with her wedding ring.

"I know exactly what it's like," she laughed. "And I know exactly what's on your mind!"

Tamsin giggled.

"I'm actually a bit worried about that," she admitted. "I mean Jon, he's really nice, but he's just so ugly! I'm not sure I want to see him naked.

"Did you, you know, *'do it'* on the first night?"

Jen laughed.

"Of course," she replied. "We *'did it'* three times on our wedding night. We did it every night for a year. Then I learnt how to say *'no'*; how to fake headaches and backaches.

"We only do it once a week now."

Tamsin's face lit up.

"Perhaps I'll fake a headache on my wedding night," she said.

Jen gave Tamsin a condescending look.

"Yeah, right!" She mocked. "Good luck with that!"

* * *

The big day arrived, and a large crowd followed Tamsin through the camp. Most of them made it past the first checkpoint, but three citizens did not.

A refugee called Keith showed his permit to the Officious Soldier, who then asked to see Keith's ID.

"This ID says your name is Keith," the Officious Soldier said.

"That's right."

"But this permit is for someone called *'Keth'*."

"The permit office misprinted it."

"No, they wouldn't do that. And I can't let you through if your ID doesn't match your permit. I'm going to have to confiscate both of these documents. Bye bye."

The second refugee to be stopped was a Flabby Girl, who was wearing asymmetrical braces. The Frustrated Soldier ran her name through his computer.

"This says that your great uncle's brother-in-law was arrested four years ago, on suspicion of being involved with the KPP," the Frustrated Soldier said. "He was accused of throwing stones."

The Flabby Girl shrugged.

"I'm afraid we can't allow terrorists into Natale."

And the third refugee to be stopped was a Scrawny Boy, who was wearing a third-hand suit he had borrowed from his cousin. The Scrawny

Boy did not want to take 'no' for an answer, so he ran through the checkpoint and sprinted up towards the castle. Two soldiers chased after him, rugby tackled him, and dragged him back to the checkpoint. The Scrawny Boy put his hands on his knees and caught his breath. Then he ran through the checkpoint again, jinked into an alley, and disappeared out of sight.

"Run little boy," the Mad Lady wailed. "Soon there'll be a checkpoint on every street. There'll be nowhere left to run. I feel it in my waters!"

"Oh shut up," the Bearded Elder shouted back. "What do you know, you batty old witch?"

The Bearded Elder walked alongside the rest of the wedding party, who eventually reached the second checkpoint. A Spotty Soldier and a Snotty Soldier were manning that post. They let some citizens through, but blocked others, without offering any explanations. Their decisions seemed to be arbitrary.

Tamsin was allowed through, but Mama Tamsin was not. Papa Tamsin was allowed through, but Toddler Tamsin was stopped. The Medicine Man, Frail Elder and Jen, were all allowed to pass. The Midwife, her husband and the Singer, were all blocked.

Those guests who made it to the temple removed their shoes, and washed their feet. They walked up the marble steps, passed the icons which hid in every hollow, and dodged a Pilgrim who was prostrate on the floor. That man kissed the ground, got up onto his knees, and took a photo of the sacred spot he had just honoured.

Tamsin waited at the front of the temple. Henna covered her arms, and a silk veil covered her face. Hundreds of citizens waited behind her.

After some moments had passed, Jon arrived on a large white horse. He dismounted his steed and walked down the central aisle.

Everyone cheered.

The Humpbacked Priest hobbled behind. He stopped every five metres to rub his bent back. He reached the front of the temple, waddled between several incense burners, and lit a joss stick in each one.

"Let these scents release Tamsin from her protective deities," he said. "Bring her into the protection of Jon's angels."

The Medicine Man went outside, pointed a gun in the air, and fired a bullet towards the sky.

Everyone stared at him.

"Well someone had to scare off the ghosts and evil spirits," he said. "And it wasn't as if any of you were going to do it."

There was a brief moment of silence. Then the congregation replied with a mixture of nods, shrugs, and approving gestures.

The Humpbacked Priest shook his head.

"Bloody Medicine Man," he muttered. "What does that schmuck know?"

Tamsin and Jon exchanged ceremonial scarves.

Jon's First Wife shed a tear. Mama Tamsin snivelled. And Jen wept with joy.

Papa Tamsin and Papa Jon walked to the front.

"My daughter comes from a proud line," Papa Tamsin told Papa Jon, with exaggerated speech and theatrical hand gestures. "She descends from honest folk, who are married to the earth and one with the stars."

"My son comes from a proud line," Papa Jon replied, with equally theatrical gestures. "He descends from honourable folk, who have goodness in their hearts and pureness in their souls."

"My daughter is the purest girl in the world. She is as fresh as a spring morning, and as innocent as a heavenly angel."

"My son is as righteous as a king, and as noble as a monk."

"My daughter is as beautiful as a rose."

"My son is a strong as an ox."

"My daughter's heart is as white as a pearl."

"My son's heart is more precious than gold."

Papa Tamsin and Papa Jon embraced.

"I'm happy to give my daughter to your son," Papa Tamsin concluded.

"I'm happy to receive your daughter into my family," Papa Jon replied.

The Humpbacked Priest smiled.

"I now pronounce you husband and wife," he said. "Mazel tov!"

Everyone cheered. Everyone clapped, sang, and threw confetti into the air. Everyone went back to their camp, where they re-joined the other guests, and celebrated in the street.

Strings of multi-coloured lightbulbs hung overhead. Pink balloons swayed in the breeze. And the smell of grilled mutton wafted around.

A Chubby Refugee stood by the barbeque, and dripped with sweat. He threw cubes of blackened meat into his mouth, as if they were sweets.

A group of boys mobbed a Cameraman. They were more interested in his camerawork, than the festivities he was filming.

Jen played an oud, and Toddler Tamsin tapped a hand-drum. The Singer cried. A group of women danced together in fits and starts. The Seductive Refugee shimmied with gyrating hips. Little girls tried to copy her. And the men chatted amongst themselves.

After many hours had passed, and after many glasses of homemade beer had been drunk, the men finally began to dance. They formed a line, placed their hands on each other's shoulders, and followed the lead of the Wrinkled Elder. They squatted together, limped together, jumped together, and skipped together.

The only man who refused to join in was the Singer.

"It's wrong," he muttered. "People are dying in our name every day. KPP rebels are hiding in caves, covered in mud, fighting for the liberation of Doomba. And we're dancing in the street? They're living off rice, and we're throwing a banquet? It's wrong. It's just not on."

But no-one paid any attention to the Singer. They danced until the sun was replaced by the moon. Then they formed a guard of honour, and cheered as Jon led Tamsin back to his family's home.

That place was the same as all the other homes in the camp. It consisted of four asbestos walls and one zinc roof. It was four metres long and three metres wide. Its floor was made of uncovered concrete.

A blanket had been pinned to the ceiling, to split the room into two. Papa Jon, Mama Jon and the First Wife, sat on one side of that blanket. They made some tea, rolled out their mattresses, and chatted about the day.

Tamsin and Jon retired to the other side of the blanket, where a line of candles had been placed on the windowsill. Two mattresses, which were covered in one white sheet, had been placed on the floor.

Jon undressed and signalled for Tamsin to do the same.

Her body tensed.

Jon approached Tamsin, stroked her arm, and looked into her eyes.

"It's going to be okay," he said. "My penis isn't too big. You'll hardly notice it."

Tamsin's muscles relaxed.

The First Wife snickered.

A beetle sat down to watch.

"Let's put the radio thingy on," Mama Jon said.

"I think that's a great idea," Papa Jon replied.

His flicked between stations, found a music channel, and turned the volume all the way up.

Pop music drowned out the sound of Jon's groans, as he arched his back and entered Tamsin. But it did not hide the sound of Tamsin's screams.

"Aaaaah!!!" She yowled.

She turned her head to the side and bit her lip.

Jon rocked back and forth, as gently as he could, for fifty three seconds. Then he rolled over, closed his eyes, and fell asleep.

Tamsin felt a thick warm liquid inside her. She sat up, pulled her knees towards her shoulders, and hugged herself.

She rocked back and forth. Then, after several moments had passed, the First Wife entered. She removed some hair from Tamsin's eyes, and kissed her cheek.

"It'll be okay," she said. "Jon's not a sexual guy. But he wants children, and I can't give them to him. If you give him a son, he'll treat you like a queen.

"Everything's going to be okay. I promise. It only hurts the first time."

Tamsin tried to smile.

The beetle disappeared between two bricks.

The First Wife took the bloodied bedsheet.

"The whole village will want to see this," she said. "You've done well. People need to know."

* * *

Tamsin had been worried about living with Jon's family. She had worried that she would be made to do backbreaking work. That she would never see her relatives. And that Jon would beat her.

None of those things came to pass.

It did take time for Tamsin to adjust to her new lifestyle. She stopped going to school, and she started life as a housewife. But things, on the whole, were good. She was only ever pressurised to do one thing.

"You need to get pregnant," Mama Jon reminded her each day. "You need to do the thingy every morning and each afternoon. You wouldn't want to stop an old lady from seeing her grandchildren before she dies, would you?"

Mama Jon gave Tamsin a knowing look.

"If you don't get pregnant within the first three months of marriage, people will start to talk. They'll say you don't have God's blessing."

Tamsin tensed her cheeks.

A lightbulb flickered.

Mama Jon massaged olive oil into Tamsin's stomach. Her strong fingers kneaded Tamsin's skin. It made Tamsin feel strangely calm.

"Dear God," Mama Jon prayed. "Bless this belly. Fill it with your bounty. Help this girl to bring forth a healthy boy."

Tamsin blinked.

"That should do it," Mama Jon concluded. "You should be pregnant within a few days."

But it was not Mama Jon who helped Tamsin the most. It was the First Wife.

"You need to loosen up before sex," she explained. "Lick your fingers and rub your clit. Stroke it. Up and down. Top to bottom. Rub it. Left to right. Side to side. Easy. Slowly. Gently.

"You'll find sex more comfortable. You may even enjoy it."

Tamsin followed the First Wife's advice. She made love to Jon every morning and every afternoon. And then, on a sunny summer's evening, she realised she was pregnant.

"It's a miracle!" Mama Jon cheered. "I'm so happy! I'm so proud of you. Let's tell everyone in the camp. Let's scream from the rooftops. God has blessed us all!"

Tamsin blushed, cringed, and turned bright red. Her embarrassment mixed in with her pride.

She could not celebrate with Jon, because no-one knew where he was. He had left that morning without saying where he was going, or when he would be back. But Tamsin did celebrate with her friends, who all came to visit.

A Freckled Refugee said, "May all auspicious signs come to this house."

A Squinty Refugee said, "I salute the God within you."

And Jen said, "Peace be upon you."

A Chirpy Refugee sprinkled some petals into a bowl of water. A Chubby Refugee lit some incense. And a Chatty Refugee shared some cakes.

Everyone wore blue jeans and white shirts. Everyone lounged around a shimmering fire. And everyone drank apple tea.

It did not take long for Jen to break into a series of odes. Sweet notes filled the air, and melodies danced from wall to wall.

"This is the cradle of civilisation," she crooned. *"We've been here as long as the sun, and longer than the stars. Our clan is as old as time itself!"*

They nattered for hours.

"I'm so happy for you," the First Wife said.

"You're going to be a great mother," Jen added.

"Can you pass the nuts?" Tamsin asked.

Everyone smiled.

Mama Jon pinched Tamsin's thigh.

The First Wife punched the air.

"It's a boy," the Squinty Refugee explained. "Pregnant mothers always want salty snacks when they're carrying a boy."

"And look at your boobs," Jen said. "The right one is larger than the left one. You're definitely going to have a boy!"

Tamsin assumed her friends were right. They were experienced mothers, and she was only a novice.

"Just don't eat from the hands of barren women," Mama Jon continued. She gave the First Wife a scornful look. "And do plenty of heavy work, to keep your body in shape. Everything will be fine. You'll have a nice healthy boy!"

"Boys *are* better than girls," the First Wife replied. "But it's not as if girls are bad. We're not like the Holies in that regard. Do you know, when people ask them how many children they have, they only give the number of boys? Girls don't count for anything in their society!"

Everyone tutted.

"Godlies are much more virtuous than those heathens," the Freckled Refugee sighed.

"Those infidels are so base," Jen agreed.

They all chuckled. They all drank some tea, and ate some biscuits. Then they all headed home.

But those friends visited Tamsin each week. They chatted, drank, and watched on as Tamsin ballooned.

"Now you're not going to give birth in one of those silly hospital thingies, are you?" Mama Jon asked during one such gathering. "We survived just fine before the Protokians built those ungodly places."

Tamsin shook her head.

"Come on!" Mama Jon continued. "You know, I gave birth to Jon whilst working in our fields? I sat down, gave birth, cut the cord between two rocks, buried the placenta, and then picked some onions.

"We don't need those hospital thingies. I don't know what they do in there, but I don't trust them one bit. What do we need their big metal machines for? We survived for thousands of years without them, thank-you very much. Nothing good ever came from the Protokians."

Tamsin shook her head again.

"Those '*big metal machines*' save lives," she said. "Blimey! Your generation is so unenlightened. Infant mortality rates have taken a nose dive in recent years. Why do you think that is?"

Mama Jon turned purple.

"No good will come of it," she said. "Nothing good ever came from the Protokians."

"Your mother knows best," the Freckled Refugee agreed. "You shouldn't trust the Holies. Just look at what they did to Doomba!"

Jen raised her eyebrows.

"I'm with Tamsin," she argued. "Hospitals save lives."

"I don't care what you think," Tamsin snapped. "It's my baby, it's my body, and it's my choice. I'm giving birth in a hospital, and that's that!"

* * *

A puddle formed between Tamsin's feet.

"Her waters have broken," the First Wife screamed.

"Let's go," Papa Jon screeched.

"Quick! Quick!" Mama Jon squealed. "Don't panic! Don't panic!"

Jon had not been seen for days, so everyone left without him.

They helped Tamsin past a Scraggly Child, who was washing the pavement, and a Scruffy Child who was taking out the rubbish. Past the only school in their camp, which had to run double shifts to keep up with demand. And past some children who were playing football, whilst Arun threw stones at them. A public phone hung off the receiver, an ice-cream van played an electronic tune, and laundry hung above the narrow street.

They approached a surprise checkpoint, which blocked the camp's exit. A row of spikes had been rolled out across the road. Two jeeps were parked on one side, and a troop-carrier was parked on the other. Twelve soldiers, who wore identical expressions, stood in between. Mounds of dirt filled the gaps.

"Stand back!" An Albino Soldier barked. He took a big step towards Tamsin and held up his palm. "Stand back or we'll shoot."

"Baby!" Tamsin said in Godliness.

"One shot, two kills," a Geeky Soldier replied in Protokian.

"Baby!" The First Wife shouted.

"Baby!" Papa Jon screamed.

"Thingamajig!" Mama Jon squealed. "Baby! Don't panic! Don't panic!"

A bullfinch panicked. It jumped off a roof and flew away.

"Stand back or we'll shoot," the Albino Soldier repeated.

The First Wife shook her fist.

Mama Jon shook her head.

Papa Jon perspired.

A bomb-defusing robot, which had ten wheels and one snout, slithered across the uneven ground. It reached Tamsin, and scanned her belly. A small light turned bright red.

"Lift up your shirt," the Albino Soldier demanded. "Show us what you've got hidden under there."

Tamsin exposed her swollen belly.

"See! I'm pregnant," she said. "There's no bomb here. Let us through. Come on!"

Tamsin replaced her shirt and put her hands on her hips.

"Can we go now please?"

"No," the Albino Soldier replied. "You're acting suspiciously. You look flustered, as if you're hiding something. And you said the b-word. So I'm going to have to detain you. You look like a terrorist to me."

Tamsin's face turned red.

"Are you serious?" She said. "Terrorists don't come to checkpoints. Come on! Think about it!"

The Albino Soldier walked up to Tamsin.

"Take your trousers off," he demanded.

"How can I?" Tamsin asked. "I'm in labour."

Her cervix began to dilate.

"I can feel my baby. He's coming!"

"Don't panic! Don't panic!"

"It'll be okay. You'll get through this. We'll be by your side, every step of the way."

The Albino Soldier clutched his gun.

"Take your trousers off," he shouted.

"Take your bloody trousers off," the Geeky Soldier echoed.

"Hurry up and take your ruddy trousers off," a Butch Soldier barked.

Papa Jon and the First Wife helped Tamsin to remove her trousers.

"Remove her shirt and pants," the Albino Soldier ordered.

Papa Jon and the First Wife did as they were told. By the time they had finished, Tamsin was completely naked. She stood in front of twelve soldiers, twenty three refugees, and seven cats. She covered her private parts and wept.

"Don't panic!" Mama Jon repeated. "Don't panic!"

Two soldiers approached Tamsin, grabbed her arms, and carried her away. They put her in the troop-carrier, and sat down beside her. They did not say a word.

After ten minutes had passed, Papa Jon joined them. He was also naked. He looked hairy and flabby.

And after twenty minutes had passed, Mama Jon joined them too. She was also naked. She also looked hairy and flabby.

But the First Wife did not join them. She had been sent home.

So Tamsin sat with her step-parents, between six soldiers, six guns and twelve grenades. She sat there for over an hour.

Tamsin had contractions every three minutes. Barbs of pain shot across her abdomen, lower back and upper thighs. They were so intense, Tamsin could barely talk. But the soldiers did not do anything to help.

"I need water," Tamsin begged. "I need drugs. I need gas and air!"

Two soldiers talked about football.

Another two soldiers talked about nail-polish.

Tamsin perspired.

"Aren't you going to do something?" Papa Jon challenged. "Let me help her. Please?"

A Teenage Soldier slapped Papa Jon with the back of his hand.

Mama Jon winced.

The vehicle's engine rumbled. Its wheels turned. It drove for thirty seconds, and then it arrived at the Natale checkpoint.

The back door swung open and Tamsin was bundled out. Papa Jon and Mama Jon landed behind her. The troop-carrier drove away.

"We need to get to the hospital," Papa Jon told the Bored Soldier. "My daughter is about to give birth."

"Permit," the Bored Soldier replied.

"It was confiscated along with my clothes."

The Bored Soldier shrugged.

"You need to let me through!"

"You need a permit."

"It's in my trouser pocket."

"Then go and get your trousers."

"I can't"

"Then I can't let you through."

The Ruddy Soldier walked over.

"An ambulance is on its way," he said. "Sit down on the floor over there. It won't be long."

It started to drizzle.

"Can we have a blanket, please?" Papa Jon asked. "It's cold, wet, and we don't have any clothes."

The Ruddy Soldier sniggered.

"What do you take us for?" He replied. "Blankets? Whatever next? You citizens! Do we look like a charity?"

Papa Jon ground his teeth, walked away, and helped Tamsin to sit beneath a tree. Mama Jon followed.

They all covered their private parts.

They all shivered.

They all waited for another hour. But no ambulance arrived.

"We could have walked to the hospital by now," Papa Jon shouted. "It's only five minutes away!"

The Bored Soldier looked at a sparrow.

The Frustrated Soldier kicked a pebble.

The Impatient Soldier shrugged.

"Shut up," he shouted. "We don't negotiate with terrorists!"

The Ruddy Soldier rolled his eyes.

"We've called the Red Moon," he explained. "They need to call the Red Sun, who need to call the Commander, who needs to investigate. He then needs to call the Red Sun, who need to call the Red Moon, who will send an ambulance. That ambulance will be delayed at three checkpoints, then it'll pick you up.

"I'm sure it'll be here soon."

Tamsin panted. She gagged. She almost choked.

Mama Jon rubbed her back.

"It's okay," she said. "Your son on his way. Don't panic! Don't panic!"

Tamsin screamed. She experienced a new contraction every minute. Her cervix was fully dilated. Her baby's head was visible.

"I want to die," she yelled. "God! Where are you? Kill me! Kill me! Save me from this shame."

Mama Jon rubbed Tamsin's back.

"Push!" She cheered. "Breathe! Push! Breathe! Push! Breathe! Push!"

Tamsin pushed.

Mama Jon cheered.

The soldiers shared a packet of crisps.

And, after thirty minutes of pushing and panting, Tamsin finally gave birth. She fell back against the tree and closed her eyes. She was cold, wet and exhausted.

Mama Jon cut the umbilical cord between two stones.

"Here you go," she said. "It's a beautiful girl."

Mama Jon took the placenta.

"I'll bury this thingy," she said. "It'll bring you good luck!"

Tamsin sucked her teeth. She cradled her baby in her arms, and looked deep into its eyes. But something seemed amiss.

Tamsin touched her baby's lip.

"She's not breathing! My baby! She's dead!"

Papa Jon took his granddaughter, checked her pulse, and bowed his head.

"It's God's will," he said. "God couldn't have wanted a birth like this."

Tamsin slouched. She looked like a ghost; naked, weightless and white. Her teeth were chattering, and her eyes were full of anguish.

Mama Jon returned, sat down next to Tamsin, and stroked her arm.

"It's okay," she consoled. "Next time will be easier. We'll give birth at home. There'll be none of this running about. There'll be none of this Protokian hospital thingy. No, no, no. It'll all be okay."

Papa Jon held his granddaughter.

Mama Jon held Tamsin's leg.

Tamsin held her head in her hands and cried.

6. ELLIE

Ellie held her head in her hands and cried.

"I don't want to do it," she wailed. "I don't want to go out. I don't want to see my friends. And I don't want to do chores.

"Children don't do chores these days. Really, mother? You're living in the Stone Age.

"There are good programs on TV. Why on earth would I want to go out? I've been at school all week. Today is my day off."

Mama Ellie took a deep breath. Her lungs inflated and her eyes bulged.

"Listen here, little missy," she said in a stern voice. "When I was your age, I had to wash my family's clothes by hand. I swear on my dead father's head; I had to scrub those clothes, bash them, rinse them, and wring them dry. I never complained once.

"But you? All you have to do is fill the washing machine and let it do your work for you. And you think that's too much? Really? You can't even drag your big fat arse away from that goggle box to buy some detergent?

"Pfft! Whatever next? I swear on my weary soul; this would have never happened in my day. Never!"

Ellie scrunched her lips together, glared at her mother, and waved her hands in a manic fashion.

"But mummy!" She wailed. "That's not fair! It's just not fair! None of my brothers have to wash their clothes. Why do you always pick on me?"

Mama Ellie ignored her daughter.

"You've got it made," she said. "You live in a house which has a flushing toilet! We have a dishwasher *and* a washing machine. We have sponges *and* mops.

"When I was your age, I had to scrub the floor with a tatty old rag. I swear on my rosary beads; when I was a girl, I had to bathe seven of my siblings in a row. So don't tell me, *'I've been at school all week'*. You're lucky to have a school to go to!

"Now get out of here. I don't want to hear another word from you until you've returned with some soap."

Mama Ellie tore the television's plug out of its socket.

A lightbulb flickered and flashed.

Ellie stormed off, slammed the door behind her, and ran into the lane.

A rope mesh hung over her head. It sagged under the weight of the rotting rubbish which some Holies had thrown from a tall block of flats. That town-centre 'settlement' was surrounded by sentry posts, which overlooked Ellie's courtyard. Those sentry posts were manned by bored teenage soldiers.

Ellie looked up at a Boyish Soldier, waved at him, and gave him a seductive wink. The Boyish Soldier stared back at her with a stony-faced expression. He looked shocked, confused and frustrated.

Ellie continued past a checkpoint on Evergreen Street, a street which was never green. Past a checkpoint on Market Square, a square which did not have a market. And past a checkpoint on Forest Road, which was nowhere near a forest.

Metal stilts held up plastic water tanks on every rooftop she passed. Solar panels looked up at those tanks. And satellite dishes faced the other way, perched on the edge of their roofs, like birds who were gazing at the sun.

New buildings were popping up everywhere Ellie looked. Natale was slowly consuming the countryside. Giant drills were turning ancient cliffs into dust. And piles of crushed cars were beginning to rust.

Ellie walked behind a van which took up the whole width of a narrow lane. Behind her, a miniature tractor pulled a cart. To her sides, boutique shops took the place of market stalls. They sold things that no-one needed, but everyone seemed to want; bath bombs and friendship bracelets, painted bowls and silk scarves, trinkets and ties.

Ellie entered a shopping centre.

A branch of Burger Prince, which had merged with Burger Queen, was being re-branded. A computer shop, which had been taken over by Dick's Sons, was being re-opened. Natale's eleventh Window Mart was opening up. And Natale's last greengrocery was closing down.

Two ladies wore heavy jackets, despite the burning sun. They ate chunks of cucumber to keep cool. Two different coffee stands played two different tunes, which clashed so much that neither song could be heard.

Hopeful typists sat on the floor, behind their typewriters, and waited for passersby to employ them. A Cobbler used a machine to repair shoes in minutes. And an Amputee dragged himself along the street.

Ellie saw twenty settlers pour out of a truck, wielding sticks, shovels and slingshots. They were accompanied by eight soldiers and four dogs.

"Evacuate your house or we'll kill you," the Militant Settler shouted in Protokian.

"If you don't leave this building we'll burn it down," Jim yelled.

"We'll set the dogs on you," a Grizzled Settler yowled. "Woof! Woof! Woof! They'll eat you alive!"

An Owlish Local leant out of a first floor window. Her face was not young, but it was wise. It was not smooth, but it was serene. The Owlish Local had big teeth which were not quite white, and feathery hair which was not quite straight. She had claw-like fingers which were not particularly clean, and pointy ears which were not particularly triangular.

A dog barked.

Ellie waited for someone to rescue the Owlish Local. But no-one came.

"Bugger orf!!!" The Owlish Local screamed in Godliness. "This is my home. Go back to your own countries. I hope God destroys *your* homes. I hope a vagina swallows *you*. Let's see how *you* like it!"

The Militant Settler stepped forward, smirked, and held a piece of paper in the air.

"The owner of this house is dead," he announced. "This property went to auction, and we bought it fair and square.

"You have no right to be here. Now leave this house, or we'll kick you out."

The soldiers watched on, like audience members at a show.

Ellie chewed her collar and clenched her fists.

A cat chased after a mouse.

"You can stick your silly piece of paper up your arse," the Owlish Local replied. "I don't care what it says. I own this house, it's been in my family for centuries, and I'm not leaving it. Never! Now bugger orf!"

The Militant Settler shook his head, walked up to the front door, and gestured for the other settlers to follow. They kicked the door off its hinges and entered, whilst the soldiers kept guard outside.

After a couple of minutes had passed, four settlers emerged. They carried the Owlish Local out on a wooden chair, which they held high above their heads.

The Owlish Local kicked and screamed.

"Do it!" She yelled. "Just do it! Hurry up and get it over with. Why are you taking so long? This is my home! I've lived here all my life.

"You bloody foreigners! You bloody Holies; coming here and taking our homes. Pfft! We should have never let you stay, with your violent ways and immoral habits. What have you ever done for us? Nothing! You're no bloody use to anyone. You bloated leeches! You circumcised ferrets! You one-dollar whores!"

She swayed, passed out, and fell off her seat. Two settlers caught her, laid her down on the ground, and went back inside. They threw five cushions, two tables and a stove, out of a first floor window. They threw a hat stand, a brown shoe and a black umbrella, out of the front door.

Ellie turned around and walked through her district. It felt like a ghost town. Three quarters of the houses had been abandoned. Settlers had occupied most of the other buildings. And only a few natives remained.

Natale had been taken in a bloodless coup, after settlers had rented every room in a town-centre hotel. They had refused to leave. They added seven stories to that building, which overlooked Ellie's home, and encouraged more settlers to join them.

Once their settlement was established, the settlers complained that they felt threatened by the locals. So Protokian soldiers closed the surrounding streets for *'security reasons'*, and erected a series of checkpoints. Locals were evicted, and the doors to their homes were welded shut. Some locals were trapped inside, and had to knock through their own walls to escape. Others were turned away when they returned from work.

Bulldozers demolished any building which was considered a *'strategical security threat'*. Settlers cheered as those homes were bulldozed. They downed beers and danced.

Then they moved into the abandoned buildings. They erected barbed wire fences around their new homes. They erected Protokian flags, which could be seen from anywhere in Natale. And they erected a giant billboard, featuring a colour poster, which said *'Love the Protokians:*

They have civilized you.'

Ellie looked up at her school, which had been renamed *'Atamow High'*. She tutted and walked on.

She walked past a row of empty homes, whose doors were all welded shut. She walked past a family of settlers, who were dumping their rubbish outside an abandoned factory. And she walked past the Economic Settler, who was jogging, with an assault rifle slung over his shoulder.

She approached a checkpoint, but chose not to pass through it. She climbed through the window of an abandoned home, clambered over its weed-covered floor, and emerged on the other side of the checkpoint. She walked past some houses which settlers had built in a generic fashion, with paint which had started to peel, and beams which had started to rot. And then she saw Tamsin, who was sitting by a boarded-up shop, with one baby in her arms, and another one in her womb.

"Hey there," she said. "Do you remember me?"

Tamsin looked Ellie up and down. She paused for a moment, stared at Ellie's face, and then nodded.

"Oh yeah," she said. "I haven't seen you in years! You're the girl who couldn't play hide and seek."

Ellie laughed.

"Look at you," she said. "The girl who couldn't fly a kite! You've got a baby in your arms and a bun in the oven."

Tamsin chortled.

"My husband wants ten children," she said. "He wants ten boys, so they can rebuild our village together."

Ellie shook her head.

"You village girls," she said. "Always serving your husbands. Pfft! You're so backwards. I bet you let your dad marry you off."

Tamsin bowed her head.

Ellie glared back at her.

"Unbelievable!" She said with mock disbelief. "Well, if you want to live your life like that, it's your choice I suppose. But I'd never let my father marry me off.

"When you throw a rock at a cat, it bares its claws. Why should us women be any different? Why should we let men throw rocks at us? This is the modern world! We should stand up for ourselves!"

Tamsin tittered. She seemed nervous and tense.

"I'm quite happy to stick to traditional values," she said.

"You're missing out," Ellie teased. "I tell you, courting is great fun.

"When I'm at school, I pass love notes between girls and boys, to help them flirt. I'm a bit of a matchmaker like that. I can tell when people fancy each other by the way they act, look at each other and giggle.

"You have to be careful of course. An unmarried girl and boy can't be seen together alone. Oh no! But we double date, that's okay. We go for picnics and walks. No-one seems to mind.

"I'm even thinking about signing up to a video dating agency. They send you boys by post! It's amazing what you can do these days. It really does knock my socks off."

Tamsin forced a smile. She shuffled from side to side, and bit her lower lip.

"You're so beautiful," Ellie continued. "Corr! If I was hot like you, I'd get all the men. I wish I had your sexy legs and big boobs."

"You look great!" Tamsin replied.

"Great? I look bloated."

"Bloated but beautiful. Your body does not sag or bulge. It's grown outwards symmetrically, like a ripe piece of fruit."

"Are you comparing me to a melon?" Ellie sneered.

"Oh no!" Tamsin protested. She turned red. "No, you're much more beautiful than that. You shine like a strawberry. You're as shapely as a star fruit. And you're sweeter than a mango."

"You're as mad as a hatter," Ellie laughed.

She smeared lipstick across her lips.

Gunfire rang out in the distance.

Tamsin grinned.

"I take after my dad," she said.

"What does he do?"

"He works for *Fizzy Stream*. They're international. My dad says, '*The opportunities are endless when you work for a multinational firm. Big companies offer real job security*'."

Ellie looked confused.

"Aren't they run by Protokians?" She asked

Tamsin held her hands out, as if to say '*What can I do?*'

"I'm not judging you," Ellie continued. "My dad works for the Protokians too. But it really pisses me off.

"The Protokians are taking over every inch of our lives, and we're passive. We let them. It's not on. We need to be more assertive."

Tamsin twisted her cheek.

"How?" She asked. "What can we do? The Holies are strong. They'll crush us if we fight them. We can't vote. And our protests all get ignored."

Ellie tapped her chin.

"Do you still play the guitar?" She asked.

"Yeah. It's been a while, but you never forget."

"Well, that's how we'll make a difference. We'll get Natale Refugee All Stars back together. We'll make Godly music, assert our Godly identity, and start a musical revolution!"

Tamsin's eyes widened. Her face brightened. And her confidence returned.

"Okay," she said. "You're on. Long live the revolution! Long live the Godlies!"

"Long live the Godlies!"

Tamsin and Ellie embraced. They walked away with smiles on their faces, and hope in their hearts.

An Elfish Soldier caressed his gun.

A leaf fell off a tree.

Ellie returned home without any detergent.

* * *

Ellie, Tamsin and Jen, rehearsed in an abandoned house several times each week. The crumbling walls vibrated with the sound of their guitar and oud, drum and tambourine. A mouse danced, and a bird sang. A crack meandered across the ceiling, a table wobbled, and a dust-ball skipped across the floor.

When Ellie wasn't playing music, she went to school. And when she wasn't at school, she did whatever she could to make herself look pretty. Seeing Tamsin, married and with children, had made her feel old and ugly. She was determined to improve her appearance.

So Ellie became a member of *Fitness Forever*, a chain of gyms which had three branches in Natale. Every morning she swam like a fish in an ocean, pounded the treadmill like a hamster in a wheel, and swung between hoops like a monkey in a tree.

By the time she was done, her body was covered in sweat, her armpits stank like rotten meat, and her hair was a tangled mess. She weighed herself. She celebrated if she had lost a pound, and cursed if her weight was unchanged. Then she showered. She covered her face in foundation, put mascara around her eyes, and spread rouge across her cheeks.

She left Fitness Forever and slinked through the gap in a wall. She scrambled through an overgrown field, which was full of rocks and tangled barbed wire. She climbed onto a ledge, circled a giant satellite dish, and strolled past a line of yellow taxis.

She passed a sign which said, '*NOTICE! Thank-you for noticing this notice. Your noticing this notice has been noted, and will be reported to the authorities.*' She passed a sign which said, '*Signpost full of signs in two hundred metres.*' And she passed a sign which said, '*This road leads to a Godly area. The entrance for Protokian citizens is dangerous*'.

She picked her way through an alley which was blocked by hundreds of parked motorbikes.

And then she approached Jen's father.

The Tape Seller still sold traditional folk music. But his activities had come to the attention of the Protokian authorities, who had interrogated him several times. As a result, the CDs he sold had to be smuggled in from abroad, copied on a computer, and distributed through a network of shady dealers.

"Hello there," the Tape Seller said. "What can I do for you?"

Ellie grinned.

"You can tell me how beautiful I look," she said.

"You've lost weight," the Tape Seller replied. "You look slender."

Ellie blushed.

"I sure do," she said. "But that's not why I came here. I came here for inspiration."

The Tape Seller chuckled.

"Take this CD," he said. "And this one. And this one. Come back if you need any more."

Ellie took the CDs.

"How much do I owe you?" She asked.

"Don't be silly," the Tape Seller replied. "You girls are doing important work, keeping our traditions alive. How could I possibly make money out of that?"

Ellie smiled, winked at the Tape Seller, and left.

She walked past an old man who was riding a donkey, and a young man who was driving a car. The old man was wearing traditional clothes, as if paying tribute to a remembered past. The young man was wearing denim jeans, which had been imported from abroad.

Ellie inhaled the sweet and sour fumes which were being excreted by a line of vibrating cars. A Trendy Youth, who was smoking a water pipe, blew fruity smoke in her direction. Her nose tingled as she passed a sweet shop which smelled of sugar, a bakery which smelled of dough, and a restaurant which smelled of boiled rice.

She arrived at her rehearsal space.

"Today we break new ground," she announced. "The revolution requires revolutionary music. It's time for us to look to the past, and walk into the future!"

She put one of the Tape Seller's discs into a CD player and hit the play button. A traditional song echoed around the room. A singer squealed like a pig who was about to be slaughtered. She sounded operatic, heartfelt and intense. A lonesome drum supplied a solemn beat. And a metallic cymbal gave an impassioned cry.

Tamsin picked up her guitar and added an upbeat rhythm. Jen played a modern riff on her oud. And Ellie danced.

Her dancing set her free. She felt that she was expressing the meaning of her country. That she was telling her story, her grandparents' story, and the story of all her ancestors.

'A weapon conflict for the sake of power,' she sang. 'When two elephants fight, it's the grass that suffers. The big fool us. We suffer. Suffer, suffer. We suffer and still we smile.'

The band played itself into a trance.

Tamsin closed her eyes and swayed from side to side. Jen rocked back and forth. Ellie shimmied across the room without even thinking. Her feet moved on their own. Her legs followed. And her torso swayed.

They jammed until the CD stopped. Then they opened their eyes, looked at each other, and fell to the ground. They were all exhausted.

"We're almost there," Ellie said. "We just need one more thing."

"What's that?" Tamsin asked.

"Just you wait and see," Ellie replied.

She winked, turned and departed.

* * *

Ellie walked into town. She passed a nervous looking donkey, who balked as cars sped by. Some children, who were riding miniature electric tanks. And a Natalian Guard, who looked like a Protokian soldier.

She bought two amps, a microphone, and an endless supply of wires. Then she went to meet her band.

Jen and Tamsin stood up when she arrived.

Tamsin looked fresher than before. She had given birth. She had left her children with the First Wife, and was relishing the opportunity to be a teenager, away from the responsibilities of motherhood.

Jen adjusted her '*Mikey*' t-shirt.

"Wow," she said. "How could you afford all this equipment?"

"I used a credit card," Ellie replied. "There's no need to worry though. There's no cow on the ice. I'll pay my bill before I get charged interest.

"It's free money! Isn't the modern world amazing?"

Tamsin rolled her eyes.

Jen rolled her shoulders.

An ant picked up a splinter.

"We do need this stuff," Ellie explained. "I've got us a gig. We're performing at the Collisian Institute of Performing Arts, *CIPA*, next Tuesday."

Tamsin and Ellie glanced at each other. They looked worried, nervous and tense.

"We're not ready," they said in unison.

"Yes, we are," Ellie replied. "Just you wait and see!"

* * *

Ellie's band rehearsed for six days in a row. And on the seventh day, they went to *CIPA*.

It was a ramshackle place, located beneath an abandoned factory. Citizens crammed into every entrance, and sat on every seat, beneath a ceiling which was covered in fans, which were all turned off. A stage stood at the front. And the Tape Seller stood at the back, selling CDs from a leather satchel. He looked like a drug dealer.

A dance act performed first.

The dancers moved with exaggerated motions. With jerky head movements, swaying limbs, and wobbling bellies. Some of them wore masks which looked like golden suns, and wigs which looked like hay. Some of them dressed up as ghosts, with black robes and white faces. Men wore skirts which swung as they danced. As they acted out folk tales, saved fair maidens, and beheaded enemies with wooden swords.

"We're on," Ellie announced. "Let's put a smile on everyone's face. Let's ignite their Godly spirit!"

Tamsin walked on stage, waved nervously, and began to strum her guitar.

The audience stared back at her.

The first song finished and no one moved. No-one made a sound. The room filled with icy-cold silence, which made Tamsin gag. Jen turned white, and Ellie turned to face her band.

"Maybe they're not ready for our contemporary style," she whispered. "Let's play a traditional one."

Jen slowly plucked her oud, Tamsin flicked a tambourine, and Ellie wailed. She screeched and she swayed.

The audience moved. They danced. And they sang out loud.

'Refugee rolling, rolling like a rolling stone. Today you settle, tomorrow you pack. Rolling for the better. Rolling for our safety. Rolling for our life. We are the clients of the UNHCR. But you've been moving us around from camp to camp. And we just want to go home.'

By the time Ellie's band left the stage, the audience were on their feet, calling out for more. And by the time their encore had finished, so was the Concert Promoter.

"How would you like a residency here?" He asked. "I'll pay you fifty dollars a show, if you perform every Tuesday night."

Ellie made an 'okay' sign with her thumb and forefinger.

"You're on," she said. "Give us sixty dollars a show, and we'll make this place famous. Citizens will be queueing up around the block!"

* * *

"It's happening!" Tamsin screamed. "It's happening! Let's go!!!"

Ellie looked at Jen. They were both confused.

"What's happening?" Ellie asked. "We're rehearsing. That's what's happening! We can't go anywhere, we need practice."

"It's happening!" Tamsin screamed. "It's happening!"

"What's happening?"

"It's happening! It's happening! We're standing up for ourselves. An uprising is sweeping the nation. It's happening! It's happening!"

Ellie paused to think.

She put her microphone down. She turned her amp off, walked across the room, and picked up her CDs. She looked into Tamsin's eyes.

She paused to think again.

She knew that uprisings were illegal. She knew she would get in trouble if she was caught taking part. She knew there would be pain and sorrow.

She had never disobeyed the government before.

So she stood there and weighed up her options, whilst an oud gently wept.

Whilst cars rattled by. *'Clickety. Clackety. Click...'*

Whilst Tamsin gestured for Ellie to follow her.

The more she tried to hold herself back, the more Ellie wanted to join the uprising. The more she resisted, the more she was tempted. She wanted to break the law, simply for the sake of breaking it.

She felt an enormous thrill. Butterflies fluttered in her stomach, and her spine tingled. Her hands shook.

"Okay," she said. "Let's do this!"

Tamsin pumped her fist.

Ellie and Jen followed her past some Bedouins, who were trapped inside a grey compound. Past some concrete camels, which were covered in snow. And past some tower blocks, which pierced the cloudy sky.

The uprising had started when heavy handed soldiers attacked a group of three hundred monks. The older monks had fought back. The army reacted; they stopped monks at checkpoints across the land. But locals came to their rescue. They waved rosary beads, KPP flags and white scarves. They marched en masse. And they chanted together.

'*Independence and freedom for Collis*', they cheered.

'*May the exiles and residents unite*'.

'*Give me my freedom*'.

The same chants echoed across the nation. They echoed between hills, along valleys, and over fields. They reached the snowy streets of Natale.

"The Protokians are no match for us," Tamsin wailed. "Look how many of us are here!"

"We'll run them out of town!" Ellie shouted.

"We'll run them wild!" Jen screamed.

A group of locals unfurled an image of the KPP's charismatic leader, Apai.

'*Long live Apai*', they cheered. '*Long live Apai. Long live Apai.*'

A Petite Local, who wore a floral dress, came out of a *View Cinema*. She was swept up by the crowd, which gushed down the street like a river. Overcome with emotion, she picked up a stone, and threw it at a soldier. She tripped, fell over, and was dragged away by a Bearded Officer.

Ellie surged ahead, engulfed by refugees and locals, villagers and townsfolk, monks and lay people, youngsters and pensioners, students and workers. There were as many women as there were men. And they all marched together through the snow.

They marched past the McRonalds, Dick's Sons and Window Mart, which lined up on one winding street. They marched past the McRonalds, Dick's Sons and Window Mart, which lined up on another winding street. And they climbed towards Natale's castle.

Sunshine reflected off the white snow. A dog sniffed another dog's anus. And a Tall Refugee, who wore long chequered socks and a plastic red nose, played a battered old accordion.

Ellie reached the castle's fence. A row of soldiers stood on the other side. More soldiers stood inside the castle itself.

The crowd chanted:

'Independence and freedom for Collis'.

'Give us our freedom'.

'Long live Apai'.

But their chants were cut short by a deafening explosion. The noise was so loud, it made Ellie jump. It was so sharp, it flushed adrenaline through her veins. And it was so sudden, it covered her skin in pimples.

Ellie turned around instinctively. Her stomach tingled, as if it had pins and needles. Her head span, as if she was dizzy. And her eyes bulged.

She looked up and saw the silhouette of a man, who was holding something metallic.

'Gun', she thought.

She took a backwards step, away from the gunman, but back towards the Protokian soldiers.

She was overcome by fear. Men with guns had surrounded her! She had nowhere to run!

Her eyes widened. Her face flattened. She glanced at the gunman, and looked into his eyes.

She focussed.

And she exhaled. She emitted a massive sigh of relief. She almost guffawed. The 'gunman' was just a teenage boy, and his 'gun' was just a camera. Ellie would have felt embarrassed, but she was far too relieved to care.

"Come back here," Jen said. She pulled Ellie close. "Where do you think you're going?"

Ellie squinted.

"Sorry," she said.

"It was only a sound bomb," Tamsin replied. "A dog barks, a lion roars, and a soldier throws a sound bomb. It's just a warning."

'Bang'.

A sound bomb exploded near a Pizza House.

'Bang'.

A sound bomb exploded near a Tisko.

'Bang'.

A sound bomb exploded near a Water Island.

Tamsin looked at Ellie.

"It's fine," Ellie said. "When you know what they are, and you see them coming, you don't react."

"That's the spirit," Tamsin replied. "We'll face down whatever those thugs, hoodlums and hooligans, have to throw at us!"

Ellie's lips curled upwards with exquisite disdain.

A dog cocked its leg and urinated on the snow.

A Dwarfish Local threw a snowball at a Giant Soldier. A Skeletal Refugee threw a snowball at a Buff Soldier. And a Scatty Girl threw a snowball at her friend.

The soldiers responded by throwing teargas grenades into the crowd. A Shaggy Soldier threw a grenade towards a Boyds Bank. A Smart Soldier flung a grenade towards a Greasy Fried Chicken. And a Goateed Soldier hurled a grenade towards Ellie.

It landed on the ground with a staccato pop. White gas sprayed up into the air. Tears flooded out of Ellie's eyes.

The Shaggy Local leapt through the crowd, landed on the grenade, and buried it beneath the snow.

A Goateed Refugee gave Ellie half an onion.

"Smell this," he said. "It'll stop the stinging."

Ellie tried to smile. But she could not even breathe. Her face was on fire, mucus had filled her nostrils, and her eyelids had slammed shut.

She stumbled, turned around, and faced her fellow citizens.

She faced young girls, who were playing cricket, using a walking stick and a ball of snow. Young boys, who were throwing snowballs back and forth. And an Energetic Girl, who was flying a kite.

The Boyish Soldier threw a tear gas grenade at an Elderly Local. The Ruddy Soldier threw one at a Crimson Refugee. And the Frustrated Soldier threw one at a Hairy Toddler.

The Tall Refugee played his accordion. A line of photographers took pictures. And a group of boys mobbed a Cameraman. They were more interested in his camerawork, than the protests he was filming.

Tear gas grenades landed near the Medicine Man, a Park's Shoes, and a Pizza Home.

The Frail Elder was carried away on a wooden trolley. A grenade hit Charlie in his head. Oliver grew mad.

He grabbed the grenade and threw it towards the soldiers. It landed near the Goateed Soldier's right foot, bounced a couple of times, and came to a sorry stop.

A Greasy Officer lifted his hand.

"Fire!" He barked.

Three soldiers stepped forward, lifted their guns, and sprayed rubber bullets above the protestors.

The crowd turned.

'*Run*', they shouted.

They stampeded down the street.

A Handsome Local fell. The crowd trampled him.

A Spotty Refugee was hit by a bullet. She rubbed her leg.

Ellie, Tamsin and Jen, turned into a side street. They dashed past a row of shops, which all had glass facades. There was a Waterrocks Books, a VMH Records, and a Rablays Bank. A Burger Queen, a Flevans Bikes, and a Tip Top Shop. Their neon signs were all covered in silver snow. Their translucent doors were all locked. Some of them were boarded up.

An Adolescent Refugee, who was wearing a black balaclava and a chequered scarf, threw a rock at a McRonalds. The rock bounced away. The Adolescent Refugee picked it up and threw it again.

He was joined by a Masked Refugee, a Hooded Local, and a Camouflaged Foreigner. They all threw stones at the McRonalds. A Ruddy Refugee stole a chair and smashed it against the storefront. A Bald Local kicked the glass.

The crowd cheered:

'*Independence and freedom for Collis*'.

'*Give us our freedom*'.

'*Long live Apai*'.

The storefront smashed.

Minute pieces of glass, which looked like shiny diamonds, spilled out across the snowy floor. Shards fell like horizontal rain. A small hole formed in the storefront.

The Masked Refugee tore at that opening until it was three feet wide. He clambered through. Ellie followed.

She picked up a chair and smashed it against a wall. She removed a mirror and threw it to the ground. She clambered over the counter, and tore a row of microwaves from their sockets.

She felt amazing. She felt elated, ecstatic and euphoric.

She felt omnipotent; more powerful than an almighty god. She felt liberated; as if a massive weight had been lifted from her shoulders. And she felt uninhibited; as if she was flying higher than a bird.

She had never felt so good. She had never had felt so free.

A deep fat fryer was thrown to the ground. A set of shelves tumbled over. Pots and pans skidded across the floor.

The crowd cheered:

'*Independence and freedom for Collis*'.

'*Give us our freedom*'.

'*Long live Apai*'.

Ellie jumped up and down. She grabbed Tamsin and hugged her. Jen joined them. They all jumped up and down together.

"The Protokians win every battle," Ellie said. "But we'll win the war!"

"Doomba will be free," Tamsin replied. "We're going home!"

The streets cleared.

They returned home.

The *Natale Times* reported on the uprising.

'*Five thousand extra soldiers were drafted in to protect Natale against disturbances of order*', it said. '*They showed great restraint to contain a mob which was full of thugs, hoodlums and hooligans*'.

* * *

The protestors had wanted the settlements to be demolished. Over the months which followed, three new settlements were built. Five new outposts were constructed. And hundreds of new settlers moved into the centre of town.

The protestors had wanted the checkpoints to be removed. Seven new checkpoints were erected.

The protestors had wanted the soldiers to move out. A thousand new soldiers moved in.

The protestors had wanted more freedom. The Protokians introduced a curfew.

Posters went up around town, which said, '*A curfew will be in place from 6pm till 6am*'. That curfew was announced on loud hailers. And it was announced on the radio.

But a group of forty nine peasants, who were sowing seeds in their fields, did not hear any of those announcements. So they stayed out until 7pm. When they returned, they were all shot dead.

The locals got the message.

They got the message when more posters appeared:

'The authorities would like to talk to the criminals who took part in the uprising. Those who inform will be exempt from punishment'.

Some locals informed on others. The local community crumbled. No-one knew who to trust.

The protestors had wanted religious tolerance. Their religion was crushed.

The Protokians pulled Godly statues to the ground. They trampled over Godly scriptures. They destroyed Godly monasteries, put CCTV cameras in Godly temples, and forced monks to fornicate with nuns.

The protestors had wanted to sustain their culture. Their culture was crushed.

The Protokians banned the Godly language. They outlawed Godly theatre, art and dance. They passed laws which made it illegal to read Godly newspapers, listen to Godly radio stations, and possess Godly books. Citizens could not even say they were from Collis.

The Protokians took the Godlies' food, hamams and carpets, and claimed them as their own. They renamed the Godlies' Tree Festival, and made it a Protokian holiday. They stole Godly science, literature and art. They said that Collis had never even existed.

They said that in Protokia there was just *'One Nation. One language. One Culture.'* They called anyone who spoke Godliness, or celebrated the Godly culture, a *'subversive element'*. They said they ought to be crushed.

But despite those policies, the Godlies clung to their culture, like helpless passengers clinging to the side of a sinking ship.

The more the Protokians suppressed the Godlies' language, the more it was spoken. Language activists distributed books on the black market. They issued a weekly journal, which they hid under the shelves at eleven branches of *HW Miths*. They read in secret, concealed their books inside other books, and passed those books from hand to hand.

When the Protokians banned traditional Godly cooking, clandestine eateries popped up selling forbidden food. When the Protokians banned images of Apai, the Collisians displayed empty picture frames in his honour. And when the Protokians stopped foreign journalists from entering Collis, the locals smuggled them in.

Ellie joined the cultural resistance. Her band performed illicit music wherever they could. They performed in citizens' homes, abandoned buildings, and hidden basements. They were always on the move. They never played at the same venue twice.

"You'll get us all killed!" Papa Ellie scolded her one night. "I work for a governmental institution. If they find out what you've been up to I'll be sacked. You'll be arrested! I demand you stop this silliness straight away.

"Pfft! You're not allowed to break the rules, Ellie. The supremacy of law is absolute!"

In the blink of an eye, Papa Ellie had puffed his chest, lifted his hand above his head, and swung his arm with all his might. His knuckles crashed into Ellie's cheek with so much power that Ellie fell to the floor. Her legs were tangled. There was a bruise on her cheek and a tear in her eye.

A moth flew into a window.

Papa Ellie panted like a cow.

Ellie straightened her hair.

"Okay," she replied. "I understand. I'll stop performing. I wouldn't want you to lose your job with the Protokians. Heaven forbid!"

She brushed herself down, left home, and performed in a closed section of the market.

"Are you okay?" Tamsin asked between sets. She had seen the bruise on Ellie's cheek, even though it was covered by a thick layer of makeup.

Ellie avoided Tamsin's empathetic gaze.

Tamsin revealed a jagged scar.

"Jon doesn't approve of our concerts either," she said. "He says I should spend more time with my children. But I feel that our music is the only thing worth living for right now. It's the only thing that sets me free."

Ellie hugged her friend.

"Me too," she said. "Me too."

Jen snorted, spat, and shook her bony finger.

"There must be more to life than this," she said. "A man was arrested last week for giving a statement to the press. A woman was arrested for no reason. What do you think they'll do to us?"

Ellie and Tamsin looked at each other with sorry eyes.

The audience called out for more.

A group of soldiers stormed in, fired some bullets into the roof, turned around, and left.

* * *

Ellie left home, waved at the Boyish Soldier, and walked through a checkpoint.

A happy dog sniffed her handbag.

An Indifferent Soldier leant on his rifle.

Ellie walked past a Pizza Home, which was being converted into a Pizza House. She walked past three different McRonalds. And she walked past a row of giant billboards, which encouraged citizens to buy things they did not need, with money they did not have:

'Live like an emperor with a Natale Resort eight bedroom villa. Take out a mortgage and move in today!'

'Drive in the fast lane with the 250mph Forgetty Payron. Available for 24 monthly instalments of $12,999.'

'Super-duper trooper pooper mobile phones! Credit options available.'

Ellie turned a corner, walked down a staircase, and meandered along a narrow alley. She looked up and saw a red sun painted on a wall. She looked down and saw a dead body on the floor. There were bullets in its shoulders, and scars on its knuckles. A cat was lapping up the blood which had pooled around its head.

Ellie squatted down. She paused, reached towards the corpse, and flipped it over.

'Aaah!!!' She screamed.

Three bugs crawled out of the corpse's eyeball.

A mouthful of blackened teeth formed a sick and twisted smile.

Ellie realised who it was.

"Tape Seller," she said. "Jen's father. Oh my."

Ellie removed her cardigan and placed it over the Tape Seller's head. She uttered a brief prayer. Then she went to Jen's shack.

"Have some tea," Jen said.

"No thank-you," Ellie replied.

"Have some tea."

"No thank-you."

"Have some bloody tea!"

"Your dad is dead!"

Jen paused. Her face turned white, her shoulders drooped, and her arms hung flaccidly by her side.

"So you don't want any tea then?" She asked.

Ellie hugged her friend.

"I'll make us a nice cup of tea," Jen continued.

She boiled some water, mixed in some tea leaves, fell to the ground and cried.

Jen mourned her father for forty days. Then she burned every hair on his body, cut him into chunks, and fed him to a pack of hungry vultures.

Ellie and Tamsin stood there in silence, bowed their heads, and closed their eyes. They did not see Jen for another six days.

"This is useless," she complained when she finally turned up to band practice. "This is as useless as an ashtray on a motorbike! We could get ourselves killed, playing this stupid music. And what exactly is it achieving? Nothing! That's what. Absolutely nothing!"

Jen kicked an amp. It fell onto its face and squealed.

"We're doing what we can," Ellie replied. "It would be cowardly to do less, and dangerous to do more."

"We need to do more," Jen protested. "We need to kick the Holies out. We can't live with them; they're too violent. And we can't let this stalemate continue; it's killing us. They're playing for time, and we're playing into their hands. They're expanding their settlements every day. We need to fight them every day, or we'll never get our country back."

"You're crazy," Ellie replied. "Fight them every day? Some of us have school. Some of us have to make ourselves look pretty, and play in a band. Some of us are occupied with other things."

"Some of us have priorities," Jen snarled. "You pretend to suffer like we do, and you sing about our pain. But you'll never understand what it's like to be a refugee, living under occupation in a foreign land. Your blood is too light. You think you've got it bad, because you're surrounded by settlements, checkpoints and soldiers. But you live in your own town, in your own home, in your own community. Your dad ain't been killed. You ain't miscarried at a checkpoint. You've got it made!"

Tamsin cowered in a corner.

The fallen amp screeched.

Ellie slapped her forehead.

"Destruction of your neighbour is destruction of yourself," she warned. "Fighting the Holies won't do you any good. If you kick the hornets' nest, you're bound to get stung."

"Kick the hornets' nest?" Jen screamed. "I live in the bloody hornets' nest! The hornets are stinging me every day! What do I have to lose by kicking a few of them? God knows they'd deserve it!"

Jen threw a chair across the room. She picked up Tamsin's guitar, lifted it above her head, and smashed it into a wall. The guitar's body hung from its neck by five strings. Jen dropped it, stormed out the building, and ran down the street.

Ellie and Tamsin both grimaced.

Gunfire rang out in the distance.

A cockroach scurried away.

* * *

Ellie was jittery for several days.

Mama Ellie decided to act.

"Look, it's fine if you don't want to talk about it," she said. "That's up to you. But you do need to be cleansed. On the name of God in heaven; there are rituals which need to be performed!"

She took her daughter by her hand, and led her through Natale.

They walked through the hamam's foyer. They undressed in a small cubicle. And they both had a full-body massage.

"You're tense," the Masseuse said.

"Life has been stressing me out," Ellie replied.

"Life has been stressing us all out. But this should help."

The Masseuse massaged olive oil into Ellie's stomach. Her strong fingers kneaded Ellie's skin. It made Ellie feel strangely calm.

"Float away," the Masseuse said. "Let all your troubles drift off into the ether. Unwind. Chill out. Let go.

"Don't worry, be happy."

Ellie relaxed.

By the time she had received a facial, manicure and pedicure, she felt like a new person. She relaxed in the hot pool, covered her face in make-up, and walked out into the world.

She walked into her classroom the next day.

"What is the differential of x^2?" The Maths Teacher asked in Protokian.

"$2x$," a Bulky Pupil replied in Godliness.

The Maths Teacher stormed across her classroom, lifted a cane above her head, and thrashed the Bulky Pupil's face. She hit the Bulky Pupil's arm, shoulder and hand.

"Don't ever speak that language in here again," she shouted. "That language doesn't even exist! Remember: *'One Nation. One Language. One Culture'*. We're all Protokian here!"

The class was silent.

A pen rolled across a table.

A note was passed to Ellie.

'Hey Ellie', it read. *'I like you. I like you a lot. Do you want to meet up after school? Tom x'*.

Ellie's eyelashes fluttered. She ran her hand through her hair, and tilted her head. She winked at Tom.

She liked Tom, and she wanted to see him after school. But she had her reputation to protect. She could not be seen alone with a boy. And she already had plans for that evening.

* * *

Ellie walked into town. She used her credit card to buy lipstick from Superb Drugs, eyeliner from Toots Pharmacy, and earrings from Accessories. Then she bought some spray paint and a balaclava.

She returned home. She waited for the sun to set, and her family to fall asleep. Then she snuck back into Natale.

She snuck back through her district, which was eerily silent, because all the other Godlies were obeying the curfew. She clambered through abandoned buildings, to avoid three checkpoints. And she zigzagged through alleys, to avoid a soldier who was on patrol.

She walked past bars, karaoke clubs and brothels, which were all jam packed with drunken Holies. Past the remains of bulldozed homes, and building sites where new houses were being built. Past green spaces, which had been covered in concrete. And past trees, which had been planted along a concrete path.

She put her balaclava over her head, and held a can of spray paint in her shaky hand.

Beneath a giant billboard, which advertised *IDEA*'s range of flat-pack furniture, she wrote: '*Sorry! The lifestyle you ordered is currently out of stock*'. The advert was in Protokian. Her graffiti was in Godliness.

Below a CCTV camera, which was spying on a group of drunken revellers, she scrawled: '*ONE NATION UNDER CCTV*'. She painted a picture of another camera, which was pointing up at the real camera.

And outside a recruiting office for the Protokian army, she scribbled: '*If at first you don't succeed – call an airstrike*'. She drew a little boy, who was wearing a gas mask.

No-one saw Ellie apart from the Mad Lady. Her nose had grown so much, it had pushed her eyes apart, and created a shadow above her mouth. Her wart had shrunk, but it was still producing pus. And her finger was still wagging.

"Red paint won't ever replace red blood," she screeched. "We're all going to die! It has been written! It can't be undone!"

"Oh shut up," Ellie replied. "What do you know, you batty old witch?"

* * *

Ellie got up the next morning and walked into town. She walked down '*Freedom Road*', '*Struggle Street*' and '*Liberation Lane*'. She walked past a majestic fountain, which was dry and covered in dust. And she walked past some camels, who had stopped to refuel at a petrol station. They were drinking murky water from a rusty trough.

A loud speaker was broadcasting the Godly call to prayer, in the Protokian language. A row of televisions, which could be seen through a row of windows, were all broadcasting the Protokian news. And a group of labourers, were all speaking Protokian. They had been told they would be sacked if they spoke Godliness. They had to assimilate to survive.

But little pockets of resistance were visible for everyone to see. Ellie passed a group of volunteers who were restoring abandoned homes, so evicted families could return to the centre of Natale. And she passed a Policeman who worked as a hacktivist in his spare time. He was talking to a Ginger Local, who had a hammer and sickle on her key-ring.

Ellie saw Jen walk past those citizens. She was wearing a pair of denim jeans, and a t-shirt which featured the *'Adigash'* logo. She was carrying a *'Beebop'* bag.

Ellie was not close enough to see the wires inside that bag. She could not hear the ticking sound those wires were making. She just looked at her friend and waved.

"Hey," she shouted. "Jen! Hey! I haven't seen you in days. Hey! Jen! How have you been?"

Jen kept on walking.

Ellie walked behind.

"Hey," she shouted.

Jen upped her pace.

Ellie started to skip.

"Jen," she shouted. "It's me!"

Jen broke into a jog. She hopped onto a bus which was full of settlers, paid the Driver, and walked inside.

Ellie stopped.

'She'll be arrested at the Protokian border', Ellie thought to herself. *'Jen doesn't have the right sort of permit'*.

Ellie watched on as the bus pulled away.

She listened as Jen shouted *'Free Collis!!!'*

She thought, *'Blimey! She's brave'*.

And then everything stood perfectly still.

Ellie could not breathe, listen or think. Her world froze. She felt paralyzed; trapped inside a vacuum which existed outside of space and time. Her face stiffened, her heart stopped, and her lungs froze.

Everything happened in slow motion.

The commuters' faces turned into black silhouettes. Then they disappeared behind a sea of yellow. A uniform, stable and pure shade of yellow. A soft shade of yellow, which had a child-like innocence, and a gentle sort of grace.

The bus's windows wobbled. They undulated in and out, like speakers which were playing a mellow tune. Then the vibrations grew. The windows moved back and forth like waves on an ocean. A crack formed in the middle of each pane. Those cracks grew outwards, like ripples on the surface of a lake.

Crack. Crack. Crack.

The windows blew out from the bus.

Tiny shards of glass, which looked like shiny diamonds, filled the sky. They flew in every direction. They bounced off one another. They danced through the air. They sparkled in the sunshine, and fell like horizontal rain.

'Boom!!!'

It took a while for the noise to reach Ellie, but when it did, it knocked her over. It was so sharp, it flushed adrenaline through her veins. And it was so sudden, it covered her skin in pimples.

Her stomach tingled, as if it had pins and needles. Her head span, as if she was dizzy. And her eyes bulged.

The noise of the explosion, and the noise of the passenger's screams, merged into one horrific howl. It sounded like the anguished death rattle of the Devil himself.

Birds jumped off their branches, rabbits jumped out of their dens, and the bus jumped off the ground.

Ellie's ears bled.

Everything bled.

Blood squirted in every direction. From the arms, which flew through the air. From the legs, which bounced across the ground. From the torsos, which rebounded off the debris. And from the body parts, which rattled around the bus.

The sky was full of fire, smoke and brimstone.

The ground was covered in lonely puddles of blood.

Jen's head landed on Ellie's lap. Ellie cradled it as if it was a baby. She stroked Jen's hair, and looked into Jen's eyes. She saw a sort of serenity which she had never seen before.

Ellie stared ahead.

Above the blackened remnants of the bus, she saw Jen's *Beebop* bag. It floated up into the air, hovered, and then drifted back down. It swayed left and right, like a weightless feather. And it landed on a Pregnant Settler, who was holding her head in her hands.

She had just miscarried.

7. ARUN

"They're terrorist," the Militant Settler said.

"Terrorists," the Economic Settler muttered.

"Terrorists," Papa Arun sputtered.

His television flashed.

'Seven settlers were killed, and twelve settlers were injured, when a suicide bomber attacked a public bus in Natale', a News Broadcaster read. *'Atamow has called it a crime against humanity.*

''This attack is an act of anti-Holism,' the prime minister told Protokian News. 'Anti-Holism is on the rise across the world. We're a persecuted minority once again. But this time we're strong. The law is on our side. And the supremacy of law is absolute! All hail the state!'

'The KPP, meanwhile, has branded the attack a 'bold and heroic act'.

'In a press release issued by the Office of Apai, they said, 'The attack carried out this morning was a natural response to the state terrorism being committed against Godly citizens every day'.'

Arun tapped his call-up card on the table.

Mama Arun made some more tea.

Their guests continued to mutter.

"Terrorists," the Orthodox Settler spat.

"Terrorists," the Pale Settler snarled.

"Terrorists," Jim grunted.

They were sat in Papa Arun's conservatory, on three sofas and two armchairs, which surrounded a table and a water pipe. A wood burning fireplace, which Papa Arun had bought from Idea, rumbled away in the corner. Papa Arun's mobile phone rested on his thigh.

When his father first bought that phone, Arun had gazed at it as if it was a spaceship from another galaxy. It looked so alien to him; so modern, futuristic and strange. But possessing it made Arun feel special. No other family in Liberation had owned a mobile phone.

That changed over the months which followed.

Three years later, pretty much everyone in their settlement owned a mobile. Those who did not were looked down upon. People thought they were weird, anti-social, and behind the times.

The Orthodox Settler's Husband, who was wearing a Mikey t-shirt, had a *Pineapple* phone in his pocket. The Owlish Settler, who was wearing an Adigash t-shirt, fiddled with his *Fokia*. And the Militant Settler's Wife, who was wearing a Beebop t-shirt, sent a text on her *Samesong*.

'*The Protokian government has raised the Terrorism Threat to 'severe',*' the News Broadcaster continued. '*It's encouraging citizens to be alert to danger at all times*'.

Mama Arun returned with a tray of teas and a plate of biscuits.

Jim threw his tea over a cat, who ran back outside.

A Wi-Fi box flashed green and red.

"We could be next," the Pale Settler said. "The fear is killing me. I can't sleep at night. I've lost five pounds. I don't want to die. I don't want our nation to die. I don't want there to be another Great Genocide."

"These citizens hate us," the Militant Settler said. "All the Godly countries hate us. The whole world hates us. They hate everything we stand for. And they want to destroy us. They want to dress us up in striped pyjamas, put us in a gas chamber, and make us inhale Zyklon gas.

"We can't just sit back and let them! When the situation is this extreme, a moderate response would be madness. Violence is the only language those thugs understand. We need to go after those bastards. We need to push the Godlies out of Collis. There are twenty-two other countries where they can live. This place is all we've got!"

"We're the chosen people," Jim agreed. "And for the first time in history, we're the strong ones. I'm not going to apologize for it. I don't see it as a problem. The Godlies need to accept that we're stuck here, with nowhere else to go. The minute they accept that, they'll have a wonderful life. We just want peace."

Arun looked up at a road map. Every road in Natale had been given a Protokian name. The areas occupied by Holies were shaded in blue.

Mama Arun looked out at a row of Holy settlements. She smiled. She looked down at the Godly areas of Natale. She scowled.

The Owlish Settler looked down at a text message.

"I don't understand why they're attacking us," the Orthodox Settler said. "My only sin is that I came back to my homeland, where my forefathers lived two thousand years ago. I didn't come here because of the politics. I came here in spite of the politics! We bought our land. We paid good money for it. I don't understand what we did wrong."

"I employ these citizens," her husband replied. "I'm nice to them. I like to think that they work with me, not for me. I pay them four times the amount they'd get in Natale. And I don't complain when they get held up at checkpoints, on their way to work. They should be grateful."

"Of course they should," the Economic Settler agreed. "We've made them rich! We've brought about increases in liberty and prosperity which would normally take millennia. Before the peaceful liberation of Collis, the Godlies lived in mud huts. Now they have TVs and computers! We give them electricity and water. They're in debt to us, and we don't complain. But what do they do? They bomb us! I just don't get those citizens. They must be deranged."

A cat walked towards the conservatory, looked at Jim, and turned around.

Arun tapped his call-up card on the table.

The television broadcast the news, but everyone ignored it. Everyone was too occupied by their conversation:

'The Protokian International Trade Treaty, 'PITT', has been ratified today. This agreement will allow firms to sue the government, in secret courts, for policies which reduce their profits.

'PITT has been hailed as a victory for the free market. Business leaders have said it'll increase efficiency, and make everyone richer. Politicians have called it a crushing blow for bureaucracy and red tape'.

Condensation dripped from the glass roof.

"Protokia is far from perfect," Papa Arun said. "And some of our government's policies are unpopular. But if Protokia is to exist, and if Holies are to have *one* place we can call home, she must be allowed to protect herself. I understand the Godlies' pain, but the onus is not just on Protokia. The Collisians have to want peace too."

"They don't want peace," the Militant Settler's wife replied. "They teach their children to hate us. The occupation is just an excuse. The truth is they can't accept other cultures. They force their children into wedlock, kill anyone who has sex outside marriage, and throw female babies in the bin! They'll never accept our liberal ways."

"Those infidels are so backwards," the Cherubic Settler agreed. "Just look at the twenty two Godly nations. Homosexuals and minorities don't have any rights there. There aren't any non-Godlies in their parliaments.

"Collisians don't know how to run a state. There never was a Collis. This land was governed by Colonisers before we took over. Their flag is copied, their history is fake, and their politicians are all corrupt.

"I tell you; we're the best thing that ever happened to them!"

The Orthodox Settler nodded.

The Economic Settler grinned.

The Militant Settler looked at Arun and his friends.

"It's down to you guys to protect us," he said. "The future of Protokia is in your hands."

Jim puffed his chest, and saluted his father.

The Pale Settler smiled, and saluted Jim.

Arun tapped his call-up card on the table.

* * *

'*The Protokian government has raised the Terrorism Threat to 'critical',*' the News Broadcaster read. '*It's promised to take extreme measures, to fix an extreme situation*'.

Arun turned the television off.

Mama Arun hugged him.

Papa Arun shook his hand.

"My boy," he said. "I'm proud of you. You're defending us all!"

Arun chewed his bottom lip.

"I'm being conscripted," he said. "It's not like I'm putting an end to global warming."

"No," Papa Arun replied. "You're putting an end to terrorism. It's far more important."

Arun rolled his eyes.

"Now what do you need to remember?" Papa Arun asked his son.

"To be friendly to everyone I meet. To take care of persecuted citizens, like the Widow took care of you."

"That's right! And who are the persecuted citizens?"

"We are."

"So who are you going to protect?"

"The Holies."

"That's my boy!"

Papa Arun shook his son's hand. By the time he let it go, Arun's hand had started to swell. It was a blotchy mix of purples and reds.

Mama Arun answered her phone.

Arun picked up his backpack, waved goodbye, and left home.

He walked past a Retired Settler who was walking her dog, and an aviary which was full of chirping birds. Past a Window Mart, a *Majestic Vines*, and a *Begg's* bakery. A row of armoured jeeps, a row of Protokian flags, and a row of astroturf football pitches.

He approached the perimeter fence, and waved to a Puny Guard. The Muscular Guard had been sacked because he was a Holy.

Arun got onto an army bus.

Jim sat down next to him.

They drove down a motorway, and gazed out at a row of billboards.

'Make the most of now!' A *Toadaphone* advert dictated.

'Share Moments! Share Life!' A *Podak* advert decreed.

'Just do it!' A Mikey advert demanded.

Arun and Jim got off the bus. They were given a set of uniforms. And they were escorted to their dorm. They sat down next to three other teenagers.

A Keen Soldier looked like a little boy grown large. He had dimpled knees and podgy forearms. It was impossible not to think of him in a school uniform, complete with grey shorts and a scatty tie.

A Muscular Soldier looked simply too big to be allowed. He looked wild. His head almost touched the ceiling, even though he was sitting down on his bed.

And a Border Soldier smelled of boiled cabbage.

"The border police are the greatest patriots," he said. "We handle the citizens who make problems for our country. Whoever comes close, and wants to make trouble, we break them. In the sun, in the rain, in the snow; we make sure they know not to mess with Protokia!"

The other conscripts looked back at the Border Soldier. They were new recruits, and they all felt slightly nervous. But the Border Soldier had served for two years. He was confident, and he dominated the room.

"It's hard work," he continued. "You're on your feet for twelve hours, with a flak jacket on your shoulders, a helmet on your head, and a bullet in the chamber. You're always working. You're freezing, and you see the Godlies in their warm cars. So you tell them to get out and open the boot, to get them cold and wet."

The Border soldier paused before he explained.

"You have your fun when you can!"

The Keen Soldier winked.

"I'd make them sit out in the rain until they got pneumonia," he said.

"Ha, ha, ha!" The Border Soldier laughed. "Well, if anyone causes us trouble, if they question us or answer us back, we bind their arms and make them sit in the mud for five or ten hours. We '*Dry them out*'.

"The Holies are the best. We make little children cry! We crush civilians between narrow grates! We make sure they know who's in charge, so they're too scared to join the KPP."

"My brother," Jim said. "You're a real hero. You've got to let those terrorists know who's the boss."

The Border Soldier sniggered.

"I can't wait to get out there," the Keen Soldier said. "I want to throw gas! I want to throw gas! I want to kill as many citizens as I can! I don't care if they're unarmed. I want to tattoo an '*x*' on my arm for every Godly I take out. I want to tattoo a smiley on my arm for every child I kill. I want to smear body parts across the walls of Natale! I want to kill, kill, kill!"

Arun winced.

"You're worse than the terrorists," he said. "You have no god!"

Jim blew smoke out through his nostrils.

"My friend," he replied. "Not this again. I'm telling you; it's a dog eat dog world. It's us or them. We need to be the hunters, not the hunted; the persecutors, not the persecuted; the lions, not the sheep.

"Come on, my brother. Pull yourself together!"

The Border Soldier glared at Arun.

"Jim's right," he said. "The Godlies aren't human. They're terrorists! They're cow-eating, peacock-worshipping, unbaptised terrorists!"

"They're terrorists! They've got sticky crotches, lice-infested hair, and breath which smells of vomit. They're terrorists!"

"They're zit faced, arse licking, pus-sucking loons!"

"They're crud infested, hog-humping dickwads!"

"They're butt-ugly schmucks!"

"They're terrorists!"

"Terrorists!"

"Terrorists!"

A bird landed on the windowsill.

Everyone looked at Arun.

Arun shrugged his shoulders.

"They're sissies," he said.

He bowed his head and sighed.

Jim sniggered.

The Muscular Soldier patted Arun's back.

"I used to be like you," he said. "I used to believe in peace. So did my two best friends. We grew up together. We played together. We worshipped together. And we believe in peace together.

"My two friends were killed together. The KPP shot them dead.

"That tragedy made me grow up. It made me understand that there will always be people who want to kill us. That not everyone likes the Holies.

"So I feel a duty to fulfil the things my friends couldn't; like coming here, joining the army, and taking it seriously.

"Serving in the army is a divine duty. We have to do it right. We can't just go around killing citizens for fun. But we've got to do it. Our friends and families are depending on us."

Everyone nodded.

Everyone spent a moment in silent contemplation.

Everyone jumped up when a Bulky Officer stormed in.

The Bulky Officer had a face which could have belonged to a medieval crusader, and a bottom which could have belonged to a whale. He looked furious. All the officers looked furious.

"Attention!" He boomed.

His steel-capped boots created a *rat-a-tat* beat as they stomped across the metal floor. His deep nasal breaths filled the air. His necklaces clinked.

"Blue heads!" He yelled. "Follow me! March! Left! Right! Left! Right! Left! Right! Left!"

Arun and his comrades followed the Bulky Officer past a row of dormitory cabins, an assault course, and a firing range.

They entered a hall which smelled of cheesy fish. New recruits stood in a grid. Officers flanked them on both sides. And a Squinty Officer stood at the front.

The Squinty Officer had a bushy monobrow, and a paper-thin moustache, which seemed to be embarrassed. It looked like it would rather be something trendier, like a sideburn or a goatee.

The Squinty Officer marched across the hall. His chest was puffed and his back was arched. His chin was lifted and his eyes were fixed. Arun did not understand his pompous ritual, but he did not have the courage to question it.

No-one said a word.

A fly got caught in a cobweb.

The Squinty Officer stopped, pivoted, and faced the room.

"Gentlemen!" He howled. "You represent the finest institution on the planet. And you'll become the finest patriots in the land.

"You'll be the difference between war and peace, terror and calm, tyranny and liberty. You'll be the saviours of the Holy race.

"But first you must train. It takes blood, sweat and tears to become the best. You've got a tough month ahead. A productive month. An honourable month. But a tough month. The toughest month of your life!"

The Squinty Officer pivoted, marched towards one wall, turned, marched across to the other wall, and then returned to the centre of the hall.

"You'll learn how to help your nation achieve its four goals; prevention, separation, preservation and legislation.

"Prevention! You will punish the Godlies before they commit crimes.

"Separation! You will segregate the Godlies before they unite.

"Preservation! You will control the Godlies before they affect our nation.

"Legislation! You will crush the Godlies before they apply the law."

The Squinty Officer walked between the new recruits. He patted a Gawky Recruit's shoulder, he stroked Arun's cheek, and he slapped the Keen Soldier's bottom. Then he returned to the front.

"Prevention!" He repeated. "Separation! Preservation! Legislation!

"The next month will be hard. You'll push your bodies further than you ever thought they could go. You'll experience pain beyond your wildest imagination. And you'll ache in places you never knew existed. But you'll be all the better for it. You'll become lean, mean, fighting machines! You'll become the greatest soldiers on the planet. You'll be ready to achieve the army's four goals.

"Prevention! Separation! Preservation! Legislation!

"Contain the Godlies and protect the Holies.

"Amen!"

"Amen!" Everyone replied.

The Squinty Officer marched away.

The other officers marched behind him.

Arun marched into a month full of early mornings, cold showers, and salty porridge; long runs, repetitive drills, and pretentious ceremonies; tactical lectures, military training, and army indoctrination.

* * *

The Terrorist Threat was set at '*super extreme*', Arun finished his military training, and his unit was sent out to protect Protokia.

"We're going to kill us some terrorists," the Keen Soldier said. "We're going to defend our nation!"

"My friends," Jim replied. "Today we become heroes!"

Arun did not say a word. He just climbed into an armoured vehicle, which was shaped like an armadillo. Its water cannon looked like a giant snout. Its front windows, which were covered with metal grilles, looked like spying eyes. And its exhaust, which stuck out of its metal shell, looked like a small tail. It emitted a smoggy mixture of carbon monoxide, nitrogen oxides and hydrocarbons.

Arun's unit drove past a *Café Hero* and a *Costly Coffee*, which were both being converted into Star & Bucks. Past a *Burger Knight* and a *Burger Bishop*, which were both being converted into Burger Queens. And past a Planner, who was planning to submit some plans to the Ministry of Planning.

They drove past citizens who were fighting to get into a single taxi, an endless series of new suburbs, and a pile of dead donkeys. Those animals weren't needed anymore. Their jobs had been taken by motor vehicles.

Arun and his comrades approached the separation wall; a barrier made up of grey concrete slabs, which were eight metres tall, and as solid as rock. Plans were afoot to extend that wall for three hundred miles along the border of Collis. Much of it cut into Collis itself. It reached the edge of Natale.

"Separation!" Jim said. "We'll segregate the Godlies before they unite."

"Preservation!" The Keen Soldier replied. "We'll control the Godlies before they affect our nation."

Jim and the Keen Soldier high-fived.

The Muscular Soldier thumbed his nose.

Arun winced.

He watched Papa Charlie, who was working with a group of Godly labourers. They uprooted a line of fig trees, dug a line of trenches, and erected a line of concrete slabs.

A line of protesters chanted.

'*From the mountains to the sea, this land of ours will be free*'.

A Ravaged Local, who had leathery skin, stepped forward.

"I've nurtured this grove for ten years!" He wailed. "I waited ten years for it to bear fruit. I enjoyed it for one year. And now you're uprooting it? You fungus covered dodos!

"I worked for thirty years to buy this land. I waited ten years for it to earn me money. You think you can just take it away from me like that? You're mad! You're the offspring of geese and guppies! You're fustylugs! You've got another thing coming!"

The Ravaged Local wagged his fist.

The Keen Soldier wagged his finger.

Jim wagged his gun.

"Forget about it," he said. "Get out of here. This land isn't yours anymore."

The Ravaged Local ground his teeth and snarled.

Jim head-butted him.

He leaned in slowly, and then he jolted forward. Temple kissed temple. Shockwaves echoed across foreheads. Kinetic energy transferred.

The Ravaged Local fell to the floor.

Jim felt a cosmic sense of elation surge through every inch of his being. A grin covered his face. His eyes opened wide. And he puffed his chest.

His comrades stood around the Ravaged Local and laughed.

Arun put his hand on that man's shoulder.

"Are you okay?" He asked.

"Du-du-does it look like I'm okay?"

Arun bit his lip.

"I can make sure they never touch you again," he said. "You just need to get out of here. Leave and don't come back. I'll make sure this never gets reported. I'll make sure you don't get into any trouble."

Arun stretched out his hand, pulled the Ravaged Local to his feet, and helped him to walk away.

Jim shook his head.

"What was that about?" He asked Arun when he returned.

"I wanted to help," Arun replied.

Jim snickered.

"Brother!" He said. "You're a nice guy. You want to be friends with everyone. I like that. But you're naïve. You need to understand that those Godlies aren't what they seem to be. They're fine on the outside, but you can't trust them. They're dangerous. You need to put them in their place."

"No," Arun explained. "I wanted to help *you*."

"Look! Those protestors are filming everything. You'd get in trouble if they reported you. I wanted to make sure that never happened."

Jim chortled.

"Really?" He asked. "In trouble with whom? A Holy doesn't punish a Holy!"

Arun sighed.

A car backfired.

Jim patted Arun's back.

They both stopped talking. They both shook their heads. And they both gazed across at some factories, which were all emitting toxic fumes.

A Begg's factory was churning out bread on a never ending conveyer belt. A components factory was producing escalators for Natale's new shopping centre. And a Fizzy Stream factory was closing down.

Having endured international condemnation for operating in

occupied land, Fizzy Stream were trying to salvage the damage done to their brand. A Manager was padlocking the gate. And Papa Tamsin was leaving for the final time. He looked both indifferent and tormented.

The Keen Soldier and the Muscular Soldier both shrugged.

Arun picked a small dandelion.

Jim approached a Small Protestor.

"Hey," he said. "You have beautiful eyes."

The Small Protestor's head jolted backwards, whilst her feet stayed fixed to the ground. She looked confused, shocked and reviled.

"Don't be shy," Jim said. "You and me, we could heal this rift. We could bring peace to Protokia. Make love not war, baby! I'd make love to you all night long!"

The Small Protestor scowled and stormed away.

A Gawky Refugee followed her.

Arun chuckled.

"That's one way to disperse the crowd," he joked. "Two down, eleven to go!"

He pointed at a Hairy Local, who had a wobbly belly and two stumpy legs. He looked as if he had grown stout too early in life.

"You should tell him that you think he's *'beautiful'*," Arun said. "And then you should approach that frail geriatric. You should ask her to make love to you *'all night long'*. We'd have this place cleared in an instant!"

Jim suppressed a smile.

A leaf fell from an uprooted tree.

The protesters chanted.

'From the mountains to the sea, this land of ours will be free'.

Three protestors laid down in a trench. The labourers worked around them. Arun and his comrades did not interfere.

They waited for the sun to set. Then the labourers left, and the protestors all followed.

Arun and his comrades retired to a watchtower.

That place, ten metres above the ground, became a home for those four soldiers. They spent many endless nights there, cramped, surrounded by sandbags, sleeping-bags and kitbags.

With just a limited supply of crackers, chocolate and canned beef, they soon grew hungry. And with little more than an MP3 player and a pile of books for entertainment, they soon grew bored.

The hunger and boredom drove them mad. Jim spent hours walking around in tiny circles, Arun rocked back and forth, and the Keen Soldier did hundreds of press-ups each night.

They made prank calls to other sentry posts. They called their commanders and hung up straight away. They used the loudhailer to curse the Godlies. And they talked. They talked about everything. They talked about their lives, their dreams, and their lovers.

"Why don't you ever speak about girls?" The Muscular Soldier asked Arun after three weeks had passed. "I tell you, courting is great fun."

Arun was being his usual quiet self; sitting with his back to the wall, fiddling with a *Rubik's Cube*, and staring up at the night-time sky.

"When I was at school, I used to pass love notes between girls and boys, to help them flirt," he replied. "I was a bit of a matchmaker like that. I can tell when people fancy each other by the way they act, look at each other and giggle."

Arun turned to face Jim.

"With him it's as easy as bread and butter," he said. "That boy fancies anything with a pulse!"

Jim punched Arun's arm.

"My brother," he said. "You don't get what you don't go after. So what if I chase a lot of girls? It's a numbers game. I end up with far more pussy than you do!"

Arun shook his head.

"I'm not sure you can call *Jabba the Hut* a 'girl'," he said. "Or the *Hunchback of Notre Dame* for that matter. Or the *Swamp Monster*. I don't think any of your girlfriends have been the slightest bit feminine."

"At least I've had girlfriends!" Jim replied.

"That's debatable!"

Jim put Arun into a headlock, and ruffled Arun's hair with his fist. The friction burnt Arun's scalp.

The Muscular Soldier guffawed.

Jim let Arun go.

"Here," the Keen Soldier shouted. "Here! Look at this!"

Everyone looked out the window. They saw the next watchtower, which was black with char. It had been burnt by a gang of youths. They saw the remnants of an olive grove, which was full of rambling cacti, burning rubbish, and rocks which had been spewed out of the earth. And they saw the wall itself. On one slat, someone had spray painted the word *'Why?'* And on another slat, Ellie was spray-painting the words, *'Peace! Love! Votes for all!'*

Ellie had been out all night.

Beneath a *TA Games* advert, which told citizens to *'Challenge everything'*, she had written, *'Challenge apartheid'*. Beneath a *Ponda Cars* advert, which told citizens to embrace *'The Power of Dreams'*, she had written, *'Dream of independence'*. And beneath a *Trite Lemonade* advert, which told citizens to *'Obey your thirst'*, she had written, *'Obey your conscience'*.

"We've encountered, encountered, encountered!" The Keen Soldier cheered.

"Engage, engage, engage!" Jim replied.

"Encounter!"

"Engage!"

"Encounter!"

"Engage!"

"Encounter!"

"Engage!"

They put on their flak jackets and helmets, loaded their guns, and skipped down the stairs.

"Brothers," Jim muttered. "Wherever you throw a rock in this god-forsaken town, there's either a cat or a bloody terrorist.

"Let's get 'em all!"

"Let's get 'em all!"

"Let's get 'em all!"

Arun shook his head.

The Muscular Soldier shook his gun.

Jim snuck up behind Ellie, and grabbed her shoulder.

"Gotcha!" He said. "Tut, tut, tut. You're coming with us!"

Jim smirked.

The Keen Soldier and the Muscular Soldier high-fived.

Ellie's heart rebounded off her ribcage. Her pulse quickened and her forehead began to sweat.

"Why?" She asked. "What for? What have I done?"

Jim sniggered.

"We've caught you red handed," he said. "You know what exactly you've done."

"It's just a bit of paint," Ellie protested.

"A crime is a crime is a crime. A murder or a slogan; it's all is the same to me. The supremacy of law is absolute! Any transgressions must be punished."

"But I've spread a message of love and peace! What law have I broken?"

"You've vandalised state property."

"No more than those firms who've plastered their adverts across every wall in town. I don't see you arresting them."

"They pay for their adverts."

"We pay with our land, labour and blood!"

"You'll you pay with every drop of blood in your body, if you don't shut up."

"I'll shut up when you give me my right to free speech and free expression."

Jim spat at Ellie.

The Keen Soldier spat on the ground.

The Muscular Soldier grunted.

"Legislation!" He barked. "Let's crush her before she applies the law!"

"Let's riddle her body with bullets!"

"Let's call this in!"

Jim pressed a button on his radio.

The Muscular Soldier knocked Ellie to the ground. She landed on her elbow. Blood poured down her arm.

The Keen Soldier rolled Ellie onto her front, and tied her arms behind her back. He grabbed a rock and smashed Ellie's head. He caught his finger. Blood streamed down his arm. But he was happy nonetheless. Capturing Ellie had made his day.

Jim cracked up with laughter.

"Look at that blow she just took," he said, as if it was the most natural thing in the world.

The Keen Soldier cracked some sunflower seeds and threw them into his mouth.

The Muscular Soldier picked his nose.

Arun winced.

'*What sort of evil people are these?*' He asked himself. He could not understand their behaviour. He felt uncomfortable, embarrassed and ashamed.

But Ellie did not react. She just exhaled. She was relieved to think that she was not being arrested for her part in the uprising, or her rebel music. She clung to those small victories. They made her feel triumphant.

She rolled onto her side, looked away from her captors, and sank into the dirt.

The radio crackled.

"Watchtower eighty three," a voice said. "What's your status?"

"We've arrested a terrorist," Jim replied.

"On what charge?"

"Graffiti. Defacing Protokian property."

"What did she write?"

"Peace, love, and votes for all."

There was a pause.

"Peace and love?"

There was another pause.

"Let her go."

"Yes sir."

Arun breathed a sigh of relief.

Ellie relaxed.

Jim had an idea. He re-tuned his radio and tried again.

"Watchtower eight three to base," he said.

"Watchtower eighty three," the radio replied. "What's your status?"

"We've arrested a terrorist."

"On what charge?"

"Graffiti. Defacing Protokian property."

"What did she write?"

"Peace, love, and votes for all."

There was a pause.

"Votes for all?"

There was another pause.

"Bloody terrorists! Bring her down to the prison."

The Keen Soldier pulled Ellie to her feet, removed her shoes, and made her march through town. She was naked, apart from the tatty jeans which covered her legs. Her shirt had been ripped from her torso when she fell. And her bra had come loose.

Her feet began to bleed.

She was marched past billboards which demanded *'Don't leave home without it'*, and billboards which demanded *'Grab a Slickers'*. Past shops with glass facades and neon signs. And past the Mad Lady, whose finger was wagging so quickly, it could barely be seen.

"Your paymasters will never be grateful," she squealed. "They'll leave you as desolate as the people you're arresting!"

"Oh shut up," Jim shouted back. "What do you know, you batty old witch?"

* * *

The *War On Terror* was felt all across Collis.

Books were burnt if they suggested that Protokia existed before the Holies took over. Statues of Holy liberators were erected throughout Natale. And loud halers were attached to lampposts. They made regular announcements:

'The Protokian government has raised the Terrorism Threat to 'unlimited'. There are no limits to what the terrorists will do to us!'

"Tell me about it," Jim said.

He led his unit towards Natale's castle. They walked over the drawbridge, through the main gate, and into a metallic portacabin.

They stood to attention and waited for the Squinty Officer to arrive.

A mild breeze caused a thin plastic window to rattle.

Arun resisted the urge to scratch his chin.

Six minutes passed. Then the Squinty Officer opened a door and marched through the room. His chest was puffed and his back was arched. His chin was lifted and his eyes were fixed.

He turned to face his men.

"Prevention!" He barked. "You'll punish the Godlies before they break the law!"

He pivoted, stepped towards one wall, span around, took two steps towards the opposite wall, and then returned to the centre of the cabin.

"Prevention! Prevention! Prevention!" He howled. "Prevention is better than cure!"

He looked the Keen Soldier up and down.

"You've done well so far," he continued. "You're an elite terror fighting unit. You've helped the army to achieve three of its key goals; separation, preservation and legislation. Your country is proud of you.

"But you need to do more. You need to work towards the army's top goal; prevention.

"Prevention! Prevention! Prevention! Prevention is better than cure!"

The Squinty Officer pivoted left, span one hundred and eighty degrees to the right, and then turned back to face the room.

"Prevention!" He barked. "You'll use two tactics to help prevent terrorism; *'Demonstration of Presence'* and *'Mapping'*.

"Demonstration of presence! You'll make sure that everyone knows you're present! Wherever they turn they'll see you, hear you, and feel you. Out in the open, hidden in the shadows, and inside their own homes. You'll be everywhere! The natives will realise they have nowhere to turn; that to join the KPP would be futile.

"Mapping! You'll search houses at random, check IDs, count rooms, and rifle through possessions. You'll record the number of citizens in each house. You'll ask embarrassing questions. And you'll report back to army headquarters, so we can assess the risks."

A fighter jet flew overhead.

A vein bulged on the Squinty Officer's forehead.

He stamped his boot and concluded his speech.

"You must do whatever you can. In the war against terror, there is no *'morality'*. You must disturb the calm. Because you're like dogs and they're like rabbits. You can chase them down holes, but they're always there. Always! You need to scare them out into the open. You need to draw them outside, engage them, and finish them off.

"Because they're terrorists. The whole lot of them. They're a bunch of bloody terrorists!"

The Squinty Officer took two big steps towards the door, pivoted right, and stared at Jim.

"Private," he barked. "You've worked hard, and hard work gets rewarded. You're promoted to the rank of 'officer'. Congratulations!"

He pivoted left, marched through the door, and disappeared into the distance.

* * *

Arun and his comrades walked through the refugee camp.

It was clear that some refugees had become rich, whilst others had become poor. God had provided for some, but not for all.

Nice cars were parked outside nasty buildings. One room shacks mingled with multistorey mansions. Palatial townhouses overlooked crumbling homes. Their conservatories were full of sofas, armchairs, water pipes, and wood burning fires. The streets were full of rubbish.

Arun walked down the camp's main thoroughfare, which had evolved into a high street. Shops with glass facades and neon signs lined up on either side. Favela style alleys appeared between branded stores.

Everything seemed cramped. Floor had been added upon floor. Most alleys were less than a metre wide. Forty thousand citizens lived in every square kilometre.

Everything seemed patched together. A school compound was fenced in by thorny branches. A clinic's roof was made from corrugated iron. And a crèche had been built using salvaged wood.

Everything seemed lifeless. It was two o'clock in the morning, the curfew was in force, and the refugees were all in bed. Arun was surrounded by thousands of citizens, yet he felt like he was in a ghost town.

"Prevention!" Jim cheered. "We'll punish the Godlies before they break the law!"

He pressed the butt of his gun into his shoulder, leant backwards, and fired into the air.

Rat-a-tat-tat.

Rat-a-tat-tat.

Rat-a-tat-tat.

Smash!

A bullet hit a water-tank. It split. Water gushed out, and poured off the roof. It looked like an oily waterfall.

Smash!

A bullet hit a rubbish bin. It made a tinny sound.

Smash!

A bullet hit a brand new *Ponda* car.

Arun grimaced.

Jim snickered.

"Demonstration of presence!" He cheered. "That'll let these terrorists know we're here!"

"Demonstration of presence," the Keen Soldier replied. "They'll all be awake now!"

He threw a stun grenade down the street. One hundred and seventy decibels of noise screamed out at the night-time sky.

The Keen Soldier pumped his fist.

The Muscular Soldier patted Arun's back.

"Demonstration of presence," he said.

He plugged his radio into a pylon, and broadcast a message over every loud-haler in the camp.

"Citizens!" He announced. "We know you're out there. We know you want to destroy Protokia. And we know you're all terrorists.

"But *you* should know one thing. We're stronger than you! We're like lions and you're like sheep. We can kill you, devour you, and tear you into little pieces. Don't say you haven't been warned!"

The Muscular Soldier pounded his chest.

The Keen Soldier grinned.

Jim sniggered.

"Come," he said. "We've demonstrated our presence. Now let's do a mapping."

He led his comrades towards a home which was three metres wide and four stories tall. Its windows were covered in bars, and its walls were covered in graffiti.

Jim kicked the door down, walked inside, and gestured for his comrades to follow. They stormed every room, dragged every resident out of bed, and shunted them all into the lounge.

Papa Jon and Mama Jon sat on a sofa. Jon and his First Wife sat on two chairs. Tamsin sat on the floor, with a baby in her arms. And Tamsin's Daughter sat in front of the television. Her grape-shaped head followed some trippy animations. Her eyes swirled. And her bushy hair swayed from side to side.

A lightbulb flickered.

A plug socket fizzed.

A moth flapped.

"We've come to castrate you," Jim said, in a stilted sort of Godliness.

Jon looked back at him in horror.

The Keen Soldier leant on his gun, which was almost as tall as he was.

Arun whispered in Jim's ear.

"Sorry," Jim said. "We've come to 'count' you."

Jon exhaled.

Papa Jon sighed.

Tamsin shook her head.

"We speak Protokian," she said.

"Good," Jim continued. "Please show us your IDs."

Jim walked around the room, and collected a handful of plastic cards.

Arun filled in a form.

The other soldiers searched the house.

"We need to check your things," Jim explained. "But don't fret. If you don't have anything to hide, you've got nothing to worry about."

Tamsin rocked her baby to sleep, as sounds echoed through her home. As wardrobes toppled over, vases crashed into walls, and picture frames skidded across floors. As lightbulbs smashed, documents scattered, and a television flew out of a window. As tables were broken, doors were unhinged, and fixings were unfixed.

Jim grinned.

"Everything is going to be okay," he said. "You've got nothing to worry about. Nothing at all. We're the good guys!"

Tamsin's Daughter cried.

'Mwah! Mwah! Mwah!' She bawled. Tears streamed down her cheeks, and her face turned red.

Jim snapped. His veins bulged, and his lips trembled.

"Don't think we'll have mercy on you just because you've got a kid!"

He boomed. "I'll kill you in front of her, if you don't shut her up!"

Tamsin stared back at Jim, as if to say '*Really?*'

Jim stared back at Tamsin, as if to say '*What?*'

Tamsin gave her baby to the First Wife, who was praying, and kneeled down next to her Daughter.

"Hey," she whispered. "It's all going to be okay. These guys will leave, and everything will go back to normal. We'll take the day off school tomorrow. We'll play hide and seek!"

She tried to hug her Daughter.

Her Daughter pushed her away.

"I don't want to play hide and seek," she said. "OMG, mummy! No-one plays hide and seek these days. Pfft. You're so ancient!"

"I'm nineteen!"

"LOL! That's ancient."

Tamsin rolled her eyes.

"Well, we'll play a different game then," she said. "We'll play whatever game you like!"

Tamsin's Daughter grinned.

"I want a *Gaystation*," she said. "And I want a war game, so I can shoot lots of helpless civilians. And I want a McRonalds for lunch. And I want a *Sappy Meal*. And I want a plastic toy.

"*Hmm! I'm lovin' it!*"

"You can have a McRonalds," Tamsin replied. "We'll all have a McRonalds together."

"Yay," Tamsin's Daughter cheered. "*Hmm! I'm lovin' you!*"

She jumped on top of her mother, and gave her a big hug.

Tamsin stared at Jim, as if to say '*Happy now?*'

Jim stared back at Tamsin, as if to say '*What? Do you want a medal?*'

Tamsin finally cracked.

"What do you want?" She screamed. "You come into my house, ransack it, sit on my sofa, and look at me as if you expect me to bring you a cup of tea. Really? Why did you even come here?"

"Because you're terrorists," Jim replied. "Because you support the KPP. Because you don't appreciate anything the Holies have done for you."

Tamsin tutted.

A Wi-Fi box flashed green and red.

The Keen Soldier returned. He waved a kitchen knife through the air. "I found this weapon," he said. "These terrorists planned to stab us!"

Jim raised his eyebrows.

"I think I know who that belongs to," he said, whilst nodding at Tamsin. "This one here is quite the trouble maker."

The Keen Soldier gave Jim a knowing look.

"I think we should arrest her."

Tamsin looked at Arun.

Arun looked back at Tamsin.

And in that instant they recognized each other. Their stomachs dropped and their hearts skipped a beat. Their bodies froze.

Arun saw the little girl who had shown him around Natale.

Tamsin saw the little boy who had played football with her friends.

Arun saw the child who had mocked him for worshipping a scroll.

Tamsin saw the child who had mocked her for worshipping fire.

Arun saw the girl who once tried to break into a prison.

Tamsin saw the boy who once broke into a stadium.

Arun saw his lost youth in Tamsin's eyes. He saw childhood days and mischievous nights. He saw the last remnants of his innocence.

Tamsin's eyes begged Arun for help. They screamed for his assistance. They pleaded for his mercy.

But voices rattled between Arun's ears.

He heard his father:

'You're putting an end to terrorism. I'm proud of you. You're defending us all'.

He heard the Squinty Officer:

'Prevention! You'll punish the Godlies before they break the law!'

And he heard the Militant Settler:

'It's down to you guys to protect us. The future of Protokia is in your hands'.

He saw Jim, the Keen Soldier and the Muscular Soldier. He felt the walls closing in on him. He tasted blood in his mouth.

He started to sweat, shake and stammer. He could not handle the pressure. The pressure to protect Protokia. The pressure to protect Tamsin. The pressure to choose.

Arun's emotions mixed within him, like liquor in a cocktail shaker. Guilt, despair and terror, merged to form one transcendent sensation. Shame and horror sploshed around his belly. Fear and fury made his saliva froth. Vulnerability made his knees knock together.

He had to make a heart-breaking choice; to betray his comrades or betray his friend.

He hated his society. He hated himself. And hated Jim for putting him in that situation. He wanted to beat Jim. He wanted to destroy Jim. He wanted to kill Jim. He wanted to see Jim's corpse, broken and twisted, in a bloody heap at his feet.

"Terrorist," Jim muttered.

"Terrorist," the Keen Soldier sputtered.

"Terrorist," the Muscular Soldier spat.

They all looked at Arun.

"Tu, tu, tu," he stuttered. "Terror."

He paused.

The television flashed blue and yellow.

Arun shook his head.

"That's my knife," he said. "I put it down in the kitchen when we first arrived. Sorry lads. That girl's not a terrorist."

Tamsin closed her eyes and thanked the lord.

The Muscular Soldier rolled his eyes.

Jim rubbed his eyes.

"Okay," he said. "I think we're done here. Thank-you for your time."

Arun left.

Jim left.

Everyone left.

Everyone followed Jim down alleys which twisted and turned, through passageways which clung to the hillside, and along lanes which squeezed in between wonky buildings.

"Why didn't you join in?" Jim asked.

Arun bowed his head.

Jim smiled, winked at Arun, and patted his back.

"Don't worry, my brother. You'll get another chance. Just you wait and see!"

He marched towards another house, kicked the door down, and

gestured for his comrades to enter.

"We'll join you in a few minutes," he said.

Jim put his hand on Arun's shoulder, and looked into Arun's eyes.

"My friend," he said. "It's up to you how you live your life. It's a free country after all. But if you continue to pally up to the Godlies, I think you'll find opportunities hard to come by. I think you'll struggle to fit in with the other soldiers."

Arun tensed his cheeks.

"You need to behave like everyone else. You can't afford to be different."

Arun puckered his lips.

"My comrade, the other soldiers don't defend Godlies. So I think it'd be for the best if you didn't either. It'll help you to be one of the lads. It'll help you to become an upstanding member of the state."

Arun winced.

"But doesn't it make you feel empty inside?" He asked. "Arresting children, chasing after innocent citizens, and searching for weapons you'll never find?

"Do you have tomatoes in your eyes? Can't you see it won't make a difference? Don't you feel guilty?"

Jim sniggered.

"No," he said. "Not at all.

"You ignore those emotions. You don't talk about them. You bottle them up. You put your head down and do whatever you can. If you don't have a dog, you go hunting with a cat. You do your duty."

Jim looked at Arun and smiled.

"I like you," he said. "Your innocence is beautiful.

"Come. My brother! Search this house. Tip over a few wardrobes. Steal some trinkets. You never know, you might even like it."

Jim winked at Arun.

Arun entered the house.

He saw the family who lived there. He saw the Keen Soldier, who was making himself a cup of coffee. And he saw the Muscular Soldier, who was drawing a red star on a door.

"My friend," Jim said. "You're up!"

Arun grabbed a chair and smashed it against a wall. He removed a mirror at threw it to the ground. He clambered over the kitchen counter, and tore a microwave from its socket.

He felt amazing. He felt elated, ecstatic and euphoric.

He felt omnipotent; more powerful than an almighty god. He felt liberated; as if a massive weight had been lifted from his shoulders. And he felt uninhibited; as if he was flying higher than a bird.

He had never felt so good. He had never felt so free.

He threw a deep fat fryer to the ground. A set of shelves tumbled over. Pots and pans skidded across the floor.

Arun's comrades cheered:

'*Long live Protokia! Long live Protokia! Long live Protokia!*'

Jim jumped up and down. He grabbed Arun and hugged him. They jumped up and down together.

"That's my boy!" Jim cheered. "Doesn't this feel amazing?"

Arun shrugged.

As he came down from his emotional high, his elation mixed with his guilt. He loved the adulation he was receiving, but he felt ashamed at the same time. He despised himself for feeling so right, when his actions had been so wrong.

He looked at a Wizened Godly, who was shaking with fear. Who was trembling so much, that his thighs jumped up and down. His settee bounced. He experienced a rapid series of involuntary convulsions, which made him look possessed. His face was bright white, and his eyes were bright red.

"Come! Come!" Jim continued. "You became a superman just now. I'm proud of you. King Arun of Natale! King Arun the Conqueror!"

The Muscular Soldier gave Arun a thumbs up.

The Keen Soldier patted Arun's back.

Jim picked Arun up, put him on his shoulders, and strutted down the street. The other soldiers skipped around him in a circle.

"He's one of our own," they sang. "He's one of our own. This boy called '*Arun*', he's one of our own."

* * *

Arun became accustomed to mappings over the weeks and months which followed.

He broke floors, turned over tables, emptied wardrobes, and threw plant pots. He shot bullets into sofas. He slaughtered sheep and horses. He killed an Egg Seller's chickens. He evicted a family, so his unit could use their house as a spy hole. He urinated on refugees from that building's first-floor window. He made children pee their pants, adults have epileptic seizures, and seniors have heart attacks.

He hesitated every now and again, and he struggled to sleep. When sleep did come, nightmares came with it. He saw a holy army of God's soldiers goose-stepping towards him, pounding holy books against their breasts, and firing bullets of fire from their eyes. He saw a cloud of bats descend from the skies, with blood dripping from their teeth, and acid spraying from their spiny wings. He saw squadrons of bears with claws like daggers, battalions of witches with long tangled nails, and legions of demented tigers with heads which spun right around.

But those nightmares did not last for long. Arun's guilt subsided. And he acclimatized to army life. Destruction became second nature to him. Petrifying innocent citizens began to feel normal.

Arun felt superior to the citizens he policed. No-one ever told him off. No-one ever told him what to do. He felt that he could do whatever he wanted. He felt that he was above the law. He felt that he *was* the law.

And so Arun joined in when his unit began to steal.

In the beginning, they only took small things; cups, ashtrays, canes, flags, broken lighters and pictures. Then they took valuable items; camcorders, mobile phones, silver platters, CD players, rings and whiskey. They even took a golden sword.

Stealing became part of their culture. They took money whenever they found it. And they were disappointed whenever they mapped a house where nothing was worth taking.

Encouraged by a surge of public support, Arun's unit began to feel entitled. Their egos grew and grew.

Their egos grew when the *Natale Express* reported on their division's contribution to state security:

'*Five thousand extra soldiers have been drafted in to protect us against terrorism. They have shown great restraint to gather intelligence about thugs, hoodlums and hooligans*'.

Their egos grew when *Protokia TV* filmed them for an evening edition of *News Today*. Arun's unit handed out doughnuts to refugees, spoke politely, and smiled for the camera. The News Broadcaster called them '*diplomatic*'.

And Arun's ego grew when his temple celebrated him. He was paraded in front of the congregation, given a standing ovation, and called a '*hero*'.

So Arun felt confident when he was called into the Squinty Officer's study. His ego had ballooned, and he expected to be promoted.

"Sit down," the Squinty Officer said.

Arun sat down.

A ladybug scuttled towards a chocolate chip cookie.

The Squinty Officer watered a bonsai tree.

"You've been stealing," he barked.

He looked Arun up and down.

His computer gurgled.

Arun shrugged.

"Do you think that's acceptable?"

"Yes sir! My commanding officer told me that I couldn't afford to be different. He told me to behave like the other soldiers. And the other soldiers steal. They say it's patriotic."

The Squinty Officer's face turned red. It was a blood-curdling shade of red. A shade of red which was so dark it was almost purple, so bold it made his face pulsate, and so loud it seemed to scream.

In the blink of an eye, he had puffed his chest, lifted his hand above his head, and swung his arm with all his might. His knuckles crashed into Arun's cheek with so much power that Arun fell to the floor. His legs were tangled. There was a bruise on his cheek and a tear in his eye.

"I'd court-martial you if you weren't so bloody innocent!" He barked. "My Lord! Tut, tut, tut."

The Squinty Officer marched over to one wall, pivoted, walked back towards the opposite wall, and then turned to face Arun.

"Tut, tut, tut," he muttered. "I'll have to assign you to a different unit."

He tapped his finger on his chin.

"Report to the *Arrest Squad* at zero eight hundred hours. And make sure I don't ever have to call you here again.

"Now bugger 'orf!!!"

* * *

'The Protokian government has raised the Terrorism Threat to 'fear everything',' the News Broadcaster read. *'Don't panic! Don't panic! Panic! Panic! Panic!'*

Arun sat on a sofa in the army common room. He looked at a Spotty Soldier, who had blotchy cheeks. And he looked at a Rosy Soldier, who was covered in tattoos.

"Bloody 'Arrest Squad'," that boy muttered. "What's the point? I'm telling you, we're not measured by arrests, we're measured by kills. We're measured by dead terrorists. The army hasn't invested in us to make arrests. Pfft. We're wasted here!"

The Rosy Soldier spat on the floor.

Arun crossed his legs.

The television broadcast the news, but everyone ignored it:

'A consortium of businesses, led by Punylever and Rablays, has used PITT to sue the government. They proved that Protokia's Competition Act has reduced their profits.

'As a result of this case, the government has revoked the Competition Act. Private firms will now be able to perform takeovers without any bureaucratic interference. They'll be able to form monopolies, and accrue whatever market share they can.

'The Chief Executive of Punylever has hailed today's ruling a 'Victory for the free market'. He's said it's sure to result in greater efficiency, and make everyone in Protokia richer.'

A lemming jumped off a cliff.

"I just want to kill terrorists," the Rosy Soldier complained. "I'm telling you, I just want to make Protokia safe."

"You're nuts," the Spotty Soldier replied. "I just want to do as little as I can, get out of here, and go on a gap year."

"I just want to go to uni," a Squat Soldier agreed. "Conscription is a joke. I want an education."

Everyone nodded.

Everyone shrugged.

Everyone jumped up when the Bulky Officer stormed in.

"Attention!" He boomed. "Blue heads! Follow me! March! Left! Right! Left! Right! Left! Right! Left!"

Arun and his new comrades followed the Bulky Officer past a row of portacabins, a parade ground, and an armoury. They entered a briefing room. And they stood to attention.

"Stand at ease," a Popeyed Officer said. "And listen up hard."

The Popeyed Officer had a muscular throat and a cavernous mouth. When he talked it looked like it was his larynx, not his brain, which was in control. His cheeks were covered by a five o'clock shadow. And his eyes were staring straight into Arun's eyes.

The Popeyed Officer was always staring at someone or something, but his eyes never blinked.

Arun's eyes watered on that man's behalf.

"Prevention!" He continued. "You'll punish the Godlies before they break the law. You'll go into Natale, arrest anyone you don't like the look of, and escort them to the prison so we can assess what risk they pose."

The Popeyed Officer stared out the window.

"You need reason for suspicion. Suspect all Godlies.

"You need evidence. Check for evidence of life.

"You need to be professional.

"You need to be arbitrary.

"And you need to make arrests!"

The Popeyed Officer stared at the door. Then he marched through it.

* * *

Arun's unit waited until three o'clock in the morning. Then they drove into Natale. They wore black paint on their hands, and black masks on their faces. They carried guns, bullets and grenades.

The Rosy Soldier banged on a door with the butt of his rifle. The door opened and Arun's new unit stormed inside. Then they shunted everyone into the lounge.

"You're a member of the KPP," the Rosy Soldier said.

He pointed at a Puny Refugee who was only ten years old.

The Puny Refugee trembled with fright.

A picture frame fell off a shelf.

"Turn around and face the wall! Put your hands up in the air! Stand on one leg!"

The Spotty Soldier went into the kitchen and made himself a cup of tea. He dropped his pants and mooned the family.

The Squat Soldier sat down, grabbed a magazine, and began to read.

The Rosy Soldier threw his helmet at the Puny Refugee.

"Oi!" He screamed. "Pick that up and give it back."

The Puny Refugee did as he was told

He was so scared he choked. He coughed. He held his throat, bent over and gagged. His eyeballs pulsated. His lips tensed. A giant vein zigzagged across his face. And a drop of blood fell from his nose.

The Rosy Soldier threw his helmet at the Puny Refugee.

"It's quite clear you're a terrorist," he said. "You're coming with us."

The Rosy Soldier blindfolded the Puny Refugee, tied his hands behind his back, and carried him outside. He dumped him, face down, onto the floor of their military jeep. Then he led his unit into another house.

"You've been throwing stones at soldiers!" He told a Squinty Refugee; a fifteen year old boy whose arm was in a plaster cast.

The Squinty Refugee looked confused.

"How possible is this?" He asked in stilted Protokian. "My hand-shoulder is in many pieces!"

"Shut up!" The Rosy Soldier barked. "How dare you answer me back? Who do you think you are? Now take your clothes off."

The Squinty Refugee undressed. He shivered, shuddered and cried.

The Rosy Soldier blindfolded the Squinty Refugee, tied his hands behind his back, and carried him outside.

He turned to face Arun.

"This is more fun than I thought it'd be," he said. "I think it's going pretty well."

Arun shook his head.

"Come! Come! We're doing our duty."

"What are we actually doing though?" Arun challenged. "What difference will these arrests actually make?"

The Rosy Soldier grinned.

"Don't you remember the suicide bomber?" He asked. "Don't you remember all those Holies who were killed?

"Well, we've arrested thousands of children since then, and there hasn't been another suicide bomber. Not one! I'm telling you; it's because of these arrests.

"Prevention! Separation! Preservation! Legislation! We're doing our duty."

Arun furrowed his eyebrows.

"I just don't want to do it," he said.

"It doesn't matter what you want to do. It matters what Protokia *needs* you to do. Be a patriot. Be a team player. Do your duty!"

"I, I, I can't," Arun stuttered. "I, I, I want to become a conscientious objector."

"A conchie? Really? You're a sandwich short of a picnic. Have you heard what happens to conchies? Blimey! You'd be better off dead."

The Rosy Soldier put his arm around Arun's shoulder.

"Come!" He said. "You'll get used to it. We'll arrest one more terrorist, and then we'll go home. Your doubts will fade away."

Arun shrugged, groaned, and entered another house.

"You," the Rosy Soldier said. He pointed at Charlie. "You're guilty of '*splitism*'. You want to split up the motherland. You're a terrorist!"

Charlie's heart pounded. Butterflies fluttered in his stomach, and his spine tingled. His hands shook.

"What evidence do you have?" Uncle Charlie asked in Godliness. "This looks bad. Bad. Very bad. This doesn't look respectable at all!"

"We have plenty of evidence," the Rosy Soldier replied in Protokian. "We have filing cabinets full of evidence! But that's none of your business. We can't reveal state secrets. We'd never show our case files to a terrorist like you.

"And don't speak Godliness to me! If I hear another word of that god forsaken language, I'll shoot you. That language doesn't even exist!"

Charlie's nervous twitch went into overdrive. His lip quivered, and his left cheek pulsated. In and out. In and out. In and out.

His left eye opened and closed at a manic rate. His eyebrow vibrated. He concentrated on his breathing.

He sat still, looked up at the Rosy Soldier, and waited.

The Rosy Soldier blindfolded him, handcuffed him, and carried him away.

"Let's go," he said.

Their jeep sped down roads which were made of cracked concrete, roads which smelled of rotting fish, and roads which turned one way and then the other. They skidded around corners, scaled steep inclines, and slid down rutted streets. They whizzed past shops with glass facades, shops with neon signs, and shops which were branded all over.

The three detainees hit their heads on the roof.

The ties around their wrists turned their hands blue.

The Rosy Soldier kicked them.

The jeep swerved around corners, jinked between roads, and then came to a sudden to a stop. The Squat Soldier removed the three detainees, and pushed them through the prison's gates.

The stars faded and the sun rose.

A cockerel crowed.

A mouse squeaked.

8. CHARLIE

Charlie was dragged towards the prison, with goose-pimples on his arms, and sweat on his brow. He looked up at the top of its wall. Tall concrete slabs stood side by side, decorated by a mixture of spikes and barbed wire. He looked at three watchtowers; gangly contraptions which looked like garden sheds on stilts. And he looked at the buildings which were painted salmon-pink, with angular roofs made from corrugated iron.

He was taken down an endless corridor, which was narrow and dark. Every surface was painted black. There weren't any doors for over a hundred metres. Orange lightbulbs flickered and flashed.

Charlie was shoved into a cell which was dank, empty and small. Five guards took pictures of him on their mobile phones. They took selfies with him by their side. Then they left, locked the door, and did not return until the following afternoon.

Charlie wet his pants. His genitals felt warm, sticky and moist. He felt ashamed. But he did not have the chance to shower. He was marched straight into '*Room 4*', where he was handcuffed to a rail.

He waited.

A cockroach crawled up his leg.

A lightbulb emitted a dull glow.

A Toothy Officer stormed in, slammed the door, and sat down in front of Charlie. His knees pressed up against Charlie's knees. His nose touched Charlie's nose. Charlie could taste that man's breath. He could smell his testosterone. He could hear his heart beat.

The Toothy Officer put his palm on Charlie's inner thigh, and slowly stroked it up towards Charlie's crotch.

"Why did you do it?" He asked.

Charlie looked scared and confused.

"Do what, sir?" He replied in fluent Protokian.

The Toothy Officer picked up a chain made of entwined wire and slapped it across Charlie's face.

"Don't hesitate!" He demanded. His protruding teeth stabbed the musty air. A tangled mix of serrated fillings and jagged fangs poked out through his crooked lips. "When I ask you a question, answer it straight away."

The Toothy Officer leaned in. His forehead touched Charlie's forehead. His eyes stared into Charlie's eyes. His hand crept towards Charlie's penis.

Charlie could smell garlic on the Toothy Officer's breath. He could smell onions, cloves and coffee.

"Why did you do it?"

"Do what, sir?"

"Do it?

"What?"

"You tell me."

"I didn't do anything, sir."

"So you say."

"It's the truth, sir."

"The truth?"

"Yes sir."

"You can't handle the truth!"

"No sir."

"Ah! Just as I thought."

The Toothy Officer leaned out, snickered, and tapped his lower lip.

'*Aaaah! Aaaah! Aaaah!*'

Screams rang out from the next room.

'*No! Please! No! Not that! Anything but that! Aaaah! No! No! No!*'

The Toothy Officer laughed.

"You'll be next," he said.

"Yes sir."

The Toothy Officer shook his head. He leaned back, away from Charlie, and scratched his eye. A sleep crystal crumbled. A nasal hair fell from his nose.

"We know all about you," he said. "You go to Atamow High."

"Yes sir."

"You work in McRonalds."

"Yes sir."

"You're a terrorist."

"No sir."

The Toothy Officer swung around, walked over to the corner of the room, and pulled a television towards Charlie. He pressed play.

Charlie watched a video, in which a group of refugees threw stones at a group soldiers.

"Which one of those terrorists are you?" The Toothy Officer asked.

"I'm not there, sir," Charlie replied.

"Who is this?"

"I don't know him."

"Who is that?"

"I don't know her."

"Which one of those boys are you?"

"I'm not there, sir."

The Toothy Officer tutted.

"Your friend has confessed," he said. "He's given you up."

"Yes sir."

"So you might as well confess."

"Confess to what, sir?"

"Confess to being a terrorist."

"No sir."

"'*No sir*'?"

"No sir."

"'*No sir*' what?"

"'*No sir*', I'm not a terrorist, sir."

"You're unbearable! I'll pour boiling water over you if you don't confess."

"Yes sir."

"'*Yes sir*'?"

"Yes sir."

"'*Yes sir*' what?"

"'*Yes sir*', you'll pour boiling water over me, sir."

The Toothy Officer whipped a knife out of his pocket and thrust it against Charlie's neck. Charlie jolted backwards. He pulled his neck away, and tilted his head up towards the roof.

Blood came to his mouth. His nose bled. He saw millions of tiny silver dots.

"Confess!"

"No sir."

"You're a terrorist!"

"No sir."

"You planned to bomb Natale!"

"No sir."

"You're a member of the KPP!"

"No sir."

"You associate with suicide bombers!"

"No sir."

"You want to destroy Protokia!"

"No sir."

The Toothy Officer shook his head. He put his knife away and paced around the room.

Charlie took a deep breath.

The television turned black.

"Sign this!" The Toothy Officer demanded.

He shoved a document onto a table, and shoved that table into Charlie's ribs.

Charlie looked at the piece of paper in front of him. It was covered in text which he could not comprehend.

"If you sign this confession, you'll be released straight away."

"What does it say, sir?"

"It says that if we catch you throwing stones again, you'll be arrested and sentenced."

Charlie bowed his head.

"I can't sign this," he said. "It wouldn't be right, sir. I don't understand this language. I don't have anything to confess."

The Toothy Officer sniggered.

"We can hold you in '*Administrative Detention*' for renewable periods of six months. We can keep you here forever! We have secret evidence!

"But if you sign this confession, we'll release you after a few weeks."

"I can't sign it, sir."

"If you go to court you'll be found guilty. The state has a 99% conviction rate! All lawyers are crooks; they turn truth into lies, and lies into truth. They'll shaft you, if they have the balls to represent you in the first place. You've got no chance."

"Yes sir."

"But if you sign this confession, we'll release you after a few months."

"No sir."

"'*No sir*'?"

"No sir."

The Toothy Officer ground his teeth. He got up and left.

After thirty minutes had passed, a Slender Guard entered. She smelled of blood and leather. Her sunglasses looked like giant black eyes, and her nose was curved like a ski jump.

"Okay," she said. "You're going home."

Charlie's eyes lit up. He felt elated. He felt ecstatic, overjoyed and thrilled.

"Thank-you ma'am," he said. "Thank-you! Thank-you! Thank-you!"

The Slender Guard led Charlie down a long corridor, unlocked a door, and shoved Charlie into a cell.

"This is your home now," she said. "Enjoy your stay at the *Devil's Hotel*."

* * *

Charlie spent three weeks in that cell. It was two metres long and one metre wide, with no ventilation, and just a bucket for a toilet. He did not see any other prisoners. He survived on a diet of watery soup.

He was tortured every day.

He was blindfolded, his penis was electrocuted, and his body was beaten. A baton was inserted into his anus. He was made to eat faeces.

He was restrained, hooded and shaken. Cigarettes were stubbed out on his skin, his hair was pulled, and his hands were put in serrated handcuffs. He was made to listen to the same nursery rhyme over and over again.

A nylon cord was tied between his testicles and his foot whenever he was interrogated. He was interrogated every day. Officers tried to make him sign false confessions. They strapped him to a chair and beat him.

It was vicious. It was ugly. It was real horrorshow.

"No!" He screamed. "No! No! No!"

He writhed and wriggled. His pelvis thrust up into the air. His head slashed from side to side. His hair became a tangled mess.

"No!" He screamed. "No! No! No!"

He gripped hold of his chair. His nails ripped through its leather armrests. His nerve endings ached. His head throbbed.

"No!" He screamed. "No! No! No!"

Urine soaked his pants.

"No!" He screamed. "Stop! Stop! Stop!"

But the daily torture sessions always continued on.

So Charlie became ill.

He complained to his guards.

"I have a headache, sir," he said.

A Gawky Guard tapped Charlie's head.

"No," he replied. "You're okay."

The other soldiers guffawed

Charlie sighed.

Without anyone to talk to, he carried the weight of his problems on his own narrow shoulders. He considered committing suicide. He became cowardly and short-tempered.

The Gawky Guard stopped laughing.

He grabbed Charlie by his arm, marched him to Room 4, and gave him some water. Charlie downed it in one. It tasted of sour chemicals.

The Toothy Officer entered, sat down in front of Charlie, and put his face in Charlie's face.

"You're a terrorist," he said.

But Charlie could not reply.

His head spun, his stomach churned, and his eyes swirled.

He looked up at the light, and saw thousands of bulbs, which were each less bright than the last. He looked across at the Toothy Officer, who seemed to have five heads. He looked down at his feet and passed out.

Angels appeared. Fairies flew around. Charlie saw a bright white light at the end of a long black tunnel.

The Toothy Officer was shining a bright white light into Charlie's eyes.

"Thank-you for coming clean," he said.

He smiled so much, his teeth pointed out of his mouth. Incisors shot one way, and molars bent back the other. They were yellow, black and greasy.

"Your confession is very much appreciated," he continued. "You've done the right thing."

"Eh?"

"The right thing!"

"I didn't confess, sir. I haven't done anything."

"That's not what this says."

The Toothy Officer held a document in the air. Charlie's eyesight was blurred, but he could still tell that it was written in a foreign language. There was an inky squiggle at the bottom of the page.

"This is all the evidence we'll need to secure a conviction."

Charlie rubbed his eyes and scratched his head.

"When is my trial, sir?" He asked.

"It's happening right now."

"Can I attend, please, sir?"

"No."

"Can I see my lawyer, please, sir?"

"No."

"Has my lawyer seen any evidence, sir?"

"Stop asking questions. Who the bloody hell do you think you are? You unvaccinated disease! You saddle-goose! You obstinate fool! How dare you question me?"

The Toothy Officer slapped Charlie's face with a metal chain.

Charlie did not say a word.

A Scarred Guard knocked on the door, waited, and then entered.

"The Legal Officer has sentenced this one to four months in jail," he said. "Shall I take him away?"

The Toothy Officer nodded.

Charlie was taken to a prison cell which contained three other prisoners, two beds, and one bucket.

He banged his head against the wall.

* * *

Charlie got to know a Crippled Prisoner, who was missing three fingers and one thumb. His hand had been maimed by an exploding gas canister. The Protokians had accused him of making a bomb.

Charlie also got to know a Girly Prisoner, who had all her fingers and all her thumbs. She had gotten arrested on purpose, after her father had forced her to wear a veil. She had picked up a knife, ran away home, and got herself detained at a checkpoint.

But Charlie did not get to know a Silent Prisoner, who sat on all his fingers and all his thumbs. No-one knew why that boy had been arrested. He never said a word. He just pissed on the floor, and sat in a pool of his own urine.

"They accused me of disrupting public order," the Crippled Prisoner explained. "Then they brought me here."

"You know," the Girly Prisoner said. "The Protokians deny this place even exists!"

Charlie sighed.

A narrow stream of urine crawled across the room.

The Scarred Guard stormed in.

"Time for work," he said. "Come on. Let's go. Chop, chop!"

The prisoners were taken out into the yard. They were shackled to the ground, given a hammer each, and made to break rocks.

They broke rocks for eight hours each day. They broke rocks in the sunshine and in the rain. They broke rocks when it was hot, when it was cold, and when it was humid. They broke rocks when they were tired, when they were depressed, and when they were ill.

Breaking rocks was part of their daily routine. It was a simple routine, which consisted of sleeping, eating, and enduring a 'struggle session'; a masterclass in indoctrination, which began with a series of shouted indictments.

"You have oppressed the people!" The Scarred Guard boomed.

"You have followed corrupt monks!" The Slender Guard screamed.

"You're terrorists!" The Gawky Guard yelled. "Terrorists! Terrorists! Terrorists!"

A prisoner was picked at random. They were dragged to the front by their ears. And they were beaten until they bled.

Then the question and answer session began.

"Who are your enemies?" The Toothy Officer asked in Protokian.

"The Godly monks and the KPP!" Everyone had to reply in unison.

"What was the best thing that ever happened to you?"

"The revolution of democracy!"

"Who liberated Protokia?"

"The Holies!"

"Who are your saviours?"

"The Holies!"

"Who do you love?"

"The Holies!"

"Long live the Holies!"

"Long live the Holies!"

"All hail the state!"

"All hail the state!"

Hundreds of prisoners grimaced, chanted in unison, and marched back to their cells. They ate, they talked, and they slept. Then they did it all again the next day.

There were only two occasions when Charlie broke that routine.

The first came after two months, when Uncle Charlie came to visit. Charlie sat with his hands tied behind his back. The Slender Guard sat with her back to the wall. And Uncle Charlie sat opposite his nephew.

"Bad, bad," he said. "Very bad. The nephew of one of the most respected burger flippers in McRonalds, here, in prison! No. No. It's just not respectable. You might as well be a secularist. Yes. Yes. Oh my!"

The Slender Guard stood up, lunged at Uncle Charlie, and slapped him across his face.

"No Godliness!" She yelled. "I'll have you arrested if you speak another word of that god forsaken language. It doesn't even exist!"

Uncle Charlie could not speak Protokian, so he just sat there in silence. He put his hands together, closed his eyes, and prayed.

Charlie looked at his uncle and smiled.

The Slender Guard looked at her watch.

"Time's up," she said. "Let's go."

She took Charlie outside to break rocks. He stood through a struggle session, went back to his cell, and went to sleep. He woke up the next morning, and broke some more rocks.

His routine did not change until the day he was due to be released, when he was marched to Room 4, and handcuffed to a rail.

He waited.

A cockroach crawled up his leg.

A lightbulb emitted a dull glow.

The Toothy Officer stormed in, slammed the door, and sat down in front of Charlie. His knees pressed up against Charlie's knees. His nose touched Charlie's nose.

Charlie could taste that man's breath. He could smell his testosterone. He could hear his heart beat.

The Toothy Officer put his palm on Charlie's inner thigh, and slowly stroked it up towards Charlie's crotch.

"You're due to be released today," he said.

"Yes sir," Charlie replied. His eyes lit up. He felt elated. He felt ecstatic, overjoyed and thrilled.

The cockroach crawled back down his leg.

The Toothy Officer grinned. It was a sinister sort of grin, with narrow eyes, narrow lips, and narrow nostrils. With teeth which poked in every direction. And with a look which seemed to say, '*I own you*'.

"But the state has branded you a threat to the security of Natale."

"Oh."

"So the Legal Officer has placed you under '*Administrative Detention*' for another three months."

Charlie stared back at the Toothy Officer. He felt helpless. He felt weak, faint and dizzy.

He choked. He could barely breathe. His heart raced, his fingers tingled, and his chest screamed out in pain.

His nervous twitch took over the left half of his face. His eye blinked, his cheek vibrated, and his lip trembled.

The Legal Officer smiled. Teeth poked out of his mouth. Hair poked out of his ears. And bogies poked out of his nostrils.

"Of course," he said. "We could just let you go."

"Yes sir," Charlie replied.

"But we'd need something in return."

"Of course sir."

"We'd need you to become an informant. We'd need you to gather information on terrorist activities in Natale, and report back to us each week."

Charlie felt the walls close in on him. He tasted blood in his mouth. He started to sweat, shake and stammer.

He could not handle the pressure. The pressure to protect his people. The pressure to protect himself. The pressure to choose.

"How could I, sir?" He asked "How could I? How could I? How could I?"

He rubbed the back of his neck.

"You bastards have stolen our land, penned us in between your settlements, and installed aquifers which are sucking up our water.

"And now you mangy rats want my help? Do you think I'm mad, sir? Do you think I want to suffer? Really sir? How could I help you? How could I justify it?"

The Toothy Officer dropped his mug.

"Do you want to know how you can justify it?" He asked. "You can justify it because it'll save you! It'll save you from prison, from poverty, and from starvation. We'll give you a blue permit. And we'll pay you too. Our money will justify your deeds. Our money will justify everything!"

A piece of mug span around on the floor.

A tear rolled over Charlie's cheekbone.

The Toothy Officer panted like a dog.

"I can't to do it, sir," Charlie whispered.

"You don't have a choice," the Toothy Officer replied. "You'll feel like a slave, but it's your only option. That or spend another three months in prison. And then another three months. And then another three months.

"If you say 'no', you'll spend the rest of life behind bars!"

The Toothy Officer filled in Charlie's release papers.

Gunfire rang out in the distance.

Charlie wagged his finger.

"What sort of future would I be building for myself? For my children?

"My own people will hate me. No-one likes a turncoat. I'll be ostracised. I'll be a social outcast! A pariah! Just like the other informants. The natives will dump their garbage in front of my house, throw rotten fruit at me, and piss in my water barrels!"

Charlie winced.

"What sort of future would I have?"

The Toothy Officer repositioned some items on the table.

"You're right," he said. "You need to make plans for your future. We wouldn't want you to spend the rest of your life struggling to get by. That's not the Protokian way!

"No. I'll arrange for you to get into Natale University. You can study any course you like there. You'll be happy.

"If you can say one thing about the Protokians, it's that we take care of our informants.

"Education! Education will save you from this mess!"

The Toothy Officer smiled.

The cockroach scuttled away.

Charlie paused to think.

"Will you pay my tuition fees?" He asked.

The Toothy Officer chuckled.

"Of course not," he said. "Don't be silly. But we'll arrange a student loan. You won't have to pay anything back until you're working."

The Toothy Officer rocked on his chair.

"You've got a bright future ahead of you, my son. I can see that now. A bright future indeed!"

Charlie grinned.

"Okay sir," he said. "We've got ourselves a deal."

He left the prison and returned home.

* * *

A quick walk through town was enough to convince Charlie that he had been right; education would save him. Educated people were thriving. He saw accountants, lawyers and bankers, wherever he looked. He saw salesmen, managers and administrators. Clerks, actuaries and analysts.

But uneducated citizens were struggling. Butchers had been replaced by stock brokers, bakers by recruitment consultants, and sweet makers by marketing executives. Those professionals, who did not produce any goods or services, seemed to look down upon the citizens who actually made things.

Charlie walked past twenty two branches of Window Mart, the chain which had bought every other supermarket in Natale. A group of sorry looking cashiers, which included Papa Tamsin, were leaving work for the final time. Their jobs had been taken by self-checkout machines.

He walked past train drivers, whose jobs had been taken by driverless trains. Past telephone operators, whose jobs had been taken by automated systems. And past insurers, whose jobs had been taken by price comparison websites.

He walked past a Peasant Farmer, who was jinking between cars, touting counterfeit CDs to stationary motorists. His son was washing windscreens and asking for donations. They had both been forced to leave their fields when *Madsanto*, an international farming conglomerate, bought all the agricultural land in Collis. Madsanto had replaced human labour with tractors, combine harvesters, and crop sprayers. They had covered the land with chemical fertilizers, pesticides, and genetically modified crops. They had turned forests into farms, removed hedgerows, and flushed chemical waste into Natale's water.

Citizens were becoming desperate. A queue had formed outside the office of a Scammer, who was offering '*Unimaginable returns for a minimal investment*'. Unemployed locals were competing to work as lorry drivers in a war zone. And some citizens were even buying lottery tickets!

Charlie approached his university, with goose-pimples on his arms, and sweat on his brow. He looked up at the top of its wall. Red bricks stood side by side, decorated with a mixture of paint and graffiti. He looked at three tower blocks; gangly edifices which housed offices and classrooms. And he looked at some buildings which were painted salmon-pink, with angular roofs made from corrugated iron.

Charlie strolled between those buildings, scanned his student ID card, and walked into a lecture hall. He sat down, removed a notepad from his satchel, and gazed at a girl in a floral dress. A coil of hair hung over one side of her face. A pendant hung from her neck.

Charlie stared at that pretty girl.

That pretty girl shook her head.

A Bespectacled Lecturer cleared her throat.

"Welcome to *Marketing 101*," she said in Protokian. "Over the months which follow, you'll learn how to serve your future employers. You'll learn how to become profitable employees. You'll become the finest patriots in the land!"

Charlie struggled to keep up. He scribbled notes on top of other notes. He looked up at the board and down at his pad. He thought about the subject matter, and he thought about the pretty girl.

He perspired.

Charlie had attended Atamow High for seven years, but the education he received had been limited. Only five teachers remained at that school after the uprising. The others had all fled in fear.

So Charlie had read to educate himself, and he had listened to the Humpbacked Priest. But he was still behind the other students. They had all graduated from high school. Most of them had gone to private schools. Very few of them worked as much as Charlie. Some of them did not have any jobs at all.

"The *'Four Ps'*!" The Bespectacled Lecturer continued. "Position, promotion, price and product."

Charlie scribbled.

"The Four Ps will help you to achieve your firms' three goals; to make profit, to make more profit, and to make even more profit!

"The Four Ps! Position! Promotion! Price! Product!

"Position! You'll target citizens who will buy things they don't need.

"Promotion! You'll convince them to buy things they don't want.

"Price! You'll entice them to buy things they can't afford.

"Product! You'll persuade them to buy things which won't last."

Charlie stared at the pretty girl.

A new slide flashed up on the board.

The Bespectacled Lecturer walked across the stage.

"Position!" She repeated. "Promotion! Price! Product!

"This module will be hard. You'll push your minds further than you ever thought they could go. You'll experience mental anguish beyond your wildest imagination. You'll struggle. But you'll be all the better for it. You'll become lean, mean, marketing machines. You'll become the greatest marketers on the planet. And you'll be ready to make loads of money.

"Position! Promotion! Price! Product!

"Sell to the Godlies and sell to the Holies!"

The Bespectacled Lecturer took a deep breath, chewed the end of her pencil, and nodded enthusiastically.

Her class nodded back.

Charlie picked up his bag, left the lecture hall, and looked around the foyer. He saw the pretty girl, who was staring into her mobile phone.

"Hu, hu, hello," he stuttered.

"Hello scribbler," the pretty girl replied without looking up.

"Scribbler?"

"You spent the whole lecture scribbling away. I've never seen anyone write so much."

Charlie giggled, gurgled, and tapped his notepad.

"This is my Pineapple EyePad!" He said.

"That's a jotter," the pretty girl replied.

Charlie shook his head.

"When I grow up I'm going to be rich like the Holies," he explained. "I'm going to buy a real EyePad. But until then, this'll have to do."

"If that pile of tatty paper is an Eyepad, my jotter is a *Woogle Plexus*," the pretty girl replied. "And everyone knows that Woogles are better than Pineapples."

"What?" Charlie shouted back with fake horror. "That's slander! Poppycock! Bunkum!"

The pretty girl giggled.

"You're cute," she said.

"You're pretty," Charlie replied.

They both smiled.

"My name's Charlie by the way."

"My name's Rosie."

Charlie paused. He felt nervous. He felt anxious, timid and tense.

His face turned red. He blushed. He trembled so much, it made him nauseous. His heart raced and his chest constricted. A hot flash shot across his torso. His nervous twitch went into overdrive.

"Wi, wi, will you be my girlfriend?" He stuttered.

"Yeah, right," Rosie replied. "I don't even know you!"

"Get to know me."

"Why?"

"Because I'm nice."

Rosie laughed.

Some students rushed by.

A Temp handed Charlie a flyer for a mortgage education program.

"What are you waiting for?" Rosie asked.

"What am I waiting for?"

"Aren't you going to ask me out for a drink?"

"Oh, of course! Would you like a drink?"

Rosie twirled her hair.

"Maybe," she said. "We'll see."

She flicked her hair behind her head, turned, and walked away.

Charlie watched her leave. He stared at her hour-glass figure. He ogled her tiny bottom. And he savoured her floral perfume.

A cat wandered into the building.

* * *

Three things occupied Charlie during the months which followed; his studying, his flirting, and his informing.

He became comfortable with technical jargon like *'branding'*, *'market share'* and *'monetisation'*. He studied *'loss prevention'*, *'market segmentation'*, *'customer preservation'*, and *'state legislation'*. He learnt how to put a price on everything.

He nagged Rosie whenever he saw her. Eventually they went out for a drink. They went out for a meal, a concert, and a night of dancing. After two months had passed, Charlie called Rosie his girlfriend, and she did not complain. After six months had passed, they moved into a flat, which they shared with six other students.

Charlie reported to the police station once a week, every week, without fail.

On his way, he walked past thirty three branches of McRonalds, which had taken over Burger Queen, Wompy Burger and Sandwich Way, to form a fast-food monopoly. He walked past eight branches of Toots Pharmacy, which had formed a pharmaceutical monopoly. And he walked past eleven branches of PC Universe, which had formed an electronics monopoly. Those monopolies had quashed the competition, suppressed supply, and increased prices. Their employees only just earned enough to survive, but their shareholders all thrived. So a few citizens had become rich, but most were still poor.

Charlie walked through six checkpoints.

He walked past a group of buskers, who were earning pennies for performing priceless tunes. A crowd watched their three dimensional performance, through the two dimensional screens on their mobile phones. Pedestrians took selfies as they walked down the street. They bumped into each other, and kept on walking.

Loudspeakers played machinegun fire and adverts:

'Bilette Razors! The best a man can get!'

Rat-a-tat-tat.

'Pony Mobiles! Don't settle for good. Demand great!'

Rat-a-tat-tat.

'Pissburg Lager! Probably the best beer in the world!'

Rat-a-tat-tat.

Charlie turned into a wide street, which was flanked by narrow pavements. He walked past trees, which burst through the concrete. And he entered a police station, which was full of criminals.

He looked into a camera.

"Name?" A robotic voice demanded.

"Charlie."

"Number?"

"54-46."

"Role?"

"Informant."

There was a pause.

Charlie scratched some plaque from his teeth.

The door buzzed, and Charlie entered an empty waiting room. He sat down on a nondescript green sofa and waited. He waited and waited and waited. He waited for an hour in all. An hour in which there was nothing to do other than stare at the second hand of a slow moving clock.

"54-46!" A voice finally rang out. "Step forward."

A door swung open and Charlie stepped through. He sat down in front of a black table. A Dark Policeman, who wore a black uniform, entered through a black door. A bright light illuminated the black floor.

"Well, well, well," the Dark Policeman said. "What do have we here then?"

"Charlie sir."

"<u>C</u>harlie, <u>H</u>otel, <u>A</u>lpha, <u>R</u>omeo, <u>L</u>ima, <u>I</u>ndia, <u>E</u>cho?"

"No, just Charlie sir."

"Hmm. Yes. Do citizens know you're spying on them, '*Just Charlie Sir*'?"

"No sir. I'm very subtle, sir. I've never given myself away!"

The Dark Policeman shook his head.

"You need to stop thinking about yourself," he said. "You need to think about others."

"Yes sir."

"Citizens need to know you're spying on them."

"Yes sir."

"They need to think that *everyone* is spying on them."

"Yes sir."

"They need to feel that they can't do anything without the state finding out."

"Yes sir."

"They need to feel that they can't break any law without getting caught."

"Yes sir."

"The supremacy of law is absolute!"

"Yes sir."

"All hail the state!"

"Yes sir."

The Dark Policeman smiled.

"So what are you going to do?"

"Tell citizens I'm spying on them."

"Don't be silly."

"Sorry sir."

"Don't be sorry."

"No sir."

"Let citizens know you're spying on them!"

"Yes sir. Definitely sir. How sir?"

"By being unsubtle. By being nosy. By interfering. By asking probing questions. By being a goddamn pain in the arse!"

"Yes sir."

"That's my boy!"

The Dark Policeman opened a drawer. He removed a ten thousand page manual on how to manage paperwork, a memo from the Minister of Pencil Pushing, and a box of luxury chocolates.

"Have a treat," he said.

Charlie took a chocolate, put it in his mouth, and chewed.

His seat creaked.

The Dark Policeman patted Charlie's head.

"Good boy," he said.

Charlie grinned like a Cheshire cat.

"Now what did you find out this week?" The Dark Policeman asked.

"The Psychology Professor is telling his students that citizens were happy before the peaceful liberation of Protokia," Charlie replied. "And there's a girl in the refugee camp, called Tamsin, who used to be in a counter-revolutionary band."

"Good boy!"

The Dark Policeman held out the box of chocolates.

Charlie threw one into his mouth. Sickly liquor slipped down the back of his throat. Bitter chocolate got stuck between his gums.

The Dark Policeman put an A4 manila envelope on the table. He removed five photos and placed them side by side.

"Do you recognize any of these citizens?" He asked.

Charlie investigated each picture in turn.

"This one works in Pizza House," he said. "I've never seen these two before. And this one is a busker, sir. He plays outside a McRonalds every morning."

Charlie stopped at the fifth photo. It was a picture of Oliver. Charlie did not want to betray his best friend, nor did he want to lie.

He felt flummoxed. He felt trapped, surrounded and lame.

His head span and his eyes swirled. His skin felt clammy. His breathing became harried. He shivered. And his heart raced.

The Dark Policeman nudged the photo of Oliver.

"And this one?" He asked. "Remember to tell us everything you know. We'll put you back in prison if you withhold information."

The Dark Policeman brushed his dark moustache.

"We know more than you realise," he said. "We know everything about you. We know about your friends, your activities, and your tastes.

We know when you're lying. And we don't like it. Not one bit!"

Charlie grimaced.

He did not want to give Oliver away. But he suspected that the Dark Policeman already knew about his friend. That this was just a test. That his testimony would not affect Oliver, but his silence would affect him.

He perspired.

His energy dissipated. His head throbbed and his stomach churned. He had to clench his sphincter, to stop his bowels from emptying. His joints ached, his muscles tensed, and his chest pounded.

His nervous twitch flared up.

"His name is Oliver, sir," Charlie said. "He's my friend. He's a good guy. He's a Protokian patriot!"

The Dark Policeman tensed his lips, looked into Charlie's eyes, and tapped the picture of Oliver.

"Where was this '*Oliver*' during the uprising?" He asked.

Charlie's stomach dropped.

He inhaled and exhaled. In and out. In and out. In and out. His peripheral blood vessels constricted. He blushed. Butterflies fluttered in his stomach, and pimples covered his skin.

His nervous twitch went into overdrive.

"I, I, I," Charlie stuttered. "He was with me, sir."

"And where were you?"

"I was in town, sir."

"What were you doing?"

"Buying oranges, sir."

"With Oliver?"

"Yes sir."

"And what happened next?"

"We got swept up in the crowd, sir. It engulfed us and carried us along."

"So you took part in the uprising then?"

"No sir."

"What happened?"

"Citizens marched around us, sir. They pushed us towards the castle."

"The castle?"

"Yes sir."

"And then what happened?"

"Soldiers threw tear gas grenades into the crowd."

"That must have been scary!"

"Yes sir."

"It must have made you angry."

"No sir."

"'*No sir*'?"

"No sir."

"Why not?"

"The soldiers were only doing their job, sir."

A moth flew into the light.

Charlie's chair squeaked.

The Dark Policeman thumped the table. He leaned over Charlie, and stared into Charlie's eyes.

"This '*Oliver*' fellow threw a grenade at a soldier, didn't he?"

"No sir."

"But a grenade did hit this '*Oliver*' on the head, didn't it?"

"Yes sir."

"And this '*Oliver*' did throw it away, didn't he?"

"Yes sir."

"He threw it at a soldier!"

"No sir."

"'*No sir*'?"

"No sir."

The Dark Policeman wiped his brow.

"Where did he throw it?"

"Away sir."

"'*Away sir*'?"

"Yes sir."

"Away where?"

"Just away, sir. The tear gas stung our eyes. It hurt. So someone had to remove the canister. It was Oliver who threw it away."

"Away?"

"Away, sir."

"Where did it land?"

"I don't know, sir."

"You don't know?"

"I couldn't see, sir. It was too crowded."

"You couldn't see?"

"No sir."

"So it could have hit a soldier?"

"I don't know, sir. I couldn't see, sir. I'm sorry, sir."

The Dark Policeman smiled.

"It could have hit a soldier," he said to himself.

He held out the tray of chocolates.

"Take one," he said. "Good boy."

Charlie shook his head.

His chair squeaked.

Everything was black, apart from the photograph of Oliver, which was illuminated by the light.

* * *

Charlie did not see Oliver that week, the next week, or the week after that.

Oliver did not turn up for his shift at McRonalds. He did not watch Natale FC's big match. And he did not appear in town.

Charlie knocked on Oliver's door, but no-one answered. No-one he spoke to had seen Oliver. No-one had heard from him in days.

Charlie worried. He felt guilty, paranoid and ashamed.

He snapped.

"I've had enough," he told Rosie, outside a Star & Bucks.

Triangular segments of amber sunlight peaked through a bushy tree. Litter swirled around. Pedestrians rushed by.

"We need to kick the Holies out! We can't live with them; they're too violent. And we can't let this stalemate continue; it's killing us. They're playing for time, and we're playing into their hands. They're becoming more powerful every day. We need to fight them every day, or we'll never get our country back."

"You're crazy," Rosie replied. "Fight them every day? You're mad!

"Confrontations won't benefit us. Let the refugees throw stones and turn to violence; it's not for us, not here, not now. Fighting won't change anything. The carrots are already cooked!"

Rosie tutted.

"If you fight back you'll be blacklisted," she continued. "You'll lose your blue permit, you won't be allowed into Protokia, and you'll end up in a low-paid job. You'll never own an EyePad or a Fastari.

"Pfft! You should be grateful to the Protokians. Look at all the wealth they've brought us! How dare you talk about fighting them? Don't be so bloody stupid.

"Rebels aren't heroes to me. They're fools!"

Rosie tapped the table, which had been made by a Protokian firm. Charlie drank a *Poka Cola*, which had been imported by a Holy. They both ignored a flyer, which called for *'Boycotts, Sanctions and Divestments'*.

The Mad Lady walked by.

"The passive will become pacified!" She wailed. "The fighters will be fought. Your debt will imprison you. Your education will never set you free. It's your destiny!"

"Oh shut up," Rosie and Charlie replied in unison. "What do you know, you batty old witch?"

They looked at each other and laughed.

A cat rubbed up against Charlie's leg.

The Mad Lady hobbled away.

"I'm going to the temple," Charlie said. "Maybe I can find solace there. It's worth a try."

Charlie had not visited the temple for weeks, he had forgotten to say his prayers, and he had suffered from nightmares as a result. He saw angry priests, ruthless ghouls and vengeful angels, every time he went to sleep.

Rosie put some cream on her lips.

"That's the most sensible thing you've said today," she replied.

Charlie finished his drink, kissed Rosie, and walked away.

He walked past a hospital, which *Supa Healthcare* had bought from the government in a cut-price deal. Past a branch of the *Post Office*, which had just been privatised. And past a gas silo, which was owned by *Exoff Imobile*, even though it had been built with taxpayer's money.

He walked past a Dog Walker, who worked for an Accountant, who was too occupied to walk her dog. Past a Cleaner, who worked for a Lawyer, who was too occupied to clean his house. And past a Nanny, who worked for a Judge, who was too occupied to raise her children.

He walked past some children, who were marching, and reciting a military chant. Past some children who were playing '*Catch*', using an undetonated grenade. And past some children who were playing '*Natives and Occupiers*', using plastic toy guns. Death, for them, was impermanent. They were shot dead one minute, and up on their feet the next.

Charlie approached the temple.

He removed his shoes and washed his feet. He walked up the marble steps, passed some religious icons, and got down on his knees to pray.

Minutes passed by in quiet contemplation. Charlie drifted off into another world. A world without Protokians, policemen or soldiers. He felt emancipated. He felt entranced, mesmerized and free.

He heard a sports car pull up outside.

The Humpbacked Priest entered. He hobbled over to the donations box, emptied its contents into a leather bag, and put that bag in his pocket.

A bead of sweat dropped from his frog-like face.

Charlie twitched. His cheek vibrated and his eye blinked.

"Good," the Humpbacked Priest said. "Praise the Lord!"

He sprinkled some petals into a font.

Charlie lit some incense.

The Humpbacked Priest said a prayer.

"What brings you here today, babushka?" He finally asked.

Charlie paused.

"Do you think religion can help us to find ourselves?" He replied. "Do you think it can strengthen us, sir? Do you think it can help us to regain our country?"

The Humpbacked Priest laughed.

"My dear boy," he said. "Without religion, we're all lost. We aren't worth bukpis! We might as well lay down in the ground and bake bagels.

"Of course religion can help us to find ourselves. Of course it can give us strength.

"But you're talking poppycock when you speak of '*regaining our country*'. Oi vey! This is our country! We never lost it. It's been here all along!"

Charlie looked at the Humpbacked Priest with hungry eyes.

A petal skipped across the floor.

The Humpbacked Priest put his sweaty hand on Charlie's shoulder.

"The Protokians have brought freedom to this land," he concluded. "And they've brought wealth which is trickling down to everyone. The Protokians are our babushkas. Our friends! So please don't talk to me about regaining countries. Oi gavelt! Please don't speak with a stiff neck in here. This is a holy place. A godly place. Not a political place. Oh yoy yoy! Show some respect! You shiksa! You nebbish! You alter cocker!"

The Humpbacked Priest raised his eyebrows and nodded towards the donations box.

Charlie tensed his cheeks, donated five dollars, and left.

A single drop of rain fell from the cloudless sky.

* * *

Rosie made some more tea.

Charlie tapped his call-up card on the table.

Their televisions continued to mutter.

"I can't do it," Charlie said. "I can't serve them. The Holies are our enemies! How could I possibly serve in their army?"

Rosie closed her eyes and took a deep breath.

"Not this again," she said. "We're powerless, kind and simple hearted people. We can't be fighting our masters; it's not in our nature. The Protokians have preserved our culture and traditions. They've made us rich. You should be grateful."

Charlie tapped his call-up card on the table.

"I could get out of it," he said. "I'd just have to pay eight thousand dollars."

Rosie shook her head.

"And where are you going to get that sort of money from?"

Charlie shrugged.

"I heard you can get fake IDs," he suggested. "You can claim you're under eighteen. And you can hide. The army can't conscript you if they can't catch you."

"They'll catch you eventually," Rosie replied.

"Not if we kick them out first."

"And do you think that's going to happen? Really?"

"I don't know. I don't know what to do. I'm being asked to choose between my country and my people! I don't know what to do."

"Choose yourself! If you join the army, you'll make contacts all over Protokia. You'll meet citizens who'll get you onto the corporate ladder. But if you refuse, you'll be blacklisted. You'll spend the rest of your life working in McRonalds. Think of yourself!"

Charlie tapped his call-up card on the table.

"Okay," he said. "Okay. Oh my!"

He put the mobile he used to talk to Holies in his right pocket. He put the mobile he used to talk to Godlies in his left pocket. He kissed Rosie, and he went out to inform.

He walked past natives who lived as prisoners in their own town, and immigrants who lived lives of total freedom. He walked past fat citizens who stuffed food into their mouths, and skinny citizens who did not have a morsel to eat. He walked past workers who produced a lot, but only consumed a little. And bosses who produced a little, but consumed a lot.

He entered a police station, which was full of criminals, and looked into a camera.

"Name?" A robotic voice demanded.

"Charlie."

"Number?"

"54-46."

"Role?"

"Informant."

There was a pause.

Charlie scratched some plaque from his teeth.

The door buzzed, and Charlie walked into an empty waiting room. He sat down on a nondescript green sofa and waited. He waited and waited and waited.

"54-46!" A voice finally rang out. "Step forward."

A door swung open and Charlie stepped through it. He sat down in front of a black table. The Dark Policeman entered through a black door, and sat down opposite Charlie.

"My dear boy," he said. "This could be the last time I see you!"

"Yes sir."

"You're being conscripted."

"Yes sir."

"So you won't be an informant anymore."

"No sir."

The Dark Policeman gave Charlie a sympathetic look.

"You look downhearted," he said.

"Yes sir."

"What's the matter?"

"I don't want to fight my people."

The Dark Policeman chuckled.

"We don't want you to fight your people either," he said. "Your people are our people. We're all family. We're all citizens of this great nation. No, we only want you to fight the guerillas; the KPP. They're nobody's people."

The Dark Policeman brushed his dark moustache.

"The villages are already full of conscripts. We've told the villagers to join our *Village Guards*, or leave home without their possessions. We've expelled whole villages! We've set whole villages on fire! But most villagers have joined us. They've changed sides overnight, en masse, like umbrellas opening in the rain. Voila! Click! Boom! All together! All at once!"

The Dark Policeman chortled.

"You won't be fighting your people," he said. "You'll be fighting with them!"

"Yes sir."

"We'll erect a statue of you in your village!"

"Yes sir."

"But if you don't sign up, we'll tell the KPP that you're an informant. They'll slaughter you. *Click*. Just like that! It's not safe. No, you'd be much safer in the army."

"Yes sir."

"So what are you waiting for?"

"Nothing sir."

"Good boy!"

The Dark Policeman passed Charlie a tray of chocolates.

Charlie sucked the hazelnut praline out of a milk chocolate shell.

His chair creaked.

* * *

Charlie turned the televisions off.

Rosie hugged him.

"My love," she said. "I'm proud of you. You're defending us all!"

Charlie chewed his bottom lip.

"I'm being conscripted," he said. "It's not like I'm putting an end to global warming."

"No," Rosie replied. "You're putting an end to terrorism. It's far more important."

Charlie bowed his head.

Rosie answered her mobile.

Charlie picked up his backpack, waved goodbye, and left.

He walked past a suited Businessman who held a briefcase, and a raggedy Tramp who held a begging bowl. Past a bus, which contained one hundred citizens, and a limousine which contained one Bureaucrat. Past a Lady who was wearing golden chains around her neck, and a Prisoner who was wearing steel chains around his ankles.

Charlie got onto an army bus.

Godly conscripts sat down around him.

They drove along a motorway, and gazed out at a row of electronic billboards.

'*Express yourself every day!*' A *Pillips* advert dictated.

'*Have a break. Have a Pit Pat!*' A second advert decreed.

'*Don't just book it. Tommy Cook it!*' A third advert demanded.

Charlie got off the bus. He was given a set of uniforms. And he was escorted to his dorm; a long cabin with a row of beds on either side.

Charlie looked around at the conscripts who were sitting on those beds. They all looked lost and forlorn. They all had long faces, sunken shoulders, and droopy heads.

But Charlie beamed with joy.

"Oliver!" He cheered.

"Charlie!" His friend cheered back.

They ran up to each other and embraced. They gripped each other so tightly, they could barely breathe. They held each other at arms' length, and gazed into each other's eyes.

"Where have you been?" Charlie asked.

"In prison," Oliver replied. "They said they'd release me if I joined the army. So here I am!"

"It's good to see you!"

"It's good to see *you*!"

They both smiled.

They both spent a moment in silent contemplation.

They both jumped up when the Bulky Officer stormed in.

"Attention!" He boomed.

His steel-capped boots created a *rat-a-tat* beat as they stomped across the metal floor. His deep nasal breaths filled the air. His necklaces clinked.

"Blue heads!" He yelled. "Follow me! March! Left! Right! Left! Right! Left! Right! Left!"

Charlie and the other new recruits followed the Bulky Officer past a row of dormitory cabins, an assault course, and a firing range.

They entered a hall which smelled of cheesy fish. New recruits stood in a grid. Officers flanked them on both sides And a Rigid Officer stood at the front. Dust nestled in the creases which ran across his face. His nostrils formed a 'v'. And his eyes were as cloudy as winter.

No-one said a word.

A fly flew into a cobweb.

The Rigid Officer raised his fist, stamped, and glared at the opposite wall.

"Rule number one!" He boomed. "You're not allowed to arrest Holies.

"Rule number two! You're to disguise yourselves as Godlies, disrupt Godlies, and bamboozle Godlies.

"Rule number three! Show no mercy! Kill anyone! Kill everyone! And always verify your kills.

"Rule number four! Innovate! Use any weapons you can. Cars, stones, household tools. The lot!

"Rule number five! Make a mess! Hack bodies into pieces. Create a gnarly halo of blood. Create a crazy balagan!"

The Rigid Officer punched the air five times.

"Rules! Rules! Rules!" He boomed. "I love rules. You love rules. We all love rules.

"The supremacy of law is absolute!

"Where would we be without the law? Nowhere! We all need rules. Never break the rules!"

The Rigid Officer marched away.

The other officers marched behind him.

Charlie marched into a month full of early mornings, cold showers, and salty porridge; long parades, repetitive drills, and pompous ceremonies; tactical lectures, military training, and army indoctrination.

* * *

Charlie enjoyed his military training; it allowed his competitive side to bloom.

"I bet I can finish this run before you," he told Oliver.

It was a crisp autumn morning. Frost glistened on the grass, and sunbeams glimmered in the sky. Golden leaves carpeted the earth, and silver clouds cloaked the heavens. Robins cheeped and sparrows chirped.

Oliver looked at Charlie and nodded.

"You're on," he replied.

He spat on his palm, and stretched it out to shake hands with Charlie.

Charlie cringed. He slowly lifted his hand towards his mouth.

Oliver swung around and ran away.

"Oi!" Charlie shouted. "Come back here, you cheeky rascal!"

He sprang into motion and chased after Oliver.

They ran down muddy tracks which were covered in twigs, icy trails which smelled of damp hay, and paths which swerved one way and then the other. They skidded around corners, scaled steep inclines, and slid down rutted hills. They whizzed past trees which pointed upwards, trees which sprawled outwards, and trees which had fallen down.

They overtook a Keen Conscript, who had a stitch. A Pink Conscript, who was struggling to breathe. And a Muscular Conscript, whose clothes were drenched in sweat.

They ran past a poster which the *Holy Defence League* had nailed to a tree. It said, '*Gas the KPP*'.

And they ran past the Rigid Officer, who punched the air and stamped his boot.

Charlie sped on ahead. But no matter how fast he ran, he could not overtake Oliver.

So Oliver made it to the finish line before Charlie. He panted, turned around, and stuck out his chalky tongue.

Charlie shrugged.

"You're the fastest conscript here!" The Popeyed Officer bellowed. He stared into Oliver's eyes.

"Yes sir!" Oliver replied. He grinned, mopped his brow, and blushed with boyish pride.

"I see potential in you!" The Popeyed Officer continued. "You've worked hard, and hard work gets rewarded. You're on track to be a member of the *Elite Squad*!

"Report to my office at zero eight hundred hours. Tomorrow, you run a double marathon!"

Oliver grimaced.

He turned and wagged his fist at Charlie.

Charlie covered his mouth and giggled.

* * *

Charlie's training concluded with a field exercise. His unit was made to police a hustings for the Protokian elections.

They marched past posters which said, '*Freedom! Democracy! Reform!*' Past posters which said, '*Vote! Make sure your voice is heard.*' And past posters which said, '*Protokia! The only democracy in the region.*'

But Godlies could only vote if they had blue permits. So whilst the Godlies constituted eighty percent of the population, they only made up nine percent of the electorate. And each party needed to receive at least ten percent of the vote, to secure representation in parliament.

Angry at that injustice, a gaggle of activists had assembled to protest. They stood to the right of a rickety wooden stage. They held up placards. They shouted, '*From the mountains to the sea, this land of ours will be free*'. And they ignored the gunfire which rang out in the hills.

Tamsin stood next to those protestors, next to a Hawker who was selling Poka Cola, and next to her three children.

"This is boring," Tamsin's Daughter said.

"This is important," Tamsin replied.

"But I'm bored."

"Well you won't be bored once we've got our land back. You'll be too busy working in our fields!"

"I don't want to work in our fields. OMG! I want an EyePhone!"

"Really? Don't you want your freedom?"

"I guess."

"So what would you rather have; an EyePhone or your freedom?"

Tamsin's Daughter looked down at her feet, ran her toe back through the dirt, and shrugged.

"I'd rather have an EyePhone, mummy," she said. "Please can I have an EyePhone? Please?"

Tamsin sighed.

"Please can I have a new war game?"

"You had a new war game six months ago."

"That one's ancient. OMG! A new one was released today. Please can I have it, mummy? Please?"

"No!"

"Please can I have a McRonalds? Please? *Mmm. I'm lovin' it*! Please can I have a Sappy Meal?"

Tamsin shook her head.

"What's wrong with my cooking?" She scolded. "When I was your age, we ate whatever we were given, and we never complained. But you! *'I want a McRonalds! I want a Pizza House! I want a Greasy Fried Chicken!'* Pfft! We didn't even eat meat when I was a girl, yet we were still content. But you! It doesn't matter what I get you; you're never satisfied."

Tamsin's Daughter giggled.

Tamsin sighed, rolled her eyes, and looked up at the sky.

Charlie's unit formed a human chain, walked towards the protestors, and escorted them away.

A Compere walked across the stage. He wore an ill-fitting shirt, which was buttoned up to the neck. And he wore a tie, which was knotted so tight, it looked like it had been put on by an enemy who was trying to strangle him.

He picked up a microphone, and used it to address the crowd.

"Hello, one and all!" He cheered. "Whoever you vote for, make sure you vote. Make sure you play your part in making this wonderful country even better. And remember; we're in this together!"

A group of paid cheerleaders, started to cheer:

'*Democracy and freedom for Protokia*'.

'*May the Godlies and the Holies unite*'.

'*Long live Atamow*'.

They were surrounded by refugees and locals, villagers and townsfolk, monks and lay people, youngsters and pensioners, students and workers. There were as many women as there were men. And they all stood together in the snow.

Sunshine reflected off that snow. A dog sniffed another dog's anus. And a Short Refugee, who wore long chequered socks and a plastic red nose, played his battered accordion.

A Giant Local threw a snowball at a Dwarfish Official. A Buff Refugee threw a snowball at a Skeletal Official. And a Ratty Girl threw a snowball at her friend.

Some of them chanted:

'*Democracy and freedom for Protokia*'.

'*May the Godlies and the Holies unite*'.

'*Long live Atamow*'.

The Humpbacked Priest hobbled across the stage, pointed at some random citizens, and then took the microphone from the Compere.

His prayer shawl was covered in advertisements. There was a Rablays eagle on his shoulder, a Window Mart sun on his chest, and a Punilever '*P*' on his crotch.

He looked at his audience, snarled and sneered:

"You may know me as your friendly neighbourhood priest. But let me tell you this; I handle my gun just as well as I handle my rosary! Oi vey! I understand politics just as much as I understand religion. And I know that there's only one man who has the Godlies' interests at heart.

"That man is Atamow! The man who liberated our nation. The man who brought us wealth beyond our wildest imaginations. The man who fights for God.

"And so I have a message for every member of my congregation. For every babushka and every bubeleh. For every balabusta and every boychick.

"My message is a simple one: that we must vote en masse! We must vote together! We must vote for Atamow!"

The paid cheerleaders all cheered:

'*Atamow! Atamow! Atamow!*'

Charlie shook his head.

A Shabby Local threw a snowball at a Scatty Refugee.

"If we vote for anyone else and Atamow wins, he won't help us. He won't invest in Natale's infrastructure, or encourage businesses to move here. Oi va voi! We'll all suffer. We might as well jump into a lake!

"So we have to vote for Atamow together. He'll reward our faithfulness. He'll make us all rich!"

The Humpbacked Priest grinned like a satisfied cat. His whiskers pointed upwards, his bottom wagged, and his head tilted to one side.

"Thank-you for circumcising your ears," he purred. "This spiel was brought to you by Star & Bucks, '*The home of great coffee*'."

Charlie shook his head.

A Messy Refugee threw a snowball at a Tidy Local.

The paid cheerleaders all cheered:

'*Atamow! Atamow! Atamow!*'

* * *

The Popeyed Officer stared into Charlie's eyes.

"Prevention!" He barked. "You'll punish the Godlies before they break the law."

The Popeyed Officer stared out the window.

"Last week, the KPP left a bomb near a Godly school. We have reason to believe that terrorist attack originated in Valley Village. And so we must attack Valley Village, to prevent them from attacking us again."

The Popeyed Officer stared at a poster.

"Prevention!" He barked. "You'll punish the Godlies before they break the law.

"You'll shoot any Godly you see with a stone. A stone is a deadly weapon! I've seen someone injured by a stone. If a Godly child holds a stone, you can shoot him in his legs. If you miss his legs and kill him, you'll be fined twenty dollars.

"If you see a Godly with a grenade, you can kill her too!

"If you see a Godly acting suspiciously, you can take him out!

"Don't show any leniency. Peace will not be achieved through leniency. Oh no! If you want peace, you need to fight in wars."

The Popeyed Officer stared at the door. Then he marched through it.

* * *

Charlie's unit marched towards Valley Village. They had bags on their backs, guns in their hands, and maps in their trouser pockets.

It was the midnight hour, and the moon was nowhere to be seen. Charlie wore a cloak of darkness as he descended down the other side of the hill.

Grass rustled in the breeze.

An owl hooted.

A wolf howled.

Rat-a-tat-tat. Rat-a-tat-tat. Rat-a-tat-tat.

The sound of KPP machinegun fire burst in Charlie's ears. He heard a bullet bounce off a rock to his right. He felt a bullet whizz above his head. And he saw a puff of dust in front of him.

He dived behind a boulder.

His heart pounded. Butterflies fluttered in his stomach, and his spine tingled. His hands shook.

His nervous twitch went into overdrive. His left cheek pulsated as quickly as the machinegun fire. In and out. In and out. In and out.

His left eye opened and closed at a manic rate. His eyebrow vibrated.

He concentrated on his breathing.

His unit waited there for hours. They looked up at the stars, and down at the earth. They looked down towards Valley Village.

When Charlie's pulse had finally settled, his unit continued down the hill. They crawled on their bellies to avoid detection. Soil stained their hands, stones tore their clothes, and thistles pricked their skin.

They slithered like snakes.

Rat-a-tat-tat. Rat-a-tat-tat. Rat-a-tat-tat.

Charlie paused. He pressed his body into the earth and closed his eyes.

A rabbit ran into its burrow.

A squirrel ran up a tree.

The sun rose.

Charlie caught his breath, paused, and then spied on his childhood village.

He saw weeds which were overgrown, and trees which had stopped growing. Houses which were empty, and bins which were full. Streets which were wet, and wells which were dry.

He saw a signpost which said, '*Welcome to Rebel Village: A village of patriots!*' A poster which said, '*There is no future which is not built in the present*'. And graffiti which said, '*Follow your dreams*'. The word '*Cancelled*' had been painted across it.

He saw four children who were painting pictures of explosive scenes, with villagers in unbreakable shackles, and Protokians in unbreachable armour. He saw three children who were playing '*Occupiers and Natives*', using pomegranate juice for blood. And he saw two children who were holding a tube bomb, which contained petrol and a wick.

"I've got the hardest throw in the village!" A Dark Boy boasted, whilst fiddling with his Poka Cola t-shirt.

"You're a real professor of the uprising!" A Blinky Girl replied, whilst fiddling with her Fokia phone.

They laughed until their eyes filled up with tears.

"Those kids are terrorists," the Pink Conscript said. "They've got petrol bombs. We need to act before they attack us!"

He looked at his comrades.

"I'm not shooting him," a Spotty Conscript replied. "Do it yourself. That kid is a Godly. I'm not killing one of our own."

Charlie tensed his cheeks.

"Well one of us has got to do it," the Pink Conscript continued. "Rules! Rules! Rules! We need to follow the rules. Never break the rules!"

Charlie spat. A globule of saliva and phlegm left his mouth with a '*plop*'. It landed on a dock leaf.

A dock leaf landed on some snow.

Some snow landed on a twig.

"We should all shoot together," Charlie suggested. "That way, we won't know who fired the fatal bullet. We can each assume it was someone else, and avoid all personal guilt."

The Spotty Conscript shrugged.

The Pink Conscript nodded.

They all lifted their guns, looked down their barrels, pulled their triggers and fired.

'*Boom!!!*'

One single sound filled the air.

Birds filled the air.

Blood filled the air.

Blood squirted in every direction. The Dark Boy's arms bounced across the ground. His legs rebounded off a wall. And his torso rattled between buildings.

The Dark Boy's head landed in front of Charlie.

A tear had formed in the corner of his aquamarine eye. It rolled over his prominent cheekbone, and dropped onto his burgundy lip.

Charlie froze. He looked at the Dark Boy's head with pale-faced horror. He realised who it was.

"My brother," he whispered. "We've shot my brother!"

He cried.

He wept.

He cradled his brother's head as if it was a baby. He stroked his brother's hair, and looked into his brother's eyes. He saw a sort of horror which he had never seen before. And he felt a demonic sort of horror himself.

He felt helpless, lost and confused.

A tear formed in his eye, rolled over his cheekbone, and dropped onto his burgundy lip.

SECTION THREE

ADULTHOOD

9. TAMSIN

Jon, the First Wife, Tamsin and her four children, lounged on their sofas. A video of a fire played on a heat-emitting screen, which Jon had bought from Idea. Jon's phone rested on his thigh.

That flat had felt like a palace when they first moved in, after twelve years of marriage. Tamsin used to *'ooh'* and *'aah'* whenever she walked into a different room. The way the lights turned on by themselves amazed her. She spent hours on her phone, changing the colour of those lights. She spent hours staring at her fridge, which re-ordered food whenever it ran out, and told her what items needed to be eaten.

Jon sank into his floating armchair, which bobbed up and down. Tamsin's Daughter injected some super-Botox into her cheeks. And Tamsin tapped her phone.

The four pillars of her telebeamer buzzed. They vibrated. Light-beams sprayed forth, creating a grey static blur, which slowly took shape. A two metre tall vision of Papa Tamsin, made solely of shaky light, wobbled from side to side.

"Well hello!" He cheered in Protokian.

Everyone spoke Protokian. Godliness had become a dead language; a cute cultural relic, resigned to the archives of history, with no place in the post-modern world.

"How's your eyesight?" Tamsin asked.

Papa Tamsin beamed with pride.

"Perfect!" He cheered. "It's never been better! It's like I was never blind. The microchips Rablays implanted into my eyes have given me twenty-twenty vision."

Tamsin grinned. She filled an electronic water pipe with apple flavoured e-tobacco, and pressed the 'on' switch. A light turned green. She passed the mouthpiece to Jon, who put it to his lips and inhaled.

The First Wife used her phone to turn the tea maker on.

Tamsin's Youngest Son looked up at his grandfather.

"Tell us about Doomba, grandpapa," he pleaded. "Go on pops! It's the best village in the world!"

Papa Tamsin smiled.

Tamsin's Youngest Son looked up at him with eager eyes. He had heard about Doomba hundreds of times before, but he still wanted to hear more. He loved it when his grandfather spoke about their ancestral village. It gave him goose-pimples.

"Ah Doomba!" Papa Tamsin sighed. "When I was a child, I thought it was the biggest place in the world. But as I grew older, it got smaller and smaller. Now the whole village fits inside my head!

"But the one thing that has never changed, is Doomba's beauty. It always was the most gorgeous place on earth. When you opened a window, you saw a view which was as beautiful as a painting! There were flowers everywhere, and we had names for each one. Our village was full of life. People gave birth every six months, just like dogs. And it was free. There weren't any laws, and we all took turns to govern. Everyone was as rich as each other. Everyone was content."

Jon inhaled some apple flavoured vapour.

Jon's First Wife poured some teas.

Tamsin's Youngest Son looked up at his grandfather.

"You're going to tell us a story, aren't you?" He asked.

"I sure am," Papa Tamsin replied.

The telebeamer whistled.

"Well, the busiest time of the year was always the grain harvest. Everyone had to work really quickly, to ensure the wheat was gathered whilst it was ripe. If you took too long it shattered, and only the birds were happy; everyone else went hungry.

"So the men cut the wheat with hand scythes, and the women gathered into it bundles. Then it was laid out in the threshing area, and a horse pulled a sledge over it. We used a big wooden fork to separate the wheat from the chaff."

Papa Tamsin grinned.

"Well, one year, when I was as young as you are now, I refused to help. I didn't want to do all that hard work!

"My dad went crazy. I'd never seen him so mad. His hair stood on end, and steam blew out of his ears! His eyes bulged so much, they almost popped out of their sockets! He grabbed me, bent me over his leg, and spanked me.

"So I decided to run away.

"But that was a dangerous thing to do, because Doomba was surrounded by ghosts. They hid in the caves, hills and orchards. They were everywhere!"

Papa Tamsin smiled.

Jon's First Wife drank some sugary tea.

Tamsin's Youngest Son called out for more.

"Tell us about the ghosts, pops. Please!" He cheered. "Please! Please! Please!"

"Okay, okay," Papa Tamsin replied. "Well, I only ever saw one ghost myself. It looked like a skeleton. It had a massive mouth, which was fixed into a permanent smile. It had holes where its eyes should have been. And it had limp legs, which dragged along the ground.

"It was the ghost of a man who had died three hundred years before. That man had lived in Doomba all his life. He loved it so much, he didn't want to leave! So he spent his afterlife there too. He lived in the fields, and protected the village from evil spirits.

"He was friendly, but not every ghost was kind. Some of them captured little children who ran away from home! They grabbed them, took them to the hills, and ate them alive! So running away was a dangerous thing to do.

"I took a mule. I wasn't supposed to ride that mule; my papa said I'd fall off. But what was I supposed to do, walk alongside it? Pfft! Of course I rode it. I rode it all the way to the sea, and went to visit my friend, the Rotund Holy.

"Only I *did* fall off. I felt like such a fool!

"The Rotund Holy helped me back to Doomba, where my mother made a compress full of olive oil, soap and raw eggs. That fixed my damaged elbow in no time.

"I tell you, the old ways are the best. We knew how to take care of ourselves in the olden days. Things weren't perfect. There were good days and bad days; days of onion and days of honey. But the ground was solid; we knew where we stood."

Papa Tamsin smiled.

"Well, that little episode taught me not to disobey my elders," he concluded. "It's a lesson you kids would do well to learn. Always do what your parents say. They know best!"

Tamsin's Youngest Son nodded.

"Yes pops," he said. "My mummy knows everything!"

Tamsin's Daughter shook her head.

"Computers know more," she muttered.

A beeping sound emanated from another room.

Tamsin used her phone to turn the oven on.

Papa Tamsin kissed the key to his village home.

"One day we'll return to Doomba," he said. "Just you wait and see!"

He fell silent. He loved Doomba so much, the thought of it struck him dumb.

Tamsin said '*goodbye*', and then turned the telebeamer off. But her television rumbled on. It was dimmed and quietened, but it could not be switched off.

'*Take a happiness pill each day*', it said. '*Keep depression far away*'.

Tamsin's Youngest Son looked up at his mother.

"Do you really want to go back to Doomba?" He asked.

"Why do you ask?" Tamsin replied.

"Because I don't want to have to use olive oil and raw eggs when I hurt myself. LOL! I want proper medicine. I want to live in a proper home, sleep on a smart bed, and have lots of gizmos. I don't want to work in the fields all day long. What sort of a life is that? OMG! Pops was right to run away!"

Tamsin laughed.

"You can live wherever you like, however you like, but don't think it'll make you happy. People were happier in Doomba than they are here."

Tamsin's Youngest Son shrugged.

"I want to play," he said.

He put on his virtual reality glasses and played hide and seek. He hid in virtual fields, orchards and caves. He climbed virtual trees, slinked between virtual plants, and crouched behind virtual rocks. He stood still and silent for minutes on end, whilst his virtual friends struggled to find him. He anticipated their every move, and snuck away whenever he was about to be caught.

"Mummy! Mummy!" He yelled. "I won again! No-one can catch me! Won't you come and play? If anyone can find me it'll be you. I love you mummy. You're the best!"

Tamsin grinned.

"I'm not wearing those virtual reality glasses," she said. "Regular glasses give me more information than I need!

"But I'll play with you in the real world, if you like?"

"The real world sucks," her son replied. He could not understand how his mother could be happy in the material realm. He assumed that growing up in a time before technology must have been hard.

"Don't you want to live in the future?" He asked.

"No."

"Why not?"

"I'm happy in the past."

"Happy?"

"Happy! Don't worry, be happy."

Tamsin's Eldest Son stormed into the room, knocked the telebeamer over, and pointed a toy gun at Tamsin's chest. His hair was uncovered, unkempt and uncombed. His tone was savage.

"Up with your hands!" He screamed "You're a traitor! You're a Godly spy! I'll shoot you! I'll vaporize you! I'll send you to prison!"

Tamsin's Youngest Daughter crawled behind. She pointed her phone at her mother, and pursed her fleshy lips.

"Traitor!" She giggled. "Spy! Prison!"

"We must do our duty," Tamsin's Eldest Son continued.

"You must calm down," Tamsin replied.

"I'll inform on you! I'll have you put away!"

"And who'll cook your dinner then? Pfft! Can't you play sensibly? Can't you play dress-up with your hologram dolls, or act out stories on your 3D tablets? I've taken out four loans to buy you toys! Why on earth would you want to lock me away?"

Tamsin's Youngest Daughter scrunched her nose.

Tamsin Eldest Son blew a raspberry.

A moth flew into a lightbulb.

* * *

Tamsin left home and walked through her camp.

She walked past glossy skyscrapers, which were packed in so tightly, it was impossible to smell the wind or see the sun. Past narrow roads, which turned into narrow alleys, as narrow towers crept forward on either side. And past the loud speakers which decorated those towers.

'*Greed is good*', they announced.

'*Is your flat bigger than your neighbours?*'

'*Don't be seen out with last year's mobile. The horror!*'

Unmanned checkpoints stretched across every road, intersected every junction, and blocked every building. But whilst their presence was intrusive, they were not disruptive. They sensed the ID card in Tamsin's pocket and allowed her to pass. She did not even have to alter her pace. Nor did she complain. No-one complained. The government tracked everyone's movements, but workers never protested. They were too occupied with other things.

Tamsin walked past twenty three checkpoints before she turned into old Natale.

Old Natale was just another district in a burgeoning metropolis which reached as far as the eye could see. Tamsin's camp was just another suburb in that conurbation. It was just one of hundreds of boroughs which squeezed in side by side, surrounded by fields of fake plastic grass.

Tamsin had questioned an Environmental Officer about that grass a week before.

"Why isn't the land just left to nature?" She had asked.

"The profit motive," the Environmental Officer replied. "The firm which produces the plastic grass makes a profit. The firm which transports it makes a profit. And the firm which installs it makes a profit. Everyone makes a profit, and so everyone is better off.

"The profit motive! It's a natural law. I tell you, without profit, nothing would ever get done."

"But who pays for it?"

"The government pays for it. The fake grass company pays their officials a commission, so they make a profit too.

"Profit! It's a jolly fine thing."

Tamsin thought about that conversation as she walked past a row of monopolies, which all made massive profits. Past twenty-five branches of Rablays, forty-five branches of Tip Top Shop, and five branches of Flevans.

Protokia had become a corporatocracy, in which every industry was run by a monopoly. It was the most profitable way.

Those monopolies faced a road which was clogged with driverless cars. Congestion was commonplace. The population had boomed so much, there was barely anywhere to move. Villagers had migrated to towns, young women had given birth, and medical advancements had kept the elderly alive.

Tamsin walked past an eighty-six year old Avatar Manager, who was wearing a touchscreen Mikey t-shirt. Past an Old Age Wellness Manager, who was talking into her wrist. And past a Telesurgeon, who was performing surgery on a person in another continent, whilst waiting for a driverless bus.

Sun beams pierced Tamsin's neck. Glass windows reflected heat onto her head. And smog shrouded her body.

Tamsin wiped her brow. She had never been so hot, but she did not complain. She had grown accustomed to climate change. She was used to the increasing temperatures, rising pollen counts, cyclones and flash floods. Public service broadcasts always kept her calm.

'*The planet may be finite*', a News Broadcaster announced each week. '*But don't worry. The profit motive is infinite! A profitable solution will be found.*'

Tamsin was so hot she felt nauseous. Her head felt faint and her legs felt frail. She almost stumbled as she walked through an automated checkpoint.

In the blink of an eye, a translucent tube shot down from above and trapped her. It happened so quickly, Tamsin did not even see it. She walked into the tube's plastic wall, bounced back, and fell onto the floor.

An ant, who was trapped with Tamsin, tried to escape.

Tamsin scratched her head.

Pedestrians streamed by.

"You've attempted to enter a Godly area," a mechanical voice rang out. It was a tinny voice, which had human characteristics. It sounded both rickety and melodic, with a local accent, and a habit of accentuating the last syllable in every sentence.

"Sorry," Tamsin replied, somewhat timorously. "Please don't hurt me."

"I'm not going to hurt you. I'm not a savage! No, I'm going to indebt you."

"You're going to fine me?"

"No. You don't have to pay a fine. You're going to be in debt."

"Who will I be in debt to?"

"No-one. A debt will be created in your bank account. You'll need to pay it off. If you don't, you won't be able to buy anything on credit. Your assets will all be confiscated."

"But if I'm not paying anyone, where will my money go?"

"It'll pay off your debt."

"What debt?"

"The debt I'm creating."

"The debt to whom?"

"The debt in your account. I'm creating it. You're paying it. Then it'll be gone."

"I don't get it."

"People have never understood debt. If they did, there'd be a revolution, and the whole system would collapse.

"But you don't have to '*get it*'. You just have to pay it."

"Oh."

Tamsin held her head in her hands.

"Can't you just rough me up a little?" She asked. "Like the soldiers used to do in the good old days. Punch me a few times, kick me about, and then let me go. It'll be done and dusted; we'll all be able to move on. There's really no need to create a debt which will last for years."

"No," the computer replied. "Debt and violence are different shades of the same colour. And, since we can indebt workers, we don't need to beat them. Debt is the only weapon we need!"

Tamsin paused. She took off her wedding ring and held it above her head.

"Take this," she said.

The computer laughed. It was a sarcastic sort of laugh, which seemed to say, '*What would I want with that?*' It was a condescending sort of laugh, which seemed to mock Tamsin for her insolence. It was a laugh which echoed all around the tube.

"Your debt has been processed," the computer concluded. "You're free to go."

The tube zoomed up as quickly as it had descended. Tamsin got to her feet, stumbled, and left the Godly area.

* * *

"I've lost my job," Tamsin told her family. "I'm afraid we're going to have to make some cutbacks. We're going to have to stop buying all these gadgets and gizmos. We're going to have to survive on a diet of rice and soup. It's the only way we'll be able to afford our interest payments."

Her family stared at Tamsin. Their stomachs dropped. Their eyes looked hollow. Confusion covered their faces.

No-one said a word.

The silence lasted for minutes.

"It's those bloody computers!" Tamsin finally said. "It's those bloody robots; coming here and doing our jobs. Pfft! We should have never let them help, with their mechanical movements and automated brains. What have they ever done for us? Nothing! They're no bloody use to anyone."

Tamsin's Daughter looked fraught.

Jon shook his head.

Tamsin went to look for a new job.

She walked past octogenarians, nonagenarians and centenarians. She walked past workers who were being indebted for driving too slowly. Past youths who were smashing windows for fun. And past firemen who were setting fire to books.

She walked past adults, who were wearing face masks to block out the smoggy air, which was thick and sticky; full of carbon monoxide and sulphur dioxide. Past children, who were holding footballs, but had nowhere to play. And past infants, who were being transported, unsupervised, by robotic prams.

She walked into a Window Mart.

"Do you have any jobs?" She asked a Chubby Assistant, who had a bulbous belly and a bulging smile. The Window Mart logo was tattooed onto her forehead, and badges were pinned to her chest. One badge said, '*Our people make the difference*'.

"Yes," she replied.

"Please can I apply?"

"Of course! Let me see your ID."

The Chubby Assistant scanned Tamsin's ID. She looked into her smart glasses. Then she looked back at Tamsin and shook her head.

"Computer says '*no*'," she said.

"Why?"

"I'm afraid I can't divulge that information. But, needless to say, the computer knows best. If it deems you unsuitable for a job at Window Mart, it must be right. I don't think you'd fit into our corporate family.

"Thank-you for shopping at Window Mart. Please come again."

The Chubby Assistant gave Tamsin a fake plastic smile. Her cheeks became so tense, they forced her lips to squeeze together. Her eyes became so wide they closed. Her eyebrows disappeared into her eye sockets.

A recorded voice promoted a special deal on genetically modified water in aisle eight.

Tamsin sighed, turned around, and left.

She walked into a McRonalds.

"Do you have any jobs?" She asked a Spotty Assistant, who had blackheads on his face and zits on his back. The McRonalds logo was emblazoned onto everything he was wearing. His name badge featured three golden stars.

"Yes," he replied.

"Please can I apply?"

"Of course! Let me see your ID."

The Spotty Assistant scanned Tamsin's ID. He looked at his smart watch. Then he looked at Tamsin and shook his head.

"Computer says '*no*'," he said.

A recorded voice advertised a special offer on Sappy Meals.

Tamsin sighed, turned around, and left.

She walked into a Rablays.

"Do you have any jobs?" She asked a Geeky Assistant, who was wearing thick rimmed glasses, and a thick layer of hair gel. The Rablays logo flashed above her head. Her electronic name badge said, '*Here to help*'.

"Yes," she replied.

"Please can I apply?"

"Of course! Let me see your ID."

The Geeky Assistant scanned Tamsin's ID. She tapped some buttons on her laser keyboard. Then she looked at Tamsin and shook her head.

"Computer says '*no*'," she said.

"What on earth do I have to do?" Tamsin screamed. "Why won't you even let me apply? I just want to fill in a form. Is that too much to ask?"

"Please madam, calm down. There's nothing I can do. It's beyond my control. Computer says '*no*'!"

"Well who the hell can say '*yes*'?"

"Head office."

"Fine."

"Have a nice day."

"Goodbye."

Tamsin stormed out the bank. She stormed past seven Toots Pharmacies, eight Star & Bucks, and nine checkpoints. She stormed past a Vertical Farmer, a Waste Data Handler, and a Body Part Maker. She stormed towards Rablays' head office, where she came across the Mad Lady.

"They own everything!" She wailed. "They own us all. We think we're free, but we're slaves. The angels have sung it in the heavens!"

"Oh shut up," Tamsin replied. "What do you know, you batty old witch?"

Tamsin entered the building. She walked through a checkpoint, approached a virtual receptionist, and looked into a camera which was shaped like a giant eye.

"Name?" A robotic voice demanded.

"Tamsin."

"Number?"

"46664."

"Purpose of visit?"

"I'd like to apply for a job."

There was a pause.

Tamsin scratched some plaque from her teeth.

The door buzzed, and Tamsin entered an empty waiting room. She sat down on a nondescript green sofa and waited. She waited and waited and waited. She waited for an hour in all. An hour in which there was nothing to do other than stare at the second hand of a slow moving clock.

"46664!" A voice finally rang out. "Step forward."

A door swung open and Tamsin stepped through. She sat down in front of a black smart table. A Dark Banker, who wore a black suit and tie, entered and sat down in front of her. An automated coffee maker poured two cups of black coffee.

"And what can I do for you?" The Dark Banker asked.

The Dark Banker possessed a tacky sort of charisma, which had earned him far more promotions than he deserved. He wore a style before substance smile. He wore cufflinks which clinked, eyes which twinkled, and aftershave which wafted around the room.

"I'd like to apply for a job, please," Tamsin replied.

"Of course! Let me see your ID."

The Dark Banker scanned Tamsin's ID. He looked at his smart table. Then he looked back at Tamsin and shook his head.

"Computer says 'no'," he said.

"Why?"

"It says you weren't productive enough in your last job."

"I was one of the most productive workers there!"

"But you weren't as productive as the machines. And in this post-modern world, where the supremacy of profit is absolute, that's all that matters. We've put a block on your ID. You won't be able to work again."

"What do you mean, 'You've put a block on my ID'? I've never met you. I've never worked for your bank. What's it got to do with you?"

The Dark Banker laughed. It was a blood-curdling sort of laugh. A laugh which was so malicious it was almost evil, so bold it made his face pulsate, and so menacing it seemed to shriek.

"You've worked for us all your life!" He guffawed. "And if you ever work again, it'll be for us. Everyone works for us. We control everything! We own everything! We own you!"

Tamsin looked down at her feet.

"I don't understand," she whimpered.

"People have never understood banking," the Dark Banker replied. "If they did, there'd be a revolution, and the whole system would collapse."

"But how can you control everything? What about the government?"

"We own the government! We own the army! We own the thought police, the work police, and the police police. We own everything! The *Bank for International Settlements* owns the world!"

"How?"

"Because we control the money supply!

"The police and the army obey the government, because of money. The government pays policemen and soldiers their wages, without which they could not survive.

"The government obeys the monopolies, because of money. The monopolies provide the government with tax revenues, without which *they* could not survive.

"And we control the monopolies, because of money. We give the monopolies loans, without which *they* could not survive. They're all in debt to us. And if they weren't, we'd just create new debts in their name. We control their bank accounts. We control the world!"

The Dark Banker beamed with gleeful superiority.

"Follow the money, find the power!" He said. "He who controls the money supply, controls the world. And we control money supply! We're in complete and total control!"

Tamsin paused.

"But the government controls the money supply," she said.

"Don't be silly," the Dark Banker replied. "They only ever controlled the supply of notes and coins. And who uses those these days? They're a cultural relic. The banks have always been able to create electronic money, the money that sits in your bank account. And that's the only money that matters!

"We've won! The profit motive has won! The bank has won! History is over. We're in complete and total control!"

Tamsin stared at the Dark Banker.

"What's stopping me from telling everyone?" She asked.

"Nothing."

"You don't mind?"

"No."

"Why not?"

"No-one will do anything."

"Yes, they will!"

"No, they won't. They're too occupied with other things."

Tamsin bowed her head.

"I really need a job," she pleaded. "I've got loans coming out of my ears, debts coming out of my eyeballs, and a whole family to feed. Surely there's something you can do?"

The Dark Banker smiled. It was a charismatic smile, with eyes which were wide, and teeth which were pearly white.

The smart table went into screen saver mode. Its surface looked like green leather.

The Dark Banker leaned in.

"You have a daughter," he said.

"I have two."

"I can see that."

"How?"

"That information is on your ID card. We know everything about you."

"Oh."

"Your eldest daughter, she's mathematical."

"Yes. She's good at maths. She's the top of her class!"

"Good. We could do with more mathematicians. They're profitable. They make great scientists, bankers and accountants."

The Dark Banker looked deep into Tamsin's eyes. He tapped his smart table, which came to life. He tapped a Rablays logo, a picture of Tamsin's Daughter, and a couple blue icons.

"Ah!" He said.

"'Ah'?"

"Voila! We have a match! Worker C33. He's a logician too. If your daughter marries C33, they're sure to have profitable babies. The bank would like that."

"Oh."

"It would make the bank very happy indeed."

"Oh."

"And if the bank is happy, it'd be able to make you happy. We'd all be happy!"

"Oh."

"We'd provide a dowry to cover the wedding, we'd halve your debts, and we'd find you a new job."

Tamsin smiled. It was a nervous smile, with eyes which were narrow, and lips which were wide.

She released an uncomfortable giggle.

The Dark Banker gave her a sympathetic look.

"It's up to you," he said. "It's a free country after all."

Tamsin pulled her earlobe.

"What job would you give me?" She asked.

"Ah! Let's see!"

The Dark Banker swiped his smart desk. He tapped an image of Tamsin's face, dragged it across the table, and dropped it onto an icon marked '*Job Allocator*'.

The smart desk made a trillion calculations in a nanosecond. Then it flashed red and white.

The Dark Banker licked his lips.

"You worked with yaks as a little girl," he said.

"Yes."

"Food production is very important. Very important indeed. We all need to eat!

"So we'll give you a job in our meat factory. You're a perfect fit! You'll be productive there. You'll be profitable. And if you work really hard, you'll be promoted. Your blood, sweat and tears, will see you rise above your peers. Because hard work is always rewarded!""

Tamsin smiled.

"Okay," she said. "I'd like that. Thank-you."

"But first," the Dark Banker concluded. "You must give us your daughter. Arrange her engagement to C33, and then you can work for us again. Everything will be hunky dory!"

Tamsin grimaced. She shook the Dark Banker's hand, turned around, and left the building.

She walked down the street in a daze. She was so dizzy, she had to sit down on a bench to recuperate. She sat next to a Social Networking Officer, who was reading a holographic newspaper. There were tiny spots on her neck, and tiny lights in her hair.

"The bankers own everything!" Tamsin told her. "The bank owns us all. We think we're free, but we're slaves. A banker told me so!"

"Oh shut up," the Social Networking Officer replied. "What do you know, you batty old witch?"

* * *

Tamsin's Daughter returned to find her house full of guests. Mama C33, a saggy lady who had droopy breasts, was sat between Tamsin and Papa C33; a meagre man whose skin was covered in liver-spots. C33, an awkward boy who had wonky eyes, was sat next to Jon.

Jon's First Wife used her phone to turn the tea maker on.

Tamsin's Daughter looked at everyone in the room.

Mama C33 looked back at Tamsin's Daughter.

"The meat is hung out for display," she announced.

Tamsin's Daughter swung her head to the side, glared at Mama C33 for the briefest of moments, and then turned back to face her mother.

"Err, yes," Tamsin stammered. "I'd like you to meet your fiancée. This is C33."

Tamsin's Daughter took a step back, looked C33 up and down, and then shook her head.

"I'm not marrying that lump of foul deformity," she said. "OMG! You've got to be kidding me!"

Tamsin gave her daughter a stern look.

"Do you want to be some sort of old spinster?" She growled. "Do you want to be some sort of old witch, left on the shelf, passed over by every man in town?"

Tamsin's Daughter put her hands on her hips.

"I don't want to be an old spinster," she snarled. "But I don't want to get married either. I'm only eighteen. I want to wait. I want to marry someone who's attractive. I want to marry someone who's rich. And I want to fall in love."

"Enough!" Tamsin snapped. "I didn't fall in love. My parents arranged my marriage, and that worked out just fine. Stop whinging!"

Tamsin's Daughter turned red.

"But mummy!" She screamed. "OMG! You're ancient! Really! I feel like I'm being enslaved by two occupiers; the Protokians and you!"

Tamsin stamped her foot.

"Well," she barked. "If that's the case, you'll be better off out of my house. It's settled!"

The First Wife handed a cup of tea to each of her guests.

The television played an advert for superhuman prosthetic limbs.

Tamsin gave her daughter a big hug. She held her daughter away, with one hand on either shoulder, and looked into her eyes.

"This will be a good marriage," she said. "The bank has calculated your compatibility. You're a perfect match! You're both logicians. You'll be happy together. You'll be productive. You'll be super profitable!"

Tamsin's Daughter wagged her finger. A tear rolled down her nose, and a bubble formed in the corner of her mouth. She looked at her mother with puppy dog eyes.

"Enough!" Tamsin growled. "You're marrying this man, and that's that.

"The dowry has been set at fifty thousand e-dollars. Fifty grand!!! That will pay for your wedding and halve our debts. Halve them!!! Do you really want our home to be repossessed? Really? Think of us for once. I think you forget that I'm unemployed."

Tamsin's Daughter shook her head.

Jon's First Wife drank some tea.

The television played an advert for nanobot implants.

* * *

Tamsin walked past a row of giant chimneys, which were all emitting toxic fumes, and then entered the Madsanto meat factory. It was one of the last remaining factories in town. Most factories had been replaced with call centres, offices or banks.

That place was massive. It was bigger than the whole of old Natale. A hologram, which was as wide as four football pitches, displayed the word '*Madsanto*' overhead. And a corporate slogan said, '*Cutting emissions, ending hunger, eliminating slaughter*'.

Meat had been grown in factories since phosphorus levels plunged. Fertilizer, which was necessary to grow animal feed, had run low. And farmland had disappeared, as towns swallowed up the countryside.

Tamsin walked past meat technicians, who added protein to muscle cells, to encourage tissue growth. Past a bioreactor, where stem cells fused together, to create muscle fibre. And past ten giant metal vats, which were thirteen stories tall, and three blocks wide. A giant metal heart hovered above those canisters. Its left ventricle pumped nutrients into each vat, and its right ventricle supplied oxygen. Its atriums sucked up waste products. Metal veins shot off in every direction.

A Bearded Manager greeted Tamsin. That man had legs which would not have looked out of place on a grand piano, and breath which smelled of chlorine gas. He was a Holy. All the managers were Holies.

"You're going to be a '*Preservation Operative*'," he told Tamsin. "Your team will work together to kill yeast and eradicate fungus."

"How?"

"By adding sodium benzoate to our vats. Or by adding collagen powder, xanthan gum or mannitol. But don't worry about that for now. Your colleagues will show you the ropes."

The Bearded Manager left Tamsin with her new team.

"Preservation!" A Keen Operative bellowed. "We control the meat before it gets out of control!"

The Keen Operative was one of four workers in Tamsin's team. The others had all been forced to work for Madsanto when their debts spiralled out of control. They had all bought things they did not need, with money they did not have.

A Frail Operative had defaulted on a business loan. She had gone out of business when her laundrette's prices were undercut by Window Mart.

"I salute the God within you," she told Tamsin.

A Skinny Operative was a video game addict, who felt an insatiable desire to own the latest releases. He was indebted as a punishment for downloading pirated games. The interest payments had crippled him.

"May all auspicious signs come to you," he told Tamsin.

And a Stout Operative, had defaulted on a payday loan, which she had taken out to buy toys for her children.

"Peace be upon you," she told Tamsin.

"Thank-you," Tamsin replied. "Peace be upon you!"

The Stout Operative showed Tamsin around the factory.

"The sodium benzoate goes in here," she said. "The collagen powder goes in there. You check the yeast levels here. You check the fungus levels there. These two vats are your responsibility."

Tamsin looked confused.

"Is that it?" She asked.

"Yep!"

"What about the xanthium gum and the mannitol?"

"Ah, we don't need any of that. There's no need to look for a cat's fifth leg. If you keep things simple, everyone will be happy."

"But checking a couple of vats won't keep me busy. What am I supposed to do all day?"

The Stout Operative chortled.

"We get our tasks done in short bursts," she said. "Then it's up to us to keep ourselves occupied. We mess about, chat, pay our bills, surf the net, daydream, and wait for the day to end."

"But aren't we supposed to be productive? To make a profit?"

"We are productive. We oversee vats which produce millions of meals each year!"

"By not working?"

"The machines work!"

Tamsin wore a blank expression.

"Look, we're measured on our output, not our efforts. It doesn't matter that we only spend one hour a day actually working. As long as we look like we're working, no-one complains. As long as we give the impression that we care, everyone's happy.

"Meat gets made and we get paid! It's a profitable state of affairs.

"The profit motive! It's a natural law. I tell you, without profit, nothing would ever get done."

Tamsin laughed.

"It sounds like nothing gets done, even with the profit motive," she said.

"That's the spirit!" The Stout Operative replied. "Come! I'll show you how to '*get nothing done*' really well."

The Stout Operative led Tamsin past a Bored Clerk, who was suffering from deep vein thrombosis, having sat at her desk for eight hours. Past a Frustrated Technician, who was suffering from repetitive strain disorder, after stirring meat solution for six hours. And past an Impatient Cleaner, who had contracted asthma, after inhaling some toxic fumes.

Those workers all earned a miniscule hourly wage. The minimum wage had been abolished when the monopolies sued the government using PITT. They had claimed that they would make more profit if they could pay their workers less.

The monopolies had also used PITT to abolish workers' rights, public sector organisations, and free healthcare.

"This is the sector 7G tea room," the Stout Operative continued. "You can come here three or four times a day without anyone complaining. But don't ever spend more than fifteen minutes in here. That sort of behaviour is frowned upon."

A tea making machine automatically poured two cups of tea.

Tamsin took a sip.

"Aah!" She said. "Just as I like it."

"That's an intelligent tea maker," the Stout Operative explained. "It scans your ID to analyse your tastes, then it makes you the perfect cuppa."

The Stout Operative snapped her fingers.

"Come!" She said. "Follow me."

They walked along a travellator which turned from white to green to orange; Madsanto's corporate colours. They took a super-speed lift to the twenty first floor. And they arrived at a long, shiny desk. The Stout Operative waved her hand above its surface, and a touchscreen computer rose up.

"You can kill a lot of time in here," she said. "You have to input data into the system, which takes about five minutes each day, but the rest of the time is yours. Most people surf the net. I'm writing a novel, and that guy's teaching himself Colonialist. Sometimes we play games. Sometimes we read."

Tamsin laughed.

"And that's it?" She asked.

"You can do other things. I once spent a whole week trying to teach myself how to cry on demand. We all like to snack, that passes the time, as does going to the toilet. I go to the toilet eight times a shift! I spend hours replying to emails, and I send love notes to an ugly guy in accounts. I'm not interested in him, but it brightens up my day to see the confusion on his face. He doesn't have a clue who's flirting with him!"

Tamsin chuckled.

"I think I've got it," she said.

"I think you'll do well here," the Stout Operative replied. "You seem passive enough. You can never be too passive! I tell you, it's the eager ones who get in trouble. Try too hard, innovate or question the system, and you'll be out on your ear in no time. But if you keep your head down, and don't do anything to rock the boat, then you'll be just fine. You'll have a long and fruitful career here at Madsanto."

Tamsin smiled.

The giant hologram flickered.

A cat climbed into a vat of meat.

* * *

The big day arrived.

The wedding party approached the *Godly Temple of Profit, sponsored by McRonalds*. They washed their feet in an ionic footbath, which bubbled and fizzed. They walked up the marble steps, passed some branded icons, and bowed down in front of a giant statue of a *McBib*.

Tamsin's Daughter waited at the front of the temple. Holographic henna covered her arms, and a holographic veil covered her face. Hundreds of workers waited behind her.

After some moments had passed, C33 arrived on a mechanical white horse. He dismounted his steed, and walked down the central aisle.

Everyone cheered.

The Humpbacked Priest followed C33 on a Segway. He stopped every five metres to rub his bent back. He reached the front of the temple, waddled between several plug-in air fresheners, and turned each one on. The smell of incense filled the hall.

"Let these scents release Tamsin from her protective deities," he said. "Bring her into the protection of C33's angels."

The Medicine Man went outside, pointed a blaster pistol into the air, and fired a laser beam towards the sky.

Everyone stared at him.

"Well someone had to scare off the ghosts and evil spirits," he said.

"And it wasn't as if any of you were going to do it."

There was a brief moment of silence. Then the congregation replied with a mixture of nods, shrugs and approving gestures.

An image of a *Filler-o-Fish* flashed up on the far wall.

The Humpbacked Priest shook his head.

"Bloody Medicine Man," he muttered. "What does that schmuck know?"

Tamsin's Daughter and C33 exchanged smartphones.

Jon's First Wife shed a tear. Mama C33 snivelled. And Tamsin wept with joy.

Papa C33 and Jon walked to the front.

"My daughter comes from a profitable line," Jon told Papa C33. "She descends from productive folk, who are married to the net and one with the web."

"My son comes from a profitable line," Papa C33 replied. "He descends from productive folk, who have goodness in their data, and pureness in their IDs."

"My daughter is the purest girl in the world. She is as fresh as a brand new skyscraper, and as innocent as a heavenly robot."

"My son is as righteous as a manager, and as noble as a clerk."

"My daughter is as beautiful as a scientifically enhanced rose."

"My son is a strong as a genetically modified ox."

"My daughter's heart is as white as computer programming."

"My son's heart is more precious than a million microchips."

Papa C33 and Jon embraced.

"I'm happy to give my daughter to your son," Jon concluded.

"I'm happy to receive your daughter into my family," Papa C33 replied.

The Humpbacked Priest smiled.

"I now pronounce you husband and wife," he said. "Mazel tov!"

Everyone cheered. Everyone clapped, sang, and threw confetti into the air. Everyone got into a driverless bus, and went to the McRonalds wedding hall.

They celebrated beneath a screen which displayed images of lights, balloons and stars. A fragrance machine produced the aroma of grilled mutton. A Chubby Logician threw cubes of artificial meat into his mouth.

Four telebeamers projected four musicians, who played one instrument each. Tamsin watched them and cried. A group of women danced together in fits and starts. A Seductive Worker shimmied with gyrating hips. Little girls tried to copy her. And the men chatted amongst themselves.

The music died down.

"This party was brought to you by McRonalds," an electronic voice announced. "*Hmm! You're loving it!*

"Please help yourselves to *Big Mocs*, *Chicken Royals* and *McFries*. And don't forget to visit one of our restaurants next time you're out. There's one on a corner near you!"

The guests ate, sang and danced, until the sun was replaced by the moon. Then they formed a guard of honour, and cheered as C33 led Tamsin's Daughter back to their matrimonial apartment.

* * *

Tamsin's home felt empty without her eldest daughter. It felt even emptier when Jon went to work in a distant town. He took the First Wife with him, and left Tamsin with her three remaining children.

Tamsin's Youngest Son played with his virtual reality glasses.

Tamsin's Eldest Son stretched out on a floating sofa.

Tamsin's television brightened. A female avatar appeared. She had buff shadows beneath her perky cheeks. And she wore an animated daffodil on her plain purple dress.

"The bank has calculated that it would be profitable for your children to attend a boarding school," the avatar announced. "It would be an efficient use of resources. Your children will develop into upstanding members of the economy."

Tamsin scowled at the avatar.

"They're not going anywhere," she protested.

"I'm afraid you don't have a choice," the avatar replied.

"Why not? You can't put me in prison for protecting my children."

"We wouldn't want to put you in prison. It wouldn't be profitable."

"So I do have a choice!"

"No, I'm afraid you don't. If you refuse to enrol your children, we'll indebt you. You'll default on your repayments and lose everything you own. Our bailiffs will repossess your children and put them in a boarding school.

"You'd be better off taking them there yourself."

The avatar smiled. It was a holier than thou smile, which seemed to say, '*What sort of an idiot are you, to think you could challenge me?*'

Tamsin's Youngest Daughter picked her nose.

Tamsin's Eldest Son rolled over.

Tamsin tugged her hair.

"Put yourself in my shoes," she pleaded. "I just want to keep my family together. Tell me, what should I do?"

The avatar shrugged.

"Not my circus, not my monkeys," it said. "Do I look like your problem solver?"

"Are you my God?" Tamsin shouted. "Am I your slave? Do I work for you?

"Where are my human rights? Show me! Show me where my human rights are, so I can go and look for them."

"Shut up!" The avatar barked back. "What can I do? What do you expect me to do? My hands are tied by the profit motive!"

"But they're my children! They've lived with me all their lives."

"Well they're not living with you anymore. Period. If you have a problem, go and speak to the family police. They're the ones in charge of you."

Tamsin tapped her phone.

The coffee machine turned on.

"Damn it!" Tamsin wailed.

She tapped her phone again.

Her telebeamer buzzed. It vibrated. Light-beams sprayed forth, creating a grey static blur, which slowly took shape. The image of a Family Policewoman, made solely of shaky light, wobbled from side to side.

There was a smile on the Family Policewoman's face, and a Rablays logo on her chest. Electronic earrings dangled from her ears, and electronic handcuffs dangled from her belt. Her forehead sparkled, and her shoelaces shone.

She was a Holy. All the family police were Holies.

"Well, well, well," she said. "What do have we here then?"

"We have a problem," Tamsin replied. "A massive problem!

"A boarding school wants to kidnap my children, an avatar is threatening to indebt my family, and you're the only person who can save us!"

"I see."

The Family Policewoman held her hand in front of her face. Icons appeared on her palm. She swiped them aside, looked at Tamsin, and shook her head.

"Computer says '*no*'," she said.

"What? When? Why?"

"It says that sending your children to boarding school would be profitable."

"But what about my family? You're the family police! You're supposed to protect families!"

"We're supposed to protect the global family. We're in it together! And we'd all be better off if your children went to boarding school.

"Thank-you for your time. And don't forget to shop at PC Universe. '*Where in the universe? It's PC Universe*'."

The telebeamer fizzled and popped. The Family Policewoman disappeared. And Tamsin's face turned a fluorescent shade of red.

A robotic vacuum cleaner skidded between her feet.

* * *

A driverless taxi arrived outside.

"Come on kids," Tamsin shouted. "It's time to go."

Tamsin's children followed her outside. They looked like zombies; with their heads bowed, and their eyes glued to their *JayPhones*. They did not utter a single word until the taxi had left.

"I don't know why you argued with that avatar," Tamsin's Eldest Son said. "The system knows best. Computers make far better decisions than people. Everyone knows that! Really mummy, sometimes I think you don't care about us at all."

Tamsin took a deep breath.

The taxi stopped, sat in traffic for three hours, and then covered the last hundred miles in twenty three seconds.

They arrived at the *Rablays Institute of Productive Education*. Two gates swung open, and Tamsin's children walked through.

A Bespectacled Teacher approached Tamsin, grabbed her hand, and shook it enthusiastically.

"Your children will do well here," he said. "We'll optimize their intelligence. We'll teach them how to operate computers, and ensure they're not clever enough to question why.

"We'll mould your children into upstanding members of an obedient and docile workforce. They'll grow into manageable employees, and eager consumers!"

Tamsin watched her children disappear out of sight.

She panted. She gagged. She almost choked.

"I want to die," she yelled. "God! Where are you? Kill me! Kill me! Save me from this shame."

Mama Jon's face appeared on Tamsin's phone.

"Don't panic!" She cried. "Don't panic! Don't panic! Don't panic!"

Tamsin panicked.

"Breathe!" Mama Jon cheered. "Inhale! Exhale! Inhale! Exhale! Inhale! Exhale!"

Tamsin huffed and puffed.

Mama Jon cheered.

The Bespectacled Teacher ate some crisps.

Tamsin's panic attack got worse. Her heart palpitated, her hands trembled, and her lips vibrated. She suffered for over thirty minutes. Then she fell back against a tree. She was cold, wet and exhausted.

A cockroach crawled up her leg.

Mama Jon looked at her step-daughter.

"It's okay," she consoled. "Life will get easier. You'll be happy again. There'll be no more running about. There'll be none of this Protokian education thingy. No, no, no. It'll all be okay."

Tamsin held her head in her hands and cried.

She returned to her empty home, sat in her empty lounge, and slept in her empty bed. She kept herself occupied. And she looked forward to going to work. It was the only place where she came into contact with other human beings.

10. ELLIE

Everything changed slowly, but everything changed.

When Ellie was first imprisoned, she was locked inside a cramped cell, out of reach of her friends and family. She was made to break rocks for eight hours each day.

She broke rocks in the sunshine and in the rain. She broke rocks when it was hot, when it was cold, and when it was humid. She broke rocks when she was tired, when she was depressed, and when she was ill.

Then, unbeknownst to her, Natale Prison was taken over by *Gee4Jess*; the monopoly provider of security services, which was owned by the bank. It teamed up with Tip Top Shop; the monopoly supplier of clothing, which was in debt to the bank. Together, they forced the inmates to produce blue denim jeans. They made lots of profit for the bank.

The inmates stitched jeans in the sunshine and in the rain. They stitched jeans when it was hot, when it was cold, and when it was humid. They stitched jeans when they were tired, when they were depressed, and when they were ill.

After a couple more years, the inmates started to hear people on the other side of a thin wall. After another year had passed, segments of that wall came down. A panel was removed one week, and a pole was removed another. That wall disappeared. The inmates were able to walk amongst the giant machines on the other side. They were able to talk to the other workers.

They talked to geriatrics, who were working for Tip Top Shop to pay off their hospital bills. To young couples, who had taken second jobs there to repay their mortgages. And to undergraduates, who were working there to keep their student loans in check.

They talked to workers who had been indebted for idleness, and workers who had been indebted for slowness. Workers who had been indebted for reading banned books, speaking Godliness, or possessing pictures of Apai. And workers who had been indebted for growing their own food, making their own furniture, or retuning their televisions.

After another year had passed, Ellie saw Tamsin in that factory. She was wearing a patched up dress. There was a defiant look in her eyes, as if she had just waved goodbye to her innocence. But, as the months passed, that look faded. Tamsin looked healthier, with chubbier cheeks and plumper arms.

"I took a second job here," she told Ellie. "To pay for my children's boarding school fees."

Tamsin held her palms up, as if to say, 'What can I do?'

Ellie picked her nail polish.

The Mad Lady walked by.

"We're all becoming machines," she wailed. "The human race is dying out. The conveyer belt told me so!"

"Oh shut up," a Straggly Worker shouted back. "What do you know, you batty old witch?"

Ellie and Tamsin looked at each other. They laughed. And they continued to natter. Tamsin told Ellie everything she had learned from the Dark Banker. And Ellie told Tamsin about her time in prison.

Gee4Jess did not mind that sort of interaction. They were happy for the inmates to mix with the debtors, as long as they were productive, and as long as they returned to their cells after each shift.

Those cells also changed.

They grew. En-suite bathrooms appeared one day after work. State of the art kitchens, with touchscreens imbedded into every surface, were added six months later. Lounges and hallways soon followed. Those cells became flats. Mortgages were created in the inmates' names.

Ellie's movements were monitored through cameras which were embedded in every wall. Her television woke her up at seven o'clock each morning, and sleeping gas put her to sleep at eleven o'clock each night. Intelligent appliances chose her food, cooked it and served it, at the same time every day. Everything followed a coercive routine, just as it had done before, but Ellie never saw a prison guard. No-one ever told her what to do. She was manoeuvred by suggestion, she did everything that was expected of her, and she never complained.

She did not even complain when she discovered she was pregnant, even though she was still a virgin.

Birth rates had been in decline for decades. Pesticides, genetically modified food, fluoridated water and radiation had all caused sperm counts to plunge. But natural pregnancies still took place, up until the 'Night of the Broken Glass', when the bank had sterilized every worker.

Since that night, pregnancies only occurred when the bank's computer calculated that they would be profitable. Women only found out they were pregnant when their televisions told them. They carried their babies for six months, then an early labour was induced, to ensure that mothers did not take any time off work.

Ellie's baby, who the bank named 'Democracy', or 'Worker 2917' for official purposes, was returned to her when she was four months old. Ellie spent two years bonding with her daughter, and with Mama Ellie, who was allowed to visit once a week.

"Massage her body with olive oil, to keep her strong," Mama Ellie always said. "Put ash under her eyelids and powder in her armpits."

"Yes mum."

"Don't use those horrible plastic dummies. On the most sacred of the Godly prophets! Wrap some grapes in a cloth and use that. Use some almonds and molasses if you can't find any grapes."

"Yes mum."

"Keep breastfeeding if you don't want to get pregnant again. I swear on my dead father's underwear; you can't get pregnant whilst you're breastfeeding!"

"Yes mum."

Whilst her mother's nagging tested Ellie's patience, she loved her company and appreciated her help. They grew closer than ever before.

Then, on one scorching hot winter's morning, Democracy was taken away to the *Rablays Baby Institute*. Mama Ellie's visits were stopped. And Ellie felt distraught.

Since that day, she had only been able to talk to her daughter through a telebeamer.

Ellie tapped her mobile phone.

A vision of Democracy wobbled from side to side. Her bushy black hair swayed. Her grape-shaped head bobbed up and down.

"Well hello!" She cheered.

"Hi honey," Ellie replied. "How are you?"

"Superhuman me!"

"You're a super human?"

"Better than humans me. OMG, mummy. You're such a homo-sapien. Homo-evolutis me!"

"A homo what?"

"'*Evolutis*' mummy. Machine me. Bank microchipped eyes!"

"What? When? Why? You're not blind. There's nothing wrong with your eyesight."

"Pfft, mummy. LOL! Old fashioned you! Everything was wrong with eyesight. It was so human."

"Human?"

"Yeah, human. Me couldn't dark see, infrared see, in or out zoom, sight record, ID use at checkpoints, or internet use to analyse surrounds. Pfft! Me could hardly use at all!"

"You could use your eyes to see."

"Barely."

Ellie's television played an advert for 3D printers.

Democracy rubbed her nose.

Ellie drank some fluoride-laden water.

"Listen here, little missy," she said in a stern voice. "When I was your age, I had to wash my family's clothes in a machine full of soap and water. I volunteered at a refugee camp, which was full of mud, diseases and poverty.

"But you? You can't even be bothered to use your god given eyes? Pfft! Whatever next? This would have never happened in my day."

Democracy laughed.

"LOL! Funny you," she said.

"Funny?"

"You nana sound."

"Your nana's a clever lady."

"That's not what you used to think."

"How do you know what I used to think?"

"Microchips."

"'*Microchips*'?"

"Microchips in eyes. They Woogled you on sight, and info gathered."

"And what information did they give you, little missy?"

"They said you were like me, when you my age."

"Oh yeah."

"Yeah! You nana challenged. You thought *she* was old fashioned. But look you! You old fashioned. You behind times too!"

Ellie chuckled.

"You'll appreciate our traditions when you're older," she said.

"You be dead then. LOL! You going to die!"

"We're all going to die."

"Not me."

"Oh yeah. And why's that?"

"Because superhuman me. Live forever me! Have artificial organs, which fail never, and synthetic blood which toxin filters. If accident, mind get new body.

"Biological life is transitory. Us superhumans immortal!

"All hail the bank!"

Democracy blew a raspberry.

Ellie scrunched her nose.

A moth flew into the electronic wallpaper.

* * *

Ellie kept herself busy. She had to, it was the law. She was reminded of that law every day, when her television repeated the bank's three corporate slogans:

'*Work is virtuous*'.

'*Idleness is evil*'.

'*Keep yourself occupied*'.

To keep its workers busy, the bank produced new cars, to create congestion. It forced people to work for sixty hours each week. And it pumped sleeping gas into the air every evening.

The bank erected giant billboards of naked models, to distract its workers. It created new fashion lines each week, so workers would spend hours choosing what to wear. And it broadcast adverts around the clock, to encourage workers to visit one of Natale's many shopping malls.

Ellie did three things to keep herself occupied. She made herself look beautiful, so men would want to make love to her. She made love to men, to satisfy her physical desires. And she listened to music, to escape the hollow nature of her existence.

Staying beautiful was easy. There was a pill or procedure for everything.

Ellie ate as much food as she could stomach. Then she took a diet pill to keep herself slender. That pill dissolved her fat, which she extracted with a long sharp syringe.

She took a pill to remove her wrinkles, a pill to widen her eyes, and a pill to keep her hair its lustrous shade of black. She sat in front of an interactive mirror, and brushed her hair for over twenty five minutes. She daydreamed, swayed, and chewed some apple-flavoured gum.

'*Buy! Buy! Buy!*' Her television buzzed. '*Don't be seen without it*'.

Ellie bit down on a mouthpiece, which whistled as it slowly whitened her teeth. She produced some foundation on her makeup printer, and smeared it across her face using a wireless airbrush. She put on a UV bracelet, patted herself down, and left her flat.

She emerged onto a smog-filled street, which hid beneath a sun-filled sky. It was fifty degrees Celsius, and people were fainting wherever Ellie looked.

Ellie looked at a giant screen, which covered the side of a giant skyscraper. It played an advert for super-human prosthetic limbs. She looked at some workers, who left a store without paying. A sensor scanned the microchips in their eyes, and debited their accounts. Ellie shook her head, and walked along the jam-packed pavement.

She walked past an Alternative Vehicle Developer, a Climate Change Reversal Specialist, and a Memory Augmentation Surgeon. A Nano Medic, a Narrowcaster, and a New Science Ethicist. A Lawyer, an Accountant, and a Salesman.

Ellie squeezed between that mass of people. She was shoved one way, and shunted back the other. She was knocked in her side, shoulder and hip.

She walked past a Window Mart where Godlies and Holies shopped side by side. They were happy to rub shoulders with their enemies, as long as they could catch a rock bottom price. But Godlies and Holies had to use separate checkouts. Godlies could only buy certain items. And Holy workers lost their jobs if they dated a Godly.

Ellie walked past hedges, which were trimmed so flat, they looked like tables. Past a branch of Rablays, where Papa Tamsin was inputting data. Past twelve checkpoints, thirteen listening posts, and fourteen robotic ants; omniscient spies who were so small, everyone ignored them.

Ellie walked into a Madsanto *'Palace of Mating'*.

She approached a screen and assessed the first person who appeared. She looked at that man, who had buckteeth and wonky eyes. Then she shook her head.

"Too ugly," she said.

She tutted, swiped left, and checked out the next man.

"His nose is too big," she said.

She swiped left again.

"Too scrawny."

"Too spotty."

"Too scatty."

"Ah!" She cheered. "He'll do. He'll do very nicely indeed!"

Ellie swiped right to select that Handsome Man, who was muscled like a maiden's fantasy, with a chiselled jaw and a heavy-duty nose. Then she waited to see if the Handsome Man had selected her.

She twisted her hair, bit her nails, and tapped her toes.

A green light flashed above her head, a scanner debited her bank account, and a door shot up into the roof. Ellie stepped forward into a room which was covered in red satin. The Handsome Man was sprawled across a four poster bed. He was almost naked. But rose petals covered his penis, and white socks covered his feet.

Ellie blushed.

The Handsome Man beckoned her forward.

"Take this," he said.

Ellie frowned.

"What is it?" She asked.

"An orgasm pill."

Ellie turned her nose up.

"What?" The Handsome Man said. "You don't expect a natural orgasm, do you? I'm good, but I'm not that good!"

Ellie laughed. She took the pill, pulled her shirt over her head, rolled her shoulders and wobbled her breasts. Her waist slinked from side to side, and her stomach shimmied in the dark blue light.

The Handsome Man ogled Ellie.

"The meat is hung out for display," he said.

Ellie giggled like a little girl. She slowly unclasped her bra, paused for effect, and then let go. Ellie jiggled her belly. Her bra fell to the floor.

The Handsome Man ogled Ellie's breasts, which were perfectly pert, thanks to the chemicals Ellie injected once a month.

Ellie tiptoed forward and jumped onto the Handsome Man, who pulled off her jeans. A button flew across the room. The Handsome Man flipped Ellie over, spread her legs, and thrust his penis inside her.

"Hang on," he said.

He popped a pill.

"This'll make me last all night."

Ellie smiled, relaxed, and closed her eyes. She moved back and forth, in time with her lover. They rocked and they rolled. They kept themselves occupied for over three hours.

"Time to go," the Handsome Man finally announced. "It's half past ten. It's almost sleep time."

Ellie nodded. She gathered her clothes as quickly as she could, got dressed and rushed out. She needed to be home by eleven, when the sleeping gas was released, because if she broke the curfew she would be indebted.

So she rushed past empty bridges, which crisscrossed each other in the sky. They were as impenetrable as the earth which supported them, and just as silent. She rushed past five giant gates, which blocked off a series of private neighbourhoods. And she rushed past a small tomato plant, which was growing between two paving slabs.

Ellie turned around. She watched on as that tomato plant swayed in the breeze, from left to right, as if it was dancing for the stars above.

She paused to think.

And then she bent down towards the plant. She crouched over its leaves, stared at its buds, and smelt its herby fragrance. She could almost taste it.

She paused to think again.

She knew that possessing a plant was a felony, for which she could be indebted. She knew she would be accused of 'profit crime' if she was caught. She knew there would be pain and sorrow.

Ellie had never disobeyed the bank before.

So she stood there and weighed up her options, whilst the plant bobbed back and forth.

Whilst the Muscular Guard tripped over his laces.

Whilst hundreds of workers ran home.

The more she tried to hold herself back, the more she wanted to take that plant. The more she resisted, the more she was tempted. She wanted to break the bank's rule, simply for the sake of breaking it.

So Ellie uprooted the plant.

She felt an enormous thrill. Butterflies fluttered in her stomach and her spine tingled. Her hands shook.

She simpered, puffed her chest, and put the seedling in her Mikey bag.

The chilly air invigorated her. The breeze kissed her neck. Three hours of sexual intercourse, and multiple orgasms, had made her feel unbeatable, indestructible and free. She felt like nothing could keep her down.

She ran back home, put her plant into a glass of water, and hid it beneath her floating bed.

It was eleven o'clock at night.

The lights went out, sleeping gas filled the room, and Ellie fell asleep. A grin covered her tired face. Images of tomato plants filled her dreams. And robotic ants crawled around in her hair.

* * *

Ellie's tomato plant grew larger over the weeks which followed. And as it grew, so did Ellie's sense of mischief. Her passivity was replaced with a burning desire to rebel.

But Ellie did not rebel. She kept herself occupied. It had become her second nature.

So instead of striking out, Ellie put a sound bubble over her head, and listened to some spherical audio; a soundless form of music, which was perfectly attuned to the listener's mood.

Sweet vibrations massaged Ellie's brain. Her auditory cortex registered the silent melodies. It sent a message to her motor cortex, which made her foot tap. And it sent a message to her cerebellum, to trigger an emotional response.

Ellie experienced all the benefits of music, in an optimised form, without hearing any actual songs.

She threw the sound bubble to the floor.

"Aaagh!!!" She screamed.

The sound bubble turned itself off, and debited Ellie's bank account.

Ellie stormed into her bedroom and unearthed her old CD player. She wiped a layer of dust from its surface, and pressed the play button. The sound of Natale Refugee All Stars filled the room.

It sounded terrible. It was screechy, and it did not match Ellie's mood. But it made Ellie smirk. That music's imperfections, humanity and personality, added something intangible yet oddly real. Her reaction did not make any sense, but Ellie did not care. She fell onto her floating bed and closed her eyes. She felt a wave of nostalgia wash over her.

Her telebeamer buzzed into life.

"What this, mummy?" Democracy squealed. "Turn infernal racket off. Pfft! Did elephant trample ear? OMG! Your generation knows nothing about music."

"Oh, sorry."

"It's not cool to sound listen, mummy."

"Well, no."

"LOL! Mummy, you funny!"

"I'm glad you think so."

Ellie laughed, flicked her hair behind her head, and got out of bed.

A robotic ant scuttled across the floor.

Ellie turned a pale shade of white.

"Ah!" She screamed. "What on earth happened to your arm?"

Democracy giggled and looked down at the stump which was hanging from her shoulder.

"Got stuck in education chamber," she said. "Get prosthetic me! Be stronger than other kids!"

"And who's going to pay for that?"

"You are!"

"No I'm not! You're far too young for a prosthetic."

"But mummy!"

"But nothing! Get yourself to a stem cell pharmacy, and ask them to grow you a replacement. It'll only take a week. And no more talk of prosthetics. You're my daughter, not my robot!"

Democracy giggled.

"Soon we'll all robots be," she said. "Soon perfection compulsory. Imaginations no more. Wholly rational be! Wholly profitable be!"

"You won't have any freedom at all!"

"OMG! Mummy! Freedom has long and terrible history. Better off without."

The electronic wallpaper changed from tartan to green.

Democracy pulled her bottom lip.

Ellie changed the subject.

"What else have you been up to at school?" She asked.

"Learnt history, mummy. Leant about how monopolies wealthed us, with bank support. About how silly people were in past, when they business managed, without decision computers. And about how slow school was before Rablays takeover."

Ellie rolled her eyes.

"Really! True! Rablays stuck thousands of cell-sized computers, called '*nanobots*', to brain. They tell me to medicine take. They pathogen exterminate. They neurone suppress, to virtual-reality create. They appliance operate. They information store, like hard drive. And they link brain to Woogle.

"Computer me! I can anything find! Any document! All know-how! Learnt more in one year, than you in ten. Ready me to workforce join!"

"But you're only six," Ellie replied.

"So what? OMG! It not profitable to school stay. And anyway, me already cleverer than you, thanks to nanobots. LOL! Me superhuman!"

Democracy giggled.

"Me more obedient than you too," she said. "Me top of Pineapple obedience class, and Madsanto passivity class. Me rule follow, uniform wear, and subordinate self. Me will perfect employee be. Me will super profitable be!"

Ellie chuckled.

"You're a regular onion," she said. "Whenever I peel a layer back, I find another layer to discover!"

"LOL," Democracy laughed. "It's true! But have to go now. Me have McRonalds inferiority class. Bye, bye."

"Goodbye!"

"All hail the bank!"

"Okay."

Ellie turned her telebeamer off, and turned her CD player on. She caressed that machine as if it was her lover.

She did not care what her daughter thought. Listening to music on that old device made her feel young; like she was performing with her band, or spraying graffiti across the walls of her town.

Ellie closed her eyes and reminisced about her youthful escapades. She dreamt about the songs she sang, and the slogans she painted. And, as she reminisced, her passivity faded away. It was replaced by a burning desire to rebel.

So Ellie put some spray paint and a balaclava into her Mikey bag. She waited for the sun to set, snuck out of her flat, and walked through the streets of new Natale.

She walked past bars, karaoke clubs and brothels, which were jam packed with drunken workers. She walked past the remains of bulldozed buildings, and building sites where new skyscrapers were being built. She walked past holographic bushes, which stuck out of a concrete path, and a concrete sculpture of a tree.

She put her balaclava over her head, and held a can of spray paint in her shaky hand.

Outside a row of four McRonalds, she drew a picture of Donald McRonald and Ricky Mouse, abducting a naked child.

Outside a Window Mart, she sketched a bottle of 'Killer Cola', an upside down Mikey squiggle, and a Pineapple logo with five bites removed.

And outside a Rablays police station, she scribbled, 'If graffiti changed anything, it would be illegal'.

A finger tapped Ellie's shoulder. Her heart jumped and her stomach dropped. She slowly turned around.

She came face-to-face with a Chiselled Policeman, who wore aftershave which smelled of musk, and a uniform which smelled of lavender. The microchip in his eye gleamed, and his earpiece glimmered.

JOSS SHELDON | 283

He was a Holy. All policemen were Holies.

"Well, well, well," he said. "What do have we here then?"

Ellie froze.

"Take this," the Chiselled Policeman continued.

Ellie took a flyer. It said, '*Graffiti is against the law. Anyone caught defacing bank property will be indebted*'.

Ellie winced. She panicked. Her heartbeat accelerated and her breathing stopped. Every muscle in her body tensed.

She stared into the policeman's eyes.

"What are you going to do?" She asked.

"Do?" The Chiselled Policeman replied. "I've already done my job. I'm a leaflet distribution operative."

"A '*leaflet distribution operative*'?"

"Yes. The police force was suffering from public sector inefficiency, so the bank took it over. It created the PR Police the very next day."

"How efficient!"

"Thank-you. Well the PR Police employed me as a leaflet distribution operative. I hand out flyers which prevent crime.

"Prevention! It's better than cure."

Ellie snickered.

"It sure is," she said.

"It sure is," the Chiselled Policeman replied.

He smiled, turned around, and walked off.

Ellie smiled, turned around, and looked back at the wall she had just graffitied. A robotic spider was removing the last drop of Ellie's paint. Her words had all disappeared.

A cat swiped its claw at the robotic spider.

A concrete leaf fell off a concrete tree.

A robot handed Ellie another flyer.

* * *

Ellie went for a walk.

Her rebellious urges had made her want to visit her childhood district. She wanted to see the McRonalds she once smashed, the checkpoints she once dodged, and the venues where her band had once performed.

But a fence surrounded the whole of old Natale, which was a Holy only area. A Rablays flag, which could be seen from anywhere in town, was raised in its centre. Ellie's family had been moved to a distant suburb.

So Ellie looked up at a floating billboard, the first in town, and shook her head. The billboard projected a three dimensional message, which said, 'Love the bank: It has made you rich'.

The sun shone brightly, and Ellie perspired.

She turned around and walked back past Natale University, which had been renamed 'The Morgan Rockchild Institute', after the Big Banker. She walked past a line of people, who were taking photos of a stuffed camel. And she walked past some motorists, who were sitting in their driverless cars, reading holographic newspapers.

"How ridiculous was it that we used to actually drive cars?" A Petite Worker asked. "What a waste of time and effort!"

Ellie pushed past a group of workers, a group of robots, and a group of climate refugees.

There were farmers whose fields had been swallowed by an ever expanding desert. Villagers whose homes had been flooded by the rising sea. And nomads whose land had been destroyed by soil erosion.

Those people mixed together with the natives, Holy immigrants and Godly refugees, who already called Natale their home. They worked for the monopolies. And they caused a wave of resentment.

"I can't stand those bloody climate refugees!" Tamsin told Ellie as soon as she arrived at work. "We should never have let them stay, with their strange ways and peculiar habits. What have they ever done for us? Nothing! They're no bloody use to anyone. And now they're taking our jobs. What chance do we have, when they're prepared to work for peanuts?

"We should expel those bloated leeches! Those circumcised ferrets! Those one-dollar whores!"

Ellie grimaced.

"You were a refugee once," she said.

"That was different," Tamsin replied.

"How?"

"I was local. I'm a Godly."

"So?"

"So I'm just like you!"

"Everyone's just like me. We're all the same deep down. We're all human."

Tamsin gave Ellie a condescending look. She tensed one cheek, raised one eyebrow, and clenched one lip.

A row of cogs spun around at top speed.

Ellie shook her head.

"We need to unite," she continued. "We shouldn't turn on each other, we should turn on the bankers. We can't live with them; they're too greedy. And we can't let this stalemate continue; it's killing us. They're playing for time, and we're playing into their hands. They're expanding their monopolies every day. We need to fight them every day, or we'll never get our lives back."

"You're crazy," Tamsin replied. "Fight them every day? Some of us have to work. Some of us have mortgages, credit card bills, and school fees to pay. Some of us have families to think about. Some of us are occupied with other things!"

"Some of us have priorities," Ellie snarled. "If you want to see your family, and if you want a life without debt, you need to fight!"

"But how?"

"By withdrawing your obedience."

"What?"

"By hitting the bank where it hurts; the bottom line. By working slowly, going home early, and refusing to buy their products."

"They'll kill us."

"We're worth more to them alive."

"No-one will join us."

"That's my main concern."

Ellie shrugged.

Tamsin scratched her nose with a paperclip.

Everyone got on with their work.

But over the weeks which followed, word began to spread. Some Godlies joined Ellie's go-slow. All the Holies worked as hard as before. Some youngsters went home early. All the older workers stayed behind. Some natives sabotaged the machines. Migrants fixed them all.

Squabbles broke out.

"You'll get us fired," a Hairy Holy cajoled.

"Let them fire us," a Hairy Godly replied. "They're nothing without us!"

"We're nothing without them," a Skinny Elder spat. "They pay our wages."

"We generate their wealth," a Skinny Youngster replied.

"They own our labour," a Scruffy Migrant scolded.

"It's our labour!" A Scruffy Native replied. "We need to take control!"

"We need to abolish debt."

"Without debt, there wouldn't be any money!"

A Pale Settler slapped a Pale Native.

A Tall Refugee pushed a Tall Local.

A Suntanned Woman kicked a Suntanned Man.

Everyone stopped working.

Everyone started shouting.

Everyone jumped up when a Bulky Manager stormed in.

The Bulky Manager looked furious. She had a face which could have belonged to a medieval crusader, and a bottom which could have belonged to a whale. She was a Holy. All the managers were Holies.

"Attention!" She boomed.

Her steel-capped boots created a rat-a-tat beat as they stomped across the metal floor. Her deep nasal breaths filled the air. Her necklaces clinked.

"Workers!" She yelled. "Listen up!

"The bank doesn't care if you're rich or poor, local or refugee, native or immigrant, male or female, young or old, religious or secular, beautiful or ugly."

She paused for effect.

She kept her feet rooted to the floor, and looked around the room. Her head moved from one shoulder to the other. She stared into the eyes of every single worker.

"The bank doesn't care if you're a Godly or a Holy!"

The Bulky Manager paused again.

"The bank only cares about your productivity. You all have the same paymaster. Don't ever forget that!"

The Bulky Manager raised her eyebrows.

Ellie took a deep breath.

Tamsin trembled.

"We've been happy to let you squabble. Hell, we've been encouraging Godlies and Holies to fight for centuries. If those disagreements keep you occupied, and stop you from turning on us, then they're a good thing. But don't ever let those disputes disrupt your work. Don't ever let them affect your productivity.

"There'll be hell to pay!

"Just remember; you're only worth what you produce. If you don't generate profit for the bank, your lives aren't worth a cent. You need to justify your existence. You need to make loads of money!"

The Bulky Manager took a deep breath.

"Thank-you for listening," she concluded. "This warning was brought to you by Poka Cola. *'Things go better with Poke'*."

* * *

The doors slid open and four members of the work police stormed into Ellie's flat.

"We've encountered, encountered, encountered!" The Spotty Soldier cheered.

"Engage, engage, engage!" The Rosy Soldier replied.

"Encounter!"

"Engage!"

"Encounter!"

"Engage!"

"Encounter!"

"Engage!"

The television played an advert for plastic flowers.

The electronic wallpaper turned pitch black.

The Rosy Soldier grabbed Ellie's shoulder.

"Gotcha!" He said. "Tut, tut, tut. You're coming with us!"

The Squat Soldier smirked.

The Spotty Soldier and Arun high-fived.

Ellie's heart rebounded off her ribcage. Her pulse quickened, and her forehead began to sweat.

"Why?" She asked. "What for? What have I done?"

The Rosy Soldier sniggered.

"We've caught you red handed," he said. "You know exactly what you've done."

The Spotty Soldier cracked some sunflower seeds and threw them into his mouth.

The Squat Soldier picked his nose.

Arun winced.

"It's quite clear that you're a terrorist," the Rosy Soldier concluded. "You're coming with us."

The Spotty Soldier blindfolded Ellie, tied her hands behind her back, and carried her outside. He dumped her, face down, onto the floor of a driverless jeep.

They waited there, beneath a thousand windows and two thousand cameras, whilst a worker set herself on fire, and a cockerel crowed.

Their vehicle turned itself on. It sped down roads which were made of cracked concrete, roads which smelled of rotting fish, and roads which turned one way and then the other. They skidded around corners, scaled steep inclines, and slid down rutted streets. They whizzed past towers which had glass facades, towers which were covered in giant screens, and towers which were branded all over.

They stopped outside a skyscraper. Fiery sunbeams reflected off of that building's glassy exterior. Ellie's hair began to steam.

She was taken down an endless corridor, which was narrow and dark. Every surface was painted black. There weren't any doors for over a hundred metres. Orange panels flickered and flashed.

She was thrown into Room 4, and handcuffed to a rail.

A cockroach crawled up her leg.

The Toothy Officer stormed in, slammed the door, and sat down in front of Ellie. His knees pressed up against Ellie's knees. His nose touched Ellie's nose.

Ellie could taste that man's breath. She could smell his testosterone. She could hear his heart beat.

The Toothy Officer put his palm on Ellie's inner thigh, and slowly stroked it up towards Ellie's crotch.

"Tut, tut, tut," he said.

Ellie wore a defiant expression.

"We know what you've done. The bank is watching you!"

"And?"

"You're guilty of profit crime!"

The Toothy Officer chomped his jowls. The uneven tips of his jagged teeth ground into each other. They almost screeched. But a thick layer of plaque lubricated the chafing, and dulled the sound. So Ellie did not react.

Ellie just exhaled. She was relieved to discover that she had not been arrested for her graffiti, for listening to real music, or for hiding a tomato plant. She clung to those small victories. They made her feel triumphant.

"I'm productive enough," she said in a confident manner. She twitched her nose, tutted, and sank bank into her chair.

"We'll see what the computer has to say about that!" The Toothy Officer cheered.

He scanned Ellie's ID, and tapped his smart table, which came to life. He tapped a Rablays logo, a picture of Ellie, and a couple of blue icons.

"Ah!" He cheered. "You make jeans!"

"Yes. And?"

"You made a thousand pairs yesterday."

"Yes."

"And you made a thousand pairs the day before."

"Yes."

"And you made six thousand pairs last week."

"Yes. So?"

"Computer says 'yes'. Six thousand pairs of jeans is productive. Very profitable indeed!"

Ellie lifted her shoulders, pushed her head forwards, and stared at the Toothy Officer.

"So I've done nothing wrong," she said. "I've been a good worker. Pfft! It doesn't matter what we do; a man's accusing finger always finds a woman. You're just the same as all the rest."

The Toothy Officer 'oohed' and 'aahed'. He swiped his smart desk. He tapped an image of Ellie's face, dragged it across the table, and dropped it onto an icon marked 'Productivity Checker'.

The smart desk made a trillion calculations in a nanosecond. Then it flashed red and white.

"Your stitching is good," the Toothy Officer said.

"Thank-you," Ellie replied.

"Your work is consistent."

"Thank-you."

"Your jeans sell for a profit."

"So I'm not a profit criminal then. Can I go home now, please? This has all been one big misunderstanding. A sorry mistake."

The Toothy Officer shook his head.

"Computers don't make mistakes," he said. "If you've been arrested for committing profit crimes, it's because you've committed profit crimes. You're guilty! Computers are never wrong."

The Toothy Officer leaned in. His forehead touched Ellie's forehead. His eyes stared into Ellie's eyes. His hand crept towards Ellie's vagina.

"Why did you do it?" He demanded.

"Do what?" Ellie replied.

"Do it?

"What?"

"You tell me."

"I didn't do anything."

"So you say."

"It's the truth."

"The truth?"

"Yes."

"You can't handle the truth!"

"Your computer can't handle the truth."

"My computer is always right!"

The Toothy Officer leaned out, snickered, and tapped his lower lip.

"Can I go now?" Ellie asked.

"No," the Toothy Officer replied. "We don't let profit criminals go. It's not profitable. And the supremacy of profit is absolute!"

The Toothy Officer tapped his smart desk.

"Ah!" He cheered. "How unusual!"

He gave Ellie a knowing glare. It contained half a smile, which was full of respect, and half a frown, which was full of disdain. His eyes widened, and his face narrowed.

The cockroach crawled back down Ellie's leg.

"What is the bank's corporate slogan?" The Toothy Officer asked.

"Work is virtuous," Ellie replied. "Idleness is evil. Keep yourself occupied."

The Toothy Officer shook his head.

"Not that one," he barked. "The other one!"

"What other one?"

"Tut! Don't you know anything?"

The Toothy Officer leaned over Ellie. He shoved his forehead into Ellie's forehead, and stared into Ellie's eyes.

Ellie almost fell out of her chair.

"Consume things you don't need," the Toothy Officer barked. "With money you don't have, to make an impression which won't last, on people you don't like!"

Ellie stared at the Toothy Officer with a look of confusion. She puckered her lips, scowled and squinted.

"I've never heard that," she said.

"We've never said it," the Toothy Officer replied.

"So how was I supposed to know about it?"

"Because it's obvious. We've covered every inch of this town with adverts encouraging you to buy things you don't need. We've provided you with a whole array of credit options to buy those things. And we've given you countless opportunities to flaunt your wealth.

"Really! Everyone else understands the need to consume more than they produce, spend more than they earn, and take on more debt than they'll ever be able to repay.

"What makes you so special? Why couldn't you be like the rest of your fellow workers? Pfft! You're clearly not a team player. You're not patriotic at all!"

Ellie shook.

"I don't understand," she said. "I thought I was accused of profit crime."

"You're quite clearly guilty of profit crime!"

"How? I've produced lots of jeans, which have made lots of profit."

"But you haven't bought enough."

"What?"

"The bank can only make profits if its workers *buy* its products. Production on its own is not enough. Hell, we have machines for that.

"How long do you think you'll be able to work in a clothes factory? People are already printing clothes on 3D printers. Factories like yours will be obsolete within months.

"No, production is not enough. You need to buy things too.

"Your lack of spending has hit the bank's bottom line. You're a disgrace. You're the worst sort of profit criminal there is. A miser!"

Ellie looked furious.

"I spend money!" She shouted. "My home is full of gadgets. I have a mortgage. I pay for music and sex. I spend lots of money. Loads and loads of money!"

"That may well be the case," the Toothy Officer replied. "But the computer says you don't spend enough, and the computer is always right."

The Toothy Officer touched two corners of his desk, and then moved his fingers in a clockwise direction. The display spun around.

"See!" He said.

Ellie looked at the numbers which were displayed on the smart desk. They formed a never ending series of columns and rows. Some numbers brightened, and others faded. Some were red and some were black. They were all so tiny, Ellie could barely see them.

She took a deep breath. She focussed on the screen. And she realised that those numbers represented every transaction she had ever made.

At the bottom were two flashing figures:

'*Lifetime income: e$709,356*'

'*Lifetime expenditure: e$678,771*'

"We live in a beautiful world," the Toothy Officer mused. "It's a beautiful thing, this marriage of costs and revenues, this supremacy of profit. But you've sullied this thing of beauty by spending less than you've earned.

"I hereby find you guilty of profit crime.

"All hail the bank!"

Ellie's stomach dropped. Her eyes were full of despair. Although she tried to hide it, her hands trembled and her heart raced.

"What are you going to do to me?" She asked.

The Toothy Officer chuckled. He laughed so much, his teeth pointed out of his mouth. Incisors shot one way, and molars bent back the other. They were yellow, black and greasy.

"We're going to indebt you!" He sang. "We're going to charge you for all the items you should have bought but didn't. And we're going to advertise you."

"Advertise me?"

"We're going to take you to prison, and we're going to advertise you until you conform. You'll be made to see reason. You'll be made to see that the supremacy of profit is absolute!"

The smart table went into screen saver mode. Its surface looked like polished oak.

A robotic ant scuttled across the floor.

Ellie held her head in her hands and cried.

* * *

The Slender Guard sat next to Ellie as they drove through Natale.

"Okay," she said. "We're taking you to prison."

Ellie cringed. She felt beaten, bleak and weary.

"Fuck you bitch," she said. "Fuck you! Fuck you! Fuck you!"

The Slender Guard gurgled.

She dragged Ellie out the jeep, escorted her into an elevator, and pushed her into her own flat.

"This is your prison now," she said. "Enjoy your stay."

Ellie looked around at her floating sofa, electronic wallpaper, and telebeamer. She furrowed her brow.

"But this is my home," she replied. "This isn't a prison."

The Slender Guard laughed.

"We don't differentiate between prisons and homes, cells and bedrooms, or prisoners and workers," she said. "We're not that unenlightened.

"No, we only care about profit. The supremacy of profit is absolute!"

"Oh," Ellie replied. She could not think of anything else to say.

An armchair floated across the room and scooped her up. She fell back into its cushioned seat, and rested her elbows on its padded arms.

"Comfortable?" The Slender Guard asked.

"Yes."

"Good. Let's begin your advertising."

Ellie's electronic wallpaper turned into one giant screen. At its centre was an avatar of Morgan Rockchild, which looked exactly like the Big Banker himself. It had the Big Banker's crooked nose, bony fingers, and bent spine.

"The bank loves you," the avatar said. "It wants to make you happy."

"I'd be happier if the bank left me alone," Ellie replied.

The Slender Guard slapped Ellie's face with a metal chain.

"Don't answer back!" She demanded. "Workers are not to talk to the Big Banker. Insubordination will not be tolerated here!"

Ellie bit her lip.

Her tea maker made her a cup of milky tea.

Her armchair massaged her shoulders.

"The bank would like to remind you just how happy it's made you," the avatar continued. "Because the bank loves you. Truly, it does!"

The avatar disappeared.

It was replaced by an image of the satin covered room in the Madsanto Palace of Mating. Ellie's legs were spread, her back was arched, and her face was a picture of bliss.

The Slender Guard put a gas mask over her head. It made her look like an alien anteater; with flat ears and a tubular snout.

A mixture of happy gas, aphrodisiac gas and orgasm gas, sprayed out of eight tiny tubes. A white cloud swirled around the room. It drifted up Ellie's nostrils.

Ellie grinned. She watched herself make love to the Handsome Man. Her eyes were clamped open, and her ears heard every sound. Every groan and every pant. Every scream, screech and shriek.

It was realistic. It was beautiful. It was real horrorshow.

Ellie felt amazing. She felt elated, ecstatic and euphoric.

Her pants moistened. Her clitoris vibrated. An orgasmic surge rushed through her body, and covered every inch of her skin.

"Yes!" She screamed. "Yes! Yes! Yes!"

Ellie writhed and wriggled. Her pelvis thrust up into the air. Her head slashed from side to side. And her hair became a tangled mess.

"Yes!" She screamed. "Yes! Yes! Yes!"

She gripped hold of her armchair. Her nails ripped through its leather. Every nerve ending in her body tingled. Her vagina buzzed.

"Yes!" She screamed. "Yes! Yes! Yes!"

Sexual juices soaked her pants.

"Yes!" She screamed. "More! More! More!"

The video stopped.

Morgan Rockchild's avatar re-appeared.

"The bank loves you," he said. "And it wants you to love it back. It wants to make you happy. Just look how happy it can make you!"

Ellie nodded furiously.

"I'm happy!" She shouted. "I'm happy! Happy! Happy! Happy! Give me more. More! More! More! Don't stop. I want more!"

Morgan Rockchild's avatar smiled, tilted its head to one side, and clicked its fingers.

Ellie's crotch thrust up into the air.

"Yes!" She screamed. "Yes! Yes! Yes!"

The avatar grinned.

"All I have to do is click my fingers," it said. "And you'll have the best orgasm you've ever had. The bank will make you happier than you've ever been. Because the bank just wants to make you happy!"

Ellie jolted forward. Every part of her being cried out for more. She felt like a drug addict, in search of another hit. She was already experiencing withdrawal symptoms. Her hands shook, her skin turned white, and her face looked gaunt.

"Click your fingers!" She shouted. "Click! Click! Click!"

The Slender Guard walked towards Ellie, stood over her, and placed a phone by her hand.

A wisp of orgasm gas swirled around a light.

The avatar tapped its fingers.

"Each time you press the beige button on your phone, an advert will be played, and more gas will be released. You'll experience a beautiful orgasm."

Ellie clenched her jaw. She tapped the beige button twenty times. She tapped it so violently, she almost broke the phone.

An advert for eye implants began.

Gas filled the room.

'Why be human, when you can be superhuman?' A narrator asked in a soothing voice. *'Glapso's microchips will help you to see the world in a whole new way.'*

Ellie felt orgasmic. Her body sang. Her limbs danced. Her torso lurched. And her hips quaked.

'Glapso's eye chips will help you to see in the dark! Glapso's eye chips will allow you to zoom in and out! Glapso's eye chips will record everything you see!'

Ellie edged closer to nirvana. Her gasps tasted of sugar. Her movements felt sublime. And her ears were bombarded by a choir of angels.

"Yes!" She screamed. "More! More! More!"

She watched a family use their eye implants to discover the world around them. A mother scanned a park for potential threats. A girl scanned a crowd for potential friends. And a boy analysed some football stats.

Ellie had an orgasmic fit. She waved her hands in the air, and kicked out with her feet. She thrashed her head from side to side. Juice saturated her crotch. Her thighs dripped, and her jeans squelched.

"Eye implants!" She screamed. "I love Glapso! I want Glapso's microchips! Eye chips! Eye chips! Eye chips! Yes! Yes! Yes!"

The advert finished.

Ellie's electronic wallpaper turned green.

Ellie reached for the phone. Her hand trembled so much, she almost dropped it. She placed it on her thigh, held it still, and pressed the beige button again.

An advert for nanobots began.

Gas filled the room.

'Why be human, when you can be superhuman?' A narrator asked in an assertive voice. *'Pineapple's nanobots will enable you to think in a whole new way. Pineapple's nanobots will tell you if you need medicine, give you enough oxygen to climb a mountain, and enhance every receptor in your body!'*

Ellie began to orgasm. Her groin felt warm and tingly. It pulsated. It throbbed with soft intensity and radiant heat.

Her body convulsed, and her mind buzzed.

"Yes! Yes! Yes!" She screamed. "I love Pineapple! I want Pineapple's nanobots! Nanobots! Nanobots! Nanobots! Yes! Yes! Yes!"

The advert finished.

Ellie's electronic wallpaper displayed a flowery pattern.

Ellie grabbed the phone. She tapped the beige button. She pressed the beige button. She thumped the beige button, over and over again.

An advert for smart beds began.

Gas filled the room.

'Why sleep, when you can have super-sleep?' A narrator asked in an eager voice. *'Idea's smart bed will give you the best night's sleep you've ever had. Idea's sensory deprivation chamber will block out distractions. Idea's motion sensors will turn your coffee maker on as soon as you awake. Idea's mood enhancers will prepare you for the day ahead.'*

Ellie climaxed. Her clitoris throbbed. Her labia majora trembled. Her labia minora shook. Her chest shook. Her whole body shook. It shivered, shuddered and shimmied.

"Yes! Yes! Yes!" She screamed. "I love Idea! I want Idea's smart bed! Smart bed! Smart bed! Smart bed! Yes! Yes! Yes!"

The advert finished.

Ellie's electronic wallpaper displayed a galaxy full of stars.

"The bank loves you," Morgan Rockchild whispered. "It wants to make you happy."

Ellie parted her stiff legs, and sank back into her armchair. She was exhausted, but she was keen. With the excitement of a child on Christmas Day, she swiped her phone and logged on to *Spamazon*. She ordered two Glapso eye implants, a thousand Pineapple nanobots, and an Idea smart bed. Hundreds of thousands of eDollars were debited from her account. An orgasmic surge flushed through her body.

"Yes!" She screamed. "Yes! Yes! Yes! More! More! More!"

Ellie rolled over and fell asleep.

The Slender Guard removed her gas mask and left the room.

The tea maker made itself a cup of milky tea.

11. ARUN

Arun sat down in his new flat, dressed in clothes he had just printed, and began to perspire. A pearl of sweat rolled over his tiny nose, and reached his chubby cheek. Arun flicked his hair behind his ears, and used his nanobots to change the opacity of his solar windows.

He turned, sat down on a floating sofa, and beamed with pride.

It had taken him years to settle in old Natale. Years of violence, years of misery, and years of pain. Years spent hiding in confiscated homes, cold and hungry, living with a strange mix of angry soldiers and outright vigilantes. Years spent working on an assortment of military missions, which came to an abrupt end whenever a politician had a change of heart. Years spent denying his conscious, his morals and his soul; not knowing who to trust, or who to avoid.

But all the dreams which sustained him during those years had finally come true. He had bought his very own flat.

Arun sat back and took it all in.

He took in the wardrobe which cleaned his clothes, the interactive mirror which monitored his health, and the fingerprint padlocks which protected his possessions. He looked at his holographic friends, electronic wallpaper, and self-cleaning carpets. And he looked at his wireless energy router, which was part of a continental grid. It powered everything in Arun's flat, apart from his model giraffe, which was still missing half a leg.

That giraffe watched Arun's robot, Napoleon, in silence.

When he first bought Napoleon, Arun had gazed at it as if it was a spaceship from another galaxy. It looked so alien to him; so modern, futuristic and strange. But possessing it had made Arun feel special. No-one else in old Natale had owned a robot.

That changed over the days which followed.

Three weeks later, pretty much everyone in his district owned a robot. Those who did not were looked down upon. People thought they were weird, reactionary, and behind the times.

But everyone used their robots differently. Arun, who lived on his own, talked to Napoleon whenever he felt lonely. And they jogged together too. Napoleon was a sporting model, whose brothers had swept the board at the last Robot Olympics. It was tall and skinny, with lifelike skin and human hair. It was programmed to cater to all of Arun's needs.

"Aren't you going to eat that?" It asked.

Arun looked down at a plate of laboratory grown meat, which sat on a bed of sautéed pomato; a vegetable which was half tomato and half potato. A glass of *Soylent*, a meal replacement shake, sat on a floating table.

"I slaved over a hot 3D printer all day, making you that," Napoleon complained.

A robotic cat curled up in a ball next to Arun's feet.

An interactive window displayed an ocean view.

Arun raised his eyebrows.

"I'm eating," he said. "Give me a chance. Blimey! You're worse than a woman!"

He stuck his fork into a piece of pomato, held it up in the air for Napoleon to see, and then put it in his mouth. He chewed slowly and deliberately. He gave Napoleon a sarcastic smile.

"Happy?" He asked.

"I'm happy if you're happy," Napoleon replied. "I just want to make you happy."

Arun finished his meal, and waited for his friends to buzz in.

The first person whose hologram appeared was the Orthodox Settler, who wore lipstick which changed colour once a minute. She was joined by her husband, whose bushy beard had turned a bright shade of white. They were followed by the Militant Settler, who wore interactive trousers, and his wife, who wore a home-printed dress. Papa Arun and Mama Arun's holograms soon followed. The Economic Settler and his lover did not. They had both been run over by a driverless tank.

The Owlish Settler scratched his new ear, which was a replacement for the ear he lost in combat. The Pale Settler ate seven chicken wings, which had all been grown on the back of one chicken. And the Cherubic Settler held his designer baby. His other child closed his eyes and played a computer game, which his nanobots generated inside his head. He experienced a high degree of movement, whilst his body remained totally still.

Those holograms were dotted around Arun's lounge. They sat on chairs which were still in their own homes. And they drank holographic cups of tea.

Arun's holographic television flashed.

'*Seven species have been wiped out, and twelve more have been endangered*', the News Broadcaster read. '*Rhinos, elephants, hedgehogs, red squirrels, brown hares, bees and turtle doves are now all extinct. Natterjack toads are set to join them.*

'*Environmentalists have blamed these extinctions on the rising levels of carbon dioxide in the atmosphere. But Morgan Rockchild has said the bank would be quick to act.*

"*This attack on our bottom line is a clear example of anti-profitism*", the Big Banker told Protokian News. '*Bees are productive members of the economy, who pollinate the vegetables we grow in our giant vats. Rablays scientists are doing everything they can to de-extinct them, and are on schedule to resurrect them by the end of the week.*

"*All hail the bank!*"

Napoleon made some tea.

Arun tapped his thigh.

His guests continued to mutter.

"Terrorists," the Orthodox Settler spat.

"Terrorists," the Pale Settler snarled.

"Terrorists," Mama Arun grunted.

The Owlish Settler shook his head

"Don't we have more important things to worry about?" He asked. "Of course unprofitable animals are being wiped out. Of course the environment's changing. The only constant is change!"

"The only constant is danger," the Militant Settler replied. "Everyone hates us! All the Godly countries hate us. The whole world hates us. They hate everything we stand for. And they want to destroy us. They want to dress us up in striped pyjamas, put us in a gas chamber, and make us inhale Zyklon gas. They want to destroy our land, our homes, and our animals. They won't rest until the Holy race is extinct!"

Arun used his nanobots to increase his mother's resolution and his father's brightness.

The Pale Settler used his nanobots to send a text message.

The Orthodox Settler grimaced.

"I fear this turmoil will send us back to the unmentionable times," she said.

"We'll all be lost, like tears in the rain," the Militant Settler agreed.

"I don't understand why they're attacking our animals," the Pale Settler screamed. "We're God's chosen people!"

They all shook their heads.

They all looked out of an interactive window.

They all watched the holographic television.

'*The bank is making cutbacks*', the News Broadcaster continued. '*It's calculated that workers in the manufacturing sector are no longer profitable. It's insisting that workers are productive at all times*'.

Arun tapped his thigh.

Condensation dripped from the ceiling.

The Orthodox Settler's Husband spilled holographic tea.

"The robots are taking over," he screamed.

"What are we going to do when they produce everything?" The Cherubic Settler screeched. "How on earth are we going to be profitable then? We can't let robots do our jobs. We have no reason to exist, other than to toil!"

"The robots are terrorists!" Mama Arun squealed.

"Terrorists!"

"Terrorists!"

"The bank will indebt us!"

"They'll send us to prison!"

"We'll lose our jobs!"

"We'll lose our homes!"

"We'll suffer!"

"We'll die!"

"Don't panic!"

"Panic!"

"All hail the bank!"

"All hail the bank!"

* * *

Arun felt confident when he was called into the Squinty Officer's study. After years in the Protokian army, and in subsidiaries like the work police, he had finally found his groove. His ego was bigger than ever before. And he expected to be promoted.

"Sit down," the Squinty Officer said.

Arun sat down. His chair moulded to his body, cupped his neck, and massaged his back.

A robotic ladybug landed on a pile of digital paper.

The Squinty Officer watered a holographic plant.

"You've been unproductive," he barked.

He looked Arun up and down.

The carpet cleaned itself.

Arun winced.

"Do you think that's acceptable?"

"No sir!"

The Squinty Officer marched over to one wall, pivoted, walked back towards the opposite wall, and then turned to face Arun.

"Tut, tut, tut," he muttered. "The bank is not happy with your output. Its computer says that you're neither productive nor profitable. You're no bloody use at all!"

The bank had been in charge of the army since it sued the government, using PITT, for printing paper money. The bank had proved that its profits had been affected. But the government was unable to pay its fine, so it gave the army to the bank as compensation.

Since that time, the bank had insisted that every mission made a profit. Any soldier who took part in an unprofitable mission was sacked.

"Your last mapping," the Squinty Officer continued. "Generated ninety seven eDollars. But it cost one hundred and twenty six eDollars in labour, and seven eDollars in fuel. See!"

A computer screen, made solely of light and colour, rose up between Arun and the Squinty Officer.

Arun read the numbers on display.

The Squinty Officer gave Arun a knowing look.

"And your last demonstration of presence cost sixty eight eDollars. Do you know how much it made?"

Arun bowed his head.

"Nothing! Absolutely nothing! It was a complete waste of time."

Arun looked down at his feet.

"You're clearly not a profitable employee."

"Bu, bu, but," Arun stuttered. "I've followed orders, sir. I've obeyed every command. And I'll do everything I'm told to do in the future."

"You don't have a future! You're sacked! Pack your bags, return your uniform, and bugger 'orf!!!

The Squinty Officer shook his head.

"This sacking was brought to you by Madsanto," he concluded. "'*Growth for a better world*'."

Arun blew hot air through his nostrils, turned around, and trudged home with clenched fists and violent steps. He felt a sort of dejection which filled his mind with energetic angst, and his body with lethargic numbness. His limbs felt heavy, and his head felt light.

On his way, he passed a dystopian expanse of buildings. Built out of old fashioned bricks, and surrounded by barbed wire, they displayed a sign which said, '*The Department of Life*'. An industrial chimney was exhaling ribbons of black smoke, which smelt of burning flesh and chargrilled terror.

Arun saw a Muscular Worker who was carrying boxes of cats inside. His arms were covered in scratches, and his ears were full of screams.

"They're killing our cats," the Mad Lady squealed. "They're killing our souls. Cats are our souls! It won't be long before they come for our bodies. It won't be long before they burn us all! I heard it on the wind."

"Oh shut up," the Muscular Worker shouted back. "What do you know, you batty old witch?"

"Yeah," a Puny Worker cheered. "Cats aren't productive. They don't do anything to justify their existence. And neither do you! Go and get a job, you drowsy old sluggard, or we'll gas you too!"

The Mad Lady stormed off towards a giant statue of Morgan Rockchild, and Arun stormed off towards his flat. He put his finger on his keypad, and waited for his door to open. But nothing happened.

Arun pressed his keypad again. But nothing moved.

"Bloody technology," he muttered. "We should never have stopped using keys."

He returned to the lobby and approached a virtual concierge, who was standing behind a virtual desk, next to a virtual plant. Lines of static flickered across its brow. Its voice crackled as it spoke.

"Hello sir," it said. "How can I help you?"

"My keypad is broken," Arun replied. "It won't let me into my flat."

The virtual concierge tilted its head, whilst it assessed the situation.

"You don't live here anymore," it replied.

"Yes I do," Arun protested. "I own flat 529h."

"But you can't afford the mortgage repayments, now you're out of work. So your flat has been repossessed."

"I don't have a mortgage."

"Yes, you do."

"Since when?"

"This morning."

"Why?"

"A mortgage was created in your name."

"But I own my flat."

"Not anymore."

"What can I do?"

"Get a job. Work is virtuous."

"But..."

"Idleness is evil."

"But..."

"Keep yourself occupied."

"But..."

"All hail the bank!"

Arun blew hot air through his nostrils, turned around, clawed his fingers and scrunched his toes. He felt a sort of despair which filled his mind with anguish, and his body with sickness. His eyesight was blurred, and his stomach felt woozy.

He meandered past a skyscraper which was building itself. Four columns supported one giant platform, which was gradually ascending. It was building twenty floors a day, atom by atom, like a giant 3D printer.

There weren't any humans on site. Robots were doing all the work. They were inspecting each floor, performing safety checks, and making minor adjustments.

Robots were also running every factory in town. They moved stock at superfast speeds, loaded and unloaded driverless trucks, maintained equipment, and secured premises. In Natale Hospital, robots were performing operations with far greater precision than humans ever had. In Natale Museum, they were bringing exhibitions to life. And in outer space, they were exploring distant planets.

But they weren't in any shops. There weren't any shops in Natale. Internet shopping and 3D printers had replaced the need for physical stores. Workers no longer went out to buy things.

Yet, after years of population growth, workers were everywhere. They walked so quickly, they were blind to the world around them. And they were also blind to Arun, who was elbowed by a depressed Nostalgist, a stressed Garbage Designer, and an anxious Media Remixer. He was shoved one way, and shunted back the other. He was knocked in his side, shoulder and hip.

As people assaulted Arun's body, adverts assaulted his eyes. Microsensors, embedded in three dimensional billboards, scanned his microchips and analysed his personality. Then they played a series of personalised adverts, which only Arun saw or heard:

'How are your interactive windows working out for you, Arun? Would you like to order some more? They'd go really well in your bathroom!'

'You could really do with a Poka Cola, Arun. You've been walking for ages.'

'Arun! Buy a McBib! It's your favourite. Mmm, you're lovin' it!'

Arun ground his teeth, took a deep breath, and exhaled. He had been walking for over an hour, but he did not know where he was heading. The crowd had agitated him, the adverts had annoyed him, and the sun had mocked him. It had lurked above his head, the king of a cloudless sky, and shot fiery beams through a hole in the ozone layer.

Arun sweated profusely. His hair was sopping wet, his back was clammy, and his clothes were drenched.

He looked around and saw Tamsin. He felt elated. And he felt that he had to get his old friend's attention. So he pointed to his chest, pointed at Tamsin, gave her thumbs up, and nodded his head.

Tamsin stared back at him.

"Hello," he shouted.

He gave Tamsin another thumbs up.

A holographic advert for a Fastari whooshed by his nose.

Tamsin chuckled.

"Are you okay?" She asked.

She stretched out her hand, pulled Arun towards her, and looked into his eyes.

Arun cried. Tears flooded over his stubbly cheeks, and left a white residue on his face. His lip quivered, and his microchips fizzed.

Tamsin hugged him.

"It's okay," she said. "It's all going to be okay."

Arun bowed his head.

"No," he said. "You're wrong. Nothing's going to be okay again."

"Come, come," Tamsin replied. "Now, now. There, there."

Arun whimpered.

"Come back to mine," Tamsin said. "You can tell me all about it."

Arun blinked his tears back into his eyes.

He followed Tamsin past some workers, who were getting younger each year. Past some bosses, who had just printed themselves new organs. And past some checkpoints, which were performing thermal scans of the area.

They entered Tamsin's flat.

"Make yourself at home," Tamsin said. "You're welcome here. What's mine is yours."

Arun passed out on top of a giant pouf.

A robotic ant crawled up his leg.

Tamsin drank some tea.

* * *

Like so many former servicemen, homelessness was not the only challenge Arun had to face. He also had to battle with unemployment, post-traumatic stress and depression.

Arun's depression made him feel helpless and hopeless, uninterested in everyday tasks, unable to sleep or eat. He became addicted to antidepressants, which briefly lifted his mood, but made him feel nauseous. He suffered from dry-mouth, blurred vision, and severe bouts of drowsiness.

Arun's life would have spiralled out of control if it was not for Tamsin. She was his rock during those dark days. She housed him, fed him, and comforted him. It was no effort on her part. With her family away, she appreciated the company. But it meant the world to Arun. Their chats helped him to come to terms with his situation.

"Why are you helping me?" He asked when he first moved in. "I'm a Holy."

Tamsin smirked.

"You helped me once, remember?" She replied. "If it wasn't for you, I'd have been imprisoned. I'd have spent years breaking rocks in the baking hot sun, locked in a squalid cell, separated from my loved ones. You saved me back then. Now it's my time to save you!"

Arun smiled. He felt proud to have helped his friend, but he also felt guilty. He felt that he should have done more to help other innocent Godlies.

He saw visions of his victims' desperate faces.

He saw the Wizened Godly, who shook with fear. Who trembled so much, his thighs jumped up and down. His settee bounced. He experienced involuntary convulsions, which made him look possessed. His face was bright white, and his eyes were bright red.

Arun saw the Puny Refugee his unit had arrested for no reason. That child was so scared he choked. He coughed. He held his throat, bent over and gagged. His eyeballs pulsated. His lips tensed. A giant vein zigzagged across his forehead. And a drop of blood fell from his nose.

Arun had flashbacks whenever he tried to act. Whenever he cleaned his teeth, he saw the ghoulish face of a beaten toddler. Whenever he ate, he saw the blood soaked clothes of a wounded woman. And whenever he washed, he saw the decapitated corpse of an elderly man.

Arun was constantly on edge. He was jumpy, easily startled, and hyper-vigilant. He was irritable, angry and confused.

"Come, come," Tamsin comforted. "Now, now. There, there."

Arun whimpered.

Tamsin hugged him.

Her tea maker made them some tea.

Tamsin counselled Arun for several weeks. She listened to Arun's stories, felt his pain, and experienced his trauma. She weaned him off his antidepressants, provided him with a shoulder to cry on, and took him out for long walks. She fell in love.

Tamsin pressed her finger against an eyelash which had fallen onto Arun's cheek, and gently stroked it away. She paused, blinked, and gazed into Arun's eyes. Arun gazed back at her. They tilted their heads and leaned in to kiss.

Tamsin's telebeamer buzzed into life. It brightened. Morgan Rockchild's avatar appeared.

"Workers!" It boomed. "The bank's super-computer has made a series of advanced calculations. It's assessed your relationship, and concluded that it's not productive. It's not profitable for you to live like this. It would generate more money if you lived in separate homes."

The avatar gave Arun a stern look.

"It's up to you how you choose to live your life," it said. "It's a free country after all. But if you continue to pally up to the Godlies, I think you'll find opportunities hard to come by. I think you'll struggle to find another job."

Arun looked down at the ground.

"You need to behave like the other Holies. You can't afford to be different."

Arun bit his lip.

He stared at the newspapers which were displayed on a smart table. The Godly Times said, *'Unproductive Holies hold back profitable Godlies'.* The Holy Express said, *'Godlies take 10,000 jobs from Holy workers'.*

Arun grimaced.

The television broadcast the news, but Arun ignored it:

'The ice-caps have melted today. Sea levels are rising, and Natale could be under water within months. But the Big Banker has told his workers not to worry.

"GDP increased by twenty percent last year', he told Protokian News. 'I don't think a little bit of water is going to derail our economic success story!"

The avatar gave Arun a sympathetic look. It held itself in a sympathetic way. And it spoke in a sympathetic tone:

"You're in a new situation, you need time to adapt. It's fine, the bank understands. But if you want to be an upstanding member of the economy, you need to be productive. You need to act like a Holy. You can't afford to associate with Godlies. It's not profitable. And the supremacy of profit is absolute!"

Arun looked at Tamsin and saw his lost youth in her eyes. He saw childhood days and mischievous nights. He saw the last remnants of his innocence.

Tamsin's eyes begged Arun to stay. They screamed for his love. And they pleaded for his friendship.

"The bank will provide you with employment and accommodation," the avatar continued. "If you leave Tamsin, the bank will take care of you. But if you stay here, you'll never work again. The bank will indebt you. You won't be able to survive."

Arun started to sweat, shake and stammer. He could not handle the pressure. The pressure to remain loyal to Tamsin. The pressure to remain loyal to himself. The pressure to choose.

He felt vulnerable. He felt exposed, conflicted and weak.

He closed his eyes.

Tamsin touched his shoulder.

"It's okay," she said. "I understand. It's a matter of survival."

Arun winced, shivered, and buried his head beneath his armpit.

"I'll leave," he finally whispered. "I'll do whatever you want. I'll do it all. I'll do it now.

"All hail the bank!"

"All hail the bank!"

* * *

"Welcome to the *'Department of Bullshit Jobs'*," a Shaven Manager told Arun. "I think you'll fit in here. You'll be an upstanding member of our corporate family. And if you work really hard, you'll be promoted. Because hard work is always rewarded!"

The Shaven Manager smiled. It was a self-satisfied smile. A smile which was not actually happy, or content, but simply smug. It was superior. It was as if the Shaven Manager knew something that no-one else knew. He sucked his lips, which created brackets around his mouth. He bit the inside of his cheeks, which made his ears stick out. And he stared straight ahead, which made his pupils move to the centre of his eyes.

"Come with me," he said.

He led Arun into an atrium which was bigger than old Natale. A hologram, which was as wide as four football pitches, displayed the words 'Cost Eradication Division' overhead. And a corporate slogan said, 'Cutting costs, ending waste, eliminating inefficiency'.

A glass coliseum surrounded that atrium. It was two hundred stories tall, with offices on every floor, and millions of cameras in every office. Workers sat in cubicles, which separated them from their colleagues. They were all occupied. Everyone was cutting costs.

There were management consultants, financial analysts, and operations executives. Actuaries, auditors and administrators. Corporate lawyers, corporate psychologists, and corporate therapists.

And then there were the accountants. There were financial accountants, forensic accountants, and taxation accountants. Junior accountants, trainee accountants and bookkeepers. Directors of finance, finance directors, and management accountants. The accountants had created their very own fiefdom.

The Shaven Manager smiled.

"Come," he said.

He led Arun into a second atrium. A hologram, which was as wide as four football pitches, displayed the words 'Revenue Procurement Division' overhead. And a corporate slogan said, 'Increasing revenues, encouraging consumption, creating demand'.

A glass coliseum surrounded that atrium. It was four hundred stories tall, with offices on every floor, and millions of cameras in every office. Workers sat in cubicles, which separated them from their colleagues. They were all occupied. Everyone was increasing revenues.

There were sales executives, telesales executives, and advertising sales executives. Advertising managers, marketing managers, and public relations managers. Pipeline specialists, customer evangelists, and lead nurturing experts.

There were financial services operatives, stock brokers, and brand development gurus. Inbound marketing strategists, partnership directors, and data analysts. Documentarians, videographers and designers.

Arun looked confused.

"What do you produce here?" He asked.

The Shaven Manager laughed. He positively guffawed. He held his belly, bent over and choked. He laughed for five minutes. Then he straightened his back, wiped his brow, and looked into Arun's eyes.

"What do we produce?" He repeated between two deep breaths. "Produce! My dear boy, we produce profit!"

Arun looked bewildered.

"But what products do you produce?" He asked. "What goods and services do you supply?"

The Shaven Manager put his hand over his mouth, to stop himself from being crippled by another fit of laughter.

"Goods and services?" He repeated. "Supply! My dear boy, we don't produce any goods or services here. Pfft! We have machines and robots for that.

"No! We don't produce products. We cut out the middle man. We only produce profits! We increase revenues, and we cut costs."

Arun looked perplexed.

"This place is the pinnacle of private sector efficiency," the Shaven Manager explained. "Just think, none of these roles would exist if it wasn't for the profit motive. These people don't produce anything worthwhile at all! They don't do anything to enrich people's lives, and yet they still have jobs. They create money out nothing! They're the most profitable people in Protokia. And they earn more than everyone else!

"My boy, without this place no-one would work. None of us would be occupied. We'd all live idle lives of leisure. Our precious human resources would be wasted. Wasted! Workers would start rival firms to compete with the monopolies. Hippy proles would start revolutions. Intelligent workers would become layabouts and chavs.

"Would we want that sort of inefficiency? Of course not! Idleness is evil. Work is virtuous. It's a right and a sacred duty. We must do everything we can to keep ourselves occupied. And, thanks to the profit motive, we can! We can all work here at the Department of Bullshit Jobs. Because there'll always be jobs for paper pushers and profiteers. Oh yes!"

The Shaven Manager smiled. It was the same self-satisfied smile he had worn when he first met Arun. It was so skeletal, it made Arun grimace. And it was so creepy, it made Arun cringe.

The Shaven Manager patted Arun's back.

They walked through a glass door, and took an elevator to floor 103. They walked past swarms of workers, who were occupied by a multitude of tasks. Past Papa Tamsin, Ellie and Charlie. And past an Administrator who had been dead for five days. A Rotund Manager was promoting her corpse, because it had spent so long at its desk, without taking a single break.

Arun walked past thousands of other workers. He could not tell what any of them were doing. He could not be sure if any of them were working at all.

He finally arrived at his cubicle.

"Here you go," the Shaven Manager said.

"Thank-you," Arun replied. "What would you like me to do?"

"Increase our revenues."

"How?"

"However you like."

"Is there any training?"

"Oh no! The Cost Elimination Division cut the training budget years ago. It saved the bank billions of eDollars!"

The Shaven Manager turned, whistled, and walked away.

Arun stared at the screen in front of him. He stared at it for ten hours. Then he returned to his brand new home.

* * *

Arun returned the next day. And the day after that. And the day after that. He returned every day for over a year.

He never did any work. He just stared at the screen in front of him, kept quiet, and counted down the hours. Then he went home.

His post-traumatic stress flared up. He saw children with tear soaked cheeks, women with bloody hands, and pensioners with chattering teeth. He saw houses which had been turned into rubble, rooms which had been turned upside down, and olive groves which had been burnt to cinders. The office floor became a sea of boiling lava, full of sea monsters who tried to grab him. The ceiling filled with fiery red clouds, full of vampire bats and killer bees.

Arun spread his arms out wide, gripped hold of his chair, and banged his head against his desk.

But no-one said a word. No-one batted an eyelid.

Days passed by and weeks passed by. Nothing changed.

Then, after several months, the bank started to heap pressure onto Arun's shoulders. Messages told him to '*Work more*', '*Work harder*' and '*Work for longer*'. A leaderboard of the most profitable workers was displayed on the electronic walls of his cubicle. Daily memos stressed the need to increase revenues. He received video calls whenever he returned home.

So Arun fudgelled. He arrived before the other workers. He stayed later than everyone else. He never took a day off. He walked around with his chest puffed and his back held straight. He spent a week's salary on a tie, which circled his neck like a noose. And he spent a month's salary on a tailored suit, which made him look suave and sophisticated.

It did not take long for things to change. His colleagues gave Arun approving looks, nods and winks. His managers patted his back. He shot up the leaderboard of profitable workers.

But he did not do any work. He just stared at his screen for sixteen hours a day. Then he went home.

The boredom made Arun numb, and the numbness made Arun despair. His life was a monotonous routine, driven by habit, law, custom and prejudice. He questioned his job, his society, and his existence. He did not believe his job was necessary. He felt that his presence at work was completely pointless.

His morale sunk to an all-time low.

So in addition to his post-traumatic stress, which caused flashbacks every day, Arun's depression also flared up. He suffered from burnout, sickness, and a crisis of confidence.

He was not alone. Most of his colleagues were also depressed. They stressed about debt, unemployment, crime, violence, terrorism, war, and global warming. They worked themselves to death.

An Asymmetrical Worker died from an epileptic fit, after she had worked for seventy two hours without a break. A Pink Worker became so depressed, he opened a window and jumped out. And a Spotty Worker killed herself whilst rushing to meet a deadline. She sprinted across the office, and tripped over an upturned piece of carpet. She slipped, stumbled, and hit her head on the corner of a desk. Her skull shattered, and juice oozed out of her brain.

Those people all returned to work the day after they had died.

The Asymmetrical Worker returned with new internal organs, which had been grown using stem cells. The Spotty Worker returned with her brain in a prosthetic head. And the Pink Worker returned because he had not actually died. He had landed in a rope net, which the bank had erected when workers first started jumping out of the windows.

All three of those workers were made to work overtime, to compensate for the time they had taken off whilst they were dead.

But they were not alone. Workers seemed to die from strokes, heart attacks and cerebral haemorrhaging, every single day.

Arun sat in his cubicle, motionless, for sixteen hours every day.

He stared at his screen every day.

Then, in a beautiful act of defiance, a worker in a distant cubicle began to hum. A worker in the adjacent cubicle joined her. A few more workers sang along.

Before too long, everyone on floor 103 was singing an ancient shanty. Individually they were quiet, but together they were deafening. They created an orchestral sound which reverberated around the office.

'On the 5th of November back in '53,
The Big Banker, sure, he sent for me.
"We brought you here sonny, 'cause we want you to know,
We've got you a cubicle in the office below".'

A rotating red light started to flash.

'But when I protested, "I'm no volunteer",
The Big Banker said, "We ain't had one this year!
But that's a wee secret, between you and me,
Everyone's a wage slave, on floor one-o-three".'

Four members of the work police, who were all Holies, entered the office. They looked around, furrowed their eyebrows, and shrugged. They were happy to allow the song to continue, as long as it did not affect the department's bottom line. And, as far as they could tell, the office was still operating profitably.

'"Oh doctor, oh doctor, I'm not feeling too well",
"Well never mind sonny, we'll very soon tell.
Try taking some pills, and drinking some tea,
You'll be fit to slave on floor one-o-three".'
The work policemen all shrugged.
'Oh Susie, oh Susie, won't you be mine?
Wage slaves' wives have a hell of a time!
You'll live like a duchess with cash in your purse,
But your dear old man will end up in a hearse.'

Sixty members of the police police, the organisation which policed the police, entered the office. They all wore black suits, black ties, and black helmets. They might have been human, or they might have been robots; it was impossible to tell. But Arun was sure that, human or robot, they were definitely all Holies.

Eight members of the police police restrained the work policemen and bundled them away. The remaining policemen fanned out, and climbed onto some desks.

"Shut up!" They shouted in unison.

They did not sound angry. There was no emotion in their voices. Their words were short, sharp and snappy. Efficient. And totally devoid of humanity.

"Shut up! Shut up! Shut up!"

The singing stopped.

Silence filled the room.

Everyone pretended to work.

Arun pretended to work. He went home eleven hours later. And he returned the next day.

But his cubicle had changed overnight. Its walls had turned black. They had been soundproofed. And a door had been installed.

Whenever a worker spoke, their nanobots vibrated, which created a sensation akin to an electric shock. It brought on temporary bouts of blindness, and permanent bouts of silence. Whenever a worker wanted to move, even to go to the toilet, they had to apply for a permit. And whenever a worker looked around, an electronic surge span their head back towards their screens.

Arun hyperventilated. His back ached, his blood boiled, and his head pounded. He felt exhausted.

He sat paralyzed in his chair for hours on end. He saw flashback after flashback. He saw desperate children with pleading eyes. Teenagers in foetal positions on the floor. Mothers cradling their dead babies. Elderly ladies being dragged by their feet. And elderly men who were having heart attacks.

Arun banged his desk. He punched his desk. He thumped his desk over and over again.

'*Bang! Bang! Bang!*'

He kicked out. He thrashed about. He screamed.

"No! No! No!"

He took a deep breath, stared at his screen, and shouted at the top of his voice:

"Fuck the fucking fucked up bank. The fuckwit fuckers can fuck off to fuck town! Fuck 'em all! I hope they all fucking die!"

Arun panted. He groaned. And he felt a presence behind him.

"Well, well, well," A gruff voice rang out. "What do have we here then?"

A Pale Policeman grabbed Arun's shoulder.

"I don't think this place is for you," he said.

"Don't worry," a Cherubic Policeman consoled, whilst wiping his runny nose. "We'll find you a job somewhere more appropriate. We're on the case! The bank loves you after all. It only wants you to be happy."

"All hail the bank!"

"All hail the bank!"

* * *

A driverless jeep took Arun to the outskirts of Natale. It drove into a gated community. And it pulled up outside a private compound.

Two cast-iron gates swung open. Arun stepped out of the jeep, and into an air-conditioned garden, which surrounded a palatial mansion.

He felt an amazing sense of liberation. The garden was covered in real grass! Not fake plastic grass, but real grass! The trees weren't made of concrete, they were organic! The bushes weren't holograms, they were alive!

Arun fell to his knees and kissed the turf. He put his nose between a tulip's petals, and inhaled its sweet pollen. He licked a dock leaf.

He felt a presence behind him.

"My brother, this is how the one percent live!"

Arun turned around.

Stood in front of him, with broad shoulders and a wide smile, was Jim. He was in the flush of middle age, with a receding hairline, and a burgeoning belly. He looked healthy. His cheeks were rosy and his skin was tight. He had enough grey hair to make him look sophisticated, but not enough to make him look old.

He burped.

"My friend, this is how the one percent live," he repeated.

"The one percent?" Arun asked.

"The one percent of the one percent! The cream of the crop. The crème de la crème. The best of the best. The leaders, shareholders and bankers. The people who actually matter!"

"Matter?"

"Matter! Not like the ninety nine percent. The great unwashed. The filthy hoi polloi. Those herpes ridden gutter rats. Those feckless scrotes, with mush for brains. Those weak and feeble proles."

Jim looked into Arun's eyes.

He waited for a response which never came.

He shook his head.

"Those mangy plebeians who'd whore out their own mothers for a dime."

He raised his eyebrows.

"Those crusty loiter-sacks, who wouldn't know class if it hit them in the face with a shovel."

Arun remained silent.

"Those half-faced fustylugs! Those sour-faced prigs! Those two-faced lubberworts!"

Jim stared at Arun. It was an aggressive stare which radiated force. It made Arun's brain feel like a receptacle of toxic waste; hot, steamy and poisonous. He felt light headed, nauseous and giddy.

"They're a bunch of sissies," he replied.

Jim cheered.

"They're a bunch of plague-infested, debt-ridden, imbecilic layabouts! Good for nothing driggle-draggles! Maggot-laden, dandruff-headed, scum buckets!"

Jim looked at Arun and grinned. He put his arms around Arun's shoulders and led him away.

"Come, my son," he said. "Come with me. A great future awaits you, here with the one percent."

They walked into Jim's mansion, and entered a lobby which was bigger than most houses. Two curved escalators, which started and finished at the same points, looped outwards as they rose. Their bannisters were covered in gold, their sides were lined with silver, and their steps were carpeted with silk.

There weren't any interactive windows in sight. But real works of art, painted by real artists, lined every wall. The floor was made of polished oak. And the ceiling was covered in diamond chandeliers.

Arun looked around, open mouthed, and in awe.

"What do you do?" He asked.

"My brother, I'm in charge of the police police!" Jim replied.

Arun paused. He digested Jim's answer. He looked pensive.

"The police police," he finally asked. "Are they robots or people?"

"Yes," Jim sniggered.

"Which ones? Robots or people?"

"What's the difference?"

Arun shrugged.

Jim snickered.

A robot cleaned a vase.

"How did you become the head of the police police?" Arun asked.

"I killed the Chief Executive of Window Mart!" Jim boasted. He puffed his chest and lifted his chin. His cheeks bulged. He took a deep breath, and then he continued:

"That man refused to let his company be indebted. So the bank asked me to solve the situation. I broke into the Chief Executive's home, crept into his boudoir, and slit his throat whilst he was sleeping.

"It was a magnificent sight. Blood sprayed up like water in a fountain, and his eyes wore a look of pure confusion. It was perfect! A real thing of beauty! Unadulterated splendour!

"The Big Banker was so happy, he put me in charge of the police police. And here I am today; an upstanding member of the one percent!"

Arun looked at Jim with a look of nervous disgust.

"My friend," Jim explained. "We live in a dog eat dog world. It's us or them. We need to be the hunters, not the hunted; the persecutors, not the persecuted; the lions, not the sheep!"

Arun shuddered.

"My brother, I'm a lion! But you? You're still a puny little sheep. I could eat you whole!"

Jim chuckled. He put one hand on his hip, and his other hand on Arun's shoulder.

"But I don't want to eat you whole. I want to make you whole! I want to make you a lion!

"Because I like you. You're a good guy. A genuine chum! A brother from another mother. You and I are like peas in a pod. And I want to bring you into my clique."

Arun looked into Jim's eyes.

"Am I going to be a member of the one percent?" He asked.

Jim laughed. It was a blood-curdling sort of laugh. A laugh which was so malicious it was evil, so bold it made his face pulsate, and so menacing it seemed to shriek.

"You?" He guffawed. "You? A member of the one percent? You? Oh, my brother, you are funny. Ha, ha, ha!

"No, you'll never be a member of the one percent. You don't have the character. Ha, ha, ha! You're too soft. You can't control your conscience. You're a Holy, and that's essential; everyone in the one percent is a Holy. But you're not ruthless. No, you'll never join the one percent."

A robot, who was wearing a suit, held out a tray of teas.

Arun looked down at the hand-stitched carpet.

Jim grinned.

"I want you to manage withdrawals at the Department of Life," he said. "I want you to be my eyes and ears. My right hand man. My man on the ground."

Jim took a deep breath.

"You'll be rich. You'll live in a gated community, with a garden full of real grass!"

Arun smiled.

"Okay," he said. "All hail the bank!"

"All hail the bank!" Jim replied.

* * *

Arun arrived at the Department of Life; a dystopian expanse of buildings, which were made out of old fashioned bricks. An industrial chimney was exhaling ribbons of black smoke, which smelt of burning flesh and chargrilled terror.

Arun watched a Scabby Guard, who was escorting a group of profit criminals. A Small Guard, who was filling in a form. And a Tall Guard, who had a hairy nose.

"Hello sir," he said. "Please follow me."

They walked beneath a sign which said, 'Work will set you free'. Through one of forty sub-camps. And past a mixture of living quarters, medical facilities, canteens, pipes and muddy roads.

A line of profit criminals marched past, with their heads bowed, and their ankles chained together. They all wore blue and white striped pyjamas. They all had shaved heads. And they all had hollow expressions.

A door slid open. Arun and the Tall Guard walked through, and stepped onto a narrow escalator. The profit criminals walked down a staircase, in an adjacent tunnel. They got undressed in an underground changing room, and walked into a metallic chamber. Its floor was white and shiny, but its walls were all stained blue. Its ceiling was covered in marks, and its lights were covered in stains.

Arun watched from an adjoining room, through a wide but shallow window. He watched hundreds of profit criminals squeeze into the chamber. He watched the Tall Guard lock the doors. And he watched Zyklon gas spray out of eight circular tubes.

He heard the screams. The deafening, menacing, blood-curdling screams. The screams which were so shrill, they made his ears bleed. So terrifying, they made him cry. And so rickety, they made snot pour out of his nose.

He saw the terror. The startling, petrifying, horrifying terror. The terror which was written across the profit criminals' bloodshot eyes, puckered lips, and choking throats.

He smelt the decay. The putrid, acidic, nauseous decay. The decaying skin, the waning limbs, and the melting bodies.

The profit criminals fell.

Their screams faded.

They were replaced by an eerie sort of absolute silence. A silence which was so complete, so comprehensive, that it was deafening. Arun could not hear a thing. He clutched his ears and collapsed.

That was when the nightmares began. Arun saw a holy army of God's soldiers goose-stepping towards him, pounding holy books against their breasts, and firing bullets of fire from their eyes. He saw a cloud of bats descend from the skies, with blood dripping from their teeth, and acid spraying from their spiny wings. He saw squadrons of bears with claws like daggers, battalions of witches with long tangled nails, and legions of demented tigers with heads which spun right around.

He saw a sorry procession of all the people he had ever abused, assaulted or arrested.

He smelt ammonia.

Smelling salts were being held to his nose. So Arun shot up, wiped his eyes, and looked around the room. He looked around at the exposed bricks which covered every wall, the robots who were carrying dead bodies, and the furnaces which had blackened doors. They looked like bakers' ovens.

"This is your workplace now," the Tall Guard explained. "You're our new *Head of Withdrawals*. It's your job to withdraw these retired workers from the economy. Twenty four robots will help you. Just make sure they burn every retiree. Make sure they don't leave a trace."

The Tall Guard saluted Arun.

"All hail the bank!" He said. Then he disappeared.

Arun frowned.

He watched his robots load body after body into a never ending line of furnaces. He did not lift a finger. His robots did all the work. They moved with automated motions, mechanical efficiency, and soulless amorality. Arun just stared at them. He stared at them for ten hours.

Arun's emotions mixed within him, like liquor in a cocktail shaker.

Guilt, despair and terror, merged to form one transcendent sensation. Shame and horror sploshed around his belly. Fear and fury made his saliva froth. Vulnerability made his knees knock together.

He hated his society. He hated himself. And he hated Jim for putting him in that situation. He wanted to beat Jim. He wanted to destroy Jim. He wanted to kill Jim. He wanted to see Jim's corpse, broken and twisted, in a bloody heap at his feet.

But he did not have the courage to dissent. So he turned around to go home.

He walked straight into Jim.

"Tut, tut, tut," Jim said. "My brother, why on earth do you want to kill me? I'm your buddy."

Jim looked genuinely hurt. His lips quivered, his eyes welled up, and his breathing became manic.

"What? Why? Where?" Arun replied. "Me? Kill you? What on earth are you talking about?"

Jim shook his head.

"Don't play games with me," he said. "My friend, I know what you were thinking. I can read your mind! My super nanobots receive signals from your nanobots. They alert me to imminent danger. Pfft! I'm not some foolish member of the ninety nine percent. I know everything!"

Arun bowed his head.

"Don't you know who I am?" Jim bellowed. "You can't kill me! You nitwit! You dipshit! You buffoon!

"I'm immortal!!!

"I have a storeroom full of spare bodies. My super nanobots protect my mind. All my knowledge, characteristics and experiences, have been uploaded to the cloud. I'll never die. No green-brained idiot like you could ever kill me. What folly! What madness! Tut, tut, tut."

Jim's face turned red. It was a blood-curdling shade of red. A shade of red which was so dark it was almost purple, so bold it made his face pulsate, and so loud it seemed to scream.

In the blink of an eye, he had puffed his chest, lifted his hand above his head, and swung his arm with all his might. His knuckles crashed into Arun's cheek with so much power that Arun fell to the floor. His legs were tangled. There was a bruise on his cheek and a tear in his eye.

Arun whimpered.

"I'm sorry," he said. "But it's this place. Please believe me! This place makes me want to do nasty things. It's filled my head with guilty thoughts."

Jim scowled

"Guilt is natural," he said. "But it goes away. The strong can overpower it. It only devours the weak.

"You're weak! And there's no place for weakness in this post-modern economy. It's not productive. It's not profitable. And that won't do. Not here, where the supremacy of profit is absolute!

"No. There's no place for you here. You'll have to be punished for your insolence. You'll have to be gassed, along with all the other profit criminals."

Jim spat on the floor.

"All hail the bank!" He shouted.

He stormed away.

A severed foot fell from a wobbly table.

Arun held his head in his hands and cried.

12. CHARLIE

It was a bright cold day in August, and the clocks were striking fifteen. Charlie sat down in his cubicle, unaware that Arun was three metres away. The cubicle walls made it impossible for workers to see their colleagues. So Charlie had not discovered that both he and Arun had followed the same career paths. That they had both left the army, homeless and penniless, and that they had both been forced to work in the Department of Bullshit Jobs.

Charlie tapped his screen.

The avatar of an Intelligence Policewoman appeared. Her face was pale and craterous, like the moon. And her fleshy mouth looked like a cow's vagina. She was a Holy. All policewomen were Holies.

Charlie saw that avatar at the beginning of every shift, because the bank had classified him as a '*Threat to corporate security*'. They made him endure a struggle session every day.

"Well, well, well," the Intelligence Policewoman said. "What do have we here then?"

"Charlie ma'am."

"Ah yes! Charlie, who are your enemies?"

"Misers and slackers, ma'am!"

"What was the best thing that ever happened to you?"

"The revolution of corporatocracy, ma'am!"

"Who liberated Protokia?"

"The bank!"

"Who are your saviours?"

"The bankers!"

"Who do you love?"

"The Big Banker!"

"Long live the bankers!"

"Long live the bankers!"

"All hail the bank!"

"All hail the bank!"

Charlie grimaced, chanted, and then began to work. He inputted data, analysed data, and wrote reports. He went home, fell asleep, and then repeated his daily routine.

The bank gave Charlie lots of work, to keep him occupied, because they did not want him to have the time to think for himself. They were worried he might rebel.

But Charlie's work was meaningless. The data he analysed was fabricated, the reports he wrote were never read, and his suggestions were always ignored. The bank made all the intelligent workers do made-up work. Its super-computer created work out of nothing, just to keep them occupied.

The Department of Bullshit Jobs kept Charlie occupied for twelve hours each day. Then he commuted home.

That commute was the only time Charlie saw any other workers. He was grateful for the human contact. Lots of workers worked from home, and never saw anyone else at all.

But Charlie rubbed shoulders with workers in the plaza outside his office, where it was always at least fifty degrees Celsius. *And* he listened to other workers' whilst he sat on a driverless bus.

He listened to a Bald Worker, who was one hundred and seventy six years old.

"I hear there's a way out," that man told a Voluptuous Worker.

The Voluptuous Worker waved her prosthetic hand. Her robotic heart pumped synthetic blood through her synthetic veins. Her artificial bacteria monitored her health.

"That's right," she replied. "There's a portal to another planet, where no-one has to work. Everyone's talking about it!"

"Machines produce everything there," an Emaciated Worker added. "Humans are free!"

"There's no Department of Bullshit Jobs!" A Tubby Worker cheered. "People don't work for the sake of working. They live for the sake of living!"

Those four workers daydreamed. Charlie daydreamed. He dreamt of Fastaris and EyePads. He dreamt about the countryside, Valley Village, and halcyon days full of leisure. He dreamt about owning a robot who satisfied his every desire.

But those daydreams were cut short by the muddled ramblings of the Mad Lady, who was wagging her finger and shaking her hand. Her nose had grown so large, it almost reached her ears. And her wart had just exploded. Pus was dripping over her hairy chin, and crystallising on her saggy neck.

"You're not going to escape!" She wailed. "You're going to die! Everyone's going to die! There are no more prophecies. Where are all the prophecies?"

"Oh shut up," the Tubby Worker shouted back. "What do you know, you batty old witch?"

But that riposte did not distract Charlie.

"You're my robot!" He cheered.

He pointed at the Voluptuous Worker.

"I'm not your robot," the Voluptuous Worker replied with disgust. "I'm not yours, and I'm not a robot either. Pfft! How rude!"

"When I get promoted, I'm going to be rich like the one percent," Charlie explained. "I'll have so much money, I'll be able to buy a real robot. But until then, you'll have to do. You're clearly more machine than human. You pretty much *are* a robot."

"I'm '*more machine than human*'? So what? Everyone knows that mechanical organs are better than natural ones."

"What?" Charlie shouted back with fake horror. "That's slander! Poppycock! Bunkum!"

The Voluptuous Worker looked flustered. She shook her head, muttered to herself, and got off the bus.

The Bald Worker laughed sarcastically.

Charlie went home, fell asleep, woke up and returned to work.

* * *

Charlie sat down at his desk and tapped his screen. An avatar appeared.

"What is virtuous?" It asked.

"Work, ma'am," Charlie replied.

"What is evil?"

"Idleness."

"What must you be?"

"Occupied."

"What are you without the bank?"

"Nothing."

"What is the bank?"

"Everything."

"What is the bank?"

"Good and wise."

"What is the bank?"

"Honest and true."

"All hail the bank!"

"All hail the bank!"

"Report to floor 101 for your quarterly review."

"Yes ma'am!"

Charlie stood up, left his cubicle, and took a lift to floor 101.

"Name?" A virtual receptionist asked in a robotic voice.

"Charlie."

"Number?"

"54-46."

"Role?"

"Revenue procurement executive."

There was a pause.

Charlie scratched some plaque from his teeth.

The door buzzed, and Charlie entered an empty waiting room. He sat down on a floating sofa and waited. He waited and waited and waited. He waited for an hour in all. An hour in which there was nothing to do, other than stare at an interactive window, which displayed a different panorama every minute.

"54-46!" A voice finally rang out. "Step forward."

A door slid open and Charlie stepped through. He sat down in front of a smart table. A Blonde Manager, who was wearing a white dress, entered through a white door. The ceiling was awash with white light.

"Have you achieved your three goals this quarter?" She asked.

"Yes ma'am," Charlie replied.

"And what exactly where your three goals?"

"To be productive, profitable and occupied."

The Blonde Manager smiled.

"They're fine goals," she said. "Three mighty fine goals indeed! Why, those are the three cornerstones of our great economy!"

"Yes ma'am."

"So how have you been productive?"

"I've analysed all the data I've been given."

"How have you been profitable?"

"I've made hundreds of suggestions to increase revenues."

"And how have you kept yourself occupied?"

"I commute for two hours, work for twelve hours, and sleep for eight hours every day!"

The Blonde Manager tutted. She flicked her hair over one shoulder, rolled her eyes, and stared at Charlie.

"There are twenty four hours in a day," she said. "And you've only accounted for twenty two of them."

"Yes ma'am."

"So what are you going to do with the other two hours?"

"Keep myself occupied, ma'am."

"Don't be silly."

"Sorry ma'am."

"Don't be sorry."

"No ma'am."

"Be more productive!"

"Yes ma'am. Definitely ma'am. How ma'am?"

"By studying. By completing another degree. By up-skilling yourself. By improving your skillset. By being a goddamn teacher's pet!"

"Yes ma'am."

"That's my boy!"

The Blonde Manager removed a box of chocolates from a drawer.

"Have a treat," she said.

Charlie took a chocolate, put it in his mouth, and chewed.

His floating seat massaged his back and shoulders.

The Blonde Manager patted his head.

"Good boy," she said.

Charlie grinned.

"You could be better though," the Blonde Manager continued.

"Yes ma'am."

"You've done exceptionally well. You're one of the best worker we've ever had! But you could be even better. You could be *more* productive. You could be even *more* profitable."

"Yes ma'am."

"You should be ashamed of yourself for not having done more."

"Yes ma'am."

"You should feel guilty."

Charlie bowed his head.

"Guilt!" The Blonde Manager cheered. "Guilt is your friend! You should feel guilty whenever you only just make a target, come second, or take a break. That guilt will drive you on to new heights. It'll encourage you to give one hundred and ten percent, and be the best you can be. It'll get you promoted. Because hard work is always rewarded!"

The Blonde Manager smiled.

Charlie nodded.

The ceiling turned from white to yellow.

"Well!" The Blonde Manager cheered. "We've assessed your performance and set your goals. We only have one more thing to do."

"Yes ma'am."

"Tell me, is there anything the bank can do for *you*? Is there anything we can do differently to make *your* life better?"

"No ma'am."

"'*No*'?"

"No ma'am. The bank is perfect. I wouldn't change it at all!"

"Good boy!"

The Blonde Manager held out the box of chocolates.

Charlie threw one into his mouth. Sickly liquor slipped down the back of his throat. Bitter chocolate got stuck between his gums.

He returned to his cubicle, wrote reports for another eleven hours, left the office, and got onto his bus.

Charlie had to take the bus home, because the bank had removed all the pavements in Natale. Forcing pedestrians to use vehicles was profitable. Anyone who wanted to go for a walk, had to buy a treadmill, and use their nanobots to generate a virtual environment.

Charlie listened to the other commuters.

"I haven't seen the Voluptuous Worker today," the Bald Worker said.

"I wonder where she's gone."

The Emaciated Worker scratched his scrawny thigh. His lips, which were slightly too small for his mouth, drew back over his stumpy teeth. And his long hair wafted around his head, like a cloud of black smoke.

"Perhaps she found the portal," he said. "Perhaps she's made it to a better place, where no-one has to work."

The Tubby Worker's eyes lit up. Her touchscreen Mikey t-shirt lit up. Her bracelet projected images onto her arm, which all lit up.

"That must be it," she said. "The Voluptuous Worker always gets on this bus. She wouldn't miss it. Not for the world! There can only be one explanation. She must have made it out!"

Those three workers daydreamed.

Charlie daydreamed.

The Bald Worker nodded.

"You're right," he said. "She was only talking about the portal just the other day. It can't be a coincidence. No, she must have escaped!"

"There's a way out of here!"

"We're going to be saved!"

"There's hope for us all!"

"All hail the bank!"

"All hail the bank!"

Charlie looked out the window.

He saw hundreds of skyscrapers which were building themselves, and thousands of unemployed builders. He saw Robot Counsellors, Quarantine Enforcers and Astronauts. He saw floating homes, underground offices, and unmanned checkpoints.

Holographic snow fell from the cloudless sky. Real snow had not fallen for years, because of global warming. But workers had been too occupied to notice.

Charlie's bus continued along its route. It hovered above the ground, which was covered in a layer of acidified seawater. All of lower Natale was covered in polluted water. When the ice caps melted, the sea levels rose, and the lowlands were flooded. Since Protokia was covered in concrete, that water had never drained away.

After an hour on the bus, Charlie entered his flat, which buzzed into life. Charlie's nanobots created a brain-computer interface, which he used to turn on the lights. Interactive surfaces displayed his vital statistics. And a moving walkway transported him to his lounge.

His 3D television flashed. The hologram of a Grey Lecturer, who was wearing a tweed blazer, stood in the middle of the room.

"Welcome to *Productivity 101*," she said. "Over the months which follow, you'll learn how to serve the bank. You'll learn how to be a super-profitable employee. You'll become the finest patriot in the economy!"

"Hang on! Hang on ma'am!" Charlie yelled. "I've only just gotten in. Give me a chance to take my shoes off."

"It's important to keep yourself motivated at all times," the Grey Lecturer continued, despite Charlie's pleas. "And the *Four Ss* will help you.

"The Four Ss! Stress! Sadness! Suspicion! Spite!"

Charlie grabbed his tablet and took notes. Even though he had completed four degrees, he still struggled to keep up. He looked up at the Grey Lecturer, and down at his tablet. He thought about the subject matter, and he thought about his job.

He perspired.

"The Four Ss will motivate you to achieve the bank's three goals; to be profitable, to be productive, and to be occupied.

"The Four Ss! Stress! Sadness! Suspicion! Spite!

"Stress! Stress will motivate you to work long hours.

"Sadness! Sadness will motivate you to meet your targets.

"Suspicion! Suspicion will motivate you to backstab your colleagues.

"Spite! Spite will motivate you to outperform your peers."

The Grey Lecturer swished her holographic cane through the air.

She lectured for another two hours. She did not stop to take a breath. She did not give Charlie the chance to ask a question. She did not even give Charlie the chance to eat his dinner.

The clocks struck eleven, sleeping gas filled the room, and Charlie fell asleep on his sofa.

A robotic ant scuttled across the floor.

The Grey Lecturer continued her lecture.

* * *

Charlie's television woke him up at seven o'clock the next morning.

He commuted into work, endured another struggle session, spent twelve hours writing reports, and then got onto his bus.

He listened to the other commuters.

"I haven't seen the Emaciated Worker today," the Bald Worker said. "I wonder where he is."

The Tubby Worker pressed some buttons on her Mikey t-shirt.

"He must have made it to the portal," she said. "He must have escaped!"

Those workers daydreamed.

Charlie daydreamed.

The Bald Worker nodded.

"You're right," he said. "He must have escaped!"

"Maybe we'll be next!"

"There's hope for us all!"

"We're going to be saved!"

"All hail the bank!"

"All hail the bank!"

Charlie looked out the window. He saw his tower, but he did not disembark. He travelled past a hundred more skyscrapers, and a thousand more checkpoints.

Those were the only two things Charlie saw. Each congested road looked exactly the same. They were all flanked by skyscrapers, which were all covered in shiny blue glass. And they all featured checkpoints, which appeared at every turn.

Charlie got off the bus when it reached Rosie's tower.

He had not seen Rosie for years. The bank had calculated that it would be profitable for them to live apart. But Charlie had never stopped loving Rosie. He thought about her every day, and dreamt about her every night. He saw her face in every mirror. And he talked to her in his sleep.

He knocked on Rosie's door.

"What are you doing here?" She asked. She looked anxious. "You can't be here. We can't be seen together. It's not profitable! And the supremacy of profit is absolute!

"Go away! Go away! You'll get us both indebted!"

"I don't care," Charlie replied. "I love you! I had to see you. We need to talk."

"Go away! Go away! Go pick mushrooms!"

"Please let me stay. Please!"

"Why? What do you want?"

"I want to talk. Because this life of ours; it's not right. We can't go on like this. We should be together."

"The bank won't allow it."

"So let's escape!"

"Escape?"

"There's a portal to another planet. People are using it every day! We can escape from the bank, the bankers, and the one percent. We can live a life of leisure. We can be together. We can be happy!"

"I am happy."

"Are you?"

"Yes. I take a happiness pill every day."

"But we can experience real, natural happiness!"

Rosie looked astonished.

"You're crazy," she replied. "Natural happiness? You're mad!

"Running away won't benefit us. Once you escape, anything can happen. It's not what we need, not here, not now."

Rosie tutted.

"You'll get caught," she continued. "You'll lose your job. You'll never get to own a robot or a Fastari. You'll disappear. You'll be wiped from the ledgers. Really! What's the point in a rebel that no-one knows about?

"Pfft! You should be grateful to the one percent. Look at all the wealth they've brought us! How dare you talk about escaping? Don't be so bloody stupid.

"Escapees aren't heroes to me. They're fools!"

Charlie froze. Only his face moved. His cheek twitched and his eye fluttered.

"But what about the environment?" He asked. "It's not safe for us to stay here. We'll be under water soon. If it gets any hotter we'll fry!"

Rosie shook her head.

"Don't worry about that," she said. "The bank will take care of the environment, just as soon as it's profitable to do so."

Rosie gave Charlie a stern look.

"Get out of my sight!" She yelled. "You can't be here. We can't be seen together. Go away! Go away! You'll get us both indebted!"

A robotic cat rubbed up against Charlie's leg.

"I'll go to the temple," he said. "Maybe I can find solace there."

Rosie smiled.

"That's the most sensible thing you've said today," she replied.

Charlie left, and got onto a bus, which drove past a giant pile of rubble; the remains of a skyscraper which had collapsed during an earthquake. Past a giant pile of dead bodies; the remains of workers who had inhaled poisonous fumes. And past a giant pile of litter, which swirled around in the breeze, and landed on every available surface.

'*Charlie*', a voice called out. The microchip in his eye was broadcasting a holographic advert, which Charlie could not avoid. '*Move into a new skyscraper! Live like a god in the clouds.*'

'*Buy an iron lung, Charlie*', another advert pleaded. Charlie saw a boy who was playing football in a dust cloud. '*You'll be able to inhale anything!*'

'*Help clean our streets*', a third advert begged. Charlie saw an eager young robot, who was litter picking. '*Do your bit, Charlie. Donate today!*'

Charlie got off the bus, walked through the *Holy Temple of Profit*, and arrived at the *Godly Temple of Profit, sponsored by McRonalds*.

He washed his feet in an ionic footbath, which bubbled and fizzed. He walked up the marble steps, passed some branded icons, and bowed down in front of a giant statue of a *McBib*.

Minutes passed by in quiet contemplation. Charlie drifted off into another world. A world without the bank, managers or debt. He felt emancipated. He felt entranced, mesmerized and free.

He heard a hover car land outside.

The Humpbacked Priest entered. He hobbled over to the donations box, and scanned it with the microchip in his eye. A thousand eDollars were transferred into his personal account.

A bead of sweat dropped from his frog-like face.

Charlie twitched. His cheek vibrated and his eye blinked.

"Good," the Humpbacked Priest said. "Praise the Lord!"

He sprinkled some plastic petals into a floating font.

Charlie used his nanobots to activate a vaporizer, which sprayed the smell of incense all around the hall.

The Humpbacked Priest said a prayer:

"Profit God in the boardroom, hallowed be your name.

"Your business come, your profit be done, in your offices, as in your factories.

"Give us this day our daily wage, and love our debts, as we have loved our creditors.

"And lead us into temptation, so that we may be too occupied to think of evil."

The Humpbacked Priest closed his eyes. He muttered to himself, swayed and bowed.

"What brings you here today, babushka?" He finally asked.

Charlie paused.

"Do you think religion can save us from the bank, sir?" He replied. "Do you think God can free us from our debts? Is there another planet where we can live? A heaven free from the Big Banker's wage slavery?"

The Humpbacked Priest picked some sweat out of his flabby neck.

"My dear boy," he said. "You've got some chutzpah; coming in here and questioning the bank. Oi vey! You clearly don't understand the holy trinity; the *Money God*, the *Invisible Hand*, and the Big Banker.

"The Money God is our mother in heaven. She's omnipotent, omniscient and benevolent. She ensures we make lots of profit.

"The Invisible Hand guides the economy. Through the profit-motive, it ensures that wealth finds its way to the most deserving workers.

"And then there's Big Banker; Morgan Rockchild. The chief executive of the bank. The prophet. The macher. The son of the Money God. The Money God's representative on earth!"

Charlie looked at the Humpbacked Priest with hungry eyes.

A McRonalds advert appeared above a branded lectern.

The Humpbacked Priest put his sweaty hand on Charlie's shoulder.

"The Big Banker is our friend," he concluded. "Our babushka! He's brought wealth which is trickling down to everyone. The bank loves us. So please don't question the sanctity of profit. Oi gavelt! Please don't talk of heavenly planets, wage slavery and debt. Please don't speak with a stiff neck in here. This is a holy place. A godly place. Not a political place. Oi yoy yoy! Show some respect! You klutz! You nafka! You pisher!"

The Humpbacked Priest raised his eyebrows and nodded towards the donations box.

Charlie engaged his microchip, transferred fifty eDollars, and left.

The Humpbacked Priest grinned, hobbled into the Holy Temple of Profit, and delivered the same message to some Holies.

* * *

Charlie's television woke him up at seven o'clock the next morning. He commuted into work, endured another struggle session, spent twelve hours writing reports, and then got onto his bus.

He listened to the Bald Worker.

"I haven't seen the Tubby Worker today," he told himself. "I wonder where she is."

The Bald Worker daydreamed.

Charlie daydreamed.

The Bald Worker nodded.

"She must have made it to the portal," he said. "She must have escaped. We're all going to be saved! All hail the bank!"

Charlie looked out the window, as the bus reached lower Natale.

At first it was able to hover above the water, which had risen during the day. But when the bus reached the town's lowest point, the water rose up around it. It reached Charlie's window. Pieces of plastic floated above Charlie's head. Charlie came face-to-face with a three-eyed fish.

Waves formed in the water. They started out as ripples; melodic patterns on the oily surface. Then those ripples grew. They turned into undulations. Those undulations turned into waves. And those waves turned into a tsunami, which was as wide as the road itself.

Everything stood perfectly still.

Charlie could not breathe, listen or think. His world froze. He felt paralyzed; trapped inside a vacuum which existed outside of space and time. His face stiffened, his heart stopped, and his lungs froze.

The earthquake happened in slow motion.

The ground vibrated. Towers swayed from side to side. Chunks of blue glass fell from the sky. Water surged down the street. And a giant wave immersed Charlie's bus.

The windows wobbled. They undulated in and out, like speakers which were playing a mellow tune. Then the vibrations grew. The windows moved back and forth, in time with the waves. A crack formed in the middle of each pane. Those cracks grew outwards, in ever increasing circles.

Crack. Crack. Crack.

The windows blew into the bus.

Tiny water droplets, which looked like shiny diamonds, filled the chamber. They flew in every direction. They bounced into one another. They danced through the air. They sparkled beneath the lights, and fell like horizontal rain.

'*Boom!!!*'

Water surged into the bus. It was so powerful, it knocked Charlie over. It was so sharp, it flushed adrenaline through his veins. And it was so cold, it covered his skin in pimples.

His stomach tingled, as if it had pins and needles. His head span, as if he was dizzy. And his eyes bulged.

He saw a broken window.

The water pressure stabilised. Charlie grabbed hold of a pillar, and heaved himself forwards, using all the strength in his body. Using all the superhuman power in his prosthetic arms. And using every nanobot in his head.

Every muscle in his body tensed. Every joint creaked. Every computer circuit buzzed.

Charlie pulled himself through the broken window. But he was caught by the current. He was whipped downstream at thirty miles an hour. He was thrown up into the sky. He glanced across at a startled bird. And he landed on top of a floating floorboard. The Bald Worker landed by his side.

The earthquake stopped.

The tsunami settled.

Charlie inhaled.

Above the remains of broken vehicles and broken buildings, which bobbed upon the water's surface, Charlie saw Oliver's Mikey bag. It floated up into the air, hovered, and then drifted back down. It swayed left and right, like a weightless feather. And it landed on a Pregnant Worker, who had just miscarried.

"Oliver!" Charlie shouted. "Oliver!"

A small piece of concrete fell from a damaged skyscraper.

A dead body surfaced between two driverless trucks.

A bus sank beneath the water's oily surface.

"Charlie?" A distant voice replied.

"Oliver!"

"Charlie!"

"Oliver!"

"Charlie!"

"Oliver!"

Charlie stood up. He looked around. And he ran in Oliver's direction.

He ran across the tops of buses, vans and cars. He ran over pieces of wreckage and pieces of people. He ran over scraps, debris and rubble.

He bobbed up and down. He bounced. Water splashed his ankles. But Charlie did not care. His clothes were already sodden, and his skin was already wet. All he could think about was Oliver. He was about to see his best friend for the first time in years.

"Oliver!"

"Charlie!"

They embraced. They gripped each other so tightly, they could barely breathe. And they gazed into each other's eyes.

"I'm so happy to see you!"

"I'm so happy to see *you*!"

They smiled.

They laughed.

They guffawed.

"What now?" Oliver finally asked.

"Now we escape!" Charlie replied.

"Escape?"

"Escape! There's a portal to another planet. People are using it every day! We can escape from the bank, the bankers, and the one percent. We can live a life of leisure. We can be friends. We can be happy!"

"I am happy."

"Are you?"

"Yes. I take a happiness pill every day."

"But we can experience real, natural happiness!"

Oliver looked astonished.

Charlie kept talking:

"Workers think they're rich, so they don't realise how unhappy they've become. They believe their lives have gotten better, and so they ignore all the ways in which their lives have gotten worse. They're too occupied to notice their discontent.

"Do you know what the deadliest disease is these days? Depression! Not cancer, not aids, not heart disease. Depression! I tell you, we were happier when we were poor. We appreciated what we had back then. And we had each other. We had time, we had nature, and we had hope."

Oliver was pale.

"You're in danger of developing a soul," he said.

"I have a soul," Charlie replied. "And so do you! Let's use them! Let's get out of here!"

Charlie had never rebelled before. So he shuddered. His twitch flared up. And his cheek vibrated so much, he had to hold his head steady.

But he felt that he had to act. That he did not have a choice. That if he stayed, his job would drive him crazy, and environmental disasters would drive him insane.

"The escape portal is near my birthplace," he said. "Don't ask me how I know. I just know it! It's there! My nanobots have worked it out. I'm telling you, the portal is in Valley Village!"

Charlie looked into Oliver's eyes.

"I bet I can make it there before you," he continued.

Oliver looked back at Charlie and nodded.

"You're on," he replied.

He spat on his palm and stretched it out to shake hands with Charlie.

Charlie cringed. He slowly lifted his hand towards his mouth.

Oliver span around and ran away

"Oi!" Charlie shouted. "Come back here, you cheeky rascal!"

He sprang into motion and chased after Oliver.

They ran over trucks which bobbed beneath their feet, beams which smelled of rotting wood, and debris which floated one way and then the other. They reached upper Natale, where the ground was still dry, and ran up roads which were full of overturned vehicles. They skidded around corners, scaled steep inclines, and slid down rutted hills. They whizzed past checkpoints which were imbedded into buildings, checkpoints which stretched across junctions, and checkpoints which hung overhead.

None of those checkpoints stopped them.

"They must have been broken during the earthquake," Charlie shouted to Oliver, who was only just ahead of him. "The movement police aren't anywhere to be seen. And there's no sleeping gas either. Fate is on our side. We're going to make it. We're going to escape!"

Oliver's eyes lit up.

They ran past a Keen Worker, who had a stitch. A Pink Worker, who was struggling to breathe. And a Muscular Worker, whose clothes were drenched. Those workers were all running towards the escape portal.

Charlie ran alongside Ellie.

"Hey," he shouted. "I know you!"

Ellie looked confused.

"You do?" She shouted back.

"Yeah! You met me on my first day in Natale. You poked me with a stick, and called me 'Donkey Boy'. Then you took me to my uncle's house."

"Oh, yeah. I think I remember that."

"Well today is my last day in Natale! I'm escaping to another planet, where no-one has to work, and everyone is free!"

Ellie panted.

"Me too!" She yelled.

"Good!" Charlie replied. "Come with us. We'll escape together."

They ran after Oliver. They ran past an advert which said, '*Gas the chavs*'. And they ran past a Rigid Worker, who punched the air and stamped his boot.

The passageway widened, between a robot who was upside down, and two jeeps which were on their sides. Charlie saw an opportunity to pass Oliver. So he swung out to the right and made his move.

He glanced at Oliver and ran past him. But, in doing so, he took his eye off the road. So he did not see an Old Lady, who stepped out from behind a broken statue. He did not see his hand smash into her nose.

Charlie turned his head when he felt the impact. He watched on in slow motion as his knuckles pushed through that woman's face. As she flew back through the air, and landed on one leg. As her knees buckled, her legs stumbled, and her elbow crashed down onto the ground.

She lay on the floor, holding her crippled arm.

Charlie stopped, turned around, and looked on in pale-faced horror.

Oliver shot off into the distance.

"Hurry up!" Ellie shouted. "We can't stop now. If we leave it too long, the checkpoints will fix themselves. The sleeping gas will knock us unconscious. Or the movement police will catch us.

"Come on! Hurry up! Let's go!!!"

Charlie looked at Ellie. He looked back at the Old Lady. He bounced on the spot. Then he ran ahead.

"I'm coming," he shouted. "Keep going. It's not far now."

He ran over the crest of a hill, and descended towards Valley Village, which had been swallowed by the urban sprawl. It was indistinguishable from the rest of Natale. The hills were all full of skyscrapers, and the roads were all surrounded by checkpoints.

Everything was covered in broken concrete. Everything was freakishly still. And everything was eerily dark. The lights had faded, the holograms had died, and the sun had set.

It was the midnight hour, and the moon was nowhere to be seen. Charlie wore a cloak of darkness as he descended down the hillside.

An operational robot fixed a broken robot.

An overturned vehicle hooted.

A broken engine howled.

Charlie's heart pounded. Butterflies fluttered in his stomach, and his spine tingled. His hands shook.

His nervous twitch went into overdrive. His left cheek pulsated as quickly as machinegun fire. In and out. In and out. In and out.

His left eye opened and closed at a manic rate. His eyebrow vibrated.

He concentrated on his breathing.

"This way!" Oliver cheered. "I think it must be this way!"

Charlie sped ahead.

He ran past corpses which were frazzled and burnt. They had been electrocuted when their nanobots malfunctioned.

He ran past holographic adverts which sputtered and spat. They had been damaged by the earthquake.

And he ran past a statue of himself. It had been erected to honour his achievements in the Protokian army.

But no matter how fast Charlie ran, he could not overtake Oliver.

So Oliver beat Charlie to their destination. He panted, turned around, and stuck out his chalky tongue.

Charlie shrugged. He looked up at a sign, which said, 'The Department of Life'.

"This must be it!" He cheered. "The Department of Life!"

"We've found the portal to another world!" Ellie chanted.

"Our lives start here!" Oliver cried. "It's time to start living. We've found the Department of Life!

"All hail the bank!"

"All hail the bank!"

They joined a long queue of eager escapees.

They looked at a robotic ant, who was writhing around on its back.

They looked at each other, and they smiled.

* * *

The queue was full of Charlie's peers. They all jumped for joy. They all clapped. And they all chattered.

"We're going to another planet, where no-one has to work!" Papa Charlie cheered.

"Robots and machines will produce everything!" Mama Charlie crowed.

"There won't be any bullshit jobs!" Uncle Charlie cried. "Yes. Yes. Good. Good. Very good."

He pumped his fist with glee.

The Night Watchman said, "We're going to live a life of leisure!"

The Wool Seller said, "We're going to make it through!"

The Toothy Officer said, "We're going to a better place!"

The Slender Guard said, "We're going to be saved!"

The Dark Policeman said, "We're going to be happy!"

The Bespectacled Lecturer said, "We're going to be free!"

"All hail the bank!"

"All hail the bank!"

A door slid open. Everyone walked through it, and skipped down a narrow staircase. They entered an underground changing room, and started to undress.

Charlie approached a Police Policeman, who was stood in the corner. He was wearing a black suit, black tie, and black helmet. He might have been human, or he might have been a robot; it was impossible to tell.

"Well, well, well," he said. "What do have we here then?"

Charlie twitched.

"I was just wondering, sir," he asked. "Why is everyone getting undressed?"

"You were born naked," the Police Policeman replied. "And you'll retire naked. It's the circle of life."

"'*Retire*', sir?"

"Retire! Your career is over."

Charlie grinned.

"I'll never have to work again, sir?" He asked.

"That's right," the Police Policeman replied.

"I'm going to be free, sir?"

"I suppose."

"I'm going to another planet?"

"No."

"'*No*', sir?"

"No."

"So where am I going?"

"Nowhere."

"'*Nowhere*', sir?"

"Nowhere."

Charlie looked confused.

"What's going to happen to me, sir?" He asked.

"You're going to die."

"'*Die*', sir?"

"Die!"

"Why sir?"

The Police Policeman chortled.

"Because you're a profit criminal," he replied. "You don't produce any profit. And that's treason. It's punishable by death."

Charlie felt a demonic sort of horror. He felt helpless, lost and confused.

A tear formed in his eye. It rolled over his cheekbone, and dropped onto his burgundy lip.

He shivered. He shuddered. His cheek vibrated and his eye blinked. He stuttered as he spoke.

"Bu, bu, but I make lots of profit, sir!" He protested. "I work really, really hard!"

The Police Policeman laughed. It was a sarcastic sort of laugh, which seemed to say, '*Are you serious?*' It was a condescending sort of laugh, which seemed to mock Charlie for his insolence. It was a laugh which echoed all around the room.

"Environmental catastrophes have generated massive costs," the Police Policeman explained. "Only those workers who generate massive revenues, can cover those massive costs. Those who don't, are no longer profitable. Our planet cannot sustain them."

"But I do produce '*massive revenues*'!" Charlie protested. "I create money making strategies every day!"

"You make lots of suggestions, that's true, but they've all been ignored. You haven't made the bank a single cent."

"What? Sir! They'd make millions if they listened to me."

"That's also true. But they haven't listened to you. They haven't made millions. So you're not profitable. You're a profit criminal. And you need to be retired!"

Charlie's eyes bulged.

"Bu, bu, but," he stuttered. "I've followed orders, sir. I've obeyed every command. And I'll do everything I'm told to do in the future. Please give me another job. I'll do any job that's profitable. Any job!"

The Police Policeman sniggered.

"There aren't any profitable jobs," he mocked. "Robots and machines produce everything. To be profitable, you need to own those machines. You need to be a banker or a shareholder. You need to be a member of the one percent."

The Police Policeman shook his head.

"Look outside," he continued. "Look at all the flooding. Look at all the earthquakes. Our planet cannot sustain you. It can only sustain the one percent. There needs to be population control. These retirements are necessary. They're profitable. And the supremacy of profit is absolute!"

The Police Policeman howled like a hyena.

"We're going to retire you!" He cried. "We're going to end your career! We're going to send you to the great retirement home in the sky! You're no longer profitable. You're a profit criminal. You don't deserve to live!"

Everyone else got undressed, folded their clothes, and combed their hair. They kept themselves occupied. And they ignored Charlie's conversation.

"Why are you telling me this?" Charlie asked.

"Why not?"

"I'll leave, sir. I'll walk out of here. I don't want to die."

"Okay."

"'*Okay*', sir?"

"Okay. Walk out of here, if that's what you want to do. It's a free country after all."

Charlie tried to turn around. His torso swung to the left, but his feet stayed rooted to the ground. His legs felt heavy, solid and firm. No matter how hard he tried, Charlie could not move them.

The Police Policeman snickered.

"I don't understand," Charlie said.

"You don't have to," the Police Policeman replied.

"But I want to, sir."

"Okay."

"'*Okay*', sir?"

"Okay."

"Please tell me why I can't leave?"

"The same reason you came here in the first place."

Charlie looked confused.

"I came here of my own free will," he said.

"No you didn't."

"I didn't, sir?"

"No."

"Oh."

Charlie raised his eyebrows.

"How did you know where to go?" The Police Policeman asked.

Charlie shrugged.

"Why were you allowed through every checkpoint?"

Charlie shrugged again.

"Why weren't you stopped by the movement police?"

Charlie kept shrugging.

"Because we wanted you to come here!" The Police Policeman cheered. "We broke through your firewall, overrode your passwords, and hacked into your nanobots. We controlled your brain! We made you think you were escaping. We made you think this place was an exit portal. And we made you enter this room.

"We controlled you! We made you come to us! And we'll make you enter that gas chamber!"

Charlie turned around. He saw a mass of naked people, who were all walking into a long metallic room.

"Thank-you for listening," the Police Policeman concluded. "And don't forget to buy your coffin from Window Mart. *'Save Money. Live better'.*"

Charlie's arms and legs moved of their own accord. Charlie couldn't do anything to stop them. He could only watch, as he undressed, folded his clothes, and walked into the gas chamber.

He looked at Ellie.

Ellie was standing with her peers. Mama Ellie, Papa Ellie and her six siblings, huddled together in a corner. Their erstwhile guests stood by their side. The Pale Teacher, Cherubic Refugee and Owlish Local, leaned up against a railing. The Concert Promoter stood amongst a group of dancers, near some protestors from the uprising. Ellie stared at the Handsome Man, and lusted after his body. She glanced across at the refugees she had met in prison, and waved at her former colleagues.

Charlie looked at Arun.

Arun was standing with his peers. Mama Arun and Papa Arun huddled together in a corner. Their erstwhile guests stood by their side. The Pale Settler, Cherubic Settler and Owlish Settler, leaned up against a railing. The Squinty Officer stood amongst a group of soldiers, near some protestors from the separation wall. Arun stared at a Beautiful Woman, and lusted after her body. He glanced across at the refugees he had sent to prison, and waved at his former colleagues.

The Godlies scowled at the Holies.

The Holies scowled at the Godlies.

"They're terrorist," the Militant Settler said.

"Terrorists," the Orthodox Settler replied.

"Terrorists," her husband agreed.

Papa Arun clenched his fists.

"We're in here because of them!" He spat.

The Keen Soldier nodded.

"They're terrorist," he said.

"Terrorists," the Muscular Soldier replied.

"Terrorists," the Rosy Soldier agreed. "They hate us! Everyone hates us! The whole world hates us. They hate everything we stand for. And they want to destroy us."

Zyklon gas sprayed out of several tubes.

Jim entered the adjacent room. He looked through a wide but shallow window. And he spoke through a rusty loudspeaker.

"The bank loves you!" He announced. "It just wants to make you happy!"

"All hail the bank!" Everyone cheered. "All hail the bank! All hail the bank! All hail the bank!"

Their cheers were replaced by screams. Deafening, menacing, blood-curdling screams. Screams which were so shrill, they made Charlie's ears bleed. So terrifying, they made him cry. And so rickety, they made snot pour out of his nose.

He experienced the most gut-wrenching terror of his life. Startling, petrifying, horrifying terror. Terror which usurped his bloodshot eyes, puckered lips, and choking throat.

He smelt the decay. The putrid, acidic, nauseous decay. The decaying skin, the waning limbs, and the melting bodies.

The other profit criminals fell.

Their screams faded.

Charlie, Arun and Ellie, looked through the window. They saw a surveillance monitor. And they saw Tamsin on its screen.

It was the last thing they ever saw.

Tamsin was standing in the queue, surrounded by a group of her peers. Mama Tamsin and Papa Tamsin were huddled together with Mama Jon, Papa Jon and the First Wife. Their erstwhile guests stood by their side. The Medicine Man, Humpbacked Priest and Singer, leaned up against a railing. Tamsin's children stood amongst a group of checkpoint soldiers, near some protestors from Natale. Tamsin stared at Jon, and lusted after his body. She glanced across at the refugees she had met in her camp, and waved at her former colleagues.

Papa Tamsin kissed the key to his village home.

A sharp breeze made the First Wife shudder.

The bright sunlight made Tamsin sneeze.

She glanced at the remains of a fallen building, and saw a strange animal in the rubble. It looked a bit like a fox, but it had bright red stripes, and a pointy grey goatee.

'*Doomba!*' She thought. '*I'm safe! Doombas bring good fortune. They protect everyone who's lucky enough to see them!*'

Tamsin smiled. She smirked. She positively beamed!

She turned to the Bedouin, and tugged his sleeve.

"Don't worry," she cheered. "Be happy!"

"Don't worry," the Bedouin replied. "Be happy!"

"Don't worry, be happy!"

"Don't worry, be happy!"

www.joss-sheldon.com

Made in the USA
Charleston, SC
15 October 2015